SPEAK FOR

ISBN- 9798700161015

By the same author

Inspector Abbs Mysteries
A Seaside Mourning
A Christmas Malice

Inspector Chance Mysteries
The Seafront Corpse
The Holly House Mystery

SPEAK FOR
THE DEAD

An Inspector Abbs Victorian Mystery

Anne Bainbridge

Gaslight Crime

PROLOGUE

'Is anybody there?'

The sitters waited in silence. Anticipation thickened about the room, as outside, mist gathered through the evening streets. Sounds gradually intruded, the ticking of the mantel clock, a phlegmatic wheeze from the old gentleman, a rumble of wheels on cobbles.

'I ask again. Is there another spirit who would speak with someone here?'

The bell began to tinkle, like a living thing, in the darkened parlour. Tentative at first, as if it took an effort to nudge with ghostly fingers. The ring was slightly muffled, coming as it did from beneath a glass dome on the sideboard.

'The spirit of a child is among us,' said Mr. Silas Dove, slowly raising his head. 'Bringing a message of comfort, long-awaited.'

His voice seemed to come from a distance, thought Rowland Ellis, a sepulchral intonation well-suited to a church. Indeed, the séance had begun with a prayer.

'A tender young soul who suffered bravely in their last illness. One greatly loved, who has left behind so much sorrow and longing.'

The lady, on his right, gasped. A chair creaked, the setting of her ring dug against his fingers. His legs inclined away from the skirts on either side. He was getting cramp.

'Is it for me? Can it be at last? Oh, it must be Eddy. Is it you, my dearest boy?'

The bell rang insistently.

'The reunion is for you, madam. Pray, do not fear to speak. The music of your voice will give strength to your dear one.'

In the faint illumination spilling around the fire-screen, Mr. Dove's head could be made out. Tilted to his left, in the manner of someone harkening to an unseen speaker.

'Is it really you, my love? This is your mama. I've always known death could not divide us for ever.'

'He is trying to tell me his name but it is difficult for a young spirit to communicate, with strangers present. Don't be shy now, Edward... Edwin... show me the letters if you are able.'

'Edmund, after his papa. Oh, don't strain him, I know it's you at last, my angel. Only tell me, are you happy?'

'Your Eddy wishes to assure you, he is truly happy. The love between you is everlasting, the anguish of separation felt only in this vale of tears. On the far side of the gulf dividing the living from the world of spirit, our loved ones dwell with our Lord Almighty in eternal peace.'

'I thought my heart would break when you left us. We miss you so. I sit in your bedroom often. Papa insisted on your things being packed away, but they're all quite safe in the attic.'

'Eddy sees you there. He watches over you and has longed to dry his mama's tears.'

'I'm so worried he's lonely without us.'

'Never lonely. He wants you to know he has lots of friends. Eddy loves to play with other spirit-children.'

'Oh, that's marvellous. He never could run and play, not with his poor twisted foot. If only I could tell your papa.'

'Everyone is whole in spirit. The old are made young again, the crippled shall walk, the dumb speak and the blind shall see. Infirmities are confined to the living. Your boy can run with ease and leap with joy.'

The lady gave a small sob. 'I'm so thankful you're not alone in heaven.'

'The connection is fading now... fading. A lady is waiting to communicate.'

'Don't go, please don't go. There's so much I want to ask.'

'Have no care, madam, your parting is over. This is but a temporary farewell. There will be ample opportunity for more private discourse.'

The bell tinkled, a fleeting ripple and gone.

Mrs Dove spoke of a sudden, her genteel voice low. 'If everyone would keep holding their neighbour's hands, our unbroken circle will assist the spirits.'

'Of course, oh, thank you, thank you.' His neighbour's sleeve rustled as she dabbed in the region of her eyes. A discreet sniff and Ellis felt her gloved fingers resume their delicate press.

'Will you approach our circle? You are among friends. My spirit-guide is bringing forth a lady, long used to patience. One who was an invalid, pious, gentle and modest. Her acceptance of her many trials was a shining example to those about her. She is showing me how she would lie on a chaise-longue with a view of her rose garden, which unhappily, she was too feeble to tend.'

His heart began to pound. Yet, this could be true of many invalids.

'Her fair locks had been much admired in her youth, becoming thin and wan as her health worsened. A second lady would lovingly comb her hair. A companion? No... a sister.'

Rowland Ellis felt his throat close like a trap. An eerie sensation fixed him, akin to icy water dripping down his backbone.

'Will you give us your name? Sophy... no, Maria... something like? Ah, I have it now. This lady wishes to speak to someone here tonight. She tells me her name is Sophia...'

ONE

London, two months later

It was gratifying to report there were no murders outstanding.

Or none, at least, likely to cause trouble, thought Chief Inspector Walter Townsend, as he packed the bowl of his pipe. A money-lender had been found on his premises, bludgeoned about the head. The killer was thought to be known but the contemptible wretch had fled, lying low in some rat-hole. They would drag him in soon enough.

While he staunchly believed the law was equal for all, it was a fact of life that reporters rarely demanded justice for the lower orders. Money-lenders were universally disliked.

His custom was to allow himself a single fill of his pipe at the end of the working day. The mixture stood on the mantelpiece in a Chinese jar, a relic of his father's time in the Royal Marines. The Townsends had a long tradition of service in the Light Infantry and he'd been expected to follow. Having no inclination for the ocean or foreign parts, he'd elected to serve his monarch on dry land, working in a place not unlike a barracks.

This was a time of evening he enjoyed, when a certain peace spread over Great Scotland Yard. Presently swathed in fog, the detectives' building stood apart from the sections edging the quadrangle, marooned to one side of the empty space he likened to a parade-ground.

Its passages were finally quiet of boots and door-bangings. A fragrant aroma of Caribbean tobacco was soothing his lungs, the last glowing coals collapsing in the grate, the clock's tick regular against the scratching of his nib.

Carrying a lantern, the Commissioner had looked in for a routine word on his way across to his house. As every evening, Townsend awaited the verbal report of his inspectors. The last of these was overdue as he sat, rapidly totting the column of figures before him.

When a knock came at last, he underlined his total, rolling the blotting-pad carefully over the ink, before bidding his subordinate to enter.

'Well? Out with it, man. I expected you a quarter-hour since.'

Ruddy-faced, bringing a whiff of damp wool with him, Sheppard's appearance was dishevelled. His demeanour spoke of a successful man.

'Pleased to report every last one of 'em are in custody at Church-street, sir. One tried to go over the roof, only I'd a division man posted by the sky-light.' Inspector Sheppard moved to warm his hands at the dying fire. 'Else we'd never have taken him in this weather. Foul out there now, worse than earlier. Mind, the fog aided our getting in and kept most of the neighbours from poking their long nebs in.'

'A satisfactory conclusion, by the sound of it. Snide coin's the very devil. Undermines the whole of society.'

'This lot were top end, it was a rare tip-off. Not a spoon to be seen. We found a whole tray of bronze medallions. The daughter fought like a cat in a sack. Baxter nearly had molten metal over his boots.'

'Was anyone injured?'

'Nothing to speak of, sir. One of 'em, an ugly cove, landed a punch on Inspector Abbs. He might've looked like the easiest way past, but he stood firm.'

'You found your new colleague useful?'

'He'll do. He's shown he can handle himself, for all there's no spare flesh on him.' Sheppard glanced down at the solid muscle tightening his waistcoat. 'He's a sharp one, sir and I'd rather a man on the quiet side than coming in all cock o' the walk.'

Townsend looked pained. 'If you mean full of bluster, say so, Sheppard, but I agree with your sentiment. Inspector Abbs has had sufficient time to learn our way of doing things. From Monday, he'll have his own dockets and take his turn with whatever comes in. He'll be out of your room shortly.'

'I don't envy Abbs. It won't be easy finding his way round the streets. No one knows him from Adam. He'll get no whispers for a long while.'

Clearing his papers, Townsend locked his drawer, pocketing his chain. 'We all had to start somewhere. His sergeant will assist him and no doubt, introduce his own informants.'

'Who will that be, sir, if I might inquire? Only, I hear we've two more second-class on the strength. A fellow from Derbyshire and one up from...'

Silencing him with his habitual flick of the hand, Townsend went to his hat-stand. 'There's a deal too much idle chatter in the inspectors'-room.' Hesitating, he made the decision he'd been weighing. 'Sergeant Grainer will accompany Abbs for now.'

Buttoning his top-coat, he caught Sheppard straightening a grin. 'I won't detain you further from making out your report, Inspector.'

'Right you are, sir.'

Folding his muffler to his satisfaction, Townsend plucked at his kid gloves. Finally, he collected his walking-stick and pointed with his pipe.

'Leave it on my desk before you go.'

~

Fog made a useful cover for foul deeds, thought Josiah Abbs, as he stretched his aching limbs. He stood at a window of his new lodgings, though there was little to be seen of the streets of St Pancras. Fanciful by nature, he'd begun to think of fog as a presence, rather than a phenomenon of weather. It even had a name here, a London particular.

Journalists wrote of fog descending on the city. It seemed to him that fog crept in like a thief. Rolling along the estuary marshes, rising from the Thames, stealing in from the countryside. Insinuating itself between gratings, along passages, dissolving through dismal courts and garden squares. Fog thickened the spittle in the throats of rich and poor alike, as it fingered round shutters and seeped under doors.

His own visage reflected in the glass, a pale ghost. When he opened the window a few inches, sounds were oddly hollow. Slow wheels bumped somewhere near, hooves slipping on greasy cobbles and hesitant footsteps, accompanied by the tapping of a stick. Some way off, came the chuffing of a locomotive, followed by an exuberant fading hoot. He couldn't tell whether it was returning or departing for the Midlands.

His landlady had expressed the hope, in her soft Scotch voice, that the railways wouldn't disturb him. She'd pointed out the great roof of St Pancras station and indicated the direction of Kings Cross. A few streets to the south, he'd already explored past the lofty arch of Euston terminus. He admired the cathedrals of steam. He'd assured Mrs Newsome truthfully, he didn't mind the sound of trains.

She'd told him the fogs would lessen as the year wore on and fewer fires added their smoke to the manufactories' chimneys. They'd reached April but it was a poor spring, winter reluctant to let go its cold grip.

Gloucester-road suited him when he came to view the sparsely-furnished rooms. A quiet street, near the old parish church. Within walking distance of the Regent's Park, and without a noisy tavern on the corner, it would do him very well.

Mrs Newsome, in her turn, appeared satisfied to let her vacant first-floor rooms to an officer from the detective-branch. He'd found that was not universally the case.

She'd assured him the omnibus ran every few minutes, but he never minded walking. Terms were more moderate away from Westminster, necessary on an inspector's pay.

He relived the taking of the bit-fakers in Bethnal Green. The Nichol had proved to be a mean quarter, tumble-down tenements and festering rubbish-heaps, worn-faced women clutching ragged children. Abbs yawned and felt his throbbing jaw.

The acrid smoke of umpteen fires was souring his lungs. A wisp of fog was floating near the gas-mantle. Weary thoughts were drifting like the blacks that would dirty the room, if he didn't raise the window.

Stacking his supper dishes on the tray, he folded the street-map he'd been studying, retrieved a saucer from the carpet and opened his door a little.

TWO

A week later

Every morning, Abbs joined a swelling tide of sober-backed clerks. The procession of men, of all ages, surged east towards the counting-houses of the City, branching south in the direction of Whitehall. More fell in step at every corner.

A good many were chewing on a fresh roll, or pie, as they walked. Street-sellers carried their wares still warm. Confectioners' and pastry-shops had a window open, where assistants waited to hand out purchases. Breakfast could be had, he saw, almost without losing pace.

A succession of morning-sweepers, so many yards apart, were regular as palings in a fence as he neared his destination. He spared a thought for their early labour, repeatedly brushing a clear path among mud and horse-dung, before hastening to their next job.

The last few days had been unfailingly grey, thin fog, half-hearted showers. Rain had woken him in the night, leaving a freshness in the air. A breeze, whipping up from the river, was dispersing rags of mist, as easily as dirt flicked from a broom.

Even at this early hour, the grand approach of Whitehall was clattering with horse-traffic of every description. Growlers, carts, delivery vans, hansoms, omnibuses and private carriages almost jostled sides, collision seeming inevitable before the day was out.

As he passed beneath the arch of Great Scotland Yard, Abbs felt its history settle about him. He wondered how long it would take for working there to seem unremarkable.

Alone in Inspector Sheppard's room, he began reading through reported sightings of drags-men, who'd been working around Hyde Park Gate. Carriage-thieves were an ever-present nuisance in the capital.

He liked Sheppard, who was proving an astute and affable colleague. A framed studio portrait of his wife stood on the desk. An engraving of Richmond Castle in Yorkshire hung on the wall, alongside the map of the Metropolis. Sheppard had emphasised he came from the North Riding town, not its inferior namesake west of London. A knock at the door interrupted his concentration.

The stranger, who entered at his summons, had a lined countenance, framed by grizzled, Piccadilly weepers. He coughed before speaking. 'Detective Sergeant Grainer, sir.'

'Good day, Sergeant. We haven't met before?'

'I mostly work with Inspector Cole, sir. He's away at present.'

'What is it you want?'

'You're to see Chief Inspector Townsend, sir, right away.'

'Do you know why?' he inquired, scraping back the chair.

'There's been a murder. Last night, in Kennington. A rate-payer, killed in his home.'

Grainer wheezed like a bellows, grasping the hand-rail, as they went downstairs. He wore an air of despondency like an old coat.

The chief inspector waved him to a seat before the desk, while Grainer took up position by the bookshelves. Glancing at the clock, Townsend wasted no time in getting to his purpose.

'Has Grainer indicated why I sent for you?'

'There was a murder last night, sir. That's all I know.'

'I trust you'll soon remedy that. We've had word from Kennington. The victim was a Mr. Rowland Ellis, an architect by profession. He was found early this morning in his own home. He'd been stabbed. There are signs the house was forcibly entered and items stolen.' Townsend looked up from the internal telegraph-form, regarding him keenly.

'Have there been other reports of house-breaking in the neighbourhood?'

'They don't say. I doubt you know Kennington yet?'

'I haven't been there, sir. A suburb south of the river, I believe?'

The chief inspector nodded. 'Comes under L Division, Lambeth. I'm assigning you to the inquiry. Sergeant Grainer will assist you.'

'Very good, sir. Have the household been questioned yet?'

Townsend made a dismissive motion with his hand. 'Talk to the local sergeant. He awaits you at the house. The body's already been taken to the mortuary. You haven't yet had occasion to go there, I think. Grainer will show you.'

'A pity. I should like to have viewed it at the scene.'

'The locals got matters underway before the Superintendent decided to request our assistance. Happens all the time, you'll find. Wait outside, Sergeant.'

They were silent until the door closed. Snatches of words drifted from outside. A deep horn blasted on the river, making Abbs flinch. Someone was whistling an air and a horse whinnied, his shoes striking against the stones as he was driven in.

'Pull that up, will you? It's like working in the midst of Piccadilly.' Townsend paused while he shut the window. 'I trust, Abbs, you feel ready to take charge? You've had a month with us.'

'I do, sir. I know I can call on your advice, if necessary, and Sergeant Grainer's assistance will be invaluable.'

'As to that...' Townsend seemed about to say something and thought better. 'A case like this can't remain on the books for long. A respectable householder struck down in his own home, it's an outrage. Men won't feel safe in their own beds, let alone their wives. The Commissioner and the public expect us to get results. That's what we're paid for.'

'Indeed, sir.'

'Your last case in Devonshire was a poisoning, I believe.'

It wasn't a question. 'Yes, sir.'

'Hmm, successfully concluded, though not without incident.'

'I very much regret what happened, sir, and take full responsibility.'

A brass stamp-box lay open on the desk. Townsend reached over and shut the lid. The sound snapped like the rap of a gavel. Being under the other man's scrutiny, as he continued, was akin to being in the witness-box. Abbs supposed he'd grow accustomed to his superior's ways, soon enough.

'It seems your former chief constable thinks highly of your competence. He attaches no blame to you, or Sergeant Reeve, on the contrary.' Abbs remained silent, noting Townsend had the facts committed to memory. 'Now, I believe I'm a fair man, but not one unduly impressed by a detective performing his given duty.'

'Understood, sir.'

'I expect dedication from my men.' Townsend swung round to the map, showing the capital's police-stations and divisions. 'Year by year, London spreads, vanquishing grass with brick. A magnificent achievement. It's our privilege to uphold the law in this great city. The dregs of the Empire and her enemies are drawn to its very heart. What's more, every country thief, sooner or later, thinks he'll try his luck here.'

'I was told the detective-branch has recently expanded, sir.'

'Lieutenant-Colonel Henderson instigated many improvements when he was newly appointed. That's no criticism of previous Commissioners. We must keep pace. As yet, district detectives are few in number. They rely on our guidance. It's as well to keep a bag packed. It may be that you'll be sent to assist a county force at short notice.'

'Yes, sir.'

'It doesn't do, Inspector, to be daunted by our great capital. We've near as many men transferred here as native Londoners. I was one of them and Sheppard's a Yorkshireman, as I don't doubt, he's informed you.'

'He has made mention, sir. I'll heed your words.'

'You'll report to me each evening. I expect to be kept fully informed of progress, and notes to be written up in full, before you go off duty. You've been allotted your own room. Grainer will show you later. You'd best be off without delay.'

There was nothing like the beginning of a case, thought Abbs, as he left.

THREE

They took a hansom, Grainer expelling air as he lowered himself on the worn seat, the folding-doors close by their knees. Their journey took them at walking pace across a crowded Westminster Bridge, free of tolls. Shortly after, the cabby called down to them, cursing that the main road was blocked by an over-turned wagon. The trap shut abruptly and he diverted them through a jumble of warehouses and timber-yards.

Mean terraces, strung with cat's-cradles of washing, were shadowed by manufactories, their chimneys belching smuts. Abbs glimpsed children playing outside a charity-school, hemmed in by grimy brick walls, steam escaping from barred windows. An over-powering stench was vile.

'Tallow,' said Grainer. 'From Belmont's, the candle-makers. Don't suppose none of them notice after a while.'

'Are you well-acquainted with Kennington, Sergeant?'

'Well enough, sir. I can find my way around.'

'What manner of people live there?'

Grainer scratched by way of consideration. Abbs drew back a meagre inch in his corner.

'Respectable, mostly clerking-class and above. This here's North Lambeth, dirt-poor but safe enough for the most part.'

'No rookery, then?'

Grainer lurched as they turned a corner. 'No, sir, 'sides, most rookeries aren't what they were ten year ago. So much getting pulled down, the rats have run eastwards, Whitechapel, like.'

'And Bethnal Green. I was there with Inspector Sheppard.'

'Heard about that, sir.' Grainer squirmed forward, peering out. 'See the streets picking up as you pull back from the river? Better income, better air, you might say. Best houses are where we're bound, near Kennington-road and the park. Not Society families but good incomes, professional men, widows living on their own means, that sort.'

As they shook off the immediate environs of the Thames, they passed streets of better terraces, small villas built in pairs. They skirted a fine square, gone up in the last century. Grainer pointed out the police-station, just off the main thoroughfare, as they passed commercial premises and shops. They turned off opposite park railings, pulling up in a quiet street of trees and tall gate-pillars.

Abbs stretched, glad to be out of the cramped confines, while Grainer obtained a grudging receipt for expenses. No great ride from Westminster and they were in another London. A nurse-maid was pushing a perambulator away from them. She turned in a gate and Wellow-road was empty, but for themselves. The street put him in mind of a painting he'd admired on his last day off. Gables and chimneys glimpsed among trees, a squat church tower, lamp-posts along the pavement. A prosperous neighbourhood, somehow faintly sinister in repose.

He shook off such foolish imagining. Possibly, the residents here didn't yet know there'd been a murder in the night. In a poor quarter, the news would have spread through lodgings like damp in winter. They'd be outside, waiting for a free show.

As the cab rattled off, he glimpsed a constable emerging from a gate. They would know soon. He could smell a gas-works and, away from the smoke-hazed river-bank, there was birdsong.

'Set up for life.' His voice doleful, Grainer joined him. The houses were positioned well back, behind low walls and hedges. Rowland Ellis's property was screened by laurel.

Abbs estimated Lindholm to have been built fifty or sixty years since. A gentleman's villa, it had traces of the elegant cottage-style of a simpler age. He liked the narrow brick and porch of decorative iron-work. Dark green shutters framed the widows, their curtains drawn. On the left-hand side, a narrow path ran between the wall and the neighbouring property.

'That doesn't make these families safe from tragedy,' he said, as they started along the short carriage-drive.

'No, sir, but they're fed and clothed while they weep. They can pay to bury their dead.'

'I take your point, Sergeant.'

The front door stood open and a parlour-maid was watching them approach, a stern, bespectacled woman in her middle years. An unfashionable household then, not over-given to appearances.

A man pushed past her, a brown billy-cock in his hand. His relief was plain as he strode up to them. 'You'll be the Yard men come to take charge?' He scarcely waited for a response as Abbs gave their

17

names. 'Sergeant Hollins of L Division, sir, stationed at Kennington-lane.' Nodding at Grainer, 'Sergeant,' he drew them to one side.

'The victim was done in with his own paper-knife.' Glancing at the servant, he lowered his voice. 'Right in the heart. A heavy sort of dagger affair, left sticking out of his chest.'

The parlour-maid tired of waiting for them and disappeared. She wasn't visibly upset, thought Abbs, but he too, didn't go by appearances.

'The killer gained entry through a side-door leading to the victim's study. That's where he was found. One of those garden-doors with the upper half glazed. He smashed the glass and turned the key from outside.'

'Is there a dog kept on the premises?'

'No, sir.' Sergeant Hollins spoke rapidly, in the manner of a man keen to hand over. Producing a large handkerchief, he mopped his face above his ginger-brown moustache, though the morning wasn't warm.

'I've set one of my constables knocking on doors. Asking if anyone was seen late last night. Thought you'd want us to make a start, sir.'

'Quite right, Sergeant, we're glad of your assistance. The family are within? I've been told very little.'

'There's no family to speak of. Only a sister by marriage, who resided with Mr. Ellis. A Miss Louisa Maitland, she's inside. He was a widower, childless, no other kin.'

Abbs looked up at the windows. Wisteria had been trained over the frontage from a gnarled trunk. He recalled his father saying it took seven years to flower. In a few weeks, the fragrant blooms would hang down, the colour of half-mourning.

'Have you questioned Miss Maitland yet?'

'Only briefly, sir, I took down the main facts. I was hampered by a gent with her, Mr. Buckley. He's Mr. Ellis's business partner. She'd sent for him and he turned up shortly after we did.'

'How is she?'

'Didn't strike me as needing a smelling-bottle. After all, there's no blood-tie.'

'I'll see where the murder took place first, then speak to them. I understand the dead man wasn't found till this morning?'

'That's right, sir, Miss Maitland was out all evening. Took a maid with her, the one you just saw. They attended a meeting at the Institute here, an improving lecture.' He jerked his head derisively. 'Mr. Ellis spent the evening in his study. The other servants didn't see him after supper. Nor did Miss Maitland, when the women came home. Didn't even bid him goodnight.'

Abbs listened intently. 'Had he requested not to be disturbed?'

'Nah, she said that was their custom. He spent most evenings sitting by himself and didn't care to be troubled. Wish I had a room away from my old woman.'

'Who saw Mr. Ellis last?'

'Miss Maitland and the parlour-maid, when he got up from the table last night.'

'Who found him, Sergeant?'

'Same maid, sir, when she went to lay the fire before breakfast. Maggie Onslow by name, she's a cool one. Couldn't get in, the study door was locked. She thought something was wrong, it was never locked. So she went round the outside of the house and found the door broken in.'

'How many servants are there?'

'Three, all female, the cook, parlour-maid and a skivvy. No carriage kept and they employ a jobbing gardener.' Sergeant Hollins reeled off the list. Abbs decided he seemed efficient.

'No one heard a sound in the night. Ain't it always the way? But mark this, sir, I set one of my lads to search the garden and he's found a snuff-box, lying under bushes by the wall. Belonged in the study. Must've been dropped by the killer, as he fled.'

Composing his features to look suitably impressed, Abbs continued. 'Had you occasion to come across Rowland Ellis, before this?'

'Never met him, sir, but I know of his business, that's well-established. Seen his name in the local 'paper over the years, giving charitable subscriptions, attending public dinners. You've been told he was an architect?'

'Nothing more.'

'He must have been nearing sixty, made his money long since. Mrs Ellis died about a year ago. I mind reading the account of her funeral.'

'What about his reputation? Was he known to be quarrelsome, a man who made enemies?'

Hollins shook his head. 'Not that I've ever heard. He disturbed a house-breaker and had the misfortune to pay for it.'

'What else was stolen?'

'Only a couple of things, they think. I had to wait till the body'd gone before I could ask the lady to look. The silver snuff-box, pair of miniature portraits in silver frames and a small bit of china from off the mantel-shelf. I have their descriptions.'

'Good. Shall we?' Abbs gestured their companion to lead the way in.

'Strikes me, sir, that's all the killer had time to pocket before Mr. Ellis confronted him.'

Hollins paused while they wiped their boots and led them through an inner hall. They passed the stairs, where an ornate gas-lamp was fitted on the newel-post.

He indicated a door with a flourish. 'In here, sir. This is where the murder took place.'

FOUR

The study was comfortably appointed. A pair of armchairs were arranged by the fireplace, one had the creases of habitual sitting, with a side-table at hand. An unusual feature was a tilted drawing-board near the window. A woman's portrait hung opposite the desk.

Abbs took in the signs of violence, which Hollins felt necessary to point out. The garden-door had its glass smashed near the brass knob. A small blood-stain disfigured the Turkey rug. Curiously, not so jarring as the jagged glass shards on the runner serving as door-mat.

'The corpse was fully dressed, lying partly across the hearth-rug here,' said Hollins. 'Sprawled half on his back and turned a bit to his left side. Left arm sticking out here, fancy handle buried in his chest.'

'Fully dressed?'

'Smoking-jacket and trousers.'

'Then he wasn't woken by a noise and came down in the night?' Frowning, Abbs looked about him. 'Mr. Ellis fell with his head towards the hall door, which would indicate his attacker was facing him thus, his back to the outer door. There doesn't appear to be any sign of a struggle.'

Hollins chewed his lips. 'Took him by surprise, I shouldn't wonder.'

'When the maid entered from outside, was the key still in the hall door?'

'Yes, sir, she saw the body, unlocked the door to the hall and hastened upstairs to wake her mistress.'

Abbs turned to Grainer. 'What do you make of it, Sergeant?'

'Either he hadn't retired, sir, or he might've gone up and not had time to undress.'

'Did you ask if Mr. Ellis's bed had been slept in?'

'Not yet sir,' said Hollins. 'These properties aren't wealthy enough to interest a cracks-man. Most of the house-breakers on this patch are known to us, but there are bound to be newcomers.'

'Have there been other break-ins in the neighbourhood?'

'Not in Kennington. Nothing recent, but there has to be a start.'

'Most house-breakers would enter through the back quarters, wouldn't you say? A larder window or pantry. Less chance of being heard. There's probably a bedroom above here. They'd wait until they thought the household was asleep. Did you inquire when Mr.

Ellis was in the habit of retiring?'

'I did, sir, apparently he slept poorly. He'd sit up late, often past midnight. Long after the rest of them were abed. All very well for those who don't have work to go to.' Hollins broke off, swinging round as the door-knob jiggled.

The man who entered was somewhere in his late forties. His air was decisive, as though he were the owner of the house.

'Ah, at last. You're the detective fellow in charge, I take it? I'm Frederick Buckley.'

Hollins stiffened. 'This gentleman is the late Mr. Ellis's business partner.'

'Inspector Abbs, sir.'

The other man appraised him openly. 'I insisted Metropolitan officers be sent for, at once. No offence, Sergeant, they have the experience. You have some register of criminals at Scotland Yard, so the press inform us? You can telegraph to every county force, if need be and hunt down the fiend who attacked Ellis?'

'The local knowledge of the Kennington police may prove the decisive factor,' said Abbs.

'Most diplomatic, Inspector. I want to see the cowardly wretch dragged to the condemned cell. I'm quite prepared to put up a reward, if necessary.'

'We'll get him, sir, never fear,' said Hollins.

'I'm glad Miss Maitland had the presence of mind to send for me. Fortunately, I hadn't left for the day. Miss Maitland is more resolute than many ladies, but she couldn't be expected to cope without assistance. She's calmer now, since I've advised her.'

'We shall be speaking to her shortly.'

'Am I able to give you any immediate information, Inspector? Only I have an urgent engagement elsewhere.'

Abbs thought quickly. Orderly in his methods, he would rather begin with the household and work outwards. Servants saw far more than employers realised.

'Do you know anything, sir, that could shed light on Mr. Ellis's murder?'

'Of course not. Is it not evident to you? Ellis was set upon by one or more ruffians. The man died defending his home. It's an outrage.'

'I have to examine all possibilities, sir. Are you aware of any enmities in Mr. Ellis's private life?'

'Certainly not. He was highly respected by everyone who knew him.'

Which was no guarantee of fair-dealing. 'What about your partnership, sir? Had your business lately been involved in any dispute?'

Buckley scowled. 'Who said such a thing?'

'No one, sir, I merely inquire.'

'In any profession, small disputes may arise from time to time. Gentlemen don't come to blows over trifling differences of opinion, I assure you. Mr. Ellis, in fact, had little to do with the day to day running of the business. He was no longer accepting commissions on his own behalf. Since his wife's illness worsened, he spent much of his time here. He'd shown no inclination to return to work since her death.'

'Even so, I shall need to speak to you further, Mr. Buckley. Might we arrange a time?'

'Very well, take my card. I shall be at my desk in the forenoon. Why you should need to, escapes me but better you ask me, than trouble Miss Maitland. She assures me she can be left in the servants' care, so I'm away to Windsor for the remainder of the day. An important client awaits me.'

Thanking him, Abbs glanced at the card he'd been passed by extended fingertip.

'I shall take my leave of you.' Closing his watch, Buckley pointed at the rug. 'Ensure that's removed before Miss Maitland sees it. She'll be down directly.'

Hollins cursed softly when the door was shut. 'Who does he think we are? Begging your pardon, sir, but he's as stiff as the wax under his nose. Anyone'd think he was off to visit the Queen, 'stead of wading ankle-deep on some building-site.'

Abbs doubted Mr. Buckley intended crossing mud in those highly-polished boots. Not if the silk cravat and gold pin were anything to go by.

'Before you came, sir, he informed me I was a servant of the public. I have my duty to perform, but I'm no man's servant.'

'An unfortunate term. We've all suffered it.' He looked at Grainer, who was fingering the wooden frame of the drawing-apparatus. 'What say you, Sergeant?'

'I've been turned away from many a front door, sir. You come to expect it of butlers, but these self-made men are worse. An' they reckon they know more about detecting than we do. Inspector Cole always gives them short shrift.'

'Does he indeed? Is there a safe on the premises?'

'No, sir, first thing I asked. Seems Mr. Ellis didn't go in for much plate. They've a few bits kept in a locked cupboard in the pantry, but there's no window. The larder window's small, you could maybe push a snakes-man through.'

Abbs looked out at a uniformed constable, standing by a shrubbery. On this side, the garden was screened from the drive by a laurel hedge and low wicket-gate. A caller could not see in the study, but there was little to bar them from walking round this side of the house.

'You've your work cut out, sir,' Hollins grinned suddenly. 'Your best hope is a witness in the small hours. Not so easy round here. We'll do our best for you but there's no coffee-stall nearer than the main road. No beggars, no street-walkers hanging round these parts. No passing trade, see.'

There was an unmistakable relish in his tone, now he was off the hook.

~

His innards squirming, Constable Latham considered his chance of bread an' dripping, washed down with hot tea in the mess-room, was dwindling by the minute. Gawd knows where he'd be sent, now the Yard men had arrived. On early turn, he'd been about to take his breakfast when Sergeant Hollins had gathered them up.

He'd been left on his own, once Benny had been sent off with the corpse. Searched the alley beyond the coach-house, glanced in the coal-house and privy. Poked under every wet bush in the garden, until he spotted the glint of silver. Made to wait here like a sentry, drips trickling down the back of his collar and his guts empty.

He thought the point of having their own detectives was no outsiders swaggering in, telling 'em they were a bunch of fools. Spitting copiously, Latham straightened his shoulders, just in time, as Hollins came out with a stranger. An older man in a worn frock-coat lagged behind.

'There, you see, sir?' Hollins was keen to impress. 'The killer climbed the wall here, dropping the box in his hurry to get away.'

The detective studied the earth, where a man might stand concealed among the shrubbery.

'Don't just stand there, Latham. Pick it up, now the inspector's seen where it lay. Good spot to climb in, sir. Nearest street-lamp's a fair way off. He'd be well hidden.'

The inspector from the Yard looked down his thin nose. A clean-shaven face, not even whiskered, he'd be taken for a school-master, were it not for a fading bruise on his jaw. Someone let him have it strong or else, he'd measured his own length. Holding the small hinged box, Latham hoped the mark was still smarting.

'Does the path, beyond the wall, lead round to the mews?'

'Yes, sir. Leads to a dirt lane running along the back of the properties, so the killer could be away in another street. The wall's much higher at the end of the garden, hiding the stable. This is where you'd choose to get over.'

'What about the tradesman's gate at the front?'

'Bolted by evening, sir. Leads to a yard by the kitchen. There's no way in the garden from there.'

Latham started as he was suddenly addressed.

'Have you found any foot-prints, Constable?'

'No, sir.'

Hollins elbowed aside a branch of drab evergreens. 'The bushes have kept the ground dry.'

Looking dubious, the inspector didn't comment. They all trooped back to the house, Hollins brushing droplets from his cape-shoulders.

'Well, Inspector, you've seen all I can usefully show you. You'll want to question the servants for yourself. I could do with being about my other duties, if you've no objection. Shall I introduce you to the lady of the house, afore I go?' Hollins stood back for the others to enter the side-door. The Yard sergeant's boots crunched on broken glass. 'Be off with you, Latham. Catch up with Rymer and start knocking on doors. You clear what to say?'

'Yes, Sarge. Did they see anyone coming or going last night.'

'Be off with you, then.'

Latham kicked the gravel as he went. He'd enjoyed seeing Hollins questioned like a scholar reciting his dates. See how he liked it. He bet Benny would've cadged a cup of cocoa at the mortuary. Maybe hot buttered toast an' all. Everyone knew they did themselves all right, those attendants down at the dead-room.

FIVE

Abbs found the air stifling in the morning-room. Hollins must have come from there when he'd first seen him. The coals were banked up, as if a servant had thought a good blaze would comfort her mistress.

Miss Louisa Maitland accepted his condolences graciously and bade them be seated. He felt obliged to take an armchair by the hearth, leaving her in sole occupancy of the sofa. He envied Grainer, taking a seat against the far wall.

The room overlooked the front garden, positioned to benefit from the early sun. There was no visible trace of its owner, though a morning-room was the usual province of the ladies of a house.

Miss Maitland offered tea and he accepted for her sake. While they waited for the tray to be brought in, Abbs wondered how often the two family members had sat together of an evening. He was beginning an impression of Rowland Ellis shut in his study, his sister-in-law solitary in the drawing-room. This would not do. As yet, he knew nothing about them.

'I regret the necessity, Miss Maitland, to trouble you with more questions.'

'I understand, Inspector. Mr. Buckley explained to me that more detective officers were sent for.'

Sombre in shabby, grey merino, Miss Louisa Maitland looked gone forty. Thin, with fine brown hair, secured painfully flat against her scalp. Abbs would have thought her composed, were it not for the black-bordered handkerchief wound tight between her fingers. He began by asking about the household, partly to put her at ease.

'In addition to Maggie, there's the cook, Mrs Emma Wilmot, and our scullery-maid, Bertha Fry.'

'How long have they been with you?'

'Cook's been here over two years, I believe and Maggie for many years. Bertha's been with us about seven months. She doesn't have followers. All three are trustworthy, I assure you.'

Abbs liked her for saying so. 'Mr. Ellis didn't keep a carriage, ma'am?'

'Not for the past year. When my sister was alive, they kept a brougham but he decided it was no longer taken out sufficiently. Mr.

Ellis found it agreeable to walk to the cab-stand on Kennington-road and we could always send out for one, if needed.'

She coloured a little, almost certainly repeating the words of the dead man. The brougham wasn't to be kept on for her convenience.

'Do you know what happened to the coachman?'

'He obtained a position with a family in Highgate. Rowland... Mr. Ellis gave him a good reference. Surely, you can't think the man held a grudge, Inspector?'

Abbs shook his head. 'I don't have suspicions of anyone, ma'am, but I'd be neglecting my duty, were I not thorough. I accept your vouching for your servants but I must question them. Dismissed servants have passed on information before now. House-breakers been known to bribe someone on the inside.'

'I'm sure that's what Sergeant Hollins suspicions but I've been an upper servant, myself. A governess.' Her eyes met his, her expression fierce. 'So I'm sympathetic to those below stairs. Too often, they're suspected of dishonesty, when their only crime is being inferior.'

'Your argument is undeniable, Miss Maitland, though I try not to bring preconceptions to my work.'

'I beg pardon, sir. For my part, I mustn't tar you with the brush of others.'

The tea-tray was brought, by Maggie, and they were silent while Miss Maitland poured.

Abbs noticed a thin curl of paper, caught behind the fire-dogs. Too flimsy for a spill, it had missed the flames. He saw a page number and a fraction of printed lettering, too little to make out any words.

'Do you wish me to repeat the events of last night, Inspector?'

'If you please. I understand you and your maid were out for the evening?'

'We accompanied my friend, Mrs Ibbotson, to a public lecture at the local Institute. She brought her parlour-maid, Edith.'

'At what time did you return?'

'It was just after ten. I can be sure because I looked at the hall clock as we came in. It's always kept good time.'

He'd noticed the handsome long-case, its hands stilled for a house in mourning.

'Will you describe what happened before you left?'

'We dined early, Mrs Ibbotson was collecting us in her carriage.

The lecture was to begin at half-past seven. Rowland usually spent the evening in his study, preferring it to the drawing-room, these past months.'

So he'd been right. 'Whereabouts is this Institute situated?'

'Not far from here on Kennington-road. We have a speaker every month and a meeting afterwards. Mrs Ibbotson is wife to our vicar. Last night, we brought a quantity of clothes donated for the needy. We were quite squashed. After refreshment, we helped to make up parcels to be distributed.'

'Did Mrs Wilmot and Bertha remain here?'

'Yes, they'll have spent the evening in the servants' quarters.'

'How did Mr. Ellis seem when you left him?'

She looked puzzled. 'Why, quite as usual. He wished me a pleasant evening and had a word about the weather.'

'He said nothing about expecting a visitor?'

'No, I'm certain he wasn't.'

'Did anything seem unusual when you came home, Miss Maitland?'

'In what way, Inspector?'

He hardly knew himself. 'Was anything out of place?'

She didn't pause to consider. 'I noticed nothing out of the ordinary. Maggie fetched my bed-candle and I went straight to my room.'

'You didn't bid Mr. Ellis good night?'

A sallow blotch suffused her cheeks for the second time. 'That wasn't our custom when my brother-in-law was closeted in his study. My sister was taken from us last June. He bore her loss heavily. We didn't see a great deal of one another, other than at table.'

Abbs nodded sympathetically, watching Grainer make a note.

'Please don't mistake me, Inspector, we were on cordial terms. I have remained here on my brother-in-law's charity. I've taken care not to trouble him in any way. At first, I hoped sharing our grief would help ease his suffering. Sadly, Rowland considered himself poor company and preferred solitude.'

'Did you hear any sound in the night, ma'am?'

'None whatsoever. The evening had been fatiguing. I slept easily and knew nothing till morning, when Maggie roused me.' For the first time, she faltered, looking down at her hands. 'Sergeant Hollins will have told you how she found my poor brother-in-law lying dead.'

'My thanks for your forbearance, Miss Maitland.' He reached for his tall hat. 'I think that's all I need ask you for the moment.'

'Forgive me, Inspector, I should like to know whether the funeral must be long delayed? There's much to be arranged.'

'Are there no distant male relatives?'

'There are no others, sir, not even a cousin. Mr. Buckley has offered his assistance. He says he'll speak to Mr. Ellis's lawyer on my behalf. My position here is somewhat awkward, until the will is read and I learn what must become of me.'

Grainer was looking openly about him, like a sale-room porter pricing his tickets. His gaze took in the grouped paintings, a davenport and a bow-fronted cabinet displaying porcelain. Abbs fixed him with a steely look, until their eyes met and he ceased.

'The usual procedure is for the coroner to release the body for burial, when he adjourns the inquest. That will take place within the next few days, as soon as can be arranged.'

'I see, thank you, Inspector.'

'I'll speak to the servants now. Then we'll need to examine the study. Do you know if Mr. Ellis's bed was used?'

'I'll go and see.' Miss Maitland rose and went to the bell-pull. 'Maggie will show you to the kitchen.'

SIX

Abbs knew many of his colleagues would leave questioning servants to their sergeant. Were he were accustomed to Grainer, he might have done the same, but he dare not miss any clue.

An unpleasant musty smell met them as they followed Maggie to the servants' quarters. It reminded him of a warehouse he'd lately helped to search, where spices lingered in stale air. They passed an open door where a girl was stirring something in a copper.

'What's that stink?'

Maggie whirled round at Grainer's mumbled remark, her north-country vowels cutting.

'She's dyeing my old gown, that's what. No good you screwing up your nose like that. What d'you expect when there's sudden death in the house? We can't all send out for new mourning.' She indicated a door at the end of the passage. 'Kitchen's through there,' and turned back smartly.

Changing his mind, Abbs spoke rapidly. 'I'll question the cook. You assist the constables in the street, Sergeant. Make certain they've listed every house where people have gone out.'

'Let's hope they're few in number.'

'However many, they'll all have to be questioned. There's a chance the killer was seen on the drive last night.'

Grainer looked sceptical. 'Thought we've established he climbed over the wall, sir?'

'That's one possibility. We won't jump to conclusions this early. The snuff-box could have been thrown, in the shrubbery, from the path. I'll find you outside when I'm done here.'

Mrs Wilmot looked a little older than her mistress. Clad in black bombazine, she thrust a yellow-back in a drawer as he walked in. The formalities done, they sat at one end of the deal table, the cook taking her carver chair, with its cushion.

He knew the division of tasks wouldn't be strictly observed, as in a larger house. Miss Maitland wouldn't be above assisting Maggie with the polishing. He wondered what manner of man Rowland Ellis had been. If he'd even noticed the female servants working constantly for his comfort.

Here in the kitchen were small signs of disorder. A skillet with a tide-mark of speckled lard. They'd had breakfast, then. A jar of used tea-leaves was left on the dresser. Carpets were unlikely to be swept that day.

The cook's wariness, Abbs decided, was probably due to having detectives in the house. An infestation of mice would be more respectable, if equally unwelcome.

'I've already recounted last night to the other one. I keep thinking it might have been me murdered. You might be standing over me with my throat cut.'

'And Miss Bertha likewise, if that were the case.'

The cook sniffed. 'She'd be under the blankets if she heard a footstep. You should see her cowering when it thunders. The master caught her at it once and took her to task. Quite right too. Cover the looking-glass, I say to her. That's only good sense, but work has to be done, come what may.'

'From serving dinner, if you would.'

Mrs Wilmot shrugged. 'No different from any other, but for Maggie off out. When she took the meat in, I dished up our supper in here. She was nipping back and forth, clearing, fetching their pudding and cheese. Soon as she'd eaten, she had to rush off with Miss M. so I gave Bertha a hand with the dishes and wiping down.'

'I see you were kept busy. Did you speak to Mr. Ellis last night?'

'No, but I wouldn't expect to see him, stuck in here. The master mostly shut himself away of an evening. He rarely rang after dinner. No need.'

'What was Mr. Ellis like, would you say?'

She unbent, leaning on her elbows. 'Must have his own way, same as any man, but a fair master, long as you were honest. Very scrupulous, he was. Always a quiet sort of gent but more so, since the mistress was taken. Doted on her, he did. Not the sort to keep a woman on the quiet. Picked at his food ever since, which is a poor thanks for all my work. Mind, come to think of it, his appetite's improved lately.'

'I see little escapes you, Mrs Wilmot. I expect you see more of Miss Maitland, discussing the meals and ordering goods?'

'Not so much as in a regular household. I know my business and she keeps out of my way. Not a farthing's wasted in this house. No butcher'll get the better of me, I know all their tricks. And no greens come in my kitchen that aren't fresh.' Nodding to herself, she finished on a triumphant note.

'What do you mean, Mrs Wilmot, by a regular household?'

'One with a proper mistress. Miss Maitland was only sister to the late Mrs Ellis.'

'Was Mrs Ellis an invalid when you came here?'

'She had a creeping affliction of the kidneys, poor lady. She died about a year after I started. A sweet-natured soul, with a face to match, unlike her sister. Died on the loveliest summer morn, with her own roses heaped on her coffin. The good are always gathered early.' Her face grew stern. 'The wicked live on.'

'Do your responsibilities include locking up at night?'

The cook drew herself up in her chair. 'I make certain the servants' quarters are secured, the master would see to the rest himself. Look, I told that sergeant, the back door was locked and bolted after the scrapings were put out. The yard gate was bolted, all the windows fastened. See for yourself, some of them are barred. Is she saying I do my duties slap-dash?'

'No one is saying that, Mrs Wilmot.'

'I should think not. It's.. it was the master paid my wages. She's lucky he let her stay here after the mistress died, if you ask me.'

Abbs thought uncharitably, he had no choice. 'Miss Maitland is Mr. Ellis's relative, surely.'

'Only by marriage, I told you. Stands to reason, you get wed, doesn't mean you want the whole pack of them to feed ever after. She doesn't try to interfere, I'll say that much. But Miss Maitland's never been used to running a house, for all she claims this is her rightful home. She was a governess, sent for to help care for the mistress. The master was a one to do his duty and she's stayed on here by his charity. Creeps about like a mouse, hoping he'd forget she's here.'

'You weren't tempted to attend the lecture last night, Mrs Wilmot?'

'No, I wasn't. I get quite enough of Mrs Ibbotson and her moralising. She's always poking about in here, when she calls. Asked to see my order-book, would you believe? Yes, you might smile, I call it a liberty. Sweeps in here, handing out tracts. Begging coins and old clothes for the needy. She'd wring more out of you than a mangle.'

The cook's small dark eyes, and rounded face, put him in mind of currants in dough. 'After you finished your work, how did you spend the remainder of the evening?'

'Sat next door, same as every night. It's the cook's parlour by rights but I invite the others to sit along with me. Not being one to stand on ceremony and I like a bit o' company. You'll want to see for yourself, I suppose? The sergeant did.'

'If you please. It would be helpful to see the lay-out of the rooms.'

Abbs followed her back in the passage. Her room was small and crowded, but better than sitting among copper pans and the row of bells. Rowland Ellis had had more consideration than many employers.

The narrow grate still held last night's ashes. A picture of simpering kittens, wearing smocks, decorated the chimney-breast. The best chair had a tunbridge work-box within reach, some darning left out.

He went to the barred window, where a small looking-glass stood on a chest of drawers. Unlike the glass hanging in the hall, it hadn't been covered with crape. His back turned to the room, he saw the cook reach down by the side of her armchair, straightening in one hurried movement.

When he swung round casually, a moment later, her hands were empty.

'Were you and Bertha together all evening, Mrs Wilmot?'

'She was under my eye till she went up to bed. That sergeant was making out she'd let someone in to rob the master, but he's wrong. Bertha knows better than to do such a wicked thing. She's got a good place here and she knows it.'

'I'm sure Sergeant Hollins wasn't casting aspersions on the girl's honesty.'

'She's all in a stew since he questioned her. Mind you go easy on her. We don't know what's to become of us now.' Mrs Wilmot patted her cap in the glass, as she joined him. 'Not much of a view, is it?'

The écru lace curtains filtered the light through their dreary shade, doing much to obscure the outside. The domestic offices were at the right-hand rear of the house, on the opposite side from the study. The cook's parlour faced north, giving on to a yard with a coal-house and swill-bin. Some rags, on a drying line, lifted in the breeze.

'Mr. Ellis rarely rang in the evening, you said?'

'No need, he'd have a full scuttle of coal and a tray of strong drink.

All a body needs to keep the cold out.'

'Did either of you hear any sounds, last night, from the rest of the house?'

'Never do, unless she's playing the piano-forte, when the master's out. You can't hear the hall-clock chime when you're sitting in here, only the bell.'

'When did you and Bertha retire?'

'Soon after Maggie came in. She saw Miss M. up, then collected her own candle. The gas doesn't run up to the attics, and a good thing too, if you ask me, else we'd be blown up in our beds. The three of us went up the back stairs together.'

'That's all, I think, Mrs Wilmot.' A thought struck him. 'Have any strangers come to the back door recently?'

'Why? You don't reckon someone's been spying out the house?'

'It's not unknown.'

'Watching us unawares, like in a penny dreadful?'

'Have there been any new tradesmen?'

'No one recent, few since the new year. Still too early for fresh stuff. An old woman came hawking fancy goods, some weeks back. I did give her a cup of tea and bought a ribbon, feeling sorry for her. Then we did have a muffin-man but I sent him away. I know stale goods when I see them.'

There was nothing more to be learned, he thought. As he went to leave, Mrs Wilmot stopped him.

'There was an odd-looking stranger, back in the autumn. Hawking Kentish cob-nuts. Very dubious-like, he had a terrible squint. I do wonder now if he was examining the locks.'

He reassured her. 'Too long ago.'

She looked disappointed. He'd seen it before with witnesses. Once the shock was passed, she was beginning to enjoy it.

~

Laboriously peeling potatoes, Bertha seemed less jumpy than Mrs Wilmot suggested. Possibly, as she was away from the cook's presence. Her large hands looked sore, with cracks and fading marks from the hot range. Drying them, she showed him the larder readily enough.

The small room was like any other, with its enamel tubs of flour

35

and raisins on curling shelf-paper. A window, high in the white-washed wall, wouldn't admit a man's shoulders. As Hollins said, it might be possible for a boy to squeeze through, but it was screened with wire mesh and clearly undisturbed. A faint earthiness, lingering on the sacks, was an improvement on the scullery.

'You didn't hear any sounds in the night?'

'Oh, no, sir, I'm always that tired, I get off soon as my head sinks in the pillow. Only I'm down first in the morning.'

'Did you go near the study?'

She shook her head. 'I'm that glad I didn't find the master. I riddle the ashes, black-lead the range, lay the fire, heat the water, make tea for Cook, do the front step...'

The girl rattled off a long list of duties before her breakfast. Grey smudges pooled beneath her eyes, young as she was.

'You don't sleep down here?'

Bertha grinned, revealing a chipped tooth. 'No, sir, this is my first place and I got a whole room to myself, under the eaves.'

Abbs nodded, touched by her gratitude. They both knew she might have been given a make-shift bed in the scullery.

'How did you get this place, Bertha?'

'Mrs Ibbotson spoke for me. She takes an interest in my ma, since Pa died.'

'Good of her. Did you like Mr. Ellis?'

'Didn't see much of him. Maggie does the study and bedrooms.'

He waited, feeling she'd nearly said more. 'Don't be afraid to say what you think.'

She lowered her voice. 'You won't peach on me?'

He glanced in the passage. Mrs Wilmot had returned to the kitchen and possibly her novel. The door was shut.

'You may depend on it.'

'I reckon he was being haunted.'

Abbs raised his eyebrows. 'What makes you say that?'

'One day, I went in to clear the breakfast-things, not thinking the master was still at the table. He was reading something and told me to carry on. Puts his pamphlet down and stares at the table-cloth while I stack the tray. All of a sudden, he looks right at me and asks, do I believe in ghosts?'

'What did you say?'

Bertha looked away. 'Told him I do. I've never seen one but I heard my Pa, after he died. None of the others did. Only me.'

Abbs studied her stubborn face. She didn't expect to be believed but she was telling the truth, as she saw it. 'What did you hear, Bertha?'

'Pa was bedridden. He'd bang his stick on the wall, when he wanted something. I heard him knocking, when the others were abed. Bang three times, like he always did. Stop and he'd do it again, till one of us went. I was too frightened to look in the front room. That's where his bed was. After a few nights, it gradually faded away and came no more. But I heard him... I know I did.'

Alone in the study while he waited for Maggie, Abbs tried to work out what the room could tell him about its owner. Invariably, if there were books, he began by browsing the titles. The green spines of *Lillywhite's Cricketers' Companion* took up much of a shelf. There were architect's pattern-books, volumes on buildings, both classical and modern, art was well represented. Mr. Darwin's famous work was there, together with other books on science and exploration, all with their pages cut. An open-minded, rational man. There were few novels.

A well-handled, first edition of *The Englishman's House* lay on the side-table beside Ellis's armchair. There was something poignant about the small signs of daily life. A bookmark placed in a familiar volume, by a reader who could never resume.

The door opened and Maggie came in, carrying a dust-pan. 'I hear you've more questions for me. All right if I sweep up the glass now and take the rug?'

'By all means, let me give you a hand with it.'

'Don't stir yourself, I can manage.'

He looked on as she made light work of rolling the rug. Tutting, she examined the carpet beneath.

'Not a speck of blood gone through, you wouldn't credit it.' Pushing her wire spectacles back with a finger, Maggie finally gave him her attention. 'What do you want to know, then?'

'Will you not sit down?' Abbs remained by the bookcase. 'It can't be agreeable for you being in here.'

'No sense making a fuss. The room'll have to be used, just the same. I've seen a few corpses carried down the street afore now.' Avoiding Ellis's chair, she perched reluctantly on its pair and answered his look. 'Grew up in a colliery town.'

'What brought you down to London?'

'Independence. I wasn't going to be a miner's wife, if any'd have me. I'd a fancy to see down south.'

'And what was your opinion, when you did?'

Maggie wrinkled her brow. 'Needn't have bothered. Daft young lass, I was. Turned out it's much like the north-country, only flatter.'

He kept meeting others who'd sought their future in the capital.

Their motives intrigued him.

'I understand these meetings at the Institute take place the first Monday of every month. Do you always attend them?'

'What difference should it make, when the house wasn't left empty? D'you say the place was being watched?'

'I don't know.'

'That's honest, I suppose. That sergeant seemed to know it all. I never miss, seeing as the mistress lets me accompany her. It's a treat to get out and I see my friend there. Lots of the ladies bring their maid. Saves them having to pick over old clothes.'

Abbs smiled to himself. She was sharper than many a sergeant. 'What was the lecture about?'

'Heathens. Given by some missionary. His wife was on the platform, next to the vicar, only she didn't have much to say for herself. Relieved to be safely back among good Christian folk, I dare say.'

Jumping up, she set about her work again. He felt uncomfortable, watching while Maggie stooped with the brush.

'Did you all sit together?'

'I'd had enough of being squashed up against the vicarage maid. She sat herself where it suited, next to an unaccompanied man. I sit with my friend at the back, so we can slip out near the end and help with the tea-urn. Gives us a chance to talk. The mistress and Mrs Ibbotson go up the front, as a rule.'

He wondered about the scrap of paper on the hearth. 'Have you removed any newspapers or periodicals from here today, Maggie?'

She treated him to a scornful look over her shoulder. 'That I have not. Touch nothing at all, the first constable said. There's the master's sherry glass, still on the side.'

'Quite right, but there are daily tasks you'd do without thinking. You might empty the ash-tray or take away yesterday's newspaper.'

'Now I take your meaning. I could straighten a room in my sleep. But see for yourself, there's yesterday's *Times*.'

'Did Mr. Ellis subscribe to any periodicals?'

Maggie pointed at the shelf containing bound volumes of *The Modern Architect*. 'Only that one. In Mrs Ellis's day, he'd come home with *All The Year Round*. She liked him to read bits to her. Haven't seen one in the house since. Anyroad, knowing that won't help you find who murdered him.'

'It's useful to have an idea of Mr. Ellis's character,' said Abbs vaguely. She looked unconvinced. 'I'm afraid I must ask you about discovering the body.' He indicated the floor-length curtain by the garden-door. 'Was this drawn across, when you reached the door?'

'All the curtains were drawn, I opened them. Soon as I drew near, I saw the glass smashed. The door was shut and the curtain pulled across roughly, the way you would in reaching from the outside.'

'Was the key still in the lock?'

'Yes, but the door opened when I turned the handle. Something was badly amiss. I knew instantly we'd been robbed, but seeing the master lying there, I couldn't believe my senses. Like a fallen waxwork, he was, his eyes staring. And the dagger...'

'Pray, take your time.'

'He used it as a letter-opener. I dusted it every morning. Brought it back from their wedding trip, they did, from Italy. He liked old buildings. That's where they bought the miniatures that hung on the chimney-breast. See where the paper's faded below the portrait? That's the mistress, Mrs Sophia Ellis, as was.'

Abbs nodded. 'I'm sorry you had such a terrible experience.'

'There's plenty have had worse. I've seen them brought out of the mine on a board. Bodies mangled and their wives waiting at the gate.' A hand to her back, above her stays, Maggie looked out at the garden. 'The master liked to leave the curtains open late. He'd step out on the path and have a cigar of an evening. I'd smell the smoke sometimes from upstairs, and sweep up the stubs next day.'

Abbs felt a stir of fellow feeling with the dead man. He rarely pulled his curtains when it was first dark, liking to look out at the night sky. 'Did Mr. Ellis leave his curtains open all night?'

'No, they were always drawn next morning. Can't understand it myself. I shut out the night, soon as the light goes. Keep the draughts out and the moths in summer.'

'When you came in here, was the lamp still burning?'

She shook her head. 'It was turned right down.'

'Thank you, Maggie. I'll have a further word with Miss Maitland. Do you know if Mr. Ellis kept a diary for his appointments?'

'I can tell you that without troubling the mistress. Black cover, to the right of the blotter.'

'It isn't here now.'

'Mostly the master left it there but I've seen him put it in his drawer, top right.'

'We'll take a look.' He took the chair behind the desk. The drawer was unlocked, but met with some resistance to pulling out in its entirety. 'It doesn't appear to be here.'

Maggie leant over the polished surface. 'That's his evening post on top. I recall the big envelope.'

He glanced in the other drawers. 'Perhaps Mr. Ellis left it elsewhere in the house. Miss Maitland may know. Can you recall when you last saw the diary?'

'It was there early yesterday, when I dusted the desk.'

Returning to the top drawer, he felt paper wedged down the side and set about tugging it free. The obstruction proved to be a crumpled, unused envelope, caught up with a visiting-card. Glancing at the Kennington address, he held it out. 'Do you know this gentleman?'

She furrowed her brow as she read. 'Silas Dove Esq. No one who called here, I've a good memory for names. Could be anyone. Gentleman who wanted his house modelling, maybe? If you've finished with me, I'll be off, then. The mistress is still in the morning-room. Knock first, if you must trouble her again.'

When she'd gone, Abbs read the card again. Below the printed lines, *Tuesday and Friday evenings at 7.00* was inscribed in a flowing hand. *Private appointments strictly by prior arrangement.* And below that, *Discretion assured.*

He placed it in his pocket-book and considered several anomalies.

EIGHT

A watery sunlight was seeping through the clouds as Abbs stood on the pavement. He was debating which direction to take, when the sound of footsteps made him look back. Bertha was coming across the gravel, wearing a shawl and old-fashioned bonnet, a basket on her arm. He waited for her to join him.

'On your way to the high street, Bertha?'

'I'm to fetch the glazier. What if he can't mend the door before nightfall? You don't think they'll come back, do you?'

'No, they won't return. You'll be with Mrs Wilmot and Maggie. You must try not to worry.'

'I can't stop fretting. We don't know what'll happen about our wages, an' mine are needed at home. Good positions are hard to come by. Cook says we won't know if we're to be kept on, till the will's read.'

There was nothing he could say. You might shut out the dark, if you had a roof over you, but the streets were always there. Their spectre haunted him at times, though Bertha wouldn't credit it. Only the prosperous could truly feel safe.

He heard himself murmuring weak platitudes and changed the subject. 'Bertha, did your mistress get you to burn any periodicals, before Sergeant Hollins arrived?'

She shook her head. 'She saw to them herself.'

There was something here, he knew it. 'When was this?'

'I don't rightly know the time. Maggie'd gone out to find a constable and the mistress sent for me in the morning-room. She told me to run and fetch Mr. Buckley, fast as I could.'

'What was your mistress doing exactly?'

'She was ripping some periodical and tossing it on the fire. There were pamphlets on the coals, torn in half. She was prodding them with the poker, so they'd burn faster.'

He kept his voice careless. 'Did you happen to see what they were?'

An uncomfortable pause. Bertha fiddled with her bonnet-string. 'I can't read.'

'Forgive me. Did you ever see your master bring home any periodicals, or did they come by post?'

'I couldn't say.'

'No matter. It's best if you don't mention this to anyone.'

Showing no curiosity, she looked beyond him, pointing down the street. 'That's the vicar's carriage.'

Abbs watched a clarence bowling towards them, the horse looking sprightly as the coachman drew up. A bearded man, in a wide-brimmed, shovel hat and clergyman's stock, stepped out on the instant. He handed down a woman, in her middling-forties, a bunch of fresh violets pinned on her mantle. She greeted Bertha briskly.

'Good day, ma'am, sir.' The girl bobbed awkwardly, her basket banging her hip.

'And you are, sir?'

The vicar had a courteous manner and a deep, sonorous voice. An asset to his calling, thought Abbs, as he replied.

'Scotland Yard,' repeated Mr. Ibbotson, when introductions had been made. 'I've this minute heard Ellis is dead. Absolutely appalling. Constable Latham hailed us. We've come to lend strength to Miss Maitland. She and Mrs Ibbotson are dear friends, though I'd do as much for any parishioner. Is your work here completed, Inspector?'

'For today, sir.'

Mrs Ibbotson took hold of Bertha's chin. 'You look wan, child, and no wonder. Were you very fearful?'

'We didn't know nothing, ma'am, till Maggie found the master slain. I'm thankful it wasn't me went in.'

'That is a mercy. Now, you must bear up like a good girl, and help look after your mistress. I shall speak to Mrs Wilmot. Beef tea is what's needed. There's nothing better for fortifying the nerves. You shall help her prepare it and take a cup yourself. Good day to you, sir. Come along, Bertha.'

'I'm to go to the shops, ma'am.'

'Nonsense, you're needed here. You can run errands later.'

Abbs replaced his hat as Mrs Ibbotson swept away, handing Bertha her umbrella. The girl followed, looking sullen.

'I'd be obliged, Inspector, if you'd relate to me the plain facts, that I might quash rumours with authority. The women and servants will be like a flock of gaggling geese, frightening anyone foolish enough to listen.'

Mr. Ibbotson stood with a fist to his beard, as Abbs briefly outlined the discovery of the murder.

'I suppose I may not ask what steps are being taken?'

'You may be assured the investigation will be thorough, sir. I don't believe in killers escaping justice.'

'Oh quite, I meant no offence. Rather, I confess to being puzzled. There've been no other houses robbed in the better part of Kennington. It would be the talk of my congregation, or am I wrong?'

'I'm told you're right, sir. There've been no other reports.'

'Mr. Ellis was comfortably circumstanced, but not a rich man. He owned no valuable collection to single him out.'

Abbs listened, making no comment.

The vicar regarded him shrewdly. 'You keep your own counsel, Inspector, rightly so. I'll inquire no more.'

'Did you know Mr. Ellis well, sir?'

'We were not intimate friends but I believe I may claim to have known him well. We met fairly often and had many a lively discourse.'

'Was Mr. Ellis a member of your congregation?'

'Not, I fear, since his wife died. Before Mrs Ellis became too weak, they both worshipped regularly. Miss Maitland is a devoted attender. She was greatly concerned about him.'

'I'm sure she'll be glad to see you and Mrs Ibbotson.'

'You have your duty, Inspector, while I must tend to the living. Do seek me out, if I may be of use to you. The vicarage is in the next street. You'll see St Edward's on the corner.'

'Thank you, Reverend Ibbotson, I may need to speak to you further. I should like a word with your coachman.'

'By all means. Tandy, this gentleman is a detective-officer from Scotland Yard. He wishes to speak with you.'

The coachman held the reins loosely against his great-coat. 'Sir.'

'Ellis was a good man, Inspector. This was an evil night's work.'

'Indeed.'

'To practicalities. God speed your labours, sir.' His stick raised in farewell, the vicar strode off towards the house.

Abbs turned back to Tandy. 'You brought Miss Maitland and her maid home last night?'

'What of it?' A well set-up fellow, Tandy craned his neck towards the house. 'What happened? Was his throat slit?'

'You'll read about it soon enough. What time did you stop here?'

'The church clock had finished chiming ten as I drew up.' Screwing round, he indicated the tower with his whip.

'Did you see anyone about?'

'Not a soul. Not that I was looking, the mist was coming in and I kept me eyes on the road. I'd have heard anyone though, so would she. Wouldn't you, eh, Poll?' He twitched the reins and the mare pricked her ears, head bobbing as if to confirm his veracity.

Down the street, Sergeant Grainer came out of a drive and peered both ways. Catching sight of Abbs, he began trudging towards him. His demeanour suggested they'd learned nothing new and his feet were sore.

NINE

The hospital mortuary felt familiar, if not agreeable, another basement room with an occupied dissection table. The same chipped enamel dishes on the shelves, a microscope, saws and pliers that would equip a carpenter. Abbs's gaze slid past the row of stoppered glass jars, their contents always resembled tripe. Enough to put a man off eating brawn for life.

The gas-lights glowed, reflecting on the shiny tiles. The drainage channel, beneath the table, had been recently sluiced, bubbles of foam clung to the iron grille. A little natural light came from a casement near the ceiling.

He'd become accustomed, in recent years, to the harsh odour of sprayed carbolic solution. Claimed to be a sure prophylactic against infection, he was still thankful he'd shaved without a nick.

A haggard-looking man, of about his own age, was by the sink, unfolding his sleeves. The ill-used frock-coat he slipped on, was decidedly well-cut. He greeted Grainer by name before offering a firm hand-shake.

'George Prentice. Welcome to Hades, Inspector.' He gestured about him with a rueful look. 'That's my name for it. It's dry, I grant you and we've no rats, but I prefer to do my ministering above ground, to patients who can still be saved.'

'Too late for this one, Doctor.' Grainer eyed the naked corpse, as if selecting his chop from a butcher's slab.

'We don't know why, but I intend to find out,' said Prentice cheerfully. 'Your man's through here.'

They followed him in a long room, where at the far end, a solitary corpse lay shrouded. A further door stood partly open. The low rise and fall of men's voices drifted in, along with a nostril-twitching whiff of coffee.

Dr. Prentice pulled back the rough sheet. They looked down at a chest that would never rise and fall again. There was surprisingly little gore.

'Three wounds, as you see. The knife was lodged in this one.'

'Is that why there was little blood?' said Abbs. 'Not a great deal was shed where the body lay.'

'Quite right. With the third wound, the knife effectively sealed the

46

laceration.' Prentice indicated with his finger. 'Hence the pooling beneath the skin. It happens that way sometimes. Stab wounds are unpredictable.'

'How much blood, would you say, was on the killer?'

'The other wounds bled freely but his linen absorbed most of it. His smoking-jacket was unfastened, the edges are stained. The clothes are parcelled for you. Some on the hand that wielded the knife, the cuff, possibly. A glove would have been stained, but probably nothing more.'

'So they'd pass unremarked in a dark street. Can you say how quick death would have been, Doctor?'

'One blow punctured this lung. Another here, caught on a rib and the final blow pierced the heart. Loss of consciousness would have been swift, with death on its heels. Are you wondering about noise, Inspector?'

'I am. From what you say, might he not even have had time to cry out?'

Prentice ran his fingers through his fairish hair. 'I can't be certain, but shock overwhelms the constitution. He'd have panicked, struggled to breathe. A moan may have been all he could utter, before his heart stopped.'

'Are there any other wounds on the hands or arms?'

'Defensive cuts? See for yourself, there are none. Dried blood on the fingers where his hands went to the knife, that's instinct. I'd say your man was attacked unawares, which suggests someone he didn't consider a threat.'

'Which hardly ties in with an intruder.' Abbs looked for a response from Sergeant Grainer. Getting none, he resumed his study of the dead man's face. Rowland Ellis had kept a head of dark-grey hair, receding at the temples. A long, lean countenance with his whiskers closely-barbered. In the *carte de visite* Miss Maitland had supplied, he'd looked intelligent. He wondered about the stilled voice. A person revealed much by their speech.

'Are you able to tell us any more from the wounds?'

'From the direction of the thrusts, you mean?' Prentice bent closer. 'Your victim was standing when he was attacked. I wasn't called to the scene. The constable said he'd been found on the floor. How was he lying exactly?'

'Half on his back and turned slightly to one side.'

'That sounds about right. Too tidy on their back and the corpse may have been moved. If you study this ragged edge, there was a slight upward tilt to the thrust, but that means nothing.'

'We can't deduce the murderer was short of stature?'

'Afraid not, nor uncommonly tall. Someone using a weapon doesn't hold it horizontally.' Stepping away, Prentice mimed slicing the air. 'The movement is so rapid.' Catching Grainer's gaze, he addressed him. 'By now, your usual companion quashes my theorising and puts me firmly in my place, does he not?'

'Inspector Cole's not a great one for other folks' theories, Doctor. You know that. He likes to work it out his own way. No offence meant. His arrest tally speaks for itself.'

'His reputation is well-known.'

'That it is. He's away in Manchester. I dare say they've even read of him up there.'

Abbs's early misgivings sank lower.

'Very like.' His voice neutral, Dr. Prentice lifted the corpse's wrist. 'The murderer was right-handed, like this fellow. Not much help to you, that.'

'It's all useful. It might eliminate someone.'

'S'cuse me, Doctor, how d'you know which hand the victim wrote with?'

Prentice showed Grainer a lump distorting the first joint of Ellis's fore-finger. 'Pressure from writing, over the decades. Rigor is well advanced in the limbs. For what it's worth, I incline to death taking place in the first half of the night.'

Thanking him, Abbs took a last look at the face, wiped of all expression. They said the eyes of the dying held the last scene they ever saw. Some men of science claimed to have proof, from experimenting on rabbits. They all contradicted one another in scathing news-print. The first murdered man he ever saw, had been a game-keeper. Long ago, when he was a constable in Norfolk. The eyes had been pecked by crows.

'If you've seen all you wish, Inspector, shall we repair to my room? I have the knife ready for you.'

'I'd welcome any theory you'd care to put forward,' said Abbs, as they crossed the dead-room. 'We're here to learn all you can tell us.'

'Little enough, I fear, on this occasion but no doubt, there'll be other times. Detective-work interests me, I admit. It would be satisfying to present you with some rare clue leading to an arrest. You must blame my partiality for reading serials.'

'You're hardly alone in that, Doctor. I like them myself.'

Returning up the shallow steps, they entered what was little more than a cubby-hole, partitioned to leave only half a window. Easing his way past shelves jammed with untidily knotted files, Prentice sat behind his desk, indicating the other chair.

'Do sit down. Drop those on the floor, Sergeant, and take the stool.' Grainer perched behind Abbs, filling the remaining space. 'I spend little time in here.' Reaching in a drawer, Prentice placed some small items on the blotter. 'You'd better take these. They belonged to your man.'

Leaving the black studs, Abbs picked up the mourning-ring, banded with black enamel. A disquieting reminder, every time you looked at your hands.

Here we are.' Prentice unwrapped the object already lying before them.

'We're told it was kept on the dead man's desk as a paper-knife.'

'A most efficient dagger, in fact. Well-honed, feel the weight.'

The blade was stained rusty-brown. Abbs sensed Grainer lean forward again. His breath was fugged.

'Ugly-looking chiv, that. Foreign curio, is it?'

'Italian, according to the parlour-maid. You said, Doctor, the third stab was to the heart. Does that imply some anatomical knowledge?'

'I saw nothing to indicate that. The middle wound was more of a scrape coming off a rib, which suggests a lack of professional skill. In my opinion, the lung received the first blow and our victim was overcome at the outset. That's why there are no defensive wounds.'

'Would you call this a frenzied attack?'

'Depends where you draw a line. I'd not say frenzied. There'd be more blows. Done in hot temper?'

'Done in desperation, Doc,' said Grainer. 'The dead man cornered a house-breaker.'

'We don't yet know the sequence of events, Sergeant. Could a woman have done it?'

'Undoubtedly. The blows were forceful and determined, but didn't require a man's strength. Your victim wasn't uncommonly tall.' Prentice grimaced, 'I've stitched up gaping wounds inflicted by the weaker sex. In both our professions, we see what women are capable of.'

'Vitriol-throwing,' said Grainer gloomily. 'That's down to a woman, like as not.'

'Not always, I think,' said Prentice.

Grainer ignored him. 'Nothing ruins a rival's face more surely. Jealousy, revenge, terrible the thoughts a woman gets in her head. They can't reason like we can.'

What drives any of us to murder? Necessity or passion, thought Abbs. And those two encompassed a good many reasons. He must find out which one had led to the death of Rowland Ellis. For failure would cling to him in the detective-branch, like the sulphurous stench of fog.

TEN

Back at the Yard, Abbs followed Sergeant Grainer along a dim passage on the first floor.

'Here we are, sir, you're last but one, next door to Inspector Cole.'

The previous occupant had left behind a taint of tobacco. Abbs took in the yellow-stained ceiling above a scratched desk and bare shelf. A dead blackbird lay in the empty grate, a bundle of dull feathers, a sightless eye and sliver of orange beak.

'I'll get rid of that, sir, must've come down this morning. I'll see about some coal an' all.'

He thanked him and Grainer left, with the dead bird dangling. The view from the sash-window overlooked the far row of buildings, where a familiar detective-sergeant leant against the wall. Hands in pockets, he seemed to be conversing idly with a stable-hand. A cabman, wrapped in his great-coat, went in the licence office. To his left, Abbs could the Commissioner's house and the back hall entrance, where two ladies were leaving.

A subdued hubbub of London entered on the sudden rush of air, screeching gulls, foul water faint on the breeze. His own modest foothold at the Yard marked a progression in unsettled months. He recalled the murders in Devonshire last autumn, his restless mood ever since. A man couldn't keep making new beginnings. Once his things were arranged, the room would do very well.

By the time Grainer returned, puffing with a full scuttle, Abbs had marshalled his thoughts on the case thus far, sending him off again to fetch tea. When they were finally settled, on either side of the desk, he asked for his sergeant's observations.

'Well, sir, usual procedure, here at the Yard, is to begin with known house-breakers and put feelers out. There's always someone will peach for a consideration.'

'You'll find your provincial counterparts do much the same.'

Grainer continued unabashed. 'If you want me to consult with Sergeant Hollins on the morrow, he'll know the likely thieves in his division. Who's behind bars, who's on the streets and where to find them. Then we shake them upside down, one by one. See what drops out.'

'Not literally, I trust. Attend to that, certainly, but first, let us have your thoughts on the murder.'

Abbs waited while Grainer splayed open his notebook and blew on his tea. Routine steps had to be taken but he couldn't shake the feeling they were pointless. That Ellis wasn't killed because he surprised a burglar. He looked away from a crumb of crust caught on the copious whiskers.

An answer of sorts came after thirst-quenching. 'You'll want me to do the rounds of the pawn-shops, sir?'

'Certainly. There must be a great many, I suppose?'

'You'd be surprised, sir, how these villains stick to their patch. A house-breaker, working Kennington way, is unlikely to cross the river. They'll head for an uncle in Lambeth, or maybe a bit further, Bermondsey or the Borough.'

'Whoever it was has little to show for their night's work.' Abbs took a sip, flinched and reached for the milk jug. Grainer must scald his windpipe. 'A pair of miniatures and a Bow figurine.'

'Silver frames'll fetch something and the china lady's said to be worth a good few sovs. He'd have reckoned on far more, had he not been caught.'

'What d'you make of the missing diary?'

'Dunno why he'd steal that. Might turn up in the house.'

'There is one obvious reason.' Abbs paused, in vain, for a pertinent comment. 'Something written therein would point to the murderer.'

'What might that be?'

'In a diary? Why, a direction or an appointment, a memorandum possibly.'

'I don't follow, sir.'

'The likelihood is the murderer took the diary,' said Abbs patiently. 'So there must be a reason. Suppose, for a moment, the murderer wasn't there to thieve.'

Grainer looked sceptical. 'Begging your pardon, sir, it doesn't add up.'

Abbs leant forward. 'There you have it, Sergeant. The facts, we've been given, don't make sense. Ellis would hardly have remained reading in his chair while someone forced the door, regardless. Nothing had disturbed him, for he'd slipped a marker in his book and placed it on the table. Are you agreed, thus far?'

The sergeant nodded sagely. 'Yes, sir.'

'The lamp-light would have shown sufficiently through the curtains to stop an intruder from breaking in. So, where did you suggest Ellis was, when the glass pane was smashed?'

Frowning, Grainer clattered his cup on the saucer. 'Still in his day-attire, so not abed.'

'He hadn't got into bed. I asked Miss Maitland. The covers were undisturbed.'

'Just retired, mayhap. At his ablutions when he heard the glass breaking and came back down?'

'Possibly, though a wise man would have grabbed a weapon. There was a stout briar in the hall-stand. Nothing was found dropped anywhere, not even his candle-stick.'

'He might've crept down in the dark, sir, not stopped to think. You might not rouse the house when they're only women.'

'True, but why no signs of a struggle? The small table hadn't over-turned. Dr. Prentice showed us, there were no marks from fending off an assailant.'

'If Mr. Ellis was still downstairs, say he'd gone in another room and the intruder was watching to see the study lamp go out. Ellis hears the glass breaking, rushes back in the room. That would account for him not having time to take up a weapon.'

'That fits, as far as it goes. If I took up house-breaking, I'd wait a good while after the last light was extinguished, lest someone was a poor sleeper.'

'Might have been good and late by the time Ellis went up. We heard he sat long in the night, sir. Our man might have done with waiting.'

'You heard what Dr. Prentice said. Do you not think it a possibility that when Miss Maitland and Maggie came home, Ellis was already dead?'

Grainer scratched his whiskers. 'Begging your pardon, sir, to put it plain, I don't. Who'd take the chance, not knowing if the rest of the house was empty?'

'Someone audacious.'

'With the other servants in the back?'

'The servants' quarters are well away from the study. And there may not have been much noise. Picture this, Sergeant. Ellis is sitting reading, his curtains open. Someone knocks softly on the garden-door. He recognises the murderer, puts his book down and lets them in. A conversation leads to a confrontation of some sort. There's possibly a cry, the sound of a body falling on the carpet. The murderer locks the inner door, pockets the small objects and the diary, turns out the lamp and leaves by the garden-door. They pull the curtain across as they go. Only *after that,* comes a single rap on the glass.'

'If you say so, sir, but I don't see it. The killer would fear being disturbed at any instant.' Grainer scrutinised the crumb on his forefinger before it vanished in his mouth. He mumbled, 'he wouldn't know the ways of the house.'

Abbs mustered his reserves of patience. 'A stranger wouldn't.'

ELEVEN

Chief Inspector Townsend's misgivings deepened as he listened to his new subordinate. When Abbs finished, he deliberately hung out the silence. Someone banged the main door and went upstairs, their footsteps weighted with the day's end. He'd assured his wife he'd leave in good time.

Inspector Abbs looked politely unconcerned as the pages of his report were turned. He would prefer some sign of anxiously awaiting his superior's approval. Frowning at the neat hand, the unblemished papers, he pushed them aside.

'Why take it upon yourself to look for Mr. Ellis's diary, in the first place? I'm at a loss as to why you thought it necessary.'

'I think it possible he knew his killer, sir. Ellis may have had a visitor last night, an appointment or an unexpected caller. His habit was to sit with the curtains open after dark. Anyone could have walked round the side of the house and seen he was alone. Someone who knew the household well, would know Miss Maitland would be out on the first Monday of the month.'

'I'm not convinced by your argument, Inspector.' He held out his palm, to strike his points on his fingers. 'First, the diary. Mr. Ellis may have left it elsewhere in the house. Did he retain a room at his business-premises? He could have taken it there. You can't prove his assailant took it.'

'Not prove, sir, no, but the parlour-maid said it was kept on his desk, or in a drawer. It was there the day before.'

'Allow me to continue. It's feasible Ellis returned to his study before retiring and disturbed the house-breaker. That would readily account for his attire, the book-mark, details you seem to consider remarkable. Good grief, man, have you never forgotten something and come downstairs again? He may have returned for his book.'

'It's possible, sir.'

'Thirdly, this notion the robbery was faked. You're certain the glass was smashed from the outside?'

'Yes, sir. I...'

He raised his hand to silence Abbs. 'You examined the curtain?'

'I did. A few splinters of glass were caught on the outer side of the material.'

'Quite consistent with being knocked out from the garden.' He watched him nod reluctantly. 'If it wasn't a genuine robbery, to what end? Do you suspect the cook or scullery-maid of wanting to murder her master?'

'No, sir, nor Miss Maitland. I've no reason to suspect any person yet, nor rule them out.'

Meeting the inspector's gaze, he felt his jaw clenching. 'If, Ellis was murdered in the early part of the evening, the lady has an alibi. Her maid can be discounted, likewise. You're arguing in circles, Abbs. I require facts. Evidence, not pointless speculation.'

'There's the matter of the periodicals Miss Maitland was burning, sir. Whatever they were, she didn't want us to see them.'

Voices intruded in the corridor. Outside, a single toll sounded the half.

He sighed. 'Think about it, man. It's obvious what sort of reading-matter they were, pornography. No doubt the lady knew they existed and was naturally horrified, taking her first chance to destroy them. Of course, she didn't want Ellis's good name ruined. There was her own reputation to safeguard. She wouldn't want the servants knowing, she destroyed them herself.' He didn't altogether care for Abbs's quizzical expression.

'I don't get the impression of Rowland Ellis as that kind of man, sir.'

'Men who practise that sort of perversion take care to keep their base nature hidden. There are two notorious streets in the Metropolis, where such disgusting publications may be readily purchased. We do our best to enforce the law, but dealers scuttle back like cockroaches. Are you acquainted with St Clement Dane's in the Strand?'

Abbs blinked in surprise. 'I've walked past the outside.'

'It's the cheek-by-jowl nature of London, that a fine Christian church must suffer a vicious quarter, close by its walls. Holywell-street, known to some as Booksellers' Row, caters for all manner of debauchery, pamphlets, engravings, volumes and so forth. Wych-street is infamous for its brothels and molly-houses. A veritable sewer of depravity.'

'I'll be surprised if Mr. Ellis frequented the area.'

'Plenty of so-called gentlemen do. After all, you say his wife was an invalid for some considerable time.' Belatedly recalling Abbs was a widower, he cleared his throat. 'Forget the periodicals, concentrate on house-breakers. Employ the local knowledge of the divisional detectives. It may pay to spread your net wider, Vauxhall, South Lambeth, Walworth. You'll have other cases to attend to. Make good use of Grainer.'

'Sir. He's working with Sergeant Hollins on the morrow.'

'Good. What does Grainer make of your theory?'

Abbs looked levelly at him. 'He agrees with you, sir.'

He found himself approving the other man's truthfulness. No dissembling, or resentment, he could see. 'How are you finding Grainer?'

'He's diligent and proving himself useful.'

He observed Abbs narrowly for the slightest hint of levity. Finding none, he continued. 'As to your suspicions, Inspector, you're new to us and keen to make your mark. I understand that, but let me make one thing clear. I won't have my detectives trying to make a name for themselves.'

'I don't quite follow, sir.'

'I speak of the self-styled, popular press. You must be aware how the so-called *Illustrated Police News* will take up an inspector. The bold hero of Great Scotland Yard one week, the most derided fool in England the next.'

Abbs nodded. 'I remember how the press pilloried Mr. Whicher, over the Road murder, sir.'

'Exactly so. I will not have my men puffed up, or lampooned by these duplicitous penny-a-liners. They do their best to make the detective-branch a laughing-stock. In short, I will not tolerate men courting publicity.'

'Understood, sir. I've no inclination to feature in fish-wrappings.'

'I'm glad to hear it. Nor will you impress me, Inspector, by wild surmisings. You'd do better not to complicate a straightforward inquiry.'

'Sir.'

'The truth is usually quite simple.'

He glanced at his tobacco-jar. His own rise through the ranks had been steady, certainly not hindered by a good family background. He knew himself to be an able administrator, an exemplary officer. Only, there was such a thing as a detective's nose. Scrupulously honest, he knew he did not possess it.

'Very well, Abbs. You may keep an open mind for now. Make a search for the diary.'

'I will, sir, and if it cannot be found?'

Persistence was another trait necessary in a detective. Again, he sighed, putting away all thoughts of his pipe.

'Inquire further into Ellis's circumstances. Speak to this Miss Maitland again. Find out who benefits from his death.'

'Thank you, sir. I've arranged to call on his partner. He denied there being any business problems, but I fancied there was something.'

'Tread carefully. Find the murderer and don't take too long. That will be all.'

As the younger man reached the door, he added a final piece of advice. 'Mark my words, Abbs. If there is more to this affair than meets the eye, money will be at the back of it.'

The sharp planes of Abbs's face were shadowed in the gas-light. Not the most robust-looking of men, he'd thought, at their first meeting.

'It very often is. I bid you good night, sir.'

He nodded in acknowledgement. 'Follow the lucre.'

TWELVE

Abbs was wryly amused, next day, to be waylaid as he entered the detectives' building. Mottram, the bearded civilian clerk, handed him several new dockets pinned to reports from other inquiries. A tang of institution polish had been added to his room overnight, marginally better than old pipe-smoke. A fresh blotter had been provided, a note about the inquest lying on top. When he'd unwrapped his desk-calendar and equipped himself with ink, his new surroundings seemed more familiar, the wooden tray laden with work.

He read and wrote undisturbed, until a constable brought him a message from the telegraph-room. As requested, Sergeant Hollins had returned to the neighbouring properties, the previous evening, and spoken to everyone they'd missed. No one had seen anything to assist them. Disappointing, but not unexpected.

Grainer, when he inquired, was also detained on other duties. The forenoon was advanced when they returned to Kennington.

The premises of Ellis and Buckley, Architects, occupied part of the ground floor of a four-storey house, situated in one of the older streets off the main thoroughfare. Well-buffed plates indicated most of the homes, in the white stucco terrace, included the consulting-rooms of professional men.

The outer door stood open and they found themselves in an office, where an elderly clerk was sealing packets and placing them on brass letter-scales. He left his stool to greet them, at once. Despite this, Grainer jabbed the brass bell-switch on the counter, stating their business in a lofty manner.

Abbs decided the absent Inspector Cole employed Grainer as a sort of foot-man, making way for an important personage. There was little sign he encouraged independent thought in his sergeant.

The clerk shook his head, his eyes distressed behind his spectacles. 'A wicked deed. What the world is coming to, I cannot say. Mr. Ellis set upon at his own fireside. The most agreeable employer I've had the good fortune to serve.' He cast an involuntary look at the door on their right.

'How long have you worked here, Mr. ...?' asked Abbs.

'Searle, sir, Henry Searle. All of eight and twenty years come Whitsun.'

'When did you last see Mr. Ellis?'

'In March, sir. Mr. Ellis called in to see us once a month. I hoped he'd return to us after Mrs Ellis was laid to rest, but alas, it wasn't to be. He kept a finger on the business, you might say, but no more.' Searle sighed. 'Not the same gentleman.'

'In what way did Mr. Ellis differ?'

'There was ever a melancholy air about him. Oh, he'd stop to inquire about my family, as he always did, but scarcely listened. He'd lost all heart.' He stopped speaking as the door opened and Frederick Buckley looked out.

'Why didn't you bring these officers straight to me, Searle? They don't want to hear your gossiping.'

'Beg pardon, sir. The gentlemen have newly arrived. I was about to show them in.'

'I detained Mr. Searle,' said Abbs pleasantly.

'Where's Dick?' Ignoring him, Mr. Buckley addressed his clerk.

'Not back, sir. You'll recall you sent him to the wharf with a message.'

'Then take those yourself. Be off with you and smarten yourself up, man. You look a disgrace.'

'At once, sir, I shall see to it.' Looking about the counter, Searle took a pen-wipe to his ink-smeared cuff and smoothed down his remaining grey hair.

Abbs felt a shaft of compassion, as the clerk dislodged some envelopes with his elbow and stooped to gather them. His knuckles were reddened.

'You'd better come in. I've no time to waste, if you have.' Mr. Buckley ushered them in a well-proportioned room, with an old-fashioned ceiling of patterned plaster. He waved them to the chairs before the desk.

Abbs looked about him as Buckley sat down. A pair of sash-windows gave on to the street. Drawings of detailed elevations hung from the picture-rail. A wooden model of a   vast building stood on a table in a corner. A section of the frontage had been painted to represent bands of patterned brickwork. Somewhere between   a Venetian palazzo and a town-hall, he supposed it to be an over-embellished manufactory.

'When is the inquest to be?' Buckley fiddled with the rim of a map-reading glass, as he spoke.

'On Friday, sir, to be held at the Kennington police-court. Notice will be in the afternoon post. You'll be required to give evidence of identity.'

'It won't take long, I suppose? Open and shut, until you apprehend Ellis's killer.'

'The inquest should be swiftly adjourned, yes, sir.'

Buckley grunted. 'Shouldn't take you long to arrest a house-breaker, if you know your business. I'm a man of my word. I'll put up a reward for information.'

'In the circumstances, I regret that won't assist us, sir. We think Mr. Ellis's murder was deliberately contrived to appear the consequence of disturbing a burglar.' Grainer contemplated his boots, disassociating himself from the statement.

The architect stared at Abbs. 'I don't follow you, Inspector. What happened was plain enough. The room was ransacked.'

'Not really, sir. Remarkably few items are missing.'

'Ellis caught the thief or gang in the act. I saw the body. A blind man could work that out, but not Scotland Yard men, apparently. What the devil makes you think this, might I ask? Ellis was an inoffensive fellow.'

'You'll understand, I cannot discuss our investigation, sir. As you're concerned about time, I suggest we move on to our questions.'

'What do you want from me?'

Abbs glanced at Grainer, his notebook at the ready. 'Will you tell us about your association with Rowland Ellis?'

'Very well. We came to know one another through mutual acquaintance in our professional body. Ellis had an abundance of work and was seeking a partner. It benefited us both to go in together. This was nine years ago.'

'Forgive me,' said Abbs, 'but would that be on equal terms?'

'I consider that an impertinent question, but in the circumstances, I suppose you've a right to know. Ellis owned sixty per cent of the business.'

'Your frankness is appreciated, sir.'

Looking down his nose, Buckley watched Grainer scribble. 'Before you ask, Ellis and I had the customary arrangement whereby, in case of death, both partners willed their share to the other. You won't find any professional men to behave differently.'

'Quite so.'

'I dare say Miss Maitland can count on getting the house. Ellis was a fair man.' Buckley's voice was indifferent. 'An annuity to go with it, if she's lucky. He had no other dependents. Mind, I wouldn't put it past him to leave a tidy sum to charity. You'll want the details of his lawyer, I presume?'

'If you please.'

Opening a drawer, Buckley tossed a card on the desk. 'The name's wrong. Charles Penfold died recently. His nephew's taken over. James, young fellow, from Cornwall, I believe he said. Ellis and I met him last month at his uncle's funeral.'

Thanking him, Abbs glanced at the inscription. 'How did this gentleman die?'

'Heart trouble. Nothing for you there, Inspector. If you'd seen old Penfold senior, he was stout as a barrel. I didn't envy the bearers.'

'Would you describe Rowland Ellis as a close friend, Mr. Buckley?'

The architect pursed his lips. 'Naturally. Partners have to get along, after all. My son and I dined with him regularly.'

'What manner of gentleman was Mr. Ellis?'

'On the starchy side, stubborn. Devoted to his wife and he went downhill as Sophia... Mrs Ellis declined. She suffered from Bright's disease, kidney trouble. He used to be a cricket bore, but since he lost his wife, Ellis gave up most pastimes.'

'I understand Mr. Ellis was a fairly recent widower?'

'Not so. In a few weeks, he'd have done his year. Frankly, I didn't consider it manly to hang on to mourning the way he did. Still wearing his hat-band. I call it ostentatious. I'm a widower myself and these set-backs have to be overcome. Many men in his position would have been looking about for another wife by now.'

Abbs thought it said much about a man, who could dismiss the death of his wife as a set-back. He wondered if Grainer, looking stony-faced, was a married man.

'You said there were no disputes arising from your commissions. Was there any difference of opinion in your partnership?'

Unexpectedly, Buckley gave a short laugh. 'Miss Maitland been talking to you, has she? Must be a strange sort of work, collecting tittle-tattle but I dare say you've no choice. Ellis and I had minor disagreements, as professional men will.'

Abbs made no comment, which generally prompted witnesses to continue.

'Ellis was a competent architect if you wanted an outmoded style. And make no mistake, many do. Suggest something fresh, he was more set in his opinions than an old dowager. No stomach for innovation. We were sometimes at odds in this way.'

'I understand, sir. Are Mr. Ellis's possessions still in his room here?'

'There's nothing of his here. He removed the remainder after his wife died. Ellis made it clear he'd lost all inclination for work and intended henceforth, to be a sleeping partner.' Buckley shrugged. 'He hadn't been here full-time for a year or two, as I told you. He was a good decade my elder and by then, my son had joined us. This room was the one Ellis used.'

'Your clerk mentioned Mr. Ellis called in each month?'

'To go over the books with me and keep abreast of new commissions. A formality only. Dig as you will, Inspector, there's nothing to uncover here.'

'A matter of being thorough, sir. When did you last see Mr. Ellis?'

'My son and I dined there about three weeks ago. That was the last time we met.' Glancing at the clock, he continued. 'Will that be all? There's nothing more I can tell you.'

'For the present,' said Abbs. Grainer tucked away his notebook, relief from servitude on his face.

'We may need to speak to you again, Mr. Buckley. Can you think of any reason why someone should want to harm Rowland Ellis, no matter how long ago?'

Getting to his feet, Buckley shook his head. 'I'd have said he didn't have an enemy in the world. My money still goes on a house-breaker. Some desperate ruffian, new to villainy mayhap, who panicked. Lashed out when Ellis accosted him.'

'Where did you spend yesterday evening, sir?'

'Come now, you don't suspect me?'

'By no means.'

'The idea's preposterous.'

'We'll be asking everyone in Mr. Ellis's circle, as a matter of routine.'

'I suppose you have your superiors to answer to. I was here all evening with my son. After we dined together, I spent the remainder of the evening adding to some notes. My son was reading. I trust that satisfies you.'

Grainer gave a lingering look at the model building, as he followed Abbs.

'Impressive, is it not, Sergeant?' Coming over, Buckley gestured with a sweep of his arm.

'I was wondering what it might be, sir?'

'Then allow me to enlighten you. This is a scale-model of the new Reading Confectionery-works. All my own design and our largest commission to date. Chosen, let me say, against considerable competition.'

'Very handsome,' said Grainer, scratching inside his collar.

'Happily, my client agrees with you. This will be the first of many. It's grow or flounder, these days. The world is changing. Only look to what we've achieved since the Queen ascended the throne. Opportunities are endless, for those with the conviction to secure them. But I detain you now, gentlemen, I'll see you out.'

~

A young man, with an unkempt beard, was now behind the counter. He was leaning over a newspaper, a bag of biscuits close at hand. Through an open door at the rear, Abbs saw a wide cabinet of shallow drawers, marked alphabetically. The corner of a drawing-frame looked similar to the one in Ellis's study.

'There you are, Father. I told old Searle he might go for his nose-bag, while he's out.'

'These officers are detectives from Scotland Yard,' said Buckley severely. 'My son, Ambrose.'

'Here about Ellis? He deserved better, poor fellow. How are your inquiries faring, Sergeant?'

'This is Inspector Abbs and his sergeant.'

'Beg pardon, Inspector, I stand corrected.' Ambrose reached for a biscuit.

'Quite all right, sir,' said Abbs.

'The police don't think Ellis was killed struggling with a house-breaker.' Buckley pressed a hand on the counter. 'They believe his murder was intended.'

His son whistled a low note. 'You mean someone paid to have it done?'

'We don't yet know, sir,' said Grainer.

'If old Rowland ever did anything to get himself murdered, I'm baffled. A more honest, good-hearted fellow you never did meet.'

'When did you last see Mr. Ellis?' said Abbs.

Buckley broke in. 'I told you, the last time we had dinner at Lindholm.'

'Actually, Father, I saw him the week after that. I did tell you. Rowland was drinking in the Horns, with some cove in an off-the-peg suit. He greeted me and said something about calling in to see you that afternoon. I told him you were away to Reading.'

'It had slipped my mind.'

'When was this precisely, sir?' Abbs asked Ambrose.

He looked at the ceiling for inspiration. 'The week before last. I have it, a Wednesday.'

'Did Mr. Ellis mention why he wished to see Mr. Buckley, senior?'

'No, could have been anything. They had some papers on the table. Don't ask me what they were.' He shrugged in a way very like his father. 'I didn't even know Ellis frequented the bar. I thought the coffee-room was more to his liking.'

Abbs was aware of Grainer looking at the street. The inner door had been propped open and a shaft of sunlight was cast across the tiles. Someone, along the pavement, was sweeping. He caught the indistinct cry of a street-seller. The sergeant and Frederick Buckley were impatient for them to be gone.

'Had you ever seen Mr. Ellis's companion before?'

'Shouldn't think so and, before you ask, I didn't hear their conversation. I was fetching drinks for the fellows I was with. Saw him again as I left. Getting in a cab.'

'Did you happen to see which way they went?'

'Heading towards the river.'

'Can you describe this man, sir?'

Ambrose grinned. 'I can do better than that for you.' They watched in silence as, reaching for a drawing-pencil and paper, he made some rapid strokes and shading. 'There you are, Inspector. About your sergeant's height. Not corpulent. I didn't see much hair. Brownish side-whiskers. His countenance was badly pitted. That was the only memorable thing about him. Think I could take likenesses for my living?'

Frederick Buckley made an exasperated sound.

'This is most helpful,' said Abbs, studying the sketch. 'I'm much obliged to you, Mr. Buckley.

'Glad to be of service.'

Abbs addressed himself to Frederick Buckley. 'Sergeant Grainer will return this afternoon, to question your other clerk.'

'Errand-boy. He won't be able to assist you. He's only been here a few weeks. The previous boy was dismissed for pilfering.'

'I liked young Billy,' said Ambrose.

His father ignored him. 'Mr. Ellis wouldn't have given Dick more than a word in passing.'

'Nevertheless, he must be seen. You'll make sure he's here?'

'Very well, if you insist.' Buckley looked at his son. 'Searle can take the afternoon post, if need be. Let him do something useful.'

Thanking them, Abbs concluded the interview.

Grainer remained silent as they made their way along the terrace.

'What d'you make of Messrs Buckley?'

'Can't say I think much to the young one in his fancy waistcoat, sir. He's a stranger to his barber.'

'As you say, he's young. Talented, if this sketch is anything to go by. What of Frederick Buckley? Does he improve on second acquaintance?'

Grainer grunted. 'He already thinks he's a fine fellow. Now, Ellis's death has more than doubled his income. There's no denying, the killer did him a good turn.'

'And he has the freedom to pursue his ambitions. It seemed to me, Mr. Buckley was keen to emphasise he and his son were together all evening.'

'Think old man Buckley did it, sir?'

'I think we must check everything people tell us. As far as possible, that is. Questioning the servants, without offending Mr. Buckley, won't be easy. We'll leave it for the moment.'

Kennington-road was crammed with horse-traffic. They paused by a linen-drapery, out of the passage of fellow pedestrians. Towards the Thames, blackened brick chimneys reached into a pall of smoke that hung over Lambeth and the heart of the Metropolis, across the river.

'Do you know the Horns, Grainer?'

'Along that way, sir.' He pointed at a passing omnibus, so hung with garish tin signs, it seemed to tilt top-heavy. 'Straight on, just past where we turned off for the house. It stands on a corner opposite the park. The Horns Hotel, used to be a coaching-inn. You can't miss it.'

'You'd better show the sketch to the landlord. Ellis's companion could be a regular.'

Grainer grimaced like he'd downed vinegar. 'Time's getting on, sir, if I'm to see Sergeant Hollins. The Chief Inspector made a rare point of it, last night. Only, we might go a-visiting. Flush a rat or two from their nests. And you want me to see the errand-boy.'

'Then call at the Horns later. You're clear what to ask this lad?'

'Yes, sir. Any remarks Mr. Ellis made to him that might throw a light.'

'Anything at all. If you can speak to him alone, so much the better. We don't know what we're looking for.' Abbs handed him the folded sketch. 'Your way now passes the cab-stand, I see. Show it to the men there, if you please.'

'Cabbies see scores of fares, sir, pock-marks an' all. They won't remember.'

'I've always found them the eyes and ears of the streets. Asking questions is our trade, Sergeant, is it not?'

'Sir.'

Abbs compared his time-piece with the clock-face projecting above a watch-maker's premises. 'I shall meet you at the police-station. Let us agree on five, that should give you sufficient time.'

The sergeant's belly protested, Abbs forestalled him as he went to speak. 'I'm sure Sergeant Hollins will spare you a cup of tea. Off you go.'

He watched Grainer trudge towards the waiting hansoms, close by a busy pie-man. Only when it was apparent the sergeant was addressing the leading cabby, did he set off in the other direction.

THIRTEEN

A row of soot-spattered awnings sagged over the shops opposite Kennington Park. Hampered behind perambulating ladies, Abbs scanned the frontages for a post-office, spotting it by the green letter-pillar nearby. A queue took up much of the interior, but his quarry had left.

He passed the Institute where Miss Maitland and Mrs Ibbotson had spent the evening. The entrance locked, a bill advertised the spring exhibition of the Surrey Floricultural Society next month. Abbs decided the lawyer would be busy lunching at this hour and he might take a short time to gather his thoughts. Dodging between slowed carriages, he crossed over to the park gates.

A few people were standing by the rear of the lodge, where cordials and cakes were being sold from an open window. Warm gingerbread wafted on the air. Henry Searle was thanking a woman as he handed back his cup. Abbs waited as he approached.

'Why, good day to you, sir. Are you looking for me?'

'Not precisely, Mr. Searle. I did wonder if I might see you, but came this way by chance.'

'If you're seeking sustenance, the lodge-keeper's wife has everything clean. No stale fare, I assure you, or there's a refreshment-house beyond the fountain.'

'I'll take your recommendation but first, will you spare me some conversation, sir?' Watching him hesitate, Abbs indicated an empty bench. 'A short time will suffice.'

'Of course, Inspector. I have several minutes in hand.'

Observing the iron slats were dry, he waited for the clerk to be seated in a corner. 'A pleasing spot.'

'Mr. Ellis liked to walk here regularly. The park is well laid-out but I miss the old days. I've known this ground all my life, three and sixty years, sir. In my boyhood, this was wild heath. Lovelier to me in its unkempt state, even as a haunt of rogues.' Searle sighed and shook his head. 'Ah me, a man shouldn't dwell on what's long gone. We live in an age of progress.'

'Mr. Buckley's words?'

'They are, sir. He is all for next year, whereas my poor, erstwhile employer had a feeling for history.'

'Did Mr. Ellis come from Kennington?'

'No, sir. I believe he spent his youth in another part of Surrey. Mrs Ellis grew up here, of course.'

'Mr. Buckley implied there's been some trouble in the business,' lied Abbs. 'He was reticent about the details. Will you enlighten me?'

An attendant pushing a bath-chair halted by them, allowing people to pass. Searle touched his hat to the elderly, female occupant.

'I'm unable to do so, Inspector. I know of nothing recent. Young Mr. Ambrose often makes some small error, for his heart's not truly in drawing plans, but nothing serious.'

'Did he have much to do with Mr. Ellis?'

'I've often heard them speak of exhibitions they'd attended. Considering their disparity in age, they got on famously. Mr. Ambrose is set on being an artist.'

'How does Mr. Buckley feel about his son's ambition?'

'That it's a precarious living, sir. Harsh words have been said but Mr. Buckley is very fond of his son. Should Mr. Ambrose become a noted painter, with a position in society, he'd be most proud of him.'

'But he won't support him in his endeavour?'

'It's natural for a father to want his son securely settled. A great pity Mr. Ellis left none to follow him.'

'Can you think of anyone with a reason to dislike Mr. Ellis?'

'Not in any respect, sir. I can't claim to know of my late employer's private life, but I would think him a staunch friend. You'll find he always dealt fairly with people. Come to think of it, I believe I can give you a good instance and answer your previous question.'

'Please do.'

'We had a claim laid against us. Oh, it must have been about three years since. It was settled as soon as Mr. Ellis came to hear of it.'

'A grievance with Mr. Buckley, then?'

Searle looked down, tracing his stick in the damp earth. 'I don't wish to tell tales, sir.'

'We need to learn all we can about Mr. Ellis. Understanding the victim will help us find his murderer.'

'Mr. Buckley told Dick, and me, that Mr. Ellis was stabbed by an intruder. Do the police think there's more to it?'

Abbs recalled the scepticism in Townsend's face. 'I believe so.'

'In that case, it's a poor return for Mr. Ellis's civility, if I cannot assist you now. It's my recollect that a manufactory, designed by Mr. Buckley, was found to be subsiding within a year. An end wall collapsed, injuring two workmen, one poor fellow was killed. The owners claimed the specifications were at fault, which we refuted.'

'Was there any truth in this claim?'

'Unhappily, yes, as it turned out. The builders we engaged had used shoddy foundations. Mr. Ellis insisted we never employ them again and paid recompense to the owners. Furniture-makers they were, like many in Globe-town.'

'This would surely damage both men's reputation, if it was widely known. Did Mr. Buckley not keep sufficient eye on his commission?'

'You must understand, Inspector, Ellis and Buckley are not builders. Workmen are hired on the spot. The architect merely visits the site, overseeing the foreman. I'm afraid unscrupulous builders are not uncommon. Mr. Buckley was badly let down.'

'Was there much ill feeling between the two partners?'

'Mr. Ellis was angered, I confess, but all was soon forgotten. As for the owners, I doubt they were concerned for their men, rather for loss of goods and their trouble. It's not unknown for buildings to have a partial collapse, I fear. The underground-railway has weakened many structures, they say.'

'My thanks to you, Mr. Searle. I hope I haven't detained you over-long.'

'My employer should be out, sir. I miss working under Mr. Ellis. Mr. Buckley is...' he hesitated. 'He does not have the same way of conducting business.'

'You're sure there's nothing else you would care to tell me?'

'I know nothing that will assist you in learning how Mr. Ellis died.'

Carefully put. Abbs knew there was no point in questioning him further. 'We shall perhaps speak again, sir.'

The sun had gone in, the air cool in this capricious April. Searle got to his feet. Rubbing his gloved hands, he gazed across the vista. Was he seeing wild tussocks and bright gorse, thought Abbs, where he saw gravel walks, edged with iron hoops?

'These days, whole streets are torn down, their successors thrown up in a month. Too much change for me, Inspector. My London is lost.'

The lawyer's room was in a surprising disarray. Books were stacked across an old walnut partners' desk, jostling a honeycomb of documents bound in red tape. A bookcase, taking up much of one wall, had its upper glass doors flung open, its shelves bare.

Black tin deed-boxes stood on the floorboards, names inscribed in gold paint. A chair had been pushed aside, leaving worn patches on the red and grey patterned carpet. A suggestion of dust suspended in the air.

Short of stature and thick-set, Charles Penfold foreshadowed the figure he'd cut in his middle years. Hands clasped behind his frock-coat, he stiffened as Abbs explained his purpose.

'The clerk should not have shown you in here. This room is not currently fit for receiving callers. I've newly taken over from my late uncle. As you see, I'm in the midst of making changes.'

'I regret the necessity to disturb your labours, Mr. Penfold.'

'I've already been informed, by Mr. Frederick Buckley, of the tragic circumstances. I shall be attending the inquest. Are you here, Inspector, to let me know the arrangements?'

'I can do so, certainly.' He waited while the lawyer made a note.

'This is a shocking event. Not at all what I expected from my late uncle's clients.'

'I dare say it was a shock to Rowland Ellis.'

'I'd heard of the criminal activity in London, but hardly expected to encounter it so nearly. I shall be having additional bolts and bars fitted. My clients entrust me with their most private documents.'

'I understand you met Mr. Ellis at your uncle's interment, sir?'

'Briefly, Inspector. He made himself known to give his condolences, but declined to attend the funeral-meats. I believe my uncle had handled his personal affairs for many years, in addition to representing both architects.'

'Did Mr. Ellis say anything else to you?'

'He intimated he'd be making an appointment with me, after I'd settled in.'

'Did he say why?'

Penfold rubbed his bare chin, encircled by his door-knocker beard. 'I believe I may tell you. Mr. Ellis wished to discuss his will.'

'With a view to adding a codicil, or making changes?'

'He did not say. Naturally, I intimated I'd be glad to assist him, as soon as I was able. I had to return to Truro to wind up my own affairs. That was the sum total of our conversation.'

'When was your uncle's funeral, sir?'

'March the fourth at Lower Norwood Cemetery. Who'd have thought Mr. Ellis would soon be buried there himself?'

'Did Mr. Ellis subsequently make an appointment?'

Penfold answered reluctantly. 'He'd lately written, proposing to see me next week, if convenient. I was about to draft a reply.'

'Might I see the letter?'

'It will be in the clerk's keeping. It was only a line, I tell you. If that's all, he can show you on your way out.'

'There is another matter, Mr. Penfold, I'd be greatly obliged if you'll tell me the provisions of Mr. Ellis's will.'

'Most unorthodox. You must be aware the deceased's will is customarily read after the funeral. The beneficiaries should be gathered together.'

'These are rare circumstances, sir. I'm investigating the deceased's murder and must pursue my inquiries without delay.'

'I fail to see how Mr. Ellis's will can be relevant.'

Abbs repeated his theory. 'So you see, the provisions of the will could provide a motive.'

'I'm greatly disturbed to hear this. But I consider it would be improper to make an exception, even for an officer of the detective-police.'

He never seemed to fare well with lawyers, thought Abbs. It would be unfortunate to have a complaint lodged against him this early. 'Your propriety does you credit, sir, but...'

'However,' Penfold spoke over him. 'As a representative of the legal profession, it would be equally wrong of me to hinder police business. On due reflection, I am prepared to bring forward the reading of the will. In these unfortunate circumstances, it may take place at Lindholm, straight after the inquest.'

'An excellent compromise. I'm obliged to you, Mr. Penfold.'

'I presume you intend to be present, Inspector?'

'I shall, sir, together with my sergeant.'

'Then I shall, take it upon myself to, inform Miss Maitland and all those concerned.'

FOURTEEN

The curtains were drawn across the front windows of Lindholm, shutting out the afternoon. A quantity of crape had been wound about the door-knocker, tied in a crimped, black bow with trailing weepers. Abbs recalled how the days between death and the funeral seemed suspended, for those remaining.

Mrs Wilmot opened the door, a black-edged envelope stiff in her hand. 'You again, as if I didn't have enough to do. It's not my place to keep answering the door. We've had an assistant from Jossey's traipsing in and out.'

'Good afternoon to you, Mrs Wilmot. Jossey's?'

Her eyes raised, as though trying to peer through her frizzled curls to her cap. 'The mourning-warehouse.'

'I see. Is Miss Maitland at home?'

'Upstairs, entertaining. And only me left to cut bread and butter. No consideration, she's let the skivvy visit her ma, when it's not her half-day till Sunday. Now she's sent Maggie off to collect the stationery. They're not the only ones who'd like to slip out for an hour. Fair's fair. I've a mind to ask her, when one of them gets back.'

'Is something amiss with Bertha's parent?'

'From what we hear, she's always ailing. The foolish girl went and dropped a dish of eggs on the carpet. Said she couldn't sleep for nightmares. Miss M. reckoned she was looking peaky and some fresh air would do her good. A sharp talking to's what she needed. Peaky, my eye.'

'Where is Bertha's home?'

'I don't know, I'm sure. Some back-street in North-Lambeth.'

Following the cook's rustling gait, Abbs doubted the efficacy of the smoky haze over-hanging the Surrey bank of the Thames. A generous mistress, though. He wondered about the contents of Ellis's will.

Miss Maitland, now clad in ready-made mourning, was sitting with her guest in the drawing-room. A tea-table, placed before them, held crumbed plates and an empty cake-stand. Mrs Ibbotson had removed her hat, a sure sign of intimate friendship and a lengthy visit. Abbs politely declined Miss Maitland's offer to ring for more hot water.

'Would you prefer me to leave, Officer?' Mrs Ibbotson fixed him with the piercing gaze of one accustomed to organising servants and the poor.

'Please stay, by all means, ma'am. I shall need to speak to you and Reverend Ibbotson.'

Her sombre costume was of good quality stuff, a black ribbon pinned on her bodice. He glimpsed a string of jet beads above her collar. The best efforts of Mrs Ibbotson's corset-maker rigidly confined her matronly figure. Abbs thought her perhaps five or six years older than her husband.

He concentrated on Miss Maitland. 'The inquest will be held on Friday at eleven, ma'am, at the local police-court. You should receive the notice from the coroner's clerk by the early evening post. I've spoken to Mr. Penfold. He's writing to you about the reading of the will. He proposes it be held here, later the same day.'

Apprehension flickered across her countenance. 'It's good of you to tell me yourself, Inspector.'

Mrs Ibbotson patted her friend's sleeve. 'That's well, my dear. We shall soon know your position. Rowland said he'd provided for you.'

'He assured me I wouldn't be without means. Those were his exact words.'

'All that matters is you'll have a roof over your head. You know you shall come straight to us, if you must quit the house. Thomas says we have ample room at the vicarage, while you look about. There are sure to be agreeable lodgings to be leased nearby.'

'Mr. Ibbotson is very good.'

'I shall have a word with Cook before I leave. The dining-room would be most suitable for Mr. Penfold's purpose. It will be sufficient to provide sherry, or perhaps the gentlemen would prefer madeira? No one will expect proper refreshments, in these unhappy circumstances.'

'You're very thoughtful, Hester but I should speak to Mrs Wilmot. I could do with something to occupy myself.'

'However it befalls, there'll be plenty to organise, soon enough. You should resume your music.'

'In case I need to seek a position?' said Miss Maitland drily. She caught his glance at the piano-forte. 'I used to play for my sister, Inspector. She found it soothing but my brother-in-law no longer cared for music. He thought it painful to be reminded.'

'There's no escaping pain in this life.' Mrs Ibbotson's voice was brusque. 'As the vicar says, we must accept what befalls us with fortitude. Trust in the Lord and look to the future.'

You could learn a great deal by letting witnesses have their head. But it was time to make clear the nature of these *unhappy circumstances.*

'Before we continue, ladies, there's a serious matter on which I must speak to you both. The police do not believe Mr. Ellis was the random victim of an interrupted burglary. I've already informed Mr. Buckley and Mr. Penfold. The likelihood is Mr. Ellis was murdered by someone known to him.'

He watched Miss Maitland's face blanch the colour of whey. Gestures could be deliberate. A skilled liar knew to relax their hands and shoulders. He didn't believe even an accomplished actress could will her complexion to drain bloodless.

Mrs Ibbotson sat carefully still. 'You mean someone of his wider acquaintance, sir?'

Abbs made no answer. He let the implication lie between them, like a Fenian bomb tossed among the tea-cups. The women exchanged glances.

'Why?' Miss Maitland shivered. 'Who would do such a terrible act? I can't believe it of anyone we know.'

'The inspector is unable to speak freely, Louie,' said Mrs Ibbotson. 'He has his work to do.' Feeling the weight of the tea-pot, she poured a cup, deftly wielded the sugar-tongs and handed it to Miss Maitland. 'Drink this. It's still warm.'

Abbs waited while she sipped, grimacing at the taste. 'You can think of no one who might believe they had a grievance against Mr. Ellis?'

'No, sir. To think my brother-in-law was slain by a thief was appalling, but this is worse.'

'Even so, it has happened,' said Mrs Ibbotson. 'It makes no difference, my dear. We place our trust in prayer.' She nodded graciously at him. 'And the best endeavours of the Metropolitan Police.'

'Make no mistake, ma'am. We shall apprehend whoever did this. There will be justice for Mr. Ellis. But I understand that's cold comfort.'

'Thank you, Inspector.' Miss Maitland recovered her composure. 'Please continue with your questions.'

'I'll endeavour to be brief. How did Mr. Ellis spend his days, since he became a widower?'

'I suppose like any retired gentleman. He spent a good deal of time occupied with his books and papers. He attended exhibitions, occasional lectures. He'd go for long walks across the city, by himself, often returning with a parcel of books.'

'Would this be art galleries, ma'am? I'm told Mr. Ellis sometimes accompanied Mr. Ambrose Buckley.'

'Yes, they shared an interest in art, despite often having conflicting views.' Her lips curved for an instant. 'Mr. Ambrose Buckley finds much to condemn in established painters. They'd argue about Mr. Charles Collins, whose works my brother-in-law admired. According to Ambrose, his subjects are too pretty by far and of no lasting merit.'

'Mr. Ellis's spirits never truly recovered,' said Mrs Ibbotson. 'He used to be fond of watching cricket, as you may see. Last summer, he didn't even visit the Surrey ground, where in happier days, he was a regular spectator.'

Abbs followed her gesture at the painting hanging above the fireplace. A depiction of cricketers playing on an elm-fringed green. He noticed the wall-paper was slightly faded above the frame. A shape that would fit the portrait of Mrs Ellis, hanging in the study.

'What about other friends and visitors, Miss Maitland?'

'I believe he corresponded with one or two gentlemen. They hadn't met for many years. As far as I know, there was no one else. He never mentioned attending galleries with anyone other than Ambrose. As for visitors, we'd have a few guests to dine occasionally, the Buckleys, the vicar and Mrs Ibbotson, of course, old Mr. Penfold until his last illness. I suspect that was for my benefit. Rowland had got out of the way of entertaining, I think.'

'Did Mr. Ellis call on any neighbours?'

Miss Maitland shook her head. 'He and my sister were content in themselves, even before her illness. I know Mr. Buckley entertained business clients when necessary. He is more out-going by nature.'

'Mr. Ellis told the vicar he had no interest in making new acquaintance,' said Mrs Ibbotson.

On his way there, Abbs had debated whether to confront Miss

Maitland about the reading-matter she'd destroyed so urgently. He decided to wait for the time being. A decision reinforced on finding she was with company. In answer to his final question, she shook her head, saying the diary hadn't turned up.

Readily complying with his request to search the study and Ellis's room, she conducted him to a large bedroom, overlooking the carriage-drive.

'You'll need more light, Inspector.' Suiting her words, she opened the curtains. 'Nothing's been touched in here. The dressing-room is through there.'

'Thank you, ma'am.'

'You know your way to the study. Please ring, if you require anything. I'll leave you to your work.'

It was a strange living, having the right to search someone's intimate possessions. Abbs had never lost that first moment of distaste, as his hands lifted and pried with minimal touch. In some eyes, he was little better than a pure-finder collecting in alleys. Even so, a dung-gatherer and a detective both had honest trades. The ugliness of life had to be cleared up by someone.

He began with a swift check of the dressing-room, with its lingering trace of macassar-oil. The dead man had been precise in his habits. A pair of horn-backed brushes aligned soldier-like. Collars, cuffs, stud-box, as though set out by a valet. In his experience, a great need for order belonged to an anxious individual. An irony not lost on him.

A rosewood writing-box stood on the old bow-fronted chest of drawers in the bedroom. He'd caught Miss Maitland's glance at it, as she left. Turning the key proved disappointing, no diary or letters.

He picked up the silver-framed picture of Ellis and the woman in the portrait, taking it near the window. Her crinoline dated them some years ago. Standing by her chair, Ellis looked a proud man, as his wife smiled happily for the photographer. But studying the likeness, Abbs read the prominent bones and hollows in her face. With hindsight, a shadow had been falling across Sophia Ellis.

The counter-pane and eiderdown were smoothed across the bed. Habit made him search beneath the mattress, though he hardly expected to find anything.

Revisiting the study, he found the room subtly altered. There was no feeling its owner would return. The hearth-rug gone. New glass in the garden-door, a hint of raw putty. The fireplace had been swept, a screen hiding its gaping emptiness. The tray of decanters had been removed. The ormolu clock was silent, a crumpled leaf fallen from a maidenhair fern.

As far as Abbs could tell, the contents of the desk were unchanged. Stationery and receipted bills at the top, a drawer fitted with a shallow tray of draughtsman's pencils, rule and compass. The bottom drawer was packed with old sketches and floor-plans.

He glanced through the last opened post. A wine-merchant's bill and a book catalogue, finally coming upon a letter written last Christmas-tide, by an elderly-sounding gentleman. It described an annual summing-up of small doings, ending with good wishes for the coming year. There was nothing more to be found at Lindholm, it seemed.

It occurred to him as he left, that an orderly man was not so likely to leave his drawer jammed. Had someone rummaged through the desk before the police came? Miss Maitland was the most obvious candidate. He wondered if Mr. Buckley had been alone in the study.

~

It took little above ten minutes to walk back along Kennington-road to the local police-station, a grimy edifice taking up a corner. Before going in, Abbs went to find the police-court in the adjoining street.

The court building was fairly new, its brick only lightly sooted, with 1869 picked out in pale stone-work above the entrance. Fortunately for the residents, Frederick Buckley had not been the architect. He passed the fire-station, where the arched stable-doors stood open. A broom was propped against the wall, someone whistling, horses snorting. Skirting rivulets of water running across the cobbles, he returned to the main street.

A tavern stood near the police-station, an oyster-seller's barrow by its green-tiled frontage. The clouds were lowering as Abbs went in beneath the blue glass lamp. The sky echoed the empty shells, discarded around the barrow.

Inside, he tried not to inhale the miasma of fear and unwashed skin. A taint that could not be masked by scrubbing with lye. His back turned, a uniformed sergeant was busy, pushing a scrawny youth against the height-gauge. An old woman slumped on the bench-end nearest the fire. The usual bills covered the walls in black lettering. Someone in the cells was kicking up a ruckus.

Before he could make himself known, Sergeant Hollins came through from behind the counter and beckoned him.

'This way, Inspector Abbs. We've not long been back ourselves.'

Long enough to empty cups and crease a *South London Journal* across the desk. Grainer got to his feet when he entered, answering to the pigeon-holes behind Abbs's head.

'Well, sir, much as I expected. Nothing to report on the identity of Mr. Ellis's companion. No one at The Horns knew either of 'em, nor did the cabbies. We've made a start on the pawn-shops.'

'A description of the missing items has been circulated,' said Hollins. 'As for your house-breaker, there's no regular customer of ours comes to mind. Most are accounted for. We've just been round the likeliest prospect, out of gaol.'

'To find he'd scarpered, sir, but not recent. His old woman told us.'

Hollins sniggered. 'Got himself on the wrong side of someone out for his blood. Left town weeks ago. Taken his new judy with him. I'm not surprised. If you'd seen his lawful wife, you'd know why he worked nights.'

'What about your informants, Sergeant?' Abbs remained standing.

'I've endeavoured to put the word out, sir. All takes time, as you know.'

'Indeed. Have you questioned the beat-constable, yet?'

'Yes, sir. He walked the length of Wellow-road, turning in about twenty after nine. No-one about. Bit of fog, he said, but clear enough to see with his bulls-eye. I did warn as much.'

'It pays to be thorough. Grainer, did you inquire if anyone at the Horns was off today?'

'I did, sir. The landlord said they were all present.'

The fellow in the cell had fallen silent. Abbs was conscious of men passing in the corridor, snatches of words. Someone put their head round the door, muttered an apology and vanished. The fire was smoking badly, tickling his throat.

He'd had sufficient of Kennington for one day. The omnibuses would be crowded. He didn't relish being jammed up top with Grainer, in the rain. The truth about the murder of Rowland Ellis was not to be found among pawn-brokers and house-breakers. He was convinced of that much.

~

The Wesleyan chapel clock struck five in the next street. Their little carriage clock was slow, but she was fond of it. Presented by the company, when they wed in Brighton. Suppressing a yawn, Jessie Dove willed their visitor to leave.

With no fire lit in the parlour kept for callers, they'd felt obliged to show her in the room they used, where a slight chemical smell lingered. Rain was spattering the window again. A spring so chilly, they were still ordering coal by the winter-load.

They'd heard a growler stop outside and watched a plain-faced woman, in her forties, get out. In an instant, the glove she'd been painting was thrust in the corner cupboard, together with brush, phial and a length of fine wire. She draped the heavy tablecloth, setting its tassels swinging. Silas pulled his frock-coat off the chair-back, fastening his collar as she went to the door. The waiting woman stood, blurred in the ridged glass.

Their caller plucked at her handkerchief with gloved fingers.

'Please, dear lady, do not distress yourself. Are you sure you won't partake of tea?'

She leant forward, concealing her irritation. 'It would be no trouble, ma'am.'

'Thank you kindly, Mrs Dove, but I cannot be away for long. I'll be missed.' Their visitor returned her attention to Silas. 'The message I seek means everything to me, Mr. Dove. If it's a question of a higher fee for all your trouble, I can pay. I've some money put by.' Her words died away as he raised his hand.

'Desist, I beg of you, ma'am. Money is of no consequence, whatsoever.'

His sorrowful expression was straight out of his rendering of the Scottish play, thought Jessie. She shivered automatically. Such an affecting speech when the Lady was dead. You could always hear a pin drop among the audience.

'I shall endeavour to explain, Mrs Smith. You must understand, when someone passes into spirit, communication is difficult at the best of times. The ability to be used, as a living channel, is given to few. It is a risky and exhausting business for the medium.'

'I don't doubt it, sir. But will you not try?'

'Alas, many a genuine medium has been unjustly vilified when they cannot give a convincing demonstration on a public stage. My answer to worldly critics is that we cannot harness the power. It flows through us at the spirits' will. I am a mere conduit, ma'am. A conductor, if you like. A lightning-rod to the heavens, nothing more.'

'I mean no disrespect, I'm sure. Only I've waited so long. I tried to explain.'

'You misunderstand me, ma'am. You say the person, from whom you hope to receive a message, has only recently departed. The problem is that the newly deceased are unable to communicate, at once, with the world of the living.'

'I did not think.' Her features looked suitably chastened.

'There is, of necessity, a period of adjustment. Those who have recently passed into the spirit-realm must accustom themselves to their new existence. Imagine, if you will, their shock. They too, must feel the sorrow of their parting from loved ones.'

'That is so very sad. How long, would you say, Mr. Dove, before the spirits may communicate?'

Their caller wore the garb of an upper servant. Jessie priced her attire with an expert eye, honed by years of fitting and altering in draughty dressing-rooms. A serviceable skirt, her mantle well-worn, though good quality. A hand-me-down for a ladies' maid, or might she be a house-keeper? Nothing hid the truth of a woman's class like gloves. Her hands might be calloused with work or soft as summer butter. However common, she was sure the name would not be her own.

'Ah, who may say, dear lady? Time, as we know it, does not exist on the other side. So much is hidden from us on this corporeal plane.

'I sometimes think, sir, that patience is the hardest virtue.'

'Take heart, ma'am. The shades of the departed are always with us. I am shortly to be appearing at a semi-public meeting here in Kennington. The audience will be carefully selected, ensuring the comfort of unattended ladies. Perhaps you would care to purchase a ticket?'

In response to the snap of his fingers, Jessie rose to fetch one of the hand-bills.

'Two eminently renowned lady mediums will be assisting me. Provided the atmosphere proves agreeable to the spirits, we are hoping for a full manifestation.'

'Oh no, that would not be possible.'

Her husband winced, as if the remark had caused him physical pain. 'Indeed, ma'am, I assure you.' He accompanied his words with a heartfelt hand to his breast. 'Marvels may be seen, if the emanations are favourable. And no nay-sayers present. There is nothing to fear.'

'Forgive me, Mr. Dove, I have never doubted it possible. I've read many accounts. I meant it is too difficult for me to get away.'

'Understood, dear lady. We can arrange a perfectly private occasion here in our humble home. As I mentioned, it is not advisable to summon the spirits without warning. I must first spend some time in preparation, clearing my mind of worldly cares. It is not judicious to have recently eaten.'

'My apologies, once more, for calling like this. I had a little time to spare, unexpectedly. I find myself so distressed.'

'Not at all, ma'am. I only regret I am unable to bring you a message this instant. We welcome all who need succour on Friday evening next, at the usual hour. If you are able to join us, I feel sure some message of comfort will be given to you then.'

Hands folded, Jessie remained by the bureau, hoping it would serve as a hint if she didn't resume her seat.

Mrs Smith picked up her reticule, hesitated. 'Tell me, Mr. Dove, does it make any difference if the person died ... violently?'

'Violently, ma'am? You mean in an accident?'

'Far worse, I fear. He was horribly attacked, sir. Murdered.'

'Out of the gentleman's way, Lachie. Move yourself, he doesn't want you under his feet. Do excuse me, Mr. Abbs.'

He smiled at his landlady, hovering by the letter-rack, and the portly, grey cat who awaited him on the bottom stair. Both peered up at him, one stern, the other's gaze unwavering.

'Please don't trouble yourself, Mrs Newsome.'

'You'll not have seen Lachie. I've been keeping him out of your way, only he's curious. He would go up and look at Mr. Snow, when he first came. He's not supposed to be in the hall.' His landlady scooped up her companion.

As he drew level, Abbs gently held out his hand. The cat's warm fur brushed against his knuckles. 'We haven't been formally introduced.'

'I can see he's taken to you. He doesn't go to everyone.'

'A handsome beast.'

'He is that.' Mrs Newsome's expression softened. 'He's been with me these past eleven years, since I lost my husband. There was I, feeling sorry for myself, without a purpose and this wee scrap was going to be drowned in the canal. I said, we'd help each other and we've rubbed along together ever since.' She hesitated, 'I hope you're comfortable here, Mr. Abbs. You'll let me know if you need anything?'

'Thank you, Mrs Newsome, I'm exceedingly comfortable and most grateful you elected to take me as a tenant. I didn't expect to find lodgings in such a well-appointed house.'

She looked gratified. Her customary severe expression derived, he thought, from wearing eye-glasses.

'Indeed, you're welcome, Mr. Abbs. It's a weight off my mind.' She looked up at the curlicues of plaster-work, Lachie settled in her arms. 'My husband loved these old houses. He always aspired to owning one. He was a master-builder, you know. I did his book-keeping for him, after we wed. Of course, they're not fashionable these days. Even thirteen year ago, he picked this house up for a song. We were close to Agar-town then, terrible slums. They were pulled down when they built the railway. He did this up lovingly. I fear he didn't get long to enjoy it.'

Later that day, Abbs recalled his landlady's words as he walked along Whitehall, nearing the austere Admiralty buildings. The first time she'd mentioned anything personal. He found himself unexpectedly moved by glimpses of strangers' lives. He wondered about his fellow tenant, away up north, according to Mrs Newsome. A commercial-traveller, perhaps.

A private carriage was drawn up outside the Pay Office, the coachman waiting to edge back among the endless horse-traffic. He watched the tall hatted passenger climb the steps, leaning on his malacca cane, his way opened by a bowing doorman. The hollow-eyed urchins, who haunted most city streets, had fallen away. Seen off from loitering near these mighty edifices of government.

From all accounts, Rowland Ellis had been a man who'd lost his purpose. What was there in his life that necessitated his removal? How did a kindly, grieving widower stand in someone's way? The will-reading would confirm an obvious answer. In all probability, the chief inspector was right. Money answered most questions.

According to Grainer, Dick, the errand-boy, had nothing useful to add, though plenty to say for himself. He'd met the dead man only once, being absent when he called in March. Mr. Ellis had confiscated his catapult, a good one which was never returned. He'd only been doing somethin' useful, taking pot-shots at the sparrows in the yard. The youth, reported Grainer, showed a pop-eyed interest in the gore of his employer's slaying, until hushed by a lily-white Mr. Searle.

He'd dispatched Grainer south of the river again, working his way through the list of pawn-brokers. Widening his search beyond the confines of Kennington. Where were the missing miniatures and figurine? If the murderer took them to fake a burglary, they'd still have to dispose of them. Foolish to hide the evidence when a chance discovery, by a servant, could be enough to hang them.

In fact, he could get no authority to search Lindholm top to bottom, certainly not the Buckleys' home or the vicarage, without already possessing other evidence. These people might only be trade, but Townsend would consider them too monied to annoy without good reason. He certainly wouldn't antagonise the Church, if it could be helped. For the inhabitants of a rookery or a mean dwelling, it would be a different story. He could tear their cupboards apart with impunity, if they had any, and if he cared to.

Abbs considered the probabilities as he turned into Great Scotland Yard, pausing while a hansom pulled up. Were incriminating items in his possession, he'd want to get rid of them on the instant. The diary could be burnt at home, but not the other things.

Dropping them from a bridge was one way. Easy at night, you'd risk being remembered by an alert toll-keeper, but that could be overcome. Westminster Bridge would be safe, but too far from Lindholm. Everyone he'd encountered, in Rowland Ellis's small circle, resided within a few streets.

He'd watched the mud-larks toiling along the river banks at low tide. Their bare feet encrusted with wet, dark slime, oozing and clinging. Sinking, as they scavenged like rats among rotting timbers and dead dogs. He smelt the churning stench every day.

The murderer would feel safe if the stolen items came in their hands. Pawned or sold, they could never be connected to the muffled figure who'd thrown them. But he would like to know...

Directly he reached his desk, Abbs scribbled instructions. Local constables would know the regulars along the Thames. He consulted the wall map to check on the likely bridges and returned across the quadrangle.

It was while he was waiting for a clerk to take his telegraph, he realised a thought was nudging at his mind. Something had been out of place in his room. His gaze had absorbed something unacknowledged by his attention.

There was little yet to be moved, the shelf still bare, save for the latest *Police Gazette,* a lone vesta-case on the mantel. Abbs studied his desk, his fingers raking his flop of hair back off his brow. The chair had been tucked in, when he pulled it out. The glass paper-weight, given him by his sister, was on the reports in his tray. But not positioned quite as he habitually did. Someone had replaced it.

No messages had been left for him. No new dockets waiting on his blotter. They'd be a reason for a constable to enter and just maybe, exercise his curiosity. The paper-weight was eye-catching, a souvenir of Hunstanton. Sheppard, or another inspector, might have dropped in with some query. Though it wasn't customary to leaf through a colleague's papers, without asking. He could think of nothing that urgent. Which left Townsend checking on his progress.

He was under no illusion about the chief inspector's opinion of him. Natural enough, he'd prefer to pick his own men. A man transferred from a county force was approved at a higher level. Townsend's demeanour suggested ex-army, though unlike the Commissioner, he retained no rank. It would be interesting to see if his superior said anything, when he made his daily report.

SIXTEEN

Waiting his turn among the people filing out, Abbs made his way from the inquest to join the others. The public benches had been tight with gawpers, avid for a free entertainment. The coroner had rebuked their fidgeting asides, calling for silence when the police-surgeon gave his evidence. A few journalists had been scribbling and no doubt, the patterers would be recounting the blood-chilling murder of Rowland Ellis by nightfall.

Sergeant Grainer was busying himself with taking snuff. He waved the tin perfunctorily at Hollins, who shook his head. It was pocketed swiftly as Grainer looked up, seeing him on the top step.

'That's that done with,' said Hollins. 'We'll keep going with the pawn-shops and jewellers. Anything more I can do for you, sir?'

'Not for the time being, Sergeant. My thanks for your assistance.'

Hollins stepped back as Grainer erupted in a widespread sneeze. 'I'll send word, directly we hear anything.'

'If you ever do, more like.'

Abbs suppressed a sigh. 'Come now, Grainer, there's no call to be despondent. It's early days and we've several lines to follow.'

'If you say so, sir. Only I don't reckon the goods'll ever turn up.'

'Make way, if you please.'

Abbs glanced back to see people obeying the strong, carrying voice. Mr. Ibbotson was escorting Miss Maitland, Mr. Buckley close behind. The three of them, sombre as a gathering of crows. Miss Maitland put up the black veil she'd worn in the witness-box. Several heads turned to get a look at her, as they halted by the detectives.

'Inspector Abbs.' Ibbotson acknowledged them. 'Good day, Hollins.'

'Afternoon, Reverend.'

Frowning, Mr. Buckley looked at his watch-face. 'So it is, ten after mid-day already. A morning gone and nothing accomplished. At least, funeral arrangements can be made now. I must be off. Are you sure I can't drop you at the house, Miss Maitland?'

'You're very good but Mr. Ibbotson is seeing me home.'

'Then I shall see you later. Will you be present, Inspector?'

'We shall, Mr. Buckley.'

'I must say, I call that unfeeling. This lady is under severe strain, as it is, without having the police peering over the lawyer's shoulder.'

'I'm sure Miss Maitland understands the necessity in these difficult circumstances,' said Mr. Ibbotson.

Scowling, Buckley took his leave, addressing himself pointedly to Miss Maitland. He set off towards the waiting carriages.

'You know Mr. Penfold is expected at three, Inspector?' said Miss Maitland. 'You and your sergeant are welcome to join us. It makes no difference to me.'

Abbs thanked her. She did look feverish, her gloved fingers clung to the vicar's arm. Though she'd answered the coroner's questions clearly, refusing the offer of a glass of water.

'Come along, Miss Louisa, Hester will be awaiting us. Miss Maitland is taking luncheon at the vicarage, Inspector. Better to be among friends.'

'You'll be at the reading, Mr. Ibbotson?'

'Mr. Penfold has summoned me, yes. Mr. Ellis informed me, some years ago, he'd set aside a legacy for the church. I'd not have been surprised, I confess, if he'd reconsidered his generosity, this last year.'

'Rowland wouldn't do that.' Miss Maitland looked up at him. 'He might have turned away from his faith, but I don't doubt that was a temporary failing. He admired St Edward's and always spoke warmly of your good works, sir.'

'Then you too, must have faith in his benefaction,' said Mr. Ibbotson. 'Come, let us be on our way.'

~

Abbs toyed with his mutton-chop. His landlady was proving an excellent cook, indeed, too generous with her helpings. Her cat had taken to visiting him, on those evenings when the smell of boiled fish rose up from the kitchen.

As they were heading in the same direction, back over Westminster Bridge, it seemed churlish to refuse the police-surgeon's good-natured suggestion.

'A decent find, this place, for those in the know,' remarked his companion. 'I come here regularly. They say you must go to the City for the best grills, as financial men always do themselves well, but this is clean and they don't spoil the meat.'

Abbs looked out from their booth. Their tablecloth was clean, the floor swept and the bill of fare modestly priced. A savoury concoction of meat and onion drifted down the long room. Not surprising, the chop-house was filling up with fellow diners. He guessed, by their apparel, some were managers or clerks.

'It was good of you to suggest it, Doctor.'

'Prentice, please. We're entitled to eat, however hard-pressed, and be all the more diligent after.' He chewed his beef-steak, washing it down with a mouthful of porter. 'You're newly arrived in London, Sergeant Grainer said?'

'So he informs everyone we meet.'

'Cheerful soul, is he not?'

'Let's just say I'd welcome more enthusiasm.' He picked up his ale. 'And faith in our eventual success.'

Prentice grinned. 'He missed his calling. Our Toby should have been a professional mourner.'

'I've been at the Yard almost two months. This is my first case here.'

Giving him a shrewd look, the police-surgeon changed the subject. 'How are you finding our mighty capital?' He sliced the remainder of his meat.

Abbs wondered if he'd be slitting a corpse later, with the same deft economy. 'Thoroughly absorbing, but a little confusing. I doubt I'll ever know where one suburb turns into its neighbour.'

'I'm not altogether sure Londoners, born and bred, could tell you. I suspect you'd get many an answer. The Metropolis is a patchwork of old villages and new towns stitched together.'

'It seems to have an endless appetite for growth.'

'Oh, undoubtedly. A market-garden one month is sure to be a brick-yard the next. Neither of us are likely to be out of customers.'

'You're not from here yourself?'

'No, I hail from Kent. Did my training at King's, there was a post on the wards at Charing Cross and I've been there ever since. Believe me, there's enough hardship to keep a man busy for a lifetime.' Prentice gazed at the diners opposite them, as an elderly waiter lowered their steaming plates. Red-eyed, he looked weary. 'My father's a physician. The idea was I'd work with him.'

As Prentice returned to his food. Abbs wondered about what wasn't said.

'Grainer said you're from Exeter?'

He shook his head, 'I'd transferred to the County Police there. I'm Norfolk-bred.'

'Ah, a restless soul. They all come here, sooner or later.'

Abbs thought of his dead wife, declaring she couldn't be parted from her family in the West Country. Leaving his home for her sake. The one impetuous act of his youth.

'Not really. Life has a way of diverting you. Otherwise, I suppose I'd still be settled in a small flint town and might never have seen London.'

'Diverted,' said Prentice slowly. 'I suppose that's what happened to me. You go somewhere, telling yourself it's only for a year or two. Comes a day when you realise, you won't go back.' He picked up his tankard. 'What made you go in for the peelers?'

'Working on the land didn't appeal. Most villagers did, we were a fair distance from the coast. My father was head-gardener on a country estate. I'd no desire to work for the big house. I think my parents hoped I'd start out as a pupil-teacher, but that wasn't for me either.'

'You must excuse me, Abbs. My curiosity runs away with me. I spend much of my time questioning the sick. It plays havoc with my manners.'

'Not at all. I suppose I wanted to do something useful.' He grinned ruefully. 'I dislike bullies.'

'Was that the nature of the gentleman in question?'

Pushing away his plate, Abbs considered. 'I think not. By all accounts, he was a fair man in his dealings.'

It was an interesting question. Did Rowland Ellis stand in someone's way, or somehow, did his own character bring about his death?

SEVENTEEN

Mr. Penfold straightened his papers needlessly, taking a sip of madeira, before resuming his reading. From his position against the wall, seated on a hard chair next to Grainer, Abbs studied the others. Heavy curtains obscured part of the window. The olive drab material, bunching on the dark floorboards, framed the company at the table like a stage.

Penfold had taken the host's chair, with Louisa Maitland on his right. Frederick Buckley sat next to her, followed by Ambrose, wearing a black arm-band. The Ibbotsons were opposite, a couple of places separating them from Henry Searle.

Mrs Wilmot and Maggie had been waiting awkwardly in the hall, until summoned in by Miss Maitland. They sat together at the far end of the dining-table. Hands clasped, Maggie sat stiffly with downcast eyes, as if in church. The cook had an air of suppressed anticipation.

The lawyer had read out the customary opening lines of Rowland Ellis's will, in a ponderous monotone. He began with legacies for several charities. Mr. Ibbotson's church was not mentioned, which suggested, thought Abbs, a larger bequest. He was surprised to see Mrs Ibbotson present.

'We now come to various other bequests, I shall begin with the household servants. To Mrs Emma Ann Wilmot, I leave a sum equivalent to one quarter's wages, provided she is still in my employ at the time of my death.' Penfold looked at the gratified recipient.

'Likewise, to Maggie Jane Onslow, I leave a sum equivalent to two months' wages, on the above condition.'

She looked up, giving a slight nod in acknowledgement.

'With your permission, Miss Maitland, there is no further need for your servants to remain.'

'As you wish, Mr. Penfold. That will be all, thank you, Mrs Wilmot, Maggie.'

'Very good, ma'am.' Now a pattern of dignity, Mrs Wilmot replaced her chair.

Penfold waited, papers raised, until the door was shut behind the two women. Before continuing, he looked round the table, like a school-master checking his pupils were attentive.

He needn't have bothered, thought Abbs. The lawyer had the rapt attention of everyone present, including surely, those who feigned indifference. Mr. Ibbotson had his arms folded. Ambrose Buckley gazed idly at the window, as he eased the back of his collar.

'To Henry Edward Searle, I leave my silver ink-stand, in gratitude for many years of loyal service.'

Searle's lips moved silently, as if repeating the last words. Turning away, he wiped his eyes.

'To Jonathan Calvert of Ghyll House, Carrdale, North Riding, I leave my books on cricket, together with my books on architecture, and my painting of our old college, in affectionate remembrance of our youth.'

Abbs recognised the name on the letter he'd read. From where they were sitting, the faces along the table were in profile. In the grey afternoon, the dining-room was gloomy, despite a good fire. The tall glass over the mantel was covered. The gasolier, suspended from a ceiling rose, threw a weak shadow across the polished wood.

'To Mrs Hester Blanche Ibbotson, I leave my garnet ring, formerly the property of my late wife, Sophia, as a token of friendship and shared remembrance.'

Mr. Ibbotson glanced at his wife, putting his hand over hers momentarily. The bequest came as a surprise to them both, thought Abbs. He glimpsed Miss Maitland's countenance, before she wiped her expression. A look of cold venom directed towards her friend.

A generous bequest for the parish church came next. To be administered by the Reverend Thomas William Ibbotson, and spent on restoring the fabric of St Edward the Confessor.

Grainer stifled an exclamation as he broke the point of his pencil. Abbs passed his own, without looking at him.

Penfold moistened his lips before continuing, tilting the document to the light. 'To my young friend, Ambrose Leigh Buckley, I leave my books on art, in the hope he may come to appreciate them.'

Stretching, Ambrose grinned. 'Not much chance of that.'

Penfold waited until he was sure no more was coming. 'And in addition, a sum equivalent to one year's wages, in order that he may devote himself to pursuing his artistic endeavours. Given with the recommendation he spend some time travelling on the Continent, in order to study classical art.'

'Well, I'll be d——d, he had me there.' Ambrose laughed, throwing back his head. 'The dear old fellow. I thought the books were all.'

'Control yourself, sir.' Frederick Buckley pressed his hands against the table-edge, his fingers white against the reddish mahogany.

'That's just it, father. I shan't have to, any more. No more drawing up doll-houses for fat philistines, thanks to old Rowley. He listened to me. He even tried to understand.'

Buckley visibly swallowed his temper. 'You had better wait outside, before you make a greater spectacle of yourself.'

Ambrose stood. 'Quite right, Father, as usual. I don't need to sit out the rest. Miss Louisa, you'll forgive me if I take my leave of you? You know I wish you well.'

Miss Maitland smiled faintly as he bent over her hand. Sketching a slight bow at Penfold and his father, Ambrose met Abbs's gaze. 'Gentlemen, ladies, I bid you all farewell.'

Buckley subsided in his chair, as his son left. 'My apologies, Penfold, Miss Maitland. My son is somewhat overwrought. I don't know what Ellis was thinking of. He should have spoken to me.'

'If we may continue...?' Penfold cleared his throat. 'We are almost at an end. We now come to the disposal of Mr. Ellis's business interests. Namely, his sixty per cent ownership of the architects' partnership, Ellis and Buckley. As is entirely usual in business...'

While the lawyer read out the formal phrases handing the business to Frederick Buckley, Abbs watched Louisa Maitland. Her gaze was fixed on the dessert-service displayed on the sideboard, her shoulders stiff with waiting.

'To my sister-in-law, Louisa Maud Maitland, I leave all my late wife's jewellery, excepting only the aforementioned ring. Also, the entire contents of my house, including furniture, plate, books, ornaments and paintings, excepting only the aforementioned books, ink-stand and painting.'

Mr. Penfold inclined to Miss Maitland as he read. Unable to see his face, Abbs could tell he was attempting to make himself agreeable.

'Furthermore, in appreciation of her sisterly kindness to my late wife, I leave unto her, all monies not otherwise aforementioned; in addition, the income from my investments, shares and securities, together with my property, known as Lindholm, for the remainder of her life, provided she does not marry.'

'And if I did wish to marry?'

Penfold coughed in some embarrassment. 'I can explain the provisions to you in detail, after your guests have departed, ma'am. That concludes the reading of Mr. Ellis's last will and testament.'

'It is a matter of indifference to me who hears, sir. I am among friends and Inspector Abbs will need to know all of it.' Miss Maitland gave him a neutral look. 'Until the murderer of my benefactor is caught, none of us can feel easy. Apart from yourself, naturally, Mr. Penfold.'

Abbs watched Henry Searle dab his handkerchief over his brow. His bony frame was shrivelled with the desire to be elsewhere. No one else was embarrassed. He knew they were listening avidly.

Penfold nodded. 'Very well, Miss Maitland, as you wish. The clause, which Mr. Ellis instructed my late uncle to include, is quite customary. In the event of your marrying, this house is to be sold immediately. All investments to be withdrawn and the entire proceeds given to Mr. Ellis's alma mata, to fund a scholarship. Otherwise, these instructions will be carried out on... ahem, on your eventual demise.'

'I'm obliged to you, Mr. Penfold. That is perfectly clear.'

'But have no fear, ma'am. While not a fortune by any means, there will be sufficient to maintain this household in comfort.'

'Ellis was a warm man,' said Frederick Buckley. He touched his moustache.

'A far-sighted gentleman, certainly. It appears the late Mr. Ellis invested in railway-shares back in the 'fifties. Unlike many, he chose companies that have prospered.'

'Did he, by Jove? He never let on. Always did hold his cards close.' Buckley pursed his lips. 'I'd have said he had too much caution.'

Miss Maitland stood, perfectly composed, as the men went to do likewise. 'Thank you, Mr. Penfold. I trust you will all stay for another glass. You too, Mr. Searle.' She smiled at him. 'If Mr. Penfold approves, I see no reason why the ink-stand cannot be wrapped for you to take away.'

Penfold inclined his head graciously. 'I see no objection, ma'am, subject to my making out a receipt.'

'Inspector? Would you and your sergeant care for some refreshment, before you depart?'

'Not on duty, thank you, Miss Maitland.' Behind Abbs, Grainer shuffled his boots. 'But I should like a word with your guests, while you're all together.'

The will revealed they had three suspects, each with a strong motive. Grainer seemed disinclined to discuss them. Instead, he pointed out the roofs of Surrey Cricket Ground, formerly frequented by Rowland Ellis. Its pavilion was overlooked by the ugly drums of the Phoenix Gas-works.

When Abbs suggested they return to the Yard by way of Lambeth, the sergeant had no choice but to agree, albeit with a resigned expression, which he ignored. They were expected to walk after all. Three miles before they could claim expenses and the bridge toll would be cheap enough.

The pavement trees and shrubberies of the better classes were left behind as they neared the Thames. Here, cramped terraces were sandwiched between looming manufactories. Two-up, two-down, coal-house and privy out the back. The sickly discharge from a brewery and soap-works hung about the streets, until the vapour from a vinegar distillery cut the air.

Both the privileged and the impoverished lived an uneasy co-existence in the great Metropolis. The streets would change within a few minutes' walk, like the turn of a child's kaleidoscope. Abbs thought about Bertha growing up among the chimneys, the grimy windows they'd passed, the wet washing strung in smoke and dust. Better to be poor in the countryside, where, at least, there was fresh air and more light.

He felt sorry for the girl. But being in service there under a year, she must have known she wouldn't be remembered in Ellis's will.

Grainer huffed his way up the slope to the toll-keeper's window. Proffering his half-penny in turn, Abbs looked about him with lively interest. The Albert Embankment was busy with carriage-traffic, but as they passed beneath the first iron tower, the suspension-bridge was surprisingly empty. Only a bandy-legged man pushing a hand-cart and some people ahead on the pavement.

'Why is it so quiet?'

Grainer leant on the parapet, catching his breath. 'On account of the approach being steep, sir. Cabbies don't like it for the horses. That many wagons have turned over, most have given up and use Vauxhall Bridge. This is left mainly for shanks's mare. Can't make much for the share-holders.'

'I suppose not.'

Abbs looked down-river at the gulls shrieking about the masts of barques, the lighters chopping small waves, heading for the opposite wharves. He caught the distant shouts of labourers moving among stacks of timber, great coal-heaps, rows of reddish-brown stoneware. A river-police patrol, from Wapping, passed below them, the four officers rowing steadily. Everywhere was commerce and money. Spreading out and pulling back like the tide.

'You should've asked me, sir.' Grainer indicated the bedraggled children, digging among pools in the wet clay. 'Before you went inquiring about that mob. I'd have put you right. Their sort won't give you their spit for nothing. Hand something valuable over to the peelers? Do me a favour. You've a deal to learn about London ways, if you don't mind me saying.'

'Oh, do speak your mind, Sergeant, by all means,' said Abbs crisply. 'Perhaps now you're ready to share your thoughts on our case?'

'We got further on today.' Grainer scratched his weepers. 'If your theory's right, sir, we've three of them with good reason to see off Ellis. Frederick Buckley gets the rest of the business, that we knew. Now Ambrose is handed enough tin to keep himself for a year and take off to foreign parts, if he likes. Swollen-headed young milksop. You could see he thought himself above working for his living. Strikes me, his pa was livid enough to stick a knife in Rowland Ellis, if he'd been there.'

'I saw it differently. Buckley was angry at his son's lack of propriety. That, and having their differences aired before the rest of us. This might be the making of Ambrose.'

'Can't see it, myself. More like he'll spend a year playing the fool. Buckley can kiss farewell to handing his business on to his son.'

'It would seem so. What of your third suspect?'

'Miss Maitland, sir. She gets a home for life and takes the rest of the pot. Very fine for the lady. My brother-in-law wouldn't leave me a bent farthing, not that he has much. But she'll have to stay an old maid to keep hold of the house.'

'A harsh restriction, but hardly unusual. Gentlemen generally do want to control the use of their money after death.'

'She must be five and forty, if she's a day. Mark you, without the house, she'll still have enough to catch a suitor of sorts. D'you reckon she's someone in mind, sir? She did ask the lawyer what the terms were.'

'I had the impression she was just making a point. She felt humiliated, I suspect. As for motive, Miss Maitland was unsure of her standing in Ellis's will. She was worried about her future. Both the Ibbotsons tried to reassure her. Too risky to commit murder for possibly very little.'

'She could've known, sir.' Grainer's voice was heavy with scorn. 'Mr. Ellis might have told her what he'd done. Propertied men like to boast about their will. There's not a woman born can't lie with the face of an angel. Besides, he was changing his will. Maybe Ellis told her, he was cutting her out.'

'Penfold said Mr. Ellis wanted to discuss his will. He might only have wanted to amend a provision in some minor way. I agree with you, though. A man is murdered, shortly before seeing his lawyer about his will. I don't believe in such coincidence. Who might have known of Mr. Ellis's intention?'

'The lawyer knew, but he's a newcomer. Besides, they make their living by keeping tight-lipped. Mr. Ellis might have told any of them, Miss Maitland, both Buckleys, the Ibbotsons.'

'Indeed, and the servants might have overheard.' Abbs looked up at the stiff wire cables. 'We don't know what was written in his missing diary. Did Ellis have an appointment that night, unbeknown to the rest of the household?'

Grainer remained silent, his sceptical visage speaking for him. Abbs watched the river, the tang of salt-water filling his lungs. He'd asked if the name on the card meant anything to the others. Only Frederick Buckley frowned, thinking he might have seen the name, Silas Dove, somewhere recently. He'd no idea where, *The Times*, possibly. A Mr. Dove had definitely never been a client.

A coffee-stall was doing brisk trade near the north end of Lambeth Bridge. The bright, polished brass urns and their smouldering charcoal, together with the pungent aroma, held out a spurious warmth in the cool, late afternoon. Customers stood around, clutching their cups and chewing on door-steps of buttered bread.

Abbs saw Grainer look them over, watching a pair of ill-clad boys as they jostled one another, ever closer. At least, he had the instincts of a long-time policeman, keeping an eye out for mug-hunters and dips. Reluctant to move off, the sergeant's gaze returned to the coffee being poured. He took pity on him.

'Fog'll be in tonight.' Grainer nodded at the sky, as they stood sipping their hot drinks. 'Don't like the way those clouds have gathered. The sea-gulls are off, look. They know. You'll get a feel for it, sir, when you've lived a time in the smoke.'

'Will it be heavy, d'you think?'

A pea-souper would ruin his plan to return to Kennington that evening. On the other hand, thought Abbs, a certain amount of cover might aid his purpose.

NINETEEN

Abbs took a cab from the stand outside the Yard. Grainer's reading of the weather had proved accurate, though the fog was patchy, a greyish-white, shifting presence. Better than the sulphurous, yellowy murk that kept pace with you, enveloping everything. Fortunate too, that he'd managed to be second in to report to Townsend. Nothing had been said about the papers on his desk being disturbed. He would take it as a warning to be careful.

He'd asked to be set down on the main road, in order to approach his destination on foot. A lamp-lighter trudged past him, shouldering his ladder, his work done for the night hours. He wondered what Grainer was doing and if, in his evenings, he gave much thought to their work. Instinct had made him say nothing about the card he'd found, or his present purpose.

Crossing the end of a street, Abbs caught sight of the beat-constable, his bull's-eye lantern held aloft. He was glad to see the figure pacing away through the gloom. Once he was in place, any inquiry about his purpose there would draw attention to his presence.

This side of Kennington, situated before the shops and park, was respectably modest. The terraced houses of Gannon-street were, like countless others, put up by speculative builders in the last twenty years or so. The sort of households that kept a maid of all work. Every home had its portion of roof, divided by a line of fire-bricks. A meagre attic window poked from the slates below the chimneys.

No one was about now, saving a small dog trotting purposefully. Home, he hoped as the creature's ribs were well-covered. Abbs watched, heartened, as the dog turned in at an open gate, scratching at a door. It opened at once, a thin shaft of gas-light and a man's voice welcomed him in.

Unlikely, he knew, that dog-thieves would haunt these streets. For the most part, they sought their ransoms from snatching pedigree animals, by day, in the fashionable squares. But dogs were always wanted for ratting or skins. There was one, at least, safe this night.

The house which interested him was the second from the corner, a street-lamp stood nearby. Curtains were pulled across both lower windows. A pale radiance diffused from the dimpled, glass panels of the door and its glazed light above. Its neighbour on the end looked empty, a '*To Let*' sign above the low wall.

He settled himself at the opening of a narrow, enclosed passage, between the houses on the opposite side. From his stance half-way along the street, he had a reasonable view of number four, provided the fog didn't thicken. A clock sounded the quarter and Abbs blessed Townsend for not detaining him.

His superior felt they were on firm ground at last. The beneficiaries of the will had to be suspects. 'Make certain of their whereabouts on the night of the murder. Bear in mind, these are people of standing,' Townsend had warned. 'Have a care not to offend them.'

Keeping away from the grimy brickwork, Abbs considered what they knew. No one had seen Ellis alive after Miss Maitland and Maggie left. The other servants denied passing the study door again that evening. Shut in their own quarters, there was no reason to do so, unless Ellis rang, which everyone said rarely happened.

No one intent on confronting Ellis would try to enter the house too late at night. Even knowing his habits, they couldn't be sure he wouldn't retire early. Murdering him in his bed would be fraught with danger. Miss Maitland's room was close by. He was convinced Ellis's body already lay in the study, when the two women came home that evening.

Would Frederick and Ambrose Buckley know Miss Maitland went to the Institute on the first Monday of the month? Was the murder premeditated? The paper-knife was on the desk, ready to be snatched up in a furious quarrel.

He started as a large rat scuffled along the wall, his tail flicking from side to side along the beaten earth. Water dripped in the tunnel. Snatches of singing came from a front parlour.

Fog was drifting waist-high, in ragged weepers along the street. Here, a window vanished, there, the wooden posts of an open porch were blurred. Footsteps were approaching, the ferrule of a walking-stick striking the kerb like a vesta.

Abbs watched a man appear, his face dark, as he passed beneath the street-lamp. He knocked at number four and went in. No chance to see who answered the door.

The hollow clop of hooves signalled an arrival from the other direction. A closed carriage drew up, two older ladies descended, sombrely dressed. The coachman moved off. More visitors came in quick succession. A gentleman arrived in a hansom. As he rapped the door-knocker, Abbs glimpsed the banding round his tall hat. More ladies went in. Their coachman touched his hat with his whip and creaked into the mist.

Abbs lowered his muffler, feeling the damp air touch his face as he crossed the street. All was quiet again, the night air strong with soot and the fresh leavings of horses. His weariness vanished. He knew what Louisa Maitland had been burning on the morning after the murder.

TWENTY

The door was opened by a slight woman in her middle years, plainly attired in dark Brunswick green. She greeted him pleasantly, revealing herself, as she smiled, to be long in the gum.

'Step inside, sir. The fog's getting worse, I believe.'

Wiping his boots, Abbs found himself in a narrow hall, furnished only with a stand for walking-sticks and a console table. A murmur of voices came from the door on the right.

'I don't believe we've had the pleasure of seeing you at one of our gatherings, sir?'

'This is my first visit, ma'am. You were recommended to me by Mr. Rowland Ellis.'

Her expression remained unchanged. No tell-tale twitch of her limbs, but he thought there was some inner reaction. He could not be sure.

'I do not recall the gentleman. Not all our visitors care to give their name. That is perfectly acceptable in the circumstances. I am Mrs Dove. You are most welcome in our home, sir. May I take your things?'

'My thanks, ma'am.'

'If you will join our other guests, Mr. Dove will be with you shortly. It is necessary for him to spend a little time in solitary contemplation, before conducting a circle.' She lowered her voice. 'The spirits can be demanding. They are clamouring to come through and speak to their loved ones. It is altogether very fatiguing for the medium.' She glanced over her shoulder before speaking, as if ghosts, lurking in the passage, should not hear her.

'I don't doubt it, Mrs Dove,' said Abbs. 'To convey messages from the dead is a truly remarkable achievement.'

'It is, sir, and please be assured, we are a good Christian household. We always begin with a prayer. Have you attended a demonstration previously?'

'None, ma'am. I confess to having been sceptical until recently but...' Abbs tailed off, biting his lip.

'Say no more, sir, I quite understand. Your candour does you credit. We have many visitors who come to us that way at first. Their doubts transformed, their burdens lifted, they return again and again.'

He was seized with an insane desire to laugh, stifling it desperately. 'I look forward immensely to receiving proof of existence beyond the grave.'

'You shall be rewarded, sir. But a word of caution, it may be that the spirits do not favour you tonight. Patience is needed, particularly for a first communication.'

He composed his expression to seem suitably crest-fallen. 'I accept that, Mrs Dove, if I must, though hope led me here.'

'Forgive me, sir, there is a weight of sadness lying heavy about you. Are you hoping to make contact with one person above all others?'

'Alas, ma'am, I have lost one who is dear to me still.'

'Then seek no further. In time, I am confident Mr. Dove will be able to bring you comfort.'

'And yourself, ma'am, may I inquire if the spirits speak through you?'

'I have some ability, sir. I am able, when in a state of trance, to produce spirit-writing between two slates secured together. The spirits tell us some people have a rapport with the other worlds. A kind of natural sympathy. Our friends are able to draw on my energy, in order to direct the planchette-board. Some, who seek guidance, are chary of attending a circle, finding these methods less fearful. Table-rapping is only one means the spirits may use to communicate in the dark. Their powers can be disturbing for the faint-hearted.'

'Is what you do not very alarming, ma'am?'

Mrs Dove's eyes closed for a second. 'I am accustomed to it, you see. I remember nothing afterwards. I am told it is akin to being a lightning-rod. But I am not a medium like my husband. Mr. Dove has a gift rare even among his peers. You know the majority of mediums are female?'

'So I've read. Mr. Rowland Ellis informed me that Mr. Dove is uncommonly accurate.'

'Indeed, everyone says so. When a gentleman is given the gift, his manifestations are far stronger. You'll have read of the remarkable powers of Mr. Dunglas Home, I don't doubt?'

'Certainly I have, ma'am. Some say his levitation has been seen by impeccable witnesses, including Mr. Trollope, the novelist. But was not Mr. Home discredited a few years since?'

'No, indeed, sir. He was wrongfully accused by a jealous old woman, who sought to recover gifts she freely made. And ungodly scientists mock and decry what they cannot understand. The spirits will never be proved false, for they do not lie. In there, sir. You'll find our guests all share a common sorrow.'

His ulster folded over her arms, Mrs Dove disappeared silently through a door along the passage. True, there was insufficient room for a hall-stand, but he did wonder.

A wisp of fog had followed him in, rising up the steep stairs. No sound from the bedrooms. An engraving, hung above the table, depicted the famous pavilion at Brighton. Reportedly disliked by the Queen for its exotic extravagance and old reputation.

The table held only a painted tray, a spray of pale wax flowers and some hand-bills advertising *An Evening of Rare Spirit Phenomena.* He pocketed one. No need to wonder the purpose of the prominent empty tray.

Abbs swiftly reckoned seven occupants of the room Mrs Dove indicated. In the way of any wintry gathering, most were grouped by the fire, which had been allowed to die down. The older ladies greeted him cordially, the younger pair, in the corner, looked nervy.

The old gentleman, in mourning, bowed. 'You are not a regular attender, sir?'

The leader of the two matrons flourished her lorgnette to inspect him. He wondered how she'd manage with her hands held. Returning the greeting, he admitted to being at a new experience. The third lady, in the background, was her paid companion, he guessed.

'You are in for a rare treat, sir,' said the matron. 'Prepare to see marvels. We were just discussing the spirit hand which appeared last week. We all saw it, glowing silvery. Mr. Dove explained afterwards, it was constructed of ether. And I actually felt it, the most gentle of touches on my shoulder. I shall never forget it.'

Recalling that he couldn't very well question her like a detective, Abbs murmured something polite, stepping back from the group by the hearth.

The other man was the one he'd seen arrive on foot. An elegant Indian, not much above thirty, he inclined his head. Abbs was about to join him by the sideboard when the door opened. As all talk ceased, Mr. Dove and his wife were among them.

At first glance, the medium looked ordinary enough, dark-haired, with a prominent widow's peak and close-barbered whiskers. He might have been a City merchant or his clerk. But when he moved and smiled among them, he had a certain presence. The trick of turning all his attention on one person, with the intensity of a lantern.

'Good evening to you all. An inclement night to be out, but happily, the fog has not deterred you from our purpose. Welcome, dear lady.' He clasped the hand of the matron, who greeted him with all the fluttering of a debutante behind her fan.

Swiftly passing a word to them all, he swung back to Abbs. 'Silas Dove, sir. You are most welcome in our home.'

Abbs took the proferred hand. The medium combined a firm, manly grip with a sincere gaze, before moving on to greet the remaining guest. The Indian's hard-edged vowels proclaimed him a native of London.

'If you would all like to take a seat, ladies and gentlemen. We shall begin shortly.' Mr. Dove gestured to the large, round table in the middle of the room. The men waited until the ladies were seated. 'Jessie, my dear, if you would prepare us.'

Lighting a candle, his wife carried it over to the sideboard. She then placed a fire-screen in front of the coals and extinguished the gas. Finally, she slipped on to a chair, without so much as a rustle.

Abbs sat facing the sideboard, the window on his right. The heavy curtains were firmly drawn. Besides the candle flame, the only light glowed round the edges of the fire-screen.

Mr. Dove began to speak. 'If you will each take the hand of your neighbour on either side. I must remind you of the importance of keeping the circle unbroken, whatever may befall. This is for your own protection and to help our friends, in spirit, draw upon the energy they need to make contact with us.' He waited while the sitters felt for their neighbours' clasp.

'We are gathered here, this night, in the name of our Lord God Almighty...' Mr. Dove uttered a short prayer, as a gentleman might say grace before dinner. 'We acknowledge that for we who dwell among this vale of tears, the parting of death is but an illusion. In the light of His infinite mercy, the shades of the departed draw near to us. For ...'

A loud rap on wood broke through the dark. Sudden as gun-shot.

Abbs felt the lady-companion's hand flinch. Breathing quickened round the table.

'Someone is approaching us. Welcome, friend.'

Silence.

The medium's voice, while not loud, was as clear as a wind instrument. Abbs had the curious sensation that the voice did not come from his left, where, he knew perfectly well, Dove was sitting.

'Be not afeared. Draw nearer. You are welcome among our circle. We are seekers after divine truth...'

Another rap on the word truth.

Someone swallowed.

'Do you wish to communicate with someone present?'

The table jolted under their arms. Someone groaned. One of the young women, thought Abbs.

Dove's breath was rasping... deep... and... slow.

After a long moment, he raised his head. *'Deception and falsehood. There is one among you who is not what they seem.'*

The voice was high, reedy. Utterly unlike Silas Dove's earlier speech.

The others were galvanised.

Abbs's heart thudded.

'Someone about this table does not seek to lift the veil between the living and departed. They have a secret purpose.'

His chest felt confined by an iron band. Cursing himself for a fool, Abbs wished he'd never ventured in this house.

'The dead draw near, yet... they... shall... not... speak.'

Someone shifted on their chair, skirts rustled.

'Beware... insincerity. False deceiver...'

A woman screamed.

The candle guttered and went out.

TWENTY-ONE

Grainer had been busy about other cases for much of the day. He'd put off telling him about the visit to Gannon-street, but it had to be faced, thought Abbs. As it turned out, if his sergeant wondered why he hadn't set a constable to watch the house, he'd kept his own counsel.

Pausing, Abbs stifled a yawn as he stood at the window. The quadrangle below had been as busy as a market-place all afternoon, the crossings of men and visitors scattering the pigeons. Trails of mist had lingered most of the day. Outdoors, everything was damp to the touch and the streets had a musty air.

Grainer recovered from his wheezy chuckle, resuming his habitual expression. 'What happened then, sir?'

'We were politely bundled out. Dove came to his senses and said it was impossible to continue with the séance that evening. The energy was unpropitious, whatever that means. Someone present was unsympathetic and the spirits wouldn't oblige. Fulsome apologies but there was nothing he could do.'

'What did the rest of 'em make of that, might I ask?'

'Disappointed, but no one seemed surprised. They assured the Doves they understood. The older ladies fussed about fetching their coachman from down the street. The Indian offered to tell him. The old gentleman feared he wouldn't find a cab in the fog. I know I couldn't.'

It had been a long, wearisome trudge back to Westminster. His spine ached with tension and standing about, the weight of his hidden life-preserver a comfort as he neared the crossing. A wise man kept his wits alert at night, particularly somewhere he was vulnerable, such as the steps up to a bridge. Finally, he'd found a cab in Parliament-street to take him to his lodgings.

'Sounds to me like they rumbled you, sir.'

'At first, I certainly thought so. I was waiting to be denounced. But nothing was said and when Mrs Dove brought my coat, she begged me not to be put off. Suggested I might like to attend the public demonstration her husband is giving. Of course, that may have been for appearance' sake.'

'You didn't get to see any parlour tricks, then? No naked female draped in a bit of gauze?'

'Not that I noticed.'

'At least, you didn't have to pay on the way in.'

'I'd like to know what made them abandon proceedings. As you point out, they lost their night's takings.'

'Can't have liked the look of you, sir. Their kind can smell a rozzer. They must live in dread of being taken up for fraud. I've read how they contrived the knocking, you know.' Grainer nodded sagely. 'With their joints. Like that, was it?'

Abbs winced as the sergeant tugged the fingers of his left hand, cracking each knuckle in turn.

'Nothing like. Besides, everyone was clasping hands.'

'My knees crack something terrible when I get up. I dare say I could do it at will, if I tried.'

'No need to demonstrate, Grainer.'

He'd given it much thought on his way back. Entertainments with illusions were wildly popular, the more incredible, the better. People liked a mystery. Some of the ladies treated spiritualism like watching a stage magician, he didn't doubt. No harm in paying to see a conjuror. Everyone understood the bargain. But he'd seen longing on some of the faces last night. Duping the grieving was a cruel trade.

'I don't care how they contrive their effects. My only interest in these charlatans is their connection to Rowland Ellis.'

'But they didn't admit to knowing him.'

'Even so, Dove's card was in his desk.'

'Seems to me, sir, there's no mystery. We know Mr. Ellis took losing his wife hard. There's no shortage of fools trying to contact their dead.'

'He stopped going to church,' said Abbs thoughtfully. 'Asked young Bertha if she believed in ghosts.'

'Do we question Miss Maitland again, sir?'

'I think we must. She claimed the card meant nothing to her, but she was burning pamphlets of some sort. I'm convinced they were on spiritualism. What else could they be? I shall see her while you're checking on the Buckleys. You're very likely right, that Mr. Ellis simply consulted them in his grief, but we can't afford to ignore any loose end.'

Grainer tapped his teeth with his pencil. 'You'd think an architect would be a rational sort of gent.'

'I share your feeling. Perhaps he was a rationalist and his interest lay in a scientific curiosity. Don't we all, at times, wonder about life's greatest mystery? A number of eminent men seek to investigate the truth. Mr. Dickens was among them, if you recall. He made no secret of his interest in all sorts of strange theories, mesmerism, for one. I recall reading about them in his own periodicals.'

'Truth be told, I never thought over-much of his ghost tales. Or his serials, come to that.'

Abbs smiled to himself. 'My picture of London came from them. Long ere I visited, I felt I knew Clerkenwell and Snow Hill, through his eyes. I wouldn't part with my volumes.'

'More money than sense, if you ask me.'

Abbs raised his eyebrows. 'Did I hear you aright, Sergeant?'

'Mr. Dickens, I mean, sir,' said Grainer hastily. 'He has his answers now. I know what I think. It's a bleedin' hard life and there's no reward in heaven. Nor hell, for the ones we swing. You just go out. Snuffed like a candle.'

TWENTY-TWO

'Policeman's back again, ma'am,' said Mrs Wilmot.

'Very well, Cook.'

Louisa Maitland was standing in what was now her drawing-room, an apron tied over her mourning-dress. The sofas were pushed back, Maggie had a feather duster in her hand. The painting over the fireplace had been taken down and propped against a stool.

'Begging your pardon, ma'am, only the boy's been, if you'd like to inspect the chops for tonight.'

Miss Maitland smiled privately. 'If you're satisfied, there's no need. Do sit down, Inspector. Would you care for a cup of tea?'

Abbs declined politely as she removed her apron and the others departed.

'It was no trouble, I assure you. Mrs Wilmot can't do enough to be obliging. You look surprised. I'm making changes to the rooms, but not the servants.'

He thought of Bertha's anxious face. 'They'll be relieved, I don't doubt.'

'I hope so. Mrs Wilmot and I have come to an understanding. She saw me as an interloper. But I can't blame her for being loyal to my sister's memory. She hasn't had an easy life.'

'In what regard, ma'am?'

'She was widowed, so had to return to being in service. It's hard for a woman to live in someone else's home, when she had her own hearth.'

'It's good of you to think of that.'

'There is always someone less fortunate than oneself, as Mr. Ibbotson preached in his sermon. Mrs Wilmot's husband was crippled from a fall. I believe his death was hastened by his injuries. Their only child was taken from them, a young lad. She sent him on an errand and he stumbled beneath a wagon.'

'How tragic.' He could almost picture it. A small boy dashing across a crowded thoroughfare. A dray-man cursing, horses rearing, iron hooves. He'd dismissed her as a foolish woman. Too easy to forget how everyone suffered, all the same.

'At least Mrs Wilmot has a home here.'

She shrugged off his remark. 'She's a very good cook. They're difficult to come by. You have more questions for me, Inspector?'

'I have, Miss Maitland. How many people would know you attend the lecture at the Institute, each month?'

She looked pensive. 'I imagine it would be widely known in Kennington. I'm a member of Mrs Ibbotson's charity-committee. We seek donations wherever we may. In theory, local shop-keepers, tradesmen, servants would all know I'd be present.'

'What about neighbours, families such as the Buckleys, would they be aware you always left the house on that evening?'

'Mrs Ibbotson has made certain our neighbours know of her charity-work. I have heard her speak of the lectures to Mr. Frederick Buckley. Unfortunately, the subjects do not engage his interest. He would know I always attend them. I take it, that is what you came to find out, Inspector?'

'Not entirely, ma'am.' He took the card from his pocket-book, holding it that she might see. 'You'll recall, I think, my asking if you knew of a Mr. Silas Dove? I mentioned the name to your guests, after the reading of the will.'

Her face hardened. 'The name means nothing to me. I told you.'

'We follow up anything that might help us. I visited this house.' Abbs let the silence linger.

She sighed. 'I see it is no use. Very well. I did not lie to you, Inspector. I hadn't seen the card before, or heard the name. When you showed me the inscription, I guessed what this man would be. Presumably, you now know.'

'That Mr. Dove claims to be a spirit-medium? Yes.'

'These persons are the worst kind of criminals, are they not?'

'That depends on their actions, Miss Maitland. If they are fraudulent, certainly. Quite a few end up exposed and fined. Persistent offenders are gaoled.'

She stared at him, her colour heightened. 'How can you possibly say *if*, Inspector? I believe them to be wicked without exception.'

'It seems to me there are two kinds. I suppose some might be sincere in their beliefs and misguided.' Abbs picked his words. 'People delude themselves. Not always for base motives.'

'You are too generous, Inspector. These so-called spiritualists deceive vulnerable people for gain. A thief is honest by comparison. The Bible tells us what happens when we die. That should be sufficient for all of us. It is not for the living to know more.'

'How often did Mr. Ellis visit Mr. Dove and his wife?'

'I don't know how far matters had gone. Back in February, he went out in the evening several times, which was unusual. He was evasive about where he went. For all I know, he also saw them by day. Did they admit to taking money from him by deception?'

'Mrs Dove denied knowing his name.'

'She must be lying.'

'It's possible Mr. Ellis didn't give his name, or used a pseudonym. I'm told that's often done.'

'Do you think this man had something to do with Rowland's death?'

'Thus far, there's no evidence to suggest that.'

'I cannot believe anyone I know is a murderer.'

'Was it spiritualist publications you destroyed before the police arrived?' said Abbs gently.

Miss Maitland bit her lip. 'How could you know?' Understanding crossed her face. 'Bertha. Of course, she saw and you questioned her.'

'Bertha is not to blame. When we spoke to you in the morning-room, I noticed a torn strip on the hearth. It was from a periodical of some sort. I asked Bertha and she merely confirmed you'd been burning some papers in a hurry. She didn't know what they were.'

'You're very observant, Inspector.'

'It's my job, Miss Maitland. Did it matter so much that we didn't see them?'

'It did to me. I hardly knew what I was doing. I suppose I panicked. Like someone hiding the washing, with unexpected callers at the door. I wanted to save my brother-in-law's reputation. I didn't want the local policemen to scoff and think him a fool. People gossip so.'

'How did you first learn of Mr. Ellis's involvement?'

'Some weeks ago, I found a pamphlet when I was straightening his room. Maggie was with me but I managed to conceal it from her. Then he came home with a periodical, taking care I didn't see the title. I began to watch. He bought more, always concealing them. He'd already stopped accompanying me to church. It seemed to me, Rowland was changing.'

'In what way, ma'am?'

'I cannot define it. He began to have sudden whims. He spoke of

113

making changes in the house. He had one or two pieces of furniture sent to auction.' Her voice was reluctant. 'He seemed more animated.'

Abbs thought of Mrs Wilmot, saying Ellis's appetite had lately improved. He was about to speak when Miss Maitland rushed on.

'I dreaded that Rowland was in the clutches of rogues. You hear of fools being bled white by these dreadful people. Making over money, even changing their wills under their influence. There was no one I could confide in. Mrs Ibbotson is my closest friend but the circumstances made it impossible. She and the vicar would have been horrified at the very mention of spiritualists. I've heard Mr. Ibbotson denounce them often enough.'

'I see your difficulty. You didn't feel you could consult Mr. Buckley?'

'No, indeed. He is not a religious man, sadly, but I knew he would have scoffed at Rowland. That would have been almost as bad. Besides, I dared not cause trouble. Even now, I hate to think of Rowland being so gullible. The thought of someone pretending to hear messages, from my dead sister, disgusts me. I loved her too, but he never thought of me.'

'Might Mr. Ellis have had a scientific interest in the possibility of existence after death? It's a topic much discussed these days. I saw he had some works on science in his study.'

'Of course, I'm aware of its popularity among sensation-seekers, Inspector. Rowland made no objection to my reading his newspaper when he'd finished with it. I cannot believe he'd visit such people in the name of scientific progress. It's obvious his grief destroyed his judgment.'

'What were the periodicals?' He couldn't help but be curious.

'I only saw the uppermost ones. A pamphlet entitled *Slate Writing - An Explanation*, another on table-rapping. A journal with some ridiculous name, *Medium And Daybreak* or something like. Does it matter? They were fit only for the fire.'

'I understand you wished to protect your brother-in-law's reputation, Miss Maitland. You'd just had a terrible shock. Nevertheless, you should have told me.'

'I see that now, Inspector.' She smiled faintly at him. 'For a policeman, you're surprisingly easy to talk to. It's been a relief to tell someone.'

'Did you go in the study that morning?'

She nodded. 'I had no choice but to steel myself. That's where he kept them. After I'd burnt them, I hurried upstairs, to be sure there were no more in his room. Bertha and Maggie had gone by then. Mrs Wilmot was in the servants' quarters.'

'I must ask you, Miss Maitland, is there anything else you've kept back?'

'Nothing, Inspector Abbs. I want Rowland's killer found as much as you.'

'Did you remove Mr. Ellis's diary?'

She shook her head. 'I give you my word, I did not. Rowland was methodical. He would always make a note of his appointments and other memoranda. If he went to these people, it would be written there. You would have found out, despite my efforts. But I was in such a taking, I forgot about his diary.'

Sergeant Grainer cursed Inspector Abbs, the long winter and his throbbing chilblains, as he trudged between the passers-by on Kennington's high street. His feet, when he'd dried them the night before, looked fit for the cat's meat-man. His toes felt like hot coals, purple as a toper's nose, they were. Mind, they were always bulbous and his soles like cracked leather. Mark of his job, bad feet.

To top it all, he'd to find time to call at the cobblers for his slightly better boots. He'd caught the inspector eyeing his shabby pair, as they sat on the 'bus. Would they drop in on Sergeant Hollins when they were done? Chance of a sit-down and a warm. Most likely not. Never mind that a body thinks better on a full belly.

He met the eyes of a young flower-seller on the corner. She gave him a smile, sweet as her cry. *Fresh up from the West country...* Her best daffs were tightly furled. The ones in the pail were already too blown, couldn't ask much for 'em. She pulled her shawl closer in the breeze. He looked at her cheap pin.

Were it the end of the day, he might've brought a bunch home for the parlour. He imagined the surprise on his sister's face. The girl would droop soon enough, like her bedraggled wares. He wondered what she did in winter, grimaced and shook her from his mind.

As he went to enter Ellis and Buckley's establishment, a surly-looking cove came out in a hurry, shouldering him aside. He cursed as a dirty great boot smote his toes. He yelled after him, shaking his fist. His assailant, clad in worn fustian, glowered over his shoulder and was off down the street.

The clerk, Searle, was at his post again, looking flustered. 'Dear me, Sergeant, are you quite all right? Is Inspector Abbs not with you today?'

'Does it look like it?' He leant against the counter, flexing his toes. 'Ignorant oaf. D'you see what he did?'

'I trust you are not hurt. Shall I get you a stool?'

'No time. Some of us have work to do. Police business won't wait, you know.'

'No, indeed, Sergeant. Then...'

He interrupted the old ditherer. 'Who was that?'

'Oh, ah, he's a builder. I'm afraid he's rather a coarse fellow and he's not in the best of tempers.'

'What's to do with him?' Not that he cared, but it gave him a minute to catch his breath.

'He wanted to see Mr. Buckley. As do you, I'm sure, Sergeant, but I fear you've had a wasted journey. I don't expect him back before late afternoon.'

'Makes no odds to me. It's his servants I'm after. How many does he keep?'

'A married couple, the Feltons live in and there's a char-woman besides. But Felton is away driving Mr. Buckley.'

'His missus'll do. What about the young Buckley, is he about?'

'You mean Mr. Ambrose Buckley?' Searle shuffled some dockets, planting them on a spike. 'Dear me, there's a sorry tale. He's gone.'

He wiped his moustache with his knuckles. Sometimes, it was like hooking a winkle out of its shell. 'Gone where? Seeing a customer?'

'No, Sergeant. Gone, as in left the business entirely. Mr. Ambrose intimated as much at the will-reading, if you recollect, but I don't think Mr. Buckley, senior, expected it to be so sudden. Packed his boxes and left a forwarding address, so Mrs Felton says.'

Remembering, he grinned. 'Fallen out with his pa, has he?'

'Oh, I don't say that, Sergeant. You mustn't mistake me.' Searle continued his straightening, all thumbs. 'Mr. Ambrose has been speaking of taking rooms with a friend for some time. Mr. Ellis's goodness to him has brought things on, that's all.'

A bell struck the quarter outside. He was to meet the inspector by the park gates.

'What sort of friend might that be?'

'A fellow artist, I believe.'

'This Mrs Felton likely to be in?'

'I saw her return a few minutes since.'

'I'll see what she has to say for herself.'

About to climb the steps to Buckeridge's front door, he glanced down the area and saw a movement. A woman was looking up at him from the barred window. Opening the gate in the railings, he went down the steps.

The door opened, revealing a stout woman, still wearing her mantle. Dressed in grey, her bosom rounded as a bolster, she put him in mind of a pigeon. He told her his business, in a no-nonsense fashion.

'You'd better come in.'

Her hat was on the kitchen table, along with a full basket. The waft of a warm loaf made his belly gripe.

'The master's not here.'

'It's you I want, missus. Some questions about the night his business-partner was murdered.' Pulling out a chair, he sat down unasked, pointing her to sit opposite.

'Does Mr. Buckley know about this? Only he won't stand for me gossiping about him.'

'He's already been questioned.' He fixed her with a stern look, as he felt for his pencil. 'Never mind your master. Your duty's to answer my questions and tell the truth.'

She drew herself up, prim and round-shouldered. 'I'm not in the habit of telling untruths. Is this going to take long?'

'Not if you speak up. Now, the Monday before last, you recall the night, I'm sure. Mr. Frederick Buckley says he was home all evening.'

'If that's what he told you, he was. Don't you take the word of a gentleman?'

The kitchen was well-equipped, with a modern range along the wall behind her. No expense spared by the look of it. Buckley was only trade, when you came down to it. He might be educated, spoke well and lived like a gentleman but he still worked for his bread. The doors of the old gentry would be firmly closed to him. Besides, a toff could lie with the best of 'em.

'In my job, we don't take anyone's word on trust. Everything has to be checked. Did he and his son eat supper together?'

Mrs Felton screwed up her face in thought. 'I'm thinking back, whether Mr. Ambrose was in. Yes, he was, so the two gentlemen dined together.'

'What time did they finish?'

'You can't expect me to recall that. They might sit over a port or brandy and soda. Mr. Buckley likes his smoke after dinner. Other times, Mr. Ambrose will go straight upstairs.'

'What for?'

'Mr. Ambrose has his own suite of rooms on the third floor.'

'Does he now? I hear he's moved out.'

She nodded reluctantly. 'Gone to Chelsea. Mr. Buckley said to keep his rooms as they are, for now.'

118

At this rate, he'd run out of time. 'After you'd cleared away, when did you see them again?'

The house-keeper folded her hands. A worn wedding-band didn't look as though it'd slip past her knuckle. 'I'm trying to make sure of the right evening. At the time, I'd no reason to take notice, more than any other.'

He tapped his pencil on his notebook. 'Think back. I haven't got all day.'

'That was the night they had best sirloin and the master only took a small helping. The next morn, I was looking at the joint, deciding what to do with the all the left-overs, when there was a great banging on the door. It was the skivvy from Mr. Ellis's house. That was how we heard he'd been murdered. I couldn't credit it. Mr. Buckley came down to learn what all the noise was about. He sent me to get Felton to bring the carriage round.'

He sighed. 'Never mind the next day. When did you see the Buckleys after dinner?'

'After I'd cleared the table, I went straight back to the dining-room and asked Mr. Buckley if he required anything else. Mr. Ambrose had already left the room.'

'Time?'

'Must have been about five-and-twenty-past eight, or a little before.'

'Did either of them ring later?'

'No. Mr. Buckley is always considerate. He's a good employer. I make sure I leave everything he might require and after I've finished in here, I'm away by half-past nine. Unless he's having people to dinner, when I stay on and Mrs. Adams helps me. She's the daily woman.'

He scratched his whiskers, confused. 'Away where?'

The house-keeper started to unpack her basket. 'We're not in the house. Felton and I live over the stable.'

A butcher's boy, in blue smock and apron, came out of the Ibbotsons' gate, his tray of clammy packages supported on his shoulder.

The vicarage was a large, modern house, built in the sham medieval style, adjacent to the old church. Now lost among suburban streets, the ancient tower had probably overlooked green meadows at the turn of the century. A welcome sign of civilisation, thought Abbs, to travellers braving the highwaymen and footpads of Kennington Common.

The bell jangled within, as he waited in the steeply-roofed porch. The studded, oak door was opened by a dark-eyed parlour-maid. On hearing his business, her superior expression vanished.

'They'll do.' She watched, hands on hips, as he wiped his boots. 'We get all sorts bringing their mud through here, wanting the vicar or the mistress.'

'Would you be Edith, by any chance?'

'That's what they call me.'

'I'd like a word with you, after I've seen your mistress.'

'Would you now? Wait there. She's busy giving Cook what for.' Edith swayed across the tiles, leaving him amused in the gloomy hall.

A tall, Oriental urn held a jumble of sticks beside the inner door. A brass-rimmed elephant's foot receptacle did likewise for umbrellas. Three hard chairs were placed against the wall, the air was cough-thick with recent polish.

Mrs Ibbotson appeared directly, showing him in a cheerless room by the front door. It was, he guessed, furnished to receive the callers Edith mentioned. The fire was unlit and his chair's horse-hair stuffing had long since settled into ridges and knobs. Doubtless, it would discourage visitors from remaining too long.

'The vicar has someone with him, Inspector, but he should be free shortly.'

'Thank you, ma'am. I won't detain Mr. Ibbotson for long. Meanwhile, perhaps I might speak to you and also your parlour-maid?'

'Edith? How can she assist your investigation?'

'She may have seen someone, from your carriage, on the night Mr. Ellis was killed.'

'I looked out when we stopped. The fog was gathering but there was sufficient light, from the street-lamps, to see. I saw no one. I'm not a fool, Inspector. It's a poor business when servants are questioned to vouch for their betters. But ...' She held up a hand to forestall his speaking. 'I accept the necessity. You have your duty.'

'We do, ma'am. These questions are simply a matter of routine, but they must be gone through.'

She nodded graciously. 'Then please continue.'

'If you would take me through the course of the evening?'

'Very well. We dined early. The Reverend Jeremiah Clark and his wife were our guests. My husband escorted them to the Institute in our carriage. They left before seven, so Mr. Clark could see where he was to speak. Tandy drove back to collect me.'

'Forgive me, did Mr. Clark and his wife know Mr. Ellis?'

She shook her head. 'They know no one in Kennington but ourselves. They're newly returned from Africa. Mr. Clark is holding a series of lectures, both to inform the public and to raise funds for further missionary work. They won't be returning. Mrs Clark has been quite worn down by the hot climate. She's cousin to the Dean of Bath and Wells, so I trust you won't find it necessary to question them.'

Abbs smiled inwardly. 'I believe you took Edith and called for Miss Maitland and her maid?'

'That is correct. Our lecture programme is educational. I see no reason why servants shouldn't learn of a wider world. It does them good to improve their minds. And to aid those less fortunate than themselves.'

'Were you together all evening?'

'Of course, though we were occupied at various tasks. After Mr. Clark's address, tea and buns were served. Those who'd come solely to hear him departed. Quite a few stayed on to help. Mostly ladies, but several gentlemen make themselves useful, fetching and carrying. The vicar escorted the Clarks home in our carriage. I spent the remainder of the evening conversing and supervising our endeavours.'

'Did you see much of the others?'

She frowned. 'Edith was gossiping, I had to find her some work. Miss Maitland and Maggie were helping to sort through clothes and blankets.'

'To give out to the needy? A kindly scheme.'

'We have use of a hall in North Lambeth, where they're distributed. We also make up parcels suitable to be sent overseas to Africa. Missionaries distribute them to the natives. You might mention to your fellow officers that donations are always wanted. I can let you have a list of their needs. In addition, we provide the deserving poor with a nourishing, hot supper, twice weekly.'

'It all sounds most benevolent, ma'am.' Privately, Abbs wondered how the poor might prove themselves worthy of eating, rather than going hungry.

Mrs Ibbotson inclined her head. 'The vicar preaches practical Christianity. I had to speak to some of my committee-ladies about the ordering. The comestibles take a great deal of managing, I assure you.'

Her manner conveyed it was meat and drink to someone of her capability. Abbs wondered if the recipients had to sing hymns for their supper.

She looked up as footsteps sounded, followed by Edith's murmur and the closing of the front door. 'There goes the parish clerk. I'll take you to my husband if you're ready.'

Pausing in the hall, she moved a collecting-tin to the front of the table, giving a meaningful rattle on the way. As she did so, a door opened and the vicar looked out.

'Inspector Abbs, good day to you. You should have told me the police were in the house, my dear. Have you been here long?'

'A few minutes only.'

'My apologies for keeping you. Had I known, my business could have waited.'

'No matter, sir. I needed to speak to Mrs Ibbotson.'

'Come in.' His wife led the way across the hall.

The vicar gestured at his fireplace. 'Do warm yourself, Inspector. I find this cold spell bracing, but I'm told, it's still unseasonably raw out.'

Thanking him, Abbs held his hands to the grate, where a good blaze warmed the room.

They were in a working study. A Bible lay open on a plain lectern. He wondered if the vicar practised his oratory there. Collected sermons, and other theology on the shelves, looked worn with handling. Crossed oars were mounted on the chimney-breast. A dishevelled newspaper was spread over the window-seat, with a pair of Indian clubs nearby.

'I perceive you weighing me, sir, from my surroundings.' Ibbotson's voice was good-humoured. 'Second nature to a detective, no doubt?' He picked up the middle frame from a row of photographs on the mantel-shelf. 'My sons. Tom, Edmund and Tertius.'

'And our daughter Violet,' said his wife, indicating a studio-portrait of a young couple, stiffly posed.

'Lately married and off our hands.'

Mrs Ibbotson fingered her jet beads, her face shadowed. 'Her husband is a stock-broker in the City.'

She misses her daughter, thought Abbs, or she's concerned for her happiness.

'The elder two follow in my footsteps,' continued Ibbotson. 'Tom, here, is a curate, already doing splendid work among the poor of Bristol. Edmund is studying at Chichester. You may have heard of Bishop Otter Clerical College, one of our oldest seats of learning. Young Tertius is away at school. I hope he might shortly follow the family calling.'

'Do you need me further, Inspector?' said Mrs Ibbotson.

'Not at present, thank you, ma'am.'

'My husband will ring for Edith when you're ready.'

Abbs thanked her, thinking he had no intention of questioning the girl in front of the vicar.

Ibbotson waved him to a seat before the desk, as the door closed. He moved a red-bound ledger to one side. 'You find me planning the future, Inspector. I'm considering how best to improve St Edward's, with Ellis's legacy. Have you seen our church?'

'Only from the outside, sir. A venerable old building. Is it in poor repair?'

'Thankfully, no longer. It was sadly dilapidated but I've made some improvements over the years. The lead is now sound, but the interior requires further restoration. I had the gallery taken down and a fine organ installed, some old glass removed. Better to let in a clear light, illuminating the word of God. Shadowy corners, like incense, have no place in churches for our modern age.'

'Did Mr. Ellis oversee the alterations?'

Ibbotson's face tightened. 'He was asked but he declined the commission. I admit to being surprised, knowing how he admired St Edward's. He suggested we needed the services of a church architect. I deemed it unnecessary. The cost would have been considerable and the work could be done by any competent builder. Now, thanks to his generosity, we shall have a tiled floor in the nave and be able to replace the worn pews.'

'Perhaps Mr. Buckley would advise you now?' said Abbs. He'd noticed a slight antipathy between the two men.

Ibbotson smiled thinly. 'I doubt he'd consider the Almighty a sufficiently grand client. Mr. Buckley does not attend any church. But I digress, what may I do for you, Inspector?'

'I've one or two questions about the night of the murder, sir. I understand you escorted Mr. Clark and his wife home. Can you recall what time you returned here?'

'Let me see,' he leant back, a thumb pressed to his beard. 'We left the Institute around a quarter before nine. Mrs Clark was fatigued, they didn't linger over refreshments. Tandy was waiting outside. We must have been back here a little before nine.'

'Whereabouts do the Clarks live?'

'Oh, their home is in Somerset. They're staying with relatives in Marylebone. I intended accompanying them to their door, but Mr. Clark kindly said there was no point in my journeying needlessly. Tandy brought me home on the way. I was glad of a little time to myself. Charitable work is best left to the ladies. They have an eye for detail, while we men oversee the whole battlefield, do we not?'

'Mr. Ibbotson, you must have given the murder some thought.'

'A great deal, Inspector. Who, among Ellis's friends, has not?'

'Might I ask your views about who might have killed him?'

Ibbotson fiddled with a stick of sealing-wax. 'I like to think of myself as a shrewd judge of character. A common failing among men. Nothing, whatsoever, suggests to me that anyone of my acquaintance could take that dread course. I wish I could assist you. For what it's worth, two thoughts occur to me.'

As he hesitated, Abbs encouraged him. 'Do go on, sir.'

'First, I don't believe a woman would kill in such a violent way. Secondly, since becoming a widower, Ellis neglected his business. Long before that, his invalid wife claimed the greater part of his attention. Make of that what you will, Inspector. I'll go no further.'

Abbs got to his feet. 'In that case, Mr. Ibbotson, I think we're finished.'

'You wish to question Edith, I believe.' He went to the bell-pull, by the fireplace. 'Shall the police be at the funeral, Inspector Abbs?'

'Sergeant Hollins will attend, sir. Prior duties prevent my being present.'

Mrs Jakes passed Abbs a tea-cup filled with a mahogany brew. Thanking the cook, he accepted a thin wedge of cake, moist with plump fruit.

'We are honoured,' said Edith, taking a generous bite of hers.

'Don't speak with your mouth full,' said the cook wearily. 'And no call to be pert, Edith. Anyone would think you never saw cake.'

'I see it all right, when I hand round upstairs. Don't often get to taste none though. Not with the mistress counting slices.'

'Take no notice, Inspector, she will exaggerate. He hasn't come here to listen to you carrying on.'

'That's where you're wrong, Cook. He's here to pick up any dirt he can.' Leaning over, she tried to see his notebook. 'If you're taking down my name, it's Rosina Whittle. Mind you put that, not Edith. That's what the mistress said I had to be when I come here, like it or lump it.'

'She never put it like that,' said the cook. 'It's a good, plain name, suitable for a parlour-maid.'

'I don't see why I had to have another. Why should we be treated different? They gave Miss Violet a pretty name. Why couldn't I keep mine?'

'Because that's how it is for servants, that's why. Told you, I worked for a family where the parlour-maid was always called Agnes and the tweeny was Ann. It saved the mistress remembering.'

Edith subsided, her cheeks flushed against her creamy skin.

Rosina suited her better, thought Abbs. A pretty, spirited girl. 'I'd like to hear about the night Mr. Ellis was killed.'

'Shocking, that was,' said the cook. 'That poor gentleman didn't deserve such a wicked end.'

'Did you ever speak to him, Mrs Jakes?'

'Only the once. Long time ago, it was. He sought me out to compliment my cooking, when they'd dined with the family.'

'What was he like?'

'Shy, I reckoned. A mite stiff in his manner, but he didn't have to thank me, just for doing my work. Showed his appreciation too. Few guests do that, I can tell you.'

She readily confirmed the time Mr. Ibbotson returned home. 'The master wanted a glass of negus to warm him and I was low on lemons. The nights are that cold. A real blackthorn winter.'

'Was that the last you saw of your master that evening? I must compliment you on your plum cake, Mrs Jakes.'

'You're very welcome.' The cook smiled at him. 'No, he rang again about a half-hour later, wanting fresh ink. Which you are supposed to keep filled, miss.'

'I did,' said Edith. 'It's her and her endless lists.'

'Who's her, the cats mother? Show some respect for your betters.' She turned back to Abbs. 'Then when the mistress came home, I took them up a tray of cocoa in the drawing-room.'

'Which meant we had to wait for ours,' said Edith, between picking up every last crumb on her plate.

'You're perfectly capable of putting it on, my girl. No good giving yourself airs because you'd been allowed out.'

'Wasn't my idea of a night out, listening to an old Bible-peddlar.' Edith grinned at him. 'Had its compensations, I s'pose.'

'You be careful if you've been batting your eyes at that young policeman. The mistress won't stand for it.'

'He wasn't even there.' She looked a picture of injured innocence.

'Or that draper's-assistant. You know the rules. No followers while you work under this roof.'

'I hear some people stay on after the lecture,' said Abbs. 'I don't suppose they all come for the instruction?'

'You suppose right. It's not exactly a penny gaff, but it's somewhere to meet. They get a stewed tea and a stale half-penny bun apiece for their ticket. An hour of boredom in the warm, a numb ...'

'Edith. I won't tell you again.'

'Sorry, Cook. And a chance to mingle if they stay on. Mind, there's a collection plate to pass on the way out. Someone stands there, watching what you give.'

Abbs thought of Mrs Ibbotson. There was no pleasant feeling of benevolence, when the do-gooder extracted your coin by force of will.

'What did you occupy yourself with, after the refreshments?'

Edith made a face. 'Sorting through grubby old rags while the ladies gossiped. I wouldn't fancy their charity. Some of those blankets weren't even off a servant's bed. They stank of horse. I'd rather go on shivering.'

'Easy to say, miss,' said Mrs Jakes. 'Excuse me.' Getting up, she moved to the range, where a pudding, tied up in string, was simmering over a pan.

He turned swiftly to Edith, as the cook fetched a fork and began prodding the muslin parcel. 'Did you see your mistress and Miss Maitland, where you were working?'

'Not more than I could help. The mistress went to sit in another room with a bunch of them. I went to speak to a friend, soon as I got the chance.'

Edith's dimpled expression dared him to inquire further. Mrs Jakes threw her a doubtful look, as she waved away the steam.

'What about Miss Maitland?'

'She was working at the other table to begin with. Didn't see her again till not long before we finished.'

'Didn't see her because you were busy yourself?'

'That's right. Aren't you taking all this down?'

'I'm only trying to get a general idea of the evening. When did you see Miss Maitland again?'

'I saw her slipping in the back way, not long before we left. About a quarter to ten, it was.'

~

Mrs Ibbotson was in the hall as he left. 'Thank you, Edith, I'll see the inspector out.'

'Yes,'m.' She gave him a look in place of a wink, as she bobbed and turned back.

'Was the girl of any assistance to you?'

'It's all useful background, ma'am.'

Mrs Ibbotson hesitated, then spoke rapidly. 'Inspector, I pray you find whoever killed poor Mr. Ellis.'

'You may be assured we're doing our utmost.' She nodded, twisting her beads, making no move to step aside. 'Was there something else, Mrs Ibbotson?'

'I tried to bring him comfort in his loss. Tell me, Inspector, are you married?'

Surprised, Abbs shook his head. 'I'm a widower, ma'am.'

'Forgive me, sir, for touching on your sorrow. I see you do understand. Sympathy is measured in rules and months, but sadness doesn't disappear when we take off our mourning. My husband said

128

Mr. Ellis should master his grief, but not everyone has the vicar's strength of purpose. Mr. Buckley said he should marry again. I don't suppose he meant to be insensitive.'

He was unsure how to reply, when the bell jangled in the porch. Hastily bidding him good day, Mrs Ibbotson answered her own door. He left, deep in thought, touching his hat to the shabby woman outside.

TWENTY-SIX

Grainer was wavering between two food-stalls by the park entrance. A greasy aroma of steaming pea soup dispersed on the cold breeze. Feeling in his pocket, he took a step towards the cups of eel-jelly.

'Later, Sergeant,' said Abbs to his back. He'd no wish to watch him wielding his spoon. 'First, we'll compare notes.' He led the way through the open gates, steering Grainer well past the lodge window, with its chalked board of fare.

He listened attentively as the sergeant summarised his questioning of Mr. Buckley's servant.

'An' I didn't take her word for it. I made her show me the lay-out of the house. He lives high on the hog, sir. Gas throughout the place, all his furniture looked on the new side. Fancy tile-back chairs at the dining-table, not a stick of mahogany.'

'You're satisfied that either one could have gone out, without the other knowing?'

'Certain, sir. The Feltons were tucked up over the stables by half-past nine. She was busy in the kitchen for the last hour. We've only Mr. Buckeridge's word for it that he stayed at home. As for young Ambrose, his rooms are on the floor above. He could come and go as he pleased. No need even to be careful on the stairs. The room he used for his painting has a door to the fire-escape. Leads down to the rear garden. He'd only to nip quietly through the gate, past the stable and away.'

'Did you find out where he's living now?'

'In my notebook, sir. Place in the back end of Chelsea, near Cremorne.'

'Good, you've been thorough.' He registered Grainer blink in surprise. 'D'you think Mrs Felton understood what you were really asking?'

'No, sir. She took it for granted we're questioning everyone. Doubt it's entered her head, one of them might have murdered Ellis.'

'From what you say, they had ample opportunity. Their only danger would be being seen in the street.'

'Not much danger, considering. Well muffled up, the fog coming in. Unless they were stood under a lamp-post, most anyone could say was they saw a figure passing by.'

Abbs repeated what he'd learned. 'Tandy can confirm the time Mr. Ibbotson returned home and Mrs Jakes saw him. No one saw him after that, until he rang for her again about half-past nine. That only gives him a half-hour or so. It's just possible that was sufficient.'

Grainer grimaced. 'I don't go much for religion, sir, but I can't see the vicar committing a mortal sin. An' he wasn't left anything, he only got money for his church. Not enough to hang for, even if he was thinking of dipping his hand in the proceeds.'

'I agree, Mr. Ibbotson is not the most likely prospect, but we can't rule out anyone yet. None of these people are fools, we mustn't underestimate them. Nor should we take it for granted the motive was money.'

Grainer grunted. 'Most times it is.'

'Chief Inspector Townsend shares your view. To return to the others, Miss Maitland or Mrs Ibbotson could have done it, provided they could get away from the Institute without being missed.'

'Looks like Miss Maitland, sir, if this maid was telling the truth.'

'Not necessarily, though I don't think Edith was lying. It's clear she was more interested in her own concerns that evening. She was doing her best to dodge both women.'

'Trying to trap some young fellow into keeping her. I know her type.'

'You haven't set eyes on her, Grainer.'

'Don't need to, sir. Miss Maitland had time. By my reckoning, she had fifty minutes. Longer even, depending on when she slipped out. How long would it take to quarrel and do the deed? A half-hour? Bit less?'

'I don't know,' said Abbs. 'The murder had the appearance of being unpremeditated. But if Louisa Maitland wanted a private interview with Ellis, she lived in his house. It only makes sense if she planned everything.'

'The maid saw her coming back.'

'Events that seem suspicious are not always so. Miss Maitland may have gone outside for some innocent reason.'

'What might that be?'

'Use your imagination, Sergeant. Or perhaps she felt overcome, wanted some fresh air.'

'If you don't reckon money alone, sir, what about lust? Could she

131

and Frederick Buckeridge be in it together?'

'It's possible. What concerns me is the blood. Dr. Prentice told us there wouldn't have been much. But even a stained glove or a spot on the cuff would take some explaining when they returned to the hall. Would either woman have the nerve to risk it?'

'We don't know what they wore that night and we can't ask,' said Grainer. He blew out a rasp of breath. 'I hate dealing with these people. If this were Lambeth, I'd search every stitch they owned. Mind, gloves can be burned.'

'We've no grounds for doing that with any of our suspects. I share your frustration, Sergeant, but we must tread carefully. Mrs Ibbotson may have been in sight the entire evening, but we cannot question her acquaintance, without more reason. We are not to antagonise these people. Our superior made that very clear.'

'It's always the way, sir. Inspector Cole says poke a stick and watch 'em scuttle. Not so easy with their class.'

Abbs made no answer as they left the shelter of their plane-tree for the main gates.

'Any of them might have done it, Grainer. All five were within a few minutes' walk of Lindholm.'

'If it was one of the women, what did they do with the stuff?'

'A good question. They might have managed to conceal the diary in a pocket, but not the rest. A piece of china and two miniatures couldn't be stuffed in a reticule. They'd have to be discarded on the way back to the Institute. I'll ask Sergeant Hollins to have a search made. It's possible they're still lying in a front garden. I should have thought of it.'

'If you say so, sir. Are we off to the station now, while we're near?'

'All in good time. Look over there.'

Grainer followed his gaze across the busy street, where the Kennington Institute had its outer doors hooked open. Two men, each carrying a bird-cage, were conversing as they went in.

'We'll take a look for ourselves.'

Abbs glanced at the poster proclaiming *A Show of Tamed Exhibits by the South London Society of Song-Bird-Fanciers.* He disliked seeing caged birds stacked on street-stalls. In this harsh, mercantile city, where men dealt in trapped linnets, even birdsong had its price.

Inside, while Grainer spoke to the caretaker, he explored the rooms off the corridor. The bird-fanciers were arranging their tables in the main hall. Canaries, chaffinches, blackbirds trilled and fluttered on every side. Observing the hall had three exits, Abbs left them to it.

Other rooms were sufficient for a smaller meeting. A notice offered classes for working-men seeking to better themselves. The kitchen door led to a rear yard where the privvies were, a third door opened on a side-path.

Still clutching a rag, the caretaker was a short, balding man, with a weak smile. He moistened his lips as Abbs approached.

'Do you live on the premises?'

'No, sir, but I'm close at hand. I live with my daughter over the iron-monger's, a few doors along. Her husband keeps the shop.'

'Were you here Monday evening last week, when Mr. Clark gave his lecture?'

The caretaker, tight against the wall, put his head on one side, rather like the birds across the passage.

'That would be the missionary gentleman. I was here before they started. I see everything's ready for them. Fill the stoves, the urn, arrange the platform and unlock the doors for the public. I was here earlier in the day to sweep and set out the chairs. Once the organisers turn up, I leave them to it.'

'Do you return to lock up?'

'That's right, I get back for the last half-hour. There's quite a bit to see to, I leave the chairs till morning. The main thing's to see to the stoves, make sure the gas is off and the building's secured. This is a responsible job and I take my duties seriously. Are you sure I'm not in trouble?' The caretaker eyed Grainer, who was standing too close.

'Just answer the inspector's questions. We don't want it minute by minute.'

Abbs motioned the sergeant to step back. 'When you returned, did you see anyone outside?'

'Not see anyone, no, but there was a young woman round the side. I heard her snigger. She wasn't alone. Some of them meet here when they're walking out.' The caretaker's voice was righteous with disapproval, his eyes bright. 'I have to keep an eye on the outside. There's no knowing what you'll see in dark corners.'

Of a sudden, Abbs was impatient to be away from the pair of them.

The grubby streets, with their sooty air, would feel cleaner somehow.

TWENTY-SEVEN

Sergeant Grainer slouched on a chair in The Clarence tavern. His mended boots, wrapped in brown paper, were dumped on the table. He contemplated the last inches of his porter, knowing to a farthing the coins in his pocket.

The public was fairly quiet for early evening, though waiters were to-ing and fro-ing, bearing laden trays to the dining-room next door. All right for some. Belching, he anticipated the remainder of warmed-up mutton stew awaiting him.

A few constables gathered at the bar, their shifts just ended. Though popular with the detective-branch, due to the Clarence neighbouring Scotland Yard, his fellow drinkers were mostly Whitehall clerks on their way home. Fortunately, he'd only seen Inspector Abbs in there once, in the company of old Sheppard.

His days were a constant trial. The pile of reports on his desk in the sergeants'-room, rarely sank lower. He wondered who would be made regular with the new man and hoped it weren't him. His thoughts weren't his own any more. Being invited to give his opinion took a deal of getting used to, so did the occasional good word. Kept him jumping like a flea.

Too weary to stir himself back in the street. The fire gave out a good warmth and the soft popping of the gas-light was sending him off.

How he loathed a bitter spring. Flower-sellers were back on the streets, like the girl with the daffs. A faint green haze was creeping over the blackened trees, like mould on Cheddar. Some days had a feeling of expectation in the air, as if something good would happen, but it never came.

The light was drawing out, but the early evenings still chilled you to the marrow. There was a bleakness in spring, the poets never wrote about.

His head nodding, Grainer swayed upright as the door banged open, releasing a draught on his back. Moments later, a shadow fell between him and the light.

'Get that down for gawd's sake. Yer look like you need it.' A fresh pot was thumped down on the table, slopping a little on the scratched wood.

A growler was setting off from outside his lodgings, as Abbs returned to Gloucester-road that evening. The front door stood open, the hall full of activity. Mrs Newsome was standing with someone, clad in a check ulster. The blacks about his cheek and left sleeve showed he'd been travelling by railway and seated by an open window.

Several parcels were deposited on the rug and a skinny boy was encumbered with a sturdy, bound trunk. Middlesbrough was written on the label.

Mrs Newsome greeted him warmly. 'Good evening, Mr. Abbs. You must excuse us being at sixes and sevens. This is Mr. Snow who lives on the second floor. He's only this minute returned home.'

Leaning on an ornate walking-stick, his fellow tenant doffed his hat with a flourishing arm and low bow. 'Edwin Snow, Esquire. Vagabond and weary traveller. Your servant, sir.' Like many a portly gentleman, Mr. Snow was surprisingly graceful and light on his feet.

'Away with you, Mr. Snow. What ever will Mr. Abbs think?' His landlady blushed, showing traces of the girl she'd once been.

'In short, sir, that I am an actor.' He emphasised his calling, rolling the second syllable.

'Josiah Abbs. Very glad to meet you, Mr. Snow.'

'And I you, sir. Abbs you say, an uncommon name.'

'It belongs to my home county of Norfolk.'

'Ah, The Theatre Royal, and the fair city of Norwich, are not unknown to me. I shall look forward to making closer acquaintance, sir, over a glass of port. There's nothing to compare for oiling the vocals.'

'Mr. Snow's been touring in the North. Mr. Abbs is an inspector at Scotland Yard, in the detective-branch. Put it in the small box-room, Caleb, if you please.'

Abbs was amused to see the lad regarding him with great interest, over the domed lid, as he staggered towards the stairs.

'D'you need a hand?'

'Can manage easy, thank you, sir. I'm stronger than I look.'

'Come through to the kitchen when you're done, Caleb. I'll find you a piece of cake. There's a letter on the table for you, Mr. Abbs.'

Escaping to his rooms shortly after, he was pleased to see the envelope bore a familiar post-mark.

~

Later, when Mrs Newsome came to remove his supper dishes, she fussed over the tray, seeming inclined to linger.

'If ever you want a cab, Mr. Abbs, young Caleb will fetch one, or run any errands. He's a trustworthy lad.'

'I'll bear that in mind, Mrs Newsome. Where would I find him?'

'He lives opposite, the rooms on the ground-floor. His mother, Mrs Fleet, helps me with the rough. She's a widow-lady, I've known them since I first came here.'

Folding his napkin, he left the table, noting his landlady still seemed reluctant to leave. 'Might I help you with anything, Mrs Newsome?'

'I did want to say that Mr. Snow couldn't be more respectable. Else I'd never have had him under my roof. He has a droll manner of speaking at times, that's just his way. I hope you won't be put off by his being on the stage?'

'By no means. Should I have heard of Mr. Snow? I've rarely had the time to go to the theatre.'

She looked doubtful. 'Well, maybe not. Mr. Snow wouldn't claim to be known throughout the land, like Mr. Kean or his father. He'll tell you himself, he's what they call a character-actor. The company tour in proper theatres, mind. You could see him for yourself. He was telling me, they're reviving *The Miller's Wife* here in the Metropolis, when they can get a booking. Don't think he frequents low gaffs.'

'I wouldn't dream of it, I assure you.'

'That's good of you, Mr. Abbs. You know how some folk can be prejudiced. I admit I didn't mention any of this, when you came to see the rooms.'

Abbs smiled at her. 'If Mr. Snow doesn't object to a detective on the premises, I've no quarrel with his profession.'

'I'm sure you'll like him. He's a most considerate gentleman. Don't think you'll be troubled when he learns his lines. Besides, he's often away for weeks on end.'

Opening the door, she clucked her tongue. 'What are you doing up here, Lachie? You'll have someone over, skulking on the landing like that. Away with you.' Her voice diminished, scolding her way

137

down the stairs.

Abbs settled by the fire and reread his letter from Ezra Duffield. Newly acquainted at Christmas, their involvement in a village mystery had begun a friendship. A neighbour of his sister, he suspected Duffield might one day become his brother-in-law.

The room had warmed up, the burble of the flames soothing, as he thought about Louisa Maitland. She didn't strike him as a woman to collapse in a swooning fit. Even so, it took a cool head to search Ellis's study, while his corpse lay sprawled on the carpet.

Once her sister had been buried, living with her brother-in-law had possibly been as awkward as being a governess. Lacking even the salary and quite as dependent on another's good opinion. She'd mentioned having no other relatives. A shame there was no brother or cousin to shelter her.

The provisions of Ellis's will were commonplace. Life could be harsh for women. Summoned on a whim or sent away again, like pieces moved on a chess-board. His thoughts strayed back to his sister. Hetty had use of her home for life, provided she remained a widow. Should she marry again, her house would pass immediately to her step-son. No man wanted to think of a stranger taking all that had been his.

Did Miss Maitland crave security enough to murder her benefactor? She claimed not to know what provision had been made for her under the existing will. But as Grainer pointed out, they had only her word for it. Her anxiety could have been an act for their benefit. It looked very much as though Ellis had been about to change his will.

Everyone believed the murderer came from outside. Was he quite wrong to suspect the murder had taken place early in the night? How much simpler for Miss Maitland to knock softly on Ellis's study door, after the servants had had time to fall asleep. Maggie and Bertha were bound to be tired out after a day's work, Mrs Wilmot too, most likely. There was the matter of what she'd hidden down the side of her chair.

The women slept two floors above the domestic quarters, at the back. The room above the study was not in use.

Miss Maitland had a dried, red line on her fore-finger. Almost healed, easily done in some small domestic mishap, slicing fruit or cut on a broken glass. That first morning, she'd been holding a handkerchief when he met her. He saw it again, entwined round her fingers, hiding any scratch.

Rubbing his brow, Abbs considered the others he'd seen that day. Mr. Ibbotson had been at pains to divert him from suspecting a woman. Was he protecting Miss Maitland, or could he possibly be directing attention away from his wife?

As he was leaving the vicarage, he'd glimpsed a softer, hesitant Hester Ibbotson. He'd assumed the garnet ring was in return for kindness to Ellis's wife. He wondered if the bequest meant something more. It seemed probable she could not have left the Institute without being missed. The likelihood was she spent the entire evening under the eyes of several women. It was unfortunate he had no grounds to question them and make sure.

Mr. Ibbotson was no admirer of Frederick Buckley. The latter's behaviour, outside the inquest, suggested the feeling was returned. Yet, it seemed to him, their antipathy stemmed from being alike. Both, in their different way, were modernisers. Forceful, energetic men, full of certainty they were right. Two people, with much in common, sometimes had a mutual distaste. Unaware they disliked seeing their own failings, reflected in the other's character.

Frederick Buckley had an obvious motive. But suppose there was something else? Ellis wanted to see Buckley. What if he'd discovered something wrong with the business? Left largely to his own devices, Buckley had every opportunity for double-dealing. Were there ways in which an architect might fiddle more money than his fees?

It made sense to look closer at the architects' practice. He could hardly question Ambrose about possible misdeeds of his father, but Mr. Searle might have his suspicions. Loyal, above all, to his dead employer, he might be persuaded to say more.

In any case, they needed to see Ambrose again. Ellis might have said something of significance, when they were alone. A stray remark could provide the clue they needed.

The funeral might prove revealing, but he'd have to leave it to Grainer. He'd have liked to watch the mourners, but Inspector Sheppard required him to give evidence. Other inquiries needed his attention. Townsend was pressing him for results. He sensed he would not be let alone much longer.

TWENTY-EIGHT

'Stands to reason, you can't go narrowing a river, just 'cause you've a mind to.' Grainer nodded towards the labourers along the Thames shore. 'It's bound to flood back, come winter. Waste o' money, if you ask me.'

Abbs, who hadn't asked, watched the scene below them. The sergeant seemed to dislike spending of the public purse on principle. He'd half-listened to a monologue begun with the under-ground railway and leading, by way of subsidence, to Mr. Bazalgette's sewers.

'I doubt Dr. Prentice would agree with you. Surely anything that will lessen the spread of disease is worthwhile?'

The omnibus had progressed at a moderate pace along the Embankment, giving Abbs time to admire the wide thoroughfare, with its avenue of young trees, alongside the busy river. Now they were slowed by the construction-works of the extension to Chelsea.

'That's what they say, sir, to justify the cost. Supposed to be opened by big-wigs next month. Ready for the Tsar's visit, no doubt. They'll never be finished in time.'

He couldn't complain now his sergeant was more talkative, thought Abbs. They were beginning to shake down together. And he doubted he was the easiest of men to work for.

After another wet morning, the rain had stopped about mid-day. Leaving their seats damp and the windows misted on the crowded lower deck. The omnibus waited to turn off past the Royal Hospital, home for old soldiers, affording them a long view of the new Chelsea Embankment.

Said in the newspapers to be a marvel of engineering, the new thoroughfare was built on reclaimed land. A great retaining wall contained the sewers and allowed them to be flushed in the Thames.

How strange it must be for the occupiers of the grand old houses they passed. Instead of giving on the river, a pebble's toss from wharves and stairs, they were now set considerably further back. Soon they would look out on constant horse-traffic. He held his handkerchief to his mouth. Perhaps lessening the stench of mud at low-tide would be some compensation.

Their view had been already been transformed by the new bridge. Opened the previous year, according to Grainer, and soon rumoured to be structurally weak. Nevertheless, the Albert Bridge looked very fine in the soft mist, wet roofs of its toll-booths gleaming and the mighty suspension chains hung with rain-drops. A steamer was passing beneath, belching dark smoke and heading up-river.

Ahead of them, labourers and carts toiled back and forth. The macadamised road surface was laid and stacks of paving slabs were ready to be set in place. Men were working on the lamp-holders and skeletal, ornamental gardens, still bare of greenery. They jolted as the horses swung into their turn.

'We get down here,' said Grainer presently. 'As well he gave me directions.'

He consulted the rough map in his notebook as they departed the terraced streets for a hugger-mugger of half-built villas and small industrial premises. A scrubby field or two remained, with the look of their days running out. Grainer pointed out the tree-tops of Cremorne pleasure-gardens by the river.

'This is it, sir.'

'Let's hope young Mr. Buckley's a man of his word. I'd hate to come all this way for nothing.' Abbs considered. He was not at ease on the water. Now he worked near the Thames, time that was overcome. 'Perhaps we might catch a steamer back.'

'He said, at the funeral, he'd be here.' Grainer screwed up his nose. 'Blowed if I'd swop this for a comfortable home.'

'It isn't what I expected, certainly.'

Abbs regarded the old brick building, set back from the lane, to one side of a neglected yard. The ghost of a vast flagged floor, broken bricks and smashed tiles were sinking among nettles.

Ambrose Buckley emerged from a door on to the walk-way, calling down to them.

'I saw you coming, Inspector. Watch out for the hand-rail, it's a tad rickety.'

Bidding him good day, Abbs climbed the wooden stair, followed by a cautious Grainer. They entered an airy room, lit by windows on two sides and a sky-light. An empty easel was set up at the far end, where a screen hid a second door.

'What was this place?'

'All that's left of an old iron foundry. Downstairs is rented by a sculptor. Up here belongs to a friend of mine. Those are his.'

Buckley gestured at a pile of canvasses turned to the wall. 'His father owns the site. It's coming down by the autumn.'

'Are you staying here until then, Mr. Buckley?'

Ambrose laughed. 'I should say not. I don't mind roughing it for a week or two, while I make arrangements. Then I'm off on my travels.'

'You're following the late Mr. Ellis's wishes?'

The young man looked sheepish. 'Up to a point. Not that I'm going to study the classical painters, as he suggested. That's asking too much but I'd like to return to Paris. After that, I'll journey south for a while. Paint the working people. They interest me more than Society bores. Do take a pew.'

Rejecting the chaise-longue with an Indian shawl draped over the back, Abbs made for a battered table under the far window. A hacked loaf and a serrated knife lay on a board, littered with cheese-crumbs. A beer bottle stood on the floor-boards by a chair-leg.

'You too, Sergeant. I see you've dried out since yesterday.' Grainer grunted as he sat down. 'I suppose the weather was appropriate.' Ambrose went on cheerfully, 'as though the day was weeping. Funerals in sunlight seem wrong, somehow. Poor old Rowland. No family at the graveside, no grandchildren to miss him. The ladies didn't attend. I do believe old Searle was the only one there who truly mourned him.'

He didn't include himself, thought Abbs. 'I was sorry to be unable to attend.'

'You missed a good spread. A first-rate cold collation. You can rely on my governor for that. He arranged a private room at The Horns. In the circumstances, he didn't think Miss Maitland would want to receive mourners at the house. Who knows the etiquette when the host's been murdered?'

Abbs cleared his throat, irritated by the lingering turpentine. The artist might return at any time. 'I'd like you to think back, if you will, to your conversations with Mr. Ellis. Did he ever say anything which, in hindsight, strikes you as significant?'

Ambrose studied them, an arm hooked over the back of his kitchen chair. 'Are you quite certain Rowland didn't try to overpower a burglar? I thought a piece of silver was found dropped near the wall?'

'Who told you that, Mr. Buckley?'

'My father had it from Sergeant Hollins.'

'A snuff-box was found. That means little, in itself.'

'Left there deliberately, you mean?'

Abbs acknowledged this with a nod. Ambrose was no fool. 'Possibly.' He glanced at Grainer, who was taking an interest in his blank page.

'He never spoke to me of being on bad terms with anyone. My father's been known to ruffle a few feathers, but not Rowland.'

'In what circumstances could you see Mr. Ellis making an enemy?'

Ambrose scratched his head. 'He wouldn't stand for someone being ill-treated without intervening. A fellow beating a woman in the street, or thrashing his horse. He'd make it his business to stop them.'

'Everyone speaks of Mr. Ellis as a kindly gentleman. I was thinking more if he posed a threat to someone. Suppose he found out about some wrong-doing? Would he consider it none of his affair and look the other way?'

'Depends what it was, Inspector. If he knew a fellow had a mistress, say, he'd be disapproving, but wouldn't go telling the wife now, would he? Any man would think that none of his business. Better the lady remained in happy ignorance.'

'Would he ever be likely to confront someone? Threaten them in some way?'

Ambrose frowned. 'He wouldn't stand for being lied to.'

'Honesty mattered a great deal to him?'

'I'll say. Look, most of us tell the odd whopper at some time. Saves trouble. But old Rowland viewed lies as poison. Made an uncommon fuss about the smallest prevarication.'

'Really?'

'You know, I've always had a suspicion his father was a welsher. He told me an aunt paid for his studies. Not his pa, though I don't believe he was dead at the time. Rowland was too free with his advice about always squaring my accounts and never, under any circumstances, signing a bill for a friend. He once said he'd seen, at a young age, the damage lies can do.'

'Did he ever speak to anyone when you were out with him?'

'Only what you'd expect. A passing word with gallery-owners, waiters, no one who mattered. When he was practising, he did, of course. When I started, he'd cart me off to various houses and sites.' He sighed extravagantly. 'It's a dull life being an architect. Worse for a lowly draughts-man. I don't know how I stood it.'

'Apart from your brief meeting at The Horns, do you recall the last time you spoke?'

'I do, as it happens. Rowland had an invitation to a gallery in St James's. He asked me to accompany him. Waste of time but he thought it might be useful for me to meet people. They were the same ghastly old landscapes. Flower-decked cottages with geese in the lane. They aren't art. Portly aldermen buy them like wall-paper. They've more talent in the frame, than the canvas. Of course, old Rowland liked them well enough.'

His voice held the casual contempt of the young. So certain of their opinion, they were unaware of giving offence. 'What did Mr. Ellis talk about?'

'Oh, nothing of consequence. Complained he'd had enough of winter, bemoaned the fog and filth. I told him the mud would be worse out of town. He kept lingering over an oil-painting. I had to work hard to dissuade him from having it.'

'What did it depict?'

'The usual twee sort of scene. Market-square in an old country town. You've seen them, I'm sure. I showed him the flaws. I fancy he saw my point in the end, for he didn't buy it. We went our separate ways outside. He asked if I'd ever had my fill of London, thought of getting away. You know, I wonder now, if his will was on his mind. Perhaps he had a premonition, he wasn't long for this world?'

'Have you recalled any more about the man with Mr. Ellis in The Horns?'

'Haven't given him a thought.' He yawned and stretched. 'His nails were clean.'

Grainer shifted, looking round the long room, distaste written on his visage. He had a regrettably brief attention-span for a detective. Abbs frowned at him.

'I notice hands, you see. Tricky things to get right, but they hold so much character. A cheap, ready-cut suit, as I think I told you. Even a barrow-boy wears them these days, but he didn't have a workman's hands. He was a clerk, bringing some papers.'

'I understand you were at home on the evening of the murder, Mr. Buckley?'

'My father and I dined together. He told you as much, Inspector.'

'Routine, sir, we have to check on everyone. Did you spend the remainder of the evening together?'

'Well, not literally. I had some letters to write. I have separate quarters on the floor above. Neither of us stirred from the house that night. Look here, I don't resent your questions. We both know my father and I benefited from the will, but you're wasting your time, Inspector.'

Thanking him for his assistance, Abbs signalled to Grainer they were done. 'Did Mr. Ellis ever mention an interest in spiritualists?'

'Good Lord, no, he wasn't that gullible. Told you, he couldn't abide liars.'

TWENTY-NINE

'Mr. Abbs, message for you.'

Abbs swung round, hearing someone call up the stairs. The detectives' building was busy with men leaving and like him, returning from a morning's leg-work.

'What is it, Mottram?' Not a telegraph, the clerk's hands were empty.

'Chief Inspector Townsend desired to see you as soon as you came in, sir. There's a note to that effect on your desk.'

'Did he say what it's about?' Abbs returned to the foot of the stairs, where the clerk hovered.

'Not to me.' Mottram's expression conveyed that Townsend wouldn't think of telling him. 'He sent for Sergeant Grainer.'

Thanking him, Abbs ran through his case-load as he walked along the corridor. Entering at Townsend's command, he nodded to Grainer, already seated.

'Sit down, Inspector.'

His superior was looking pleased with himself. Abbs eased his limbs. Presumably, he'd done nothing wrong.

'You'll be glad to hear there's been a development in the Ellis murder. Not before time, I might add. Message from Sergeant ...' Townsend picked up the telegraph-form before him, 'Hollins. One of the stolen items has turned up in Bermondsey.'

'Bermondsey?'

Impatience flickered across Townsend's face. 'M Division. Lies back from the Surrey bank, over London Bridge. A working-class district.'

'Some distance from Kennington?'

'Just far enough,' said Grainer. 'Known for leather-workers and tailoring.'

'If I might continue, Sergeant. Earlier today, a pawn-broker accepted a china figurine, which matches the description of the one taken from the Ellis house. Brought to him by a woman. Fortunately, he must be an honest fellow, for his kind. He recalled a constable coming round, checked the list of stolen items and sent word to Kennington.'

He hadn't expected this. Abbs's mind raced with the implications.

'Well, Abbs? Real progress, is it not? Sergeant Hollins requests instructions. He assumes you'll want to question the fellow, yourself. I'm minded to think you may hand further inquiries to him. It turns out a perfectly simple crime, after all.' Townsend rubbed his neat Van Dyke beard, awaiting a response.

'I'd prefer to continue with the case myself, sir.'

'Surely, now you accept Mr. Ellis died at the hands of a house-breaker? An appalling tragedy, but a common or garden matter. For myself, I regard it a pity we put an end to transporting convicts. A harsher punishment, in fact, than a quick death with the rope.'

Grainer nodded solemnly. 'Quite agree, sir. We don't want 'em.'

'Mind, if they don't hang, they wish they'd never turned to crime when they're breaking rocks on the Moor. I've visited Princetown, you know. I wouldn't recommend it. The inclement weather up there's like a sentence. I pitied the villagers.'

Abbs took an even breath. The course of his working life at the Yard might be determined in these few minutes. 'With respect, sir, I should still like to continue. After the work we've already done, Sergeant Grainer and I are best placed to see the case through to the finish.'

Townsend flicked his hand, the way you'd brush off a fly. 'You both have other inquiries needing your attention. Doubtless, this Sergeant Hollins is perfectly capable of questioning a pawn-broker. He'll have his informers. He'll find the murderer in time.'

The urgency to appease journalists and frightened house-holders no longer mattered, then, thought Abbs. Grainer looked sideways at him, unexpectedly sympathetic. One last try.

'It seems to me, sir, that the figurine turning up doesn't necessarily change anything. The murderer would have to dispose of what he took from the study. We don't know how it came to end up at the pawn-shop. I still believe Rowland Ellis was murdered by someone who knew him.'

Townsend glanced at his ash-tray, his hand straying to his mouth. He was in want of tobacco. Abbs wondered, in passing, where the beaten brass bowl came from. Turkey perhaps? He forced himself to concentrate.

'I've given you my decision, Inspector. Instruct Sergeant Hollins accordingly. I was telling Grainer, he'll remain with you for the time being. Sheppard has been asking for more assistance with this spate of attacks in Green Park. They can't be allowed to continue. He's in the building now. I suggest you both join him.'

'As you wish, sir. May I take the telegraph?' Schooling his expression to be neutral, Abbs held out a hand.

Hesitating, Townsend passed it to him and reached for the top folder on his tray. 'That is all, Inspector. Sergeant. I won't detain you from your duties.'

~

Looking up-river, the magnificent Houses of Parliament, with its three towers, dominated the Victoria Embankment. Its sand-coloured stone, and ranks of tall windows, seemed to gleam, despite the flecking of blacks and a grey afternoon. The Clock Tower pointed pencil-like, above the pinnacled roofs. Abbs consulted its face.

Some yards off, an old man slumped, his back to the parapet. Bundled about with so many layers of ragged attire, he appeared far bulkier than his frame. His low-brimmed hat, gone beyond brushing, tipped at an angle misleadingly cheery. His dull stare fixed in the direction of the fine carriages passing.

The Thames was a shifting, parting, watery highway, constantly rippling through the heart of the city. Here, not so busy as down-river below London Bridge, where the masts of ocean-ships fringed the vast docks. Yet more crowded than the great thoroughfare clattering at his back. He'd felt better than anticipated on the steamer from Chelsea, back to Westminster.

Smoke, from the chimneys on the Surrey-shore, drifted into the thin mist. Lighter-men called out as they steered their craft, their long sweeps carving waves past floating timber logs, lashed in rafts, bumping on the far wharves.

Penny-boats ferried between the banks, dodging coal-barges, wherries with stained sails, passenger-steamers and skiffs. Collision seemed inevitable but was ever averted, head-way gained against the current, foaming wake cleaving arrow-heads across the cloud-coloured water. Eddying gulls screeched about masts and perched on bollards. Some urchins were dragging rope free of the stinking mud.

Abbs wondered why a man must always be working his way through an invisible list of tasks. In the depths of night, when sleep was elusive, they paraded past the dark. They were waiting each morning to be done and done again, like convicts' feet pounding the mill.

The only task he wanted to pursue was finding out who murdered Rowland Ellis. Sergeant Hollins would search diligently for an unknown house-breaker and do no more.

The chill of the stonework seeped through his hands. Hurrying from the Yard, he'd neglected to pick up his gloves. Everyone had been questioned about their whereabouts on the night of the murder. Grainer had elicited nothing new from watching the funeral. A search of alleys and shrubberies on the direct route between Lindholm and the Institute had been fruitless.

Now, when something fresh had turned up, he was ordered to leave it be. No doubt now who had looked through the papers on his desk. Townsend had intercepted the telegraph, meant for him, in the same high-handed way.

Should he do as he was told, or follow his inclination and risk censure, even dismissal? His grasp on his new life was precarious. Disobeying a direct order would hardly endear him to Townsend.

A gloomy future drifted by with the river. The ignominy of leaving Great Scotland Yard for the last time. Running out of savings to pay Mrs Newsome. Selling his books and the walnut bookcase, his one good piece of furniture. Leaving the Metropolis, a few months after he'd come here to make a new start. The disappointed face of Hetty, who would gladly take him in, but would worry about him. What else could he do for a living?

A hooter blew, making him jump. The brass funnel of a river-launch glinted as it spewed black smoke.

Abbs smelt the unwashed body as he drew near, the weeks of weather the old man wore about him like a shawl. As he fumbled handing him a shilling, their eyes met. Not yet forty, he'd wager, beneath the grime. They were much of an age.

Stepping perilously near the trotting horse-traffic, he hailed a cabby. If he was to keep pace with his given duties, there was no time to be lost.

THIRTY

'I'd draw you a map, only I don't rightly know myself,' said Sergeant Hollins. 'Bermondsey is a bit of a warren. If you call at the local station-house, that's on Bermondsey-street, they'll direct you.'

'I don't have much time this afternoon. Valentine-place, you say? Not far from the leather market. I'll find it.' Abbs realised he must look doubtful, for Hollins continued.

'Tell you what, Inspector. How about if I send young Latham along with you? He's the one who inquired there in the first place.'

'That would be useful. I'm obliged to you. If you're sure you can spare one of your men?'

'This one I can. He might learn something.' Hollins glanced at the clock. 'He was on earlies, he'll be in the mess-room.' Throwing open the door, he stuck his head out and bawled at a subordinate. 'Winkle out Latham and send him in, will you?'

A moment later, the constable joined them. Like many a man obliged to stand still, he was too aware of his hands.

'We've met before,' said Abbs. 'You found the snuff-box.'

'S'right, sir.'

'Stand up straight when the Inspector's speaking to you. Shoulders back. You make a sack of spuds look smart.' As he spoke, Sergeant Hollins swept the crumbs on his desk to the floor. 'Latham had the beat past Lindholm till latterly.'

'Did you know Mr. Ellis, Constable?'

'No, sir. Leastways, only to bid good day to.'

'Do you recall anything about comings and goings at the house?'

The pustules on Latham's chin stood out more, as he coloured. 'I'd pass him taking his lady wife out in the brougham, now and again. Always wrapped in shawls, she was, whatever the weather. That's all I ever saw, sir.'

'The Yard are turning the inquiry over to us. But the Inspector, here, wants a look at the pawn-broker for himself. Inspector Abbs is new to the Metropolis, so I want you to accompany him.'

'Go there now, Sarge?'

'I don't mean yesterday.'

'I won't take up any more of your time. This is very good of you, Sergeant Hollins,' said Abbs. 'My thanks for your assistance. Here's my hand on it.'

Hollins wiped his on his worsted jacket before shaking heartily. 'Glad to be of help, sir. We like the Yard to know we're not all dolts in the divisions. I was certain all along it was a house-breaker. Like I said, it's my belief he scared himself silly, sticking his chiv in a gentleman. They're not killers as a rule.'

'You may be right, Sergeant.'

'Nah, he's gone to earth or scarpered. But if he is still this side of the river, we'll find him. Someone always peaches in the end. Might be worth inquiring if the late Mr. Ellis's partner will put up a reward. He was all mouth right after the murder, but there's been no sign of the blunt.'

A discordant rendering of an Irish air was coming from the corner of Kennington-road, where an old woman was turning a barrel-organ. Grinning all the while, bobbing like an automaton as she wrung the handle. A man's cap on the ground invited coins. Abbs was glad she kept no unfortunate monkey, holding a cup at the onlookers.

The harsh, jerky music jangled down the street as they approached the cab-stand. Two cabs in quick succession, and no claiming expenses, but speed mattered. As it was, he'd have to fudge an account of his afternoon when he made his nightly report to Townsend. Constable Latham looked somewhat disgruntled at his errand. A short journey would be preferable to stilted conversing on an omnibus. Hang the cost.

As they rattled back towards the Thames, then swung eastwards, Abbs plucked from his memory, a chance remark made by Mrs Jakes. 'Do you know Edith, the vicarage parlour-maid, Constable?'

His long limbs crammed uncomfortably, Latham stiffened further. 'Er, sort of, sir.'

'I remember what it's like on the beat. My old sergeant used to say a good constable needs to know every living body on his patch, down to who keeps which cat.'

Latham nodded. 'We're supposed to know the occupants of every house, sir.'

'I started out a village bobby, so it was easy enough. Not so simple in the Metropolis, I dare say.'

'S'right, sir, hard to keep track when the houses are let. But properties near the Park don't change hands for years.'

'I expect you get to know all the downstairs. Which Cooks will give you a cup of tea and so forth?'

He effected not to notice as his companion coloured. A rosy complexion was a curse to a young fellow, particularly when he had to uphold the law.

'Every once in a while, sir. Not often.'

'I haven't forgotten what it's like to be shut out in wind and rain, Constable. And local gossip can be useful. I believe the vicar and his wife are known for their charity. Were you made welcome in their kitchen?'

'Not them, sir. Mrs Jakes wouldn't begrudge a warm and a bite, but Edith says Mrs Ibbotson scrutinises her books. Makes her account for every last farthing.'

'So you didn't become acquainted with Edith there?'

'Met her in the street, sir, when she was on an errand.'

Recalling Edith, or rather, Rosina, Abbs could imagine. 'Did your beat take in Mr. Buckley's house?'

'No, sir, it ended at the front boundary of the Park. I'd never set eyes on him, before the body was found.'

'No matter. What about Mrs Wilmot? Ever invited in the kitchen at Lindholm?'

'Now and again,' said Latham, his voice cagey.

'A talkative woman, I thought.'

'A rare old gossip. Free with her baking, if she thought she could get some titbit out of you. Liked to read the tea-leaves, if the parlour-maid weren't about.'

'Did she indeed?' said Abbs thoughtfully. 'Maggie didn't hold with such things?'

'That Miss Maitland didn't and she'd snitch to her.'

As they rumbled through Bermondsey, they passed a succession of industrial premises. An oil cloth-makers, engine-works, glue manufactories, a cooperage, their names on boards or written in the iron-work of double gates. Housing for the workers was shoe-horned between warehouses and large yards.

In recent weeks, Abbs had explored enough of London to know the most noxious industries thronged along the Surrey-shore. The buildings of governance, Buckingham Palace, the inns of court, museums, theatres and parks were mostly north of the Thames. They must be about ten minutes' walk from the river-bank, he guessed, roughly south of the Tower.

They'd driven into a foul stench. Impossible to avoid recognising the stink of piss. He fancied droplets seemed to cling in the damp air about them. Stale as a full chamber-pot, laced with putrefying flesh and the sting of lime. He coughed, swallowing down phlegm. Behind the high walls, the street was full of tanning-pits.

Smirking, Constable Latham caught his eye. 'Too rich for you, sir?'

Their cab halted as a cart left a tannery. Hereabouts, the cobbles were slicked with a reddish-brown mud. Pasted on the wheel-spokes and smearing the carter's leggings, Abbs realised the earth was bloody, flecked with matted hair and tufts of wool. He glimpsed a great mound of bark shavings and another of pure, being shovelled by unfortunate labourers. Small wonder, every workman seemed to be smoking a short-stemmed pipe.

'D'you want the police-station first, sir?'

'No, we'll go straight to the pawn-brokers.'

Latham called up to the cabby accordingly. Their way led them past a great warehouse of patterned brick, taking up much of a row. Carts and wagons were leaving from an arch at either end. As they went by, a quadrangle and booths could be seen within.

'That's the leather market, sir. Skins this end, dressed leather the other side. Pawn-shop's off the next street.'

Among the workmen, in stained hide aprons and gaiters, Abbs noticed several gentlemen coming and going, prosperous in tall hats and tailored top-coats. As Inspector Sheppard was wont to say, *Where there's muck, there's brass.*

THIRTY-ONE

They descended from the cab in Long-lane, a busy street of shops and stalls. Latham led the way along a short place, blocked off by a wall liberally pasted with bills. Beyond a cordwainers' with its cast-iron boot sign, the three brass balls denoting a pawn-broker hung above a wide shop frontage. Its windows were edged with catches, whereby iron-barred cages might be fitted at night.

Before going in, Abbs studied the window displays and what could be made out of the interior. A woman was being served, some kind of garment draped over the counter. Her drooping shoulders suggested resignation.

All manner of household objects were arrayed before them. Large goods included clocks, a dinner service, a fiddle and bow, a valise and a stuffed owl in a glass case. Small items such as pocket-watches, buckles, hat-pins, an ivory rattle, were laid out between. Someone had arranged them all as artistically as an Oxford-street emporium. A notice claimed good prices would be paid for gold and silver.

The woman emerged, putting a ticket in her shabby reticule. They entered, the bell jingling as Abbs closed the door.

Behind the counter, a young woman was folding a man's jacket, her lips pursed as she tugged at a seam.

'Good day.' She waited, her expression guarded.

At a nod from Abbs, Latham stepped forward and explained their purpose. 'We received a message from Mr. Glossop. He's expecting a detective to call. Is he here, miss?'

She glanced up before speaking. Following her gaze to where a display of walking-sticks and fishing-rods had been attached to a beam, Abbs saw a small looking-glass placed unobtrusively among them. Angled to show the counter, to someone in the room behind.

As she hesitated, a man filled the open doorway, his approach silent. He looked in his fifties, though his complexion was stretched infant-smooth. He was possibly the most corpulent man Abbs had ever seen, not being one to frequent side-shows.

'Carry on, Lucy. I'll attend to this.'

'Very well, Pa.'

Taking the jacket, she moved to the back of the room, where rows of clothes and boots were arranged, in appearance, a cut above a dolly-shop. Ducking between suits hanging from the beams, she set about the new pledge with a clothes-brush.

'This is Mr. Abner Glossop, the proprietor, sir.'

'Very prompt, sir,' said the pawn-broker, addressing himself to Abbs. 'From the detective-branch at Scotland Yard, eh? Serious, then. A weighty matter. I have the item of interest for you.'

'Thank you Mr. Glossop. If we might see the china? Then I'd like to hear about the woman who brought it in.'

The pawn-broker nodded, setting his several chins moving. He gave the appearance of having no neck, his head being wedged erect by his high-winged collar. 'And so you shall. Lucy...'

'Yes, Pa?'

He pointed his finger as the young woman hastened before him. 'The door.'

She put up the latch, turning a hanging label to the inside.

'Fetch the figurine. Careful, girl.'

Abbs looked about him while Lucy disappeared in the back. Latham was casting an eye over a glass-topped case of rings, its contents finer quality than the gewgaws in the window. Behind the counter, he noticed a stout bludgeon propped against the wall. A barred wall-cupboard held an assortment of silver-ware. He suspected a fire-arm might also lie in a convenient drawer.

Lucy returned, carrying an object wrapped in cloth, setting it down with both hands.

'Did the woman bring it to you in that?'

She shook her head. 'It's ours. She had it in newspaper.'

'Out of the way, girl.' Abner Glossop unwrapped it and stood back. 'Behold. As dainty a piece of Chelsea porcelain, as ever you'll find. Wouldn't look out of place in Osborne House, that wouldn't.'

Abbs studied the figurine. A girl in the dress of a century ago, one delicate hand holding out her skirt, the other carrying a basket of exquisitely modelled flowers. Her pose was so life-like, a suggestion that she was about to dip and turn on her toes. The milk-white porcelain of the costume was picked out in tiny bunches of blue ribbons, matching those tying her wide-brimmed hat. The effect was both elegant and gay, the artistry of the modeller speaking to them down the years.

'I see you appreciate it, Inspector. Daisy-fresh, ain't she? Like she was done yesterday.'

'Indeed.' Abbs almost winced when the pudgy hand plucked the figurine in the air, flicking a dark-rimmed fingernail against the china.

'Rings true.' Glossop up-ended the piece, showing the mark. 'Raised anchor, that's an early mark. Soon as I saw this dainty lady, I knew she was far from her rightful home.'

'You assumed it was stolen?'

'Nay, I wouldn't necessarily think that. The woman who brought it in was a drab body, but you hear all sorts in this line. Women, long in service, might get left a keep-sake. Passed down in the family. Then there's folk who've gone down in the world. Managed to hang on to a good piece from the grand-parents. Sooner or later, they all pay a visit to Uncle.' He smiled, all but smacking his lips.

'What's it worth?' said Latham.

'Every last thing is only worth what someone'll give you for it. In an auction-room, a deal more than she could ever earn. Or you, lad.'

'What time did the woman come here?' Abbs readied his notebook and pencil.

'Between ten and the quarter.'

'Will you describe her?'

'Middling height, forties, worn face.'

'Hair colour, dress, if you please. Any distinguishing features?'

'None whatsoever. Take yourself out in the street, Inspector, and you'll see her walk by ten thousand times over. So dull, they're invisible.'

Abbs frowned. 'The shade of her hair, Mr. Glossop?'

'Wearing an old bonnet, wasn't she? Not in fashion since the old queen died. Some strands of mousy at her temples. A dark plaid dress, green, with a brown shawl.'

'Which one of you served her?'

'I dealt with her.'

'What did she say?'

'What would I give her for it? Nothing more.'

'Do you ask how people came by their possessions, if they're uncommonly valuable?'

Glossop smiled benevolently at him. His eyes, ringed with short creases and fat, remained cold as pebbles.

He smiled too much, thought Abbs, and it wasn't down to

156

nervousness. Glossop treated his girl as if she were a small dog, scurrying at his heels.

'I'm not obliged to, by law, but I generally do inquire. Always looking to do the blue-bottles a good turn.'

A likely story. 'What did the woman tell you, Mr. Glossop?'

He shrugged. 'Like I said, been in the family.'

'How did she strike you in her manner?'

'Furtive. But then, they all are. Whether it's hocking the old man's Sunday suit without him knowing, or soaping off their own wedding-band. They're desperate for the tin. Avid to know what I'll let 'em have. This one certainly was.'

'What did you offer her?'

'Half a sov, take it or leave it. She wanted more, of course. When I wouldn't budge, she snatched it up.'

'Could she sign her name?'

'See for yourself.' He snapped his fingers. Lucy slid an open ledger along the counter. The pawn-broker turned the book towards them, pointing to the fourth from last entry.

Abbs read the name aloud. 'Mrs Smith, 10, Belmont St, Bermondsey.'

'Lies. Ain't no such place. I know every street hereabouts. As for Mrs Smith, you wouldn't believe how often she drops in. Along with her sister Mrs Grey, an' her cousin Mrs Jones.'

'Had you ever seen her in here before, Mr. Glossop?'

'Not I, but Lucy, here, reckons she was in the once. Don't you, girl?'

She nodded but didn't speak, glancing at her pa.

'Miss Glossop?'

'She came in last February, when it was sleeting. My father was gone to the bank. I looked back, the name and street are the same.' Taking the ledger, she flicked through the earlier pages, showing him the entry.

'Thank you. You have a good memory, miss. You must see many customers. Have you particular cause to remember this woman?'

'She brought in a skirt. Afterwards, I found she'd overlooked a handkerchief in the concealed pocket. Best cambric, lace-edged and embroidered with violets.' Her voice was faltering. 'It was so pretty, I kept it for myself.'

'She knows better now,' said the pawn-broker. 'Only fessed up earlier. If the skirt weren't redeemed, that wipe was mine. Serves you right, girl, if these two run you in for thieving.'

'My only interest is in the woman,' said Abbs. Lucy gave him a grateful look. 'Did she claim her skirt, Miss Glossop?'

'She never came for it. I think she just wanted the money. It was a good skirt, grey merino. It went quickly.'

'Better than her own attire?'

'A good deal. Plain, but you can always tell quality.'

'Could she be a ladies' maid, with an old garment belonging to her mistress, d'you think?'

Lucy shook her head. 'She wasn't dressed well enough. A ladies' maid wouldn't miss the handkerchief.'

A well-reasoned point. Ladies' maids and companions were sometimes given their mistresses' old clothes to wear or sell. But it would be second nature for them to check pockets.

'Did this woman wear spectacles?'

'Not that I saw.'

'What was her accent like?'

'Ordinary. Not quality.'

'My thanks, Miss Glossop. Your impressions are most useful.'

She smiled faintly. 'The handkerchief was embroidered L in one corner. I didn't think it would hurt if I kept it.'

'Why didn't you tell me, then?' said Glossop. His reasonable tone made it all the more shocking when his hand flicked out, catching Lucy a hard blow beside her eye.

~

'Best sit inside, Latham, lest that gets dropped on the stair.'

'F'you say so, sir. I'll go with the old men.'

Abbs could feel the younger man's impatience, coming off him like steam from a bake-house. He sounded finicky to himself, but the bumping and swaying on the knife-board was no seat for clutching valuable porcelain, nor the steep climb up the iron stair. The piece was the property of Miss Maitland and worth more than the Commissioner would care to reimburse from public funds. Especially when he was meant to be off the case.

'Ask Sergeant Hollins to send me word, if Glossop doesn't turn up to make his statement.'

Latham gave a satisfied grin. 'He'll do what he's told, sir, after the way you roasted him.'

'We shall see. My thanks for your assistance, Constable.'

Abbs watched him duck inside the lower deck of the omnibus, the figurine parcelled and tucked securely beneath his arm. Latham had been wide-eyed at his outburst. Despite his blistering rebuke to the pawn-broker, he'd just about held a grip on his tongue. Knowing that afterwards, Glossop might make his daughter suffer the more. Doubtless, he'd shortly be the talk of Kennington police-station.

Angry as he was at seeing the girl struck, he knew he'd unleashed his frustration with Townsend on the loathsome pawn-broker. As the passengers climbed aboard, he consulted his pocket-watch, gave a last look to Long-lane and set off for the river.

The Yard was a good distance from Bermondsey. He could cross the river at London Bridge, via a dog-leg maze of streets. But the way, as the crow flies, was by means of the Tower Subway beneath the Thames. Not over-keen on confined spaces below ground, he understood Dr. Prentice's dislike of working in a basement. Nevertheless, he was determined to venture through and broaden his knowledge of the Metropolis.

How was he to find the woman at the pawn-brokers'? That was the question preoccupying him as he walked briskly northwards, guided by the masts soon visible at street-ends and the banshee-wails of whirling gulls.

They'd attempted to pick up her trail, inquiring of a newspaper-seller and a girl hawking whelks by Valentine-place. The cabbies, at the nearby stand, might have seen her pass by. They'd done their best to be helpful, to no avail. The assistants at the pastry-cook's, by the omnibus-stop, could not pick out one woman, even if they'd served her.

The pawn-broker was right about the anonymity of a lower-class woman of middling years. With no bright attire, in the new, gaudy dyes, to make her memorable, no one would see her among the crowded streets.

For the present, it seemed there was nothing else he could do. And yet, thought Abbs, as he reached the river-bank, something was nagging at him. Some scrap of information, he'd had from the

Glossops, had reminded him of something. What that memory was, he couldn't grasp, try as he might. The only thing to do, when this happened, was to stop probing. He knew from long experience that the thought would surface, like a splinter, in its own time.

He was determined to solve the case, himself. Not for his own worth, because somewhere under this lowering sky, dwelt a murderer. Someone who might feel safer as the days went by. Someone who might find a need to kill again. Every detective knew, once that terrible Rubicon had been crossed, the second time was easier.

He arrived at the pungently named Pickle Herring stairs. Paying his half-penny at the booth, he descended down a well-lit, spiral staircase, finding himself in a dim, cast-iron tunnel stretching straight ahead, the way out unseen.

The footway was busy at the end of the afternoon. How unsettling it must be when empty, but for oneself. A row of gas-lights, spread at intervals, did little to dispel the gloom. The thought of all that water, and boats passing overhead, was disconcerting. But narrow as this was, he preferred being on his feet to the sensation of the underground-railway, where he'd rarely ventured.

Where did the unknown woman fit in? The simplest answer was she had nothing to do with Rowland Ellis's death. His murderer had thrown away the figurine and she had found it. In that case, did she also have the miniatures?

Their footfalls echoed with a metallic clang. The voices of the people coming towards him sounded hollow. Shadows moved, huge on the rounded walls. There were two other possibilities. She was the murderer, or an accomplice. Much hinged on whether the skirt had ever belonged to Louisa Maitland. Many women's names began with the letter L.

He discounted Bertha for her youth. In theory, Miss Maitland, Maggie or Mrs Wilmot could fit the vague description. Not Maggie, he thought, for she wore spectacles. She had a habit of pushing them higher and he'd noticed the pink groove they left on the bridge of her nose.

There was Hester Ibbotson and Jessie Dove, all the women were much of an age. One fact he knew, thanks to Lucy Glossop. The woman pawned the skirt in February and never redeemed it. She'd been in want of money.

That might indicate a servant, but he couldn't rule out any of the women. Maybe Miss Maitland had run out of savings from her governess's salary. Mrs Ibbotson and Mrs Dove would only have pin-money from their husbands. He could feel a draught of air now and hear footfalls on the end stair.

As he ascended in turn, coming out in cool daylight, he thought of the clothing, collected by the ladies at the Institute, for the deserving poor. He needed to pay another visit to Lindholm.

THIRTY-TWO

The air was still chilly for April. Sparrows, flitting in and out of the hedges, were the surest sign of spring, as Abbs walked through the residential avenues of Kennington. It wouldn't do to turn up too early. He'd managed to time his arrival for mid-morning, once again passing the butcher's boy, calling with the orders he'd collected after breakfast.

No one came to the door at Lindholm, so he ventured through the tradesman's gate on the right-hand side. Across the small yard, where a rag-rug hung on the line, the door to the servants' quarters stood open. The linoleum in the passage had been mopped. Wiping his boots, Abbs stepped in and knocked on the kitchen door. Mrs Wilmot's voice bade him come in.

The cook was tying the strings of a clean holland apron over her black bombazine. The one she'd taken off was thrown over a chair-back.

'Oh, it's you, Inspector. You gave me a turn. I thought it was the boy with the veg. Was that you at the front door? I was on my way.'

Bertha was poised with a knife in her hand. A decapitated rabbit lay on the table before her. A basin held a lump of glistening flesh. Another brace lay to one side, still intact and strung together.

'It was, Mrs Wilmot. I was hoping to see Miss Maitland.'

'You've had a wasted journey. There's only we two here. The mistress won't be back for a good while. She's gone to Oxford-street and taken Maggie with her.'

'Was Miss Maitland there yesterday? I was that way, myself, and thought I glimpsed her.'

'Wasn't her. The mistress hasn't stirred all week until today. I told her the fog'll be in by mid-afternoon, but they set off early. It's not like she can't afford a cab. Cup of tea? It's fresh made.'

Thanking her, Abbs watched her pour, then took his cup and saucer to lean against the dresser, well out of the way.

Hands now on hips, the cook frowned at Bertha. 'Not like that, girl. Give me patience, I've just shown you. Gently or you'll spoil it. Fur's worth money, but not if it's hacked to bits.'

'I'm trying, Cook.'

Abbs watched as Bertha inserted the point of the knife and

continued to cut. A smeared chopper had been used to take off the head.

'Take the weight off your feet, Inspector.'

'I won't, thank you, Mrs Wilmot. I can see you're busy.'

'Please yourself. Is there any news on who killed the master? I suppose you won't tell us if there is?'

'Inquiries are continuing.' He'd noticed how many Londoners asked a question they instantly answered themselves.

'What brings you here, then?'

'I wanted to ask about the clothing Miss Maitland helps to sort out, at the Institute. On the night Mr. Ellis was killed, I believe some was donated from this house?'

'That's right. The master finally let the last of Mrs Ellis's things go. He'd been parting with them bit by bit. Unhealthy I call it. Stale clothing won't keep the dead close. Only brings in the moths.'

She pressed her lips, as if thinking of her own dead. Bertha made a clatter putting down the knife. Inserting her hands in the rent fur, she tugged.

'Keep going, put your back into it or you'll be there all night. Do it right and it'll come away, easy as shelling peas.'

Abbs looked away from the slippery flesh. The sound of tearing was like attending a post-mortem. He wondered why hearing could be worse than seeing.

'Did Miss Maitland donate any of her own things?'

The cook shook her head. 'She didn't have much to wear. That's why she's gone up west.'

'I see.' He thought he was beginning to.

'The master said she might go through the linen-cupboard. She found some old towels and a pair of sheets on the thin side. The poor can do sides to middle, years of wear in them. The only things the mistress ever donated were what she wore as governess, that was after twelfth night. Good quality when they were new, but serviceable. Plenty of wear left in them for someone, mind.'

'Miss Maitland knew she wouldn't need them again?'

'That's what I said at the time. The master might have sent her on her way. Didn't I say that very thing, Bertha? That was Mrs Ibbotson's doing. She talked her into getting rid of them.'

Bertha cursed, putting her finger to her mouth.

'What did I tell you, you clumsy girl.' Mrs Wilmot darted round the table and seized her by the wrist. 'Away with you, before you drip on the fur.'

'It ain't my fault. The knife slipped.'

'Go and put it under the tap. Quickly.'

Taking her place as the girl fled, the cook stretched, pulled, sliced some clinging membranes and lifted out the carcass. Dangling it on the board in one deft, continuous movement.

Returning to his side of the table, she wiped her hands on the discarded apron. The sound of running water stopped.

Bertha appeared in the doorway, holding out her hand. 'I can't find a clean rag.'

'No, and your nose lives on the end of your face. Don't s'pose you can find that either. Use your hankie.'

'Allow me.' Abbs offered his own.

Mrs Wilmot gave it an appraising glance. 'No, shame to spoil it. That's fine work.'

'My sister's.'

The cook fished in Bertha's apron pocket, produced a crumpled handkerchief and tied it on her finger.'

'Ow, that's too tight.'

'Has to be. Don't make a fuss. It's nothing, but small cuts can bleed freely. Thank the Inspector, then.' She gave the girl a small push, her manner not unkind.

'Thank you, all the same, sir.'

Abbs smiled at her. 'Do the poor get given handkerchiefs too?' He sipped his tea, his manner careless.

'Course not,' said Mrs Wilmot. 'Rags is one thing they're not short of. The ones I see use their sleeve. Mind you, the mistress lost a handkerchief a while back. Maggie looked everywhere, but never did find it. That might have gone in a charity-bundle by mistake, she reckoned. I say the laundress had it. Took a fancy to it or sold it. She denied it, but then she would.'

'Thank you, Mrs Wilmot. That was very welcome.' Abbs replaced his cup on the tray. 'I suppose small things might easily be mislaid in the laundry. Did it matter?'

'I said that an' all, but it was one of a set Mrs Ibbotson gave her for Christmas. The mistress didn't want to give offence. Lace-edged it

164

was, worked all over with violets. Mrs Ibbotson often wears them.'

'Her daughter's called Violet,' said Bertha. 'I like the primrose one best.'

'I've told you before,' said Mrs Wilmot, 'it's no use you mooning over pretty things.'

Perched on the edge of a stool, the girl scowled. Her colour was deathly pale.

~

While he was in the kitchen, a hand-cart had appeared on the carriage-drive. The wicket-gate, leading round past the study, now stood ajar. *Geo. Ruddock, Jobbing Gardener, of Forder Lane, Kennington* was evidently at work. On impulse, Abbs decided to have a word with him.

Rowland Ellis's study had changed again. Looking through the window, he saw the traces of its erstwhile owner were being stripped away. The cumbersome drawing-board was gone. The armchairs by the fire had been shifted. All accoutrements of writing were no longer on the desk-top. The ink-stand, he recalled, had gone with Henry Searle. The bookshelves had gaping holes, some volumes sideways to prop up the remainder.

The gardener was weeding a flower-border. Abbs relished the scent of damp, newly-turned earth. The figure in coarse, fustian breeches, and a battered waistcoat, straightened up, revealing a short, brawny fellow, younger than he expected.

Dragging off his cap, the gardener introduced himself in return. 'George Ruddock. Proper terrible what happened but I can't tell you nothing. This is my first time here since afore Christmas. Miss Maitland sent word I was to start back. None of them round here keep me on regular through winter. Not enough work.'

'What d'you turn your hand to?'

'Whatever jobs I can get. Some walling, carpentry, I put up that arbour for Mr. Ellis. Tree-work, selling logs. Main thing is to work all the hours I can through summer and put something by, to tide me over.'

Abbs nodded. So many people needed more than one job to survive, he knew he was fortunate. He admired the arbour.

'Mrs Ellis loved her roses.'

'You've been coming here some time?'

'Must be five years.'

'Did you like Mr. Ellis?'

Ruddock considered, rubbing his hair, which was already thinning. 'He always paid promptly, which you can't say for all of them. A real demon for tidiness. Everything had to be just so. Paths swept, briars all tied in. Nothing allowed to seed where it felt like it. Nature doesn't always want to be neat.'

'No, indeed.'

'He let me have the logs from the copper beech there.' He pointed to the broad tree stump, near the edge of the lawn. 'That was good of him. Had to get a mate in to help me chop it down. And his horse and cart to take it all away. There was a right to-do about that having to come down, I can tell you.'

'A pity to lose an old tree. I can see it must have been a size. Was it dying?'

'No, it was old, but perfectly sound. A real beauty. Mr. Ellis wanted it down. He would have it the roots were too near the house. Couldn't see it myself.'

'I suppose an architect would be cautious.' Looking back, it seemed to Abbs the tree would have been sufficient distance from the foundations. They were near the wall dividing the garden from the stable.

'It was Miss Maitland made all the fuss. Pleading with him 'bout how long the tree'd been there. I kept my head down. Pretended I didn't hear. One time, I heard her raging to the maid about Mr. Ellis. I'd never have thought a lady like her had such a temper. She was spittin' feathers.'

Abbs raised his eyebrows. 'What was she saying?'

'That Mr. Ellis was making an excuse to justify killing the tree. He wanted it gone 'cause he hated the leaves going everywhere. An' he couldn't do it when Mrs Ellis was alive. God rest her soul.'

'D'you think she was right?'

'I couldn't say. It's true he didn't like fallen leaves on the paths or the lawns. Not even on the borders. Like I say, he would have every last one swept up and they blew everywhere. Kept me busy all autumn.'

'Mr. Ellis had his way about the tree,' said Abbs thoughtfully.

'Oh, he always had his way. I learnt not to make any suggestions, just do his bidding. Fair enough, it was his garden. He was a decent old cove. Poor devil, whoever would have thought he'd be murdered?'

'Allow me to top up your glass. You look, if I may say, to be a man sorely in need of rest.'

Abbs thanked him as Mr. Snow leant forward with his decanter. He sat up himself, pushing his flop of hair from his aching brow. 'It's been a long day. This is uncommonly good of you.'

'By no means. I'm glad we find ourselves in sympathy, as fellow-tenants of the good-hearted Mrs Newsome. Take your ease, sir.'

He'd done his neighbour an injustice. Mr. Snow's company was proving unexpectedly stimulating. They'd conversed freely on subjects as diverse as the recent election, the dreadful news of the Cheshire pit disaster and the merits of favourite novels. Now, a natural lull had fallen. Mr. Snow had the happy art of sitting in a comfortable silence.

Returning the decanter to its twin in the tantalus, his neighbour strolled over to the far window and looked out. The generously proportioned room mirrored his own quarters directly below, overlooking Gloucester-road, with the bedroom behind.

'The fog's worse than ever. Traffic's slowed to walking pace.'

'There seems no logic to it. I can't tell foretell foggy weather, if it will clear by morning or last for days. My sergeant says I'll get a feel for it, when I've been here longer.'

'In short, my dear sir, you'll learn to detect small signs in the elements. Where would we Englishmen be without the weather to remark upon? It is how strangers signal cordiality when travelling in a railway-carriage, if you'll excuse my pun.'

He had a curious way of seeming to put a flourish on some of his remarks, much as he did when he bowed. A declaiming actor's voice with a rich timbre. It reminded him of another voice with a remarkable range, that of Mr. Silas Dove.

'I hazard a guess this will blow away by the morrow. In the meantime, it's no night to be out.' Adjusting the curtains, Mr. Snow then added a shovel of coal to the fire, before resuming his chair.

'We're certainly snug in here.'

'To return to Mr. Dickens, it is a night fit for one of his ghostly tales.' The damper rattled as new flames leapt towards the chimney.

'Do you believe in ghosts?' said Abbs, on impulse.

'What makes you ask, I wonder? Your question seems to have a particular emphasis.'

'I recently met someone who styles himself a spirit-medium.'

'In connection with your work?'

He nodded, reluctant to say more.

'Ah, then I won't inquire further. As to answering your question...' To his surprise, Mr. Snow did not at once continue. Adopting a pensive air, he set his glass in the hearth.

'All theatrical folk are aware of unworldly spirits, my dear sir. Perhaps our calling requires us to be attuned to feeling. We're more sensitive to atmosphere than most.'

Abbs examined his companion's face for any glint of amusement. The dark eyes, beneath arched brows, were perfectly sincere.

'I know actors are said to be superstitious. Don't you always say *the Scottish play* instead of Ma...' He broke off as Mr. Snow held up a hand, half-rising.

'Do not say it, I beg of you.'

'I beg your pardon.' He managed to remain grave-faced.

'You are quite correct, Mr. Abbs. That name is best left unsaid.'

'How do you manage when putting on that play?'

'To use the name when rehearsing demands it, is supposedly permissible. But it is not to be said idly, even within a theatre, lest it invoke misfortune. Like most of my number, I prefer to take no chances.'

'I shall remember that, Mr. Snow. From whence does the custom originate?'

'The play in question is said to have a curse upon it. Unlucky since its first performance, in 1606, if I remember aright. I, myself, have played a ghost in the Scottish play in several runs over the years. The shade of Banquo. You'll no doubt recall.'

'Oh, indeed,' said Abbs hurriedly. He hoped Mr. Snow didn't expect him to know of a specific performance. 'But who first spoke of a curse? Is there more to the story?'

'Ah, the keen questions of a detective. You will not be put off. It has been passed down that Shakespeare used fragments of real spells in his speeches written for the witches. Supposedly, real witches, of the time, took exception to this. Some of their number laid a curse on the play which holds to this day, with the caveats I mentioned.'

'An intriguing legend. At the risk of sounding tedious, is there any evidence of the curse?'

'The first actor cast as the Lady is said to have died before the opening night and Shakespeare, himself, took his place. There have been numerous instances of accidents and misfortune in companies staging the play. Too many to be coincidence. I can testify to more than one.'

'I can understand actors are superstitious, when their livelihood depends on successful plays,' said Abbs, 'but ghosts are another matter.'

Mr. Snow looked into the flames, as if scrying through his own past. 'I've never worked in an old theatre that did not have its lingering shade. The play-houses, of the last century, seem to have the past imprinted in their very walls and drapery. A dressing-room, when it's quiet, without the laughter and squabbles of the other players, can be an eerie place. Easy to feel you're being watched from the shadows beyond the lamp. Many a player has heard footsteps behind the flats, when they're last to leave and the stage-doorman swears he's never left his cubby-hole.'

'Forgive me, I mean no offence, but would not actors be susceptible to their imagination?'

His companion smiled at him. 'No offence taken, sir. Imagination is both a blessing and a curse. You would have to be there, Mr. Abbs. There are many accounts of theatricals being alone on stage, sensing a presence watching from the front of house. It might be from a box or the empty stalls. Not only actors, it happens to visitors and stage-hands setting out props. Some productions are beset by accidents. Some old theatres have a malign feeling to them. Others seem to welcome us with benevolent arms.'

'What about new theatres? They seem to be opening all over the place.'

'The new play-houses I've worked in are quite devoid of atmosphere. It seems to me, these strange happenings take time to come forth.'

Abbs wondered why Louisa Maitland would make a great fuss about a tree. When she was, by her own admission, anxious to be self-effacing and little trouble to Rowland Ellis. As he pondered, sipping his port, he heard more tales of theatre hauntings, an actor-manager who hanged himself in a dressing-room, a deadly fall from the flies.

Most horrifying, was the story Mr. Snow told of the Scottish play put on many years ago, in Gloucester. About an actress who caught her costume in the limelight. He was one of those who came running in answer to her screams. The flames quickly smothered, she died of burns two days later. Truly, the stuff of nightmares.

THIRTY-FOUR

Abbs blotted his initials and placed the report on the tray. Then set about tidying his desk, returning the *Blue Book* to its place behind him. His shelf was no longer bare, holding a sheaf of other London directories, last month's *Bradshaw* and the latest *Police Gazette*. Outside, the daily sounds of the Metropolis were becoming familiar, scarcely noticed as he worked. He realised the mournful fog-horn, sounding at intervals throughout the forenoon, had stilled. Stretching, his thoughts returned to the Ellis murder.

He'd had a feeling the handkerchief belonged to Louisa Maitland. But she wasn't the woman at the pawn-broker's. It looked as though the woman had been given the skirt from charity, sometime in January, when Miss Maitland donated her work-attire. In February, the unknown woman had pawned it in Bermondsey, giving a false address. She probably lived in the poorer part of Kennington or Lambeth, the area where the charity parcels were given out.

He was inclined to think the woman had found the figurine, discarded by the murderer. Even so, they needed to find her. The truth about Ellis's death would only emerge when they'd cleared everything confusing out of the way.

Frowning, Abbs groped for whatever was nagging at his memory. There was a connection he hadn't made. Soon, he must report to Townsend, explaining why he'd ignored his orders. No use feeling settled in his room at the Yard. One slip and he'd be on the Great Eastern to his sister's, his possessions packed in a trunk.

Someone knocked. At once, the knob rattled and Grainer backed in, gingerly bearing a tray. 'Cup o' tea, sir? Thought you might be ready.'

'I am, indeed, thank you.'

Grainer was on his best behaviour since their interview with Townsend, showing an unspoken sympathy. They had, after all, a shared grievance at being taken off the case. Maybe Grainer cared more about his work than he'd given him credit for. Abbs considered telling him he'd continued to investigate. It would be useful to talk over what he'd found out, but hardly fair to involve his sergeant.

'Starting to clear outside. Just as well. They found a corpse washed up by Blackfriars Bridge earlier. Two fell in Regent's Canal last night.'

Grainer blew on his tea and gulped some down. 'Dead-rooms'll be full again.' Said with a gloomy relish.

A sobering thought, how many people were injured or killed in the fog. Collisions were common, people knocked down, even with horse-traffic at walking pace. But the greatest danger, he'd soon learned, was drowning. Simply running out of the unseen street. A step into air, terror, a splash, threshing, cold, choking...

Abbs eyed Grainer thoughtfully. He always seemed to know what was going on. Scraps gleaned from the sergeants'-room, his acquaintance on the streets, no doubt, and the public bar of the Clarence.

'Have you heard anything of how Sergeant Hollins is faring?'

He looked up in surprise. 'No, sir. Not our pigeon now, is it?'

'Frustrating, is it not? A murderer's still on the streets.'

'To my mind, there's no sense fretting, sir. The Chief Inspector makes the decisions. He moves the rest of us around as he sees fit. Me more'n most.'

Inspector Sheppard's remarks came back to him. "Nobody wants to be landed with Grainer. He's a cross we all have to bear, periodically. Townsend shuffles him round to cover leave and sickness. Mostly he works with Cole, who treads on anyone lower rank."

Abbs felt a twinge of shame. He was as keen as his colleagues to rid himself of Grainer, but who knew how life had sapped his enthusiasm? To get made up to sergeant, he must have been alert and dedicated once. Maybe he'd be the same in twenty years.

'Tell you what I did hear, sir. That Dove fellow, the medium, he gave a public performance in Kennington the other night. Supposed to have made an apparition appear. Daft women nearly pissing themselves, you know how they love being frightened. He's made now, they'll be queueing in droves. Course, it's all gammon, but they say he's trickier than most of his kind.'

He should have questioned Silas Dove and his wife, in a proper manner, instead of making a fool of himself at a séance. Jessie Dove had made no reaction to Rowland Ellis's name but there'd been something in her eyes, for an instant. Recognition was hard to hide.

~

The fog had thinned sufficiently, by early afternoon, to journey through the streets without mishap. The air was hung with a gauze-like mist which dulled the edges, giving the streets the appearance of being beneath the glass roof of a railway-terminus, with the engines steaming. Hard outlines of buildings and carriages were smudged, a statue loomed wraith-like on its stone plinth, and the horses exhaled their warm, visible breath, adding to the vapour.

The pavements smelt of damp, hot meat and fried fish. Root-sellers were hawking primroses, their delicate bouquets dug up entire and carted in from the country. A weak sunlight was attempting to pierce the mist and the temperature had risen. There seemed more vigour in the crowds, a haze of greenery between the grey, a hoarse cheeriness about the newspaper-sellers. That indefinable sense that spring was asserting itself over winter.

May-day was now nearer than March. With any luck, they might soon shake off the long months of cold and murk for the annual sweeps' holiday, blossom and clear skies. Abbs looked forward to the return of the cherry-girls and his first summer in London.

As he turned into Gannon-street, it was at once apparent something was going on down the far end. A maid, holding a duster, was craning her neck from a front garden. Further along, a rag and bottle man had left his hand-cart askew on the pavement, sacks spilling over. Collecting bones from a woman at her gate, he was pointing along the terrace. Over the road, another woman was at her upper window, lace curtain edged back. A sense of foreboding took him.

A growler was waiting near the corner, a bunch of men, in worsted suits and waistcoats, were milling around. He took in the notebooks, their lively air, the faces turned to one door. They were watching the spiritualists' house.

The front door was shut. As he reached them, Abbs saw that, in daylight, the paint-work of number four was dull maroon, in need of freshening. The small diamond of flower-bed was trodden with boot-prints, by the tiled path.

'What's happened?' He addressed the nearest fellow, whose checked jacket reeked of tobacco.

'Word is, it's murder. The bogeys are inside but they won't tell us nothing. You live along here?'

Abbs didn't answer, as he caught sight of a man talking to the cabby.

The Indian from the séance inclined his head in recognition, he looked faintly amused. Hemmed in, Abbs was about to move towards him when the door opened.

A youngish, plain-clothes man came down the short path, as the others surged closer to the gate. His billycock crammed on short, curly hair, not a great deal over regulation height, he addressed them confidently.

'On your way, all of you. There's nothing to see here. The inspector wants this area cleared. Apply to the station-house later. They'll give you what you're after.'

'Have a heart,' said one of the men, mining his ear with his pencil. 'We'll miss the evening edition. Blimey, we're stood on the spot. We can't go back with nothing.'

'Who's in charge?' came a voice from the back.

'Inspector Cole.'

Someone groaned. A bearded man called out. 'Why's the Yard been summoned? Is it murder? Give us something to go on for gawd's sake.' A chorus added to this appeal.

'All right, all right.' Grinning, the detective held up his hand for silence. 'A woman's been found dead. Might be manslaughter. That's all I can tell you now.'

'You can't give us half a tale. How was it done?' Called a young fellow, scarcely whiskered.

'Her old man did it,' said another, to a round of laughter. 'He was provoked.'

Abbs watched as the detective officer suddenly noticed him. Improving his posture, his face wiped of humour.

'There's nothing funny about death.' He raised his voice. 'That's it for now. Be off with the lot of you.'

'Bleedin' crumbs. We was told murder.'

The journalists reluctantly did as they were told, moving off in consultation. When Abbs looked again, the Indian had vanished. A few paused, looking back towards the other houses.

'And don't bother the neighbours,' called the detective. 'They can't help you. Hook it.' He watched them out of sight, before nodding to Abbs and throwing open the gate. If he was surprised, he didn't show it. 'Good to see you again, sir.'

'How are you, Sergeant Reeve?' said Abbs.

THIRTY-FIVE

The front door opened again, a tall, burly figure filling the doorway.

'I see we have a visitor. Don't stand on ceremony, Sergeant. Show the Inspector in.'

Reeve threw him an apologetic look as Abbs entered the hall. Both doors were open. On the left, he glimpsed a parlour, with a gate-leg table, before following Inspector Cole in the room where the séance took place.

'Bad news travels faster than good. This what you come to see, Inspector?' Jabez Cole waved an arm at the fireplace, his eyes watchful.

The body of Mrs Dove was sprawled on the carpet, a creased, saxe-blue dress, one slipper fallen off. The dead eyes were open. Dr. Prentice rose from his knees, his open bag by his feet. He wiped his hands on a cloth. It flashed across Abbs's mind irrelevantly, that the doctor was performing the same action when they met.

'Good day, Abbs. Nasty head wound, poor creature.'

Abbs looked from the gash on her temple to the smears of dried blood on the corner of the hearth. Saw again his crushed eggshells at breakfast.

Cole stood before the window, blocking much of the light. His broad-shouldered shape put Abbs in mind of a playing-card. The rug, in the middle of the floor, was rumpled. A few tiny specks among the threads appeared to be glinting.

Acknowledging the police-surgeon, Abbs answered Inspector Cole. 'I didn't know until I saw the commotion outside. It was obvious something was badly wrong.'

'Kennington tossed it to us like a red-hot spud. I hear they already have their hands full with a dead architect.'

He looked evenly at Cole. The corners of his mouth were turned up, though his colleague couldn't be said to be smiling. 'Where is Silas Dove?'

The inspector shrugged. 'The spirit-botherer? Where would you be? Scarpered. Just happened to be passing, were you, Inspector?'

'I came to speak to the Doves. The architect, in question, had some connection with them.'

Cole's thick eyebrows drew together. 'A little bird told me that wasn't your concern any longer. I must have been misinformed.'

Abbs was aware of Reeve in the corner behind him, his jaw set. Dr. Prentice was studying the corpse. A footfall sounded in the passage. He looked round as a uniformed constable appeared in the doorway.

'Well?'

'Nothing out of the ordinary, sir. The alley's hard-surfaced, no footprints. I secured the gate.'

'The way the fog was last eve,' said Cole, 'a parade of Astley's stallions could have ridden in the front and none would have seen 'em. But I favour the husband.'

'Who discovered the body?' said Abbs.

'Char-woman. No one let her in so after knocking for a bit, the old dame went round the alley. Claims the gate and back door were unlocked. You had a job to stop her snivelling long enough to tell her tale, eh, Doc?'

'She'd had a shock,' said Prentice. 'Not everyone is as inured to bodies as you, Inspector.'

'Likewise your good self. Where's this van of yours got to?'

'Caught up in 'traffic, I would assume. Do you need me any longer? If not, I won't wait. The attendants know their business.'

'Hold your horses, Doc. What we all want to know, even the Constable and Sergeant here, is did she trip or was she shoved on her way?'

'I can tell no more than you. You may never know without a confession. She was being attacked, there are clear indications.' Prentice's voice lost its stiffness as he slipped into his professional manner. 'You see the bruising at her jaw.' He included Abbs, who stepped closer to view the cold flesh. 'There may be bruising on the arms when I have her on the table. Regard the...'

'The Inspector here doesn't need to know.' Cole spoke over him. 'Whether her old man was just giving her what for and she fell, or whether he meant to throttle her, it comes to the same thing. He'll swing for her, either way. I could find it in my heart to pity him, if she goaded him too far. A woman's tongue can be sharper than a razor. We all know that. Not Mrs Cole, mind, don't think that for an instant. We are in harmony, like two bees making honey.'

'I hope I can enlighten you in due course, Inspector. I can examine the body at four. Will you be attending?'

The police-surgeon addressed the wall-paper beyond Inspector Cole's ear. Abbs thought he looked pallid.

'I'll be there. You can lay on the tea and toast after, Doctor. Now then, gentlemen, some of us have work to do. This is my pigeon, Abbs, so I won't keep you.' He turned, the tweed folds of his ulster swinging. 'Don't idle there, lad. Get next door. See if the neighbours heard any row.'

'Sir.' The constable left smartly.

'As for you, Reeve, talking of idle, time you earned your keep. Dr. Prentice will be wanting a cab. Go and find him one, if it won't tax your wits. I'll sure the good doctor here will give you a lift, Abbs.'

Townsend listened to his account in impassive silence. His mood was usually easy to read, but the shutters could come down. This was one of those times. The ticking of the mantle clock seemed ominous as the seconds stretched out. The drumming fingers were irritating, but no outburst came.

Abbs waited, his future wavering in the balance. In the circumstances, he had no choice other than to relate his unauthorised activities. They said confession was good for the soul. He hoped it wouldn't prove his last act at Scotland Yard.

'You actually attended this séance. And saw fit not to include this in your report.'

'I did, sir. It was in my own time.'

'No such thing, Inspector, when you're in the midst of an inquiry.'

'No, sir.'

'You discussed this with Grainer.'

Abbs nodded. They weren't questions. Townsend did not sound surprised. He supposed his superior had heard most things across his desk. You didn't get to be a detective of senior rank and be easily disconcerted.

'You've shown a modicum of sense in coming to me now, albeit belatedly. You'll be interested to learn, no doubt, that I've known of your exploit all along.'

He understood instantly. Townsend saw that he did.

'Sergeant Grainer is of an unfortunately garrulous disposition. He is accustomed to relaying all he hears to Inspector Cole. A good detective might be expected to discover this for himself.'

Abbs winced inwardly at a formidable hit. He was learning as much about Townsend as Grainer. His superior was right, of course. He should have realised.

'The rest, I did not know. Presumably, you did not disclose your irregular inquiries to Grainer. From now on, Inspector, I require your reports to detail all your investigations. Not an abridged version you think will suffice for me.'

'Understood, sir.'

'Using your own judgement will not extend to defying my explicit instructions. When I give an order, I expect to be obeyed fully and without question. Do I make myself clear?'

'You do, sir.'

'Good. And, as far as possible, keep Mottram informed of your whereabouts. All of you are lax in that respect.'

'I'll do that, sir.'

'At least, you weren't wasting police time. I don't deny you've furthered the inquiry.' Townsend sighed heavily. 'There are several thorns in my side, Abbs. I should prefer you not to be one more.'

'That wasn't my intention, sir.'

'I believe you, but I won't have insubordination. I, too, have to answer to those above me.'

'Yes, sir.'

'Then we'll consider the matter closed. Tell me, do you smoke a cigar?'

Smoking held no attraction for him, but in the interest of diplomacy. 'Rarely, sir.'

'Well, indulge yourself now, man. You look as though you could do with one.' Pushing a carved box towards him, Townsend rose and went to the mantel-shelf.

A minute or two later, they sat in silence until Townsend's pipe was drawing to his satisfaction. A scattering of spent matches filled the ash-tray. The mingled scents of tobacco filled the air about the desk.

'That's better.' Townsend exhaled a stream of smoke. 'Now, you don't strike me as credulous. You don't believe any of this poppycock about raising the dead, do you?'

'Certainly not, sir. I wish more could be done to protect those who do.'

'Quite so. We get convictions for taking money by fraudulent means, but they achieve little. A fine they can easily afford, a few lines in the press. These vultures move elsewhere, change names and begin anew. I'd see more of them gaoled for a first offence.'

'I agree, sir. I can think of no other instance where fraud is ambiguous to prove. Where victims are anxious to assist in their own entrapment. They may even bear witness for those who duped them.'

'Hmm. What's more, the whole business is so damnably popular. It shows no sign of ever going away. I blame these meddling pseudo-scientists. Some friends of Mrs Townsend proposed to attend a private demonstration. She wished to accompany them. I forbade her to have anything to do with it. Good grief, I'd sooner she went to a penny-gaff.'

Abbs examined his cigar, which was of the cheaper sort, kept, presumably, for visitors. Their discussion having gone better than he hoped, it seemed wise to remain silent.

Townsend glanced at the clock, as though an invisible Mrs T. might be reminding him of the hour left before dinner. Abbs knew for a fact, having made certain, he was the last to report.

'Inspector Cole is not best pleased. I sent him to look into Mrs Dove's death. He feels you're poaching on his preserves, as it were. What say you, Abbs?'

'I feel, sir, that Mrs Dove's death must be connected in some way to Rowland Ellis. It's too much coincidence.'

'Inspector Cole is sure her husband is responsible. He may well be right. You seem to have a dislike of the simplest answer. Do you believe Dove murdered Ellis?'

'I don't know, sir. He is the most likely suspect for his wife's death but I don't feel we should take that for granted.'

'We'll know when we find him. It would be naive to think an innocent man would have stayed put to face us. This is my decision. Inspector Cole will remain in charge of Mrs Dove's death and the search for her absconded husband.'

'Sir.'

'We now have a good idea of when Mrs Dove died. Apparently, there are signs of hasty packing at the house. A cabman has been found who knew Dove by sight. He took him to Charing Cross that evening. Thinks it was about five and twenty past eight when he dropped him off. The booking-clerks don't recall a man answering Dove's description, but the trains were still busy.'

'Making for a Channel port?'

'Precisely. Fortuitously, much of the Kent coast is fog-bound and the Dover steamers aren't expected to make their early crossing. Cole and Sergeant Reeve are on their way to Folkestone tonight.'

His drink with Reeve must be postponed, then. Abbs felt his words with caution. 'And the Ellis inquiry, sir?'

'This second death does put a different complexion on matters. Too complicated for the division.'

'I believe it would pay to investigate the suspects further, sir, while

Sergeant Hollins concentrates on house-breakers.'

Townsend drew on his pipe. 'What about this woman who pawned the skirt? Miss Maitland might be able to tell you who received the garment. It seems to me, this female may be an accomplice.'

'Then may I question Miss Maitland again, sir?'

'I suppose it's an improvement that you ask.' He examined the bowl of smouldering tobacco. 'She has to be the chief suspect for the obvious reason. And you've discovered the lady has a considerable temper. Did I not say, it's likely all about money?'

'You did, sir.'

'Everything in this city comes down to money, Abbs. How many detectives our betters in parliament will allow us, the street-walkers hawking their bodies. God save us, even infants can be bought. Only the rich need never think of money. They do, I suppose, they rarely seem to feel they have sufficient.'

'Indeed, sir. We have three suspects who benefited financially from Mr. Ellis's death. I should like to take a closer look at the architect's practice.'

'Something fishy in the books, eh? You're a persistent fellow, Abbs. Very well, you may resume your inquiries. Let us say another week. And remember my orders.'

'Thank you, sir. I will.'

'No officer wants an unsolved case on his record. Particularly, when he's newly joined us, so I'm minded to give you more rope.' Townsend pointed the stem of his pipe at him. 'Take heed, lest you hang yourself with it.'

'Understood, sir.'

'Ensure your inquiries don't conflict with Inspector Cole's. He'll be back on the morrow.'

'I'll bear that in mind.'

'That would be wise,' said Townsend drily. 'Predictably, none of the neighbours saw or heard anything.'

'The house, on one side, is to let, which doesn't help.'

'Nor the weather. It was closing in when I returned from luncheon. Fog is no friend to the detective-branch.'

'No, indeed.'

'I suppose you'll have to question the penny-a-liner, the half-caste, I mean.'

'You said you knew of him, sir?'

'His name's March, I believe. I can't tell you which scurrilous rag he scribbles for. You'll track him down in Fleet Street. Ask Sheppard, he knows most of them. Be careful. Journalists will twist anything you say for profit. Best not take Grainer.'

THIRTY-SEVEN

The fog was gone by the time Abbs left the Yard, on his way to the mortuary. Washed away by light, persistent rain, heavying the tweed on his shoulders. He did not mind the wet. He and Chief Inspector Townsend had come to some accommodation, by what means, he was unsure. Possibly, due to his superior's dislike of Inspector Cole. He'd have liked a free hand with Jessie Dove's death but, at least, he might continue with his own case.

For his part, he acquitted Townsend of rifling through his papers. Grainer had been away from the Yard, that left the possibility of Jabez Cole snooping. He didn't know how curious his colleague was, but he wouldn't put it past him.

Since his arrival, he'd had little to do with Inspector Cole. They'd been introduced in the inspectors'-room, where Cole had offered an iron hand-shake and a flint-eyed gaze, before turning his broad back. Until today, their paths had barely crossed since. He rather hoped the Kentish ports would keep Cole occupied for some time.

Horse-traffic clopped briskly, at intervals, along The West Strand. Dusk had fallen and carriage-lamps flared against the shadows, silhouetting the driver on his box. The shops were half-empty, rain streaking their plate-glass windows, gas-jets hissing, illuminating weary assistants and cheerful, blurred displays. Outside the Lowther arcade, a uniformed beadle was seeing off a shabby girl and boy, lingering at the gaily-painted toys.

The air reeked of soot and a fresh breeze from the river, carrying a hint of the sea, way down by the Essex marshes. Turning into Agar-street, shadowy figures were huddled in the recessed doorway of a shuttered post-office. Young ones breathing on the glass between them and happiness. Grown ones faring no better than a colony of hedge-sparrows. The discordant notes of tuning instruments blew from a nearby theatre.

Dr. Prentice was conversing with a porter at the hospital entrance. Seeing Abbs, he broke off and greeted him. 'Splendid. You had my message. I wasn't sure it would reach you this evening.'

'It was good of you, though I shouldn't be here.'

'There are one or two features... I thought you'd be interested.' Prentice led the way down to the dissection-room.

Yawning, he shrugged off his damp coat. 'Here we are again. Seems a long while since we left Kennington. I came up from Hades for air.' He indicated the body on the slab, draped in a much-laundered sheet. 'She's here.'

Removing his hat, Abbs noted the 'she'. Wondered if the police-surgeon was one of those doctors who felt over-much for their patients. If he was, Prentice would burn out too soon, like a poorly-strung candle. He had the gritty-eyed look of one who'd been up much of the night.

Prentice gently lowered the sheet, revealing the head and naked shoulders of the corpse of Jessie Dove. Freeing each arm in turn, he placed them at her sides.

Abbs studied the bruising on the side of her cheek and jaw. The pinched weals from finger-tips, not clear enough for him to judge, by size, whether the attacker was male or female. Her bare shoulders were like alabaster, retaining a softness long gone from her face.

'I'll just turn these down.' Prentice moved between the gas-jets. 'Now, watch this.' He indicated the right hand.

As Abbs looked, a few speckles glowed silver, shimmering in the dark. 'What is it?'

'Eerie, is it not? Like marsh gas.'

'Some kind of chemical?'

'Phosphorus.'

'Really? Then there was some on the rug. I caught the glint.'

'Spilt drops, probably, as I think this was. I only found them by chance, examining her hands through a magnifier. My own shadow was sufficient to give me a hint.'

'You're most thorough, Doctor.' Abbs waited while he turned up the light, releasing a head-achy trace of gas.

'Prentice, please. I always inspect the nails. They often have something to tell. I gathered the husband and wife claimed to be spirit-mediums. I'll wager they used phosphorus in their performance.'

'A woman, who'd attended their séances, told me they'd seen a disembodied glowing hand. She was utterly thrilled.'

Prentice nodded. 'People see what they want to see. Oil of phosphorus rubbed to the wrist. Like all conjuring tricks, nothing once you know how it was done.'

'Is this something they could readily buy?'

'Not from a druggist's. I dare say they'd extract it themselves by soaking matches. Invisible, so long as it's not in dim light. Heat gives a particular glow. If someone warmed their hands at the fire, for instance and slipped their treated hand in their pocket, they could produce it, in the dark, to remarkable effect.'

'Everything has a rational explanation?'

'I'd say so, but I'm no church-goer. The only miracles I see are when someone lives, I expected to die. And that's their constitution. Come, that's not all I have to show you. This corpse hid a further surprise.'

'Indeed?'

Prentice fetched an enamel dish from the shelf. 'Take a look at this.' His voice was grim. 'You can touch it without risk of infection. It's been washed in carbolic.'

Abbs peered at a small bell, of the sort found on a dog-collar. 'Where did you find this?' He looked at the surgeon, with a growing sense of dread.

'Lodged at the back of the poor woman's mouth.'

'That's horrible.'

'I think Inspector Cole was wrong. Whoever did this wasn't trying to throttle Mrs Dove, as he put it. The bruises are all wrong. Her throat is unblemished. They were shoving this in her mouth and holding it closed, until she swallowed.'

They were silent a moment. Abbs became aware of the rain on the window-light, high up at street-level. A gutter sounded blocked. Water was dripping down the outside wall. A pipe gurgled. He swallowed, his throat tight.

'You know,' said Prentice slowly, 'whoever did this must have hated her. Else, why do it?'

'I know what you mean.' Abbs considered his suspects. No one among them seemed capable of such an act. But he knew what canker could hide behind a mild face.

'They left behind a clue.' Returning to the shelf, Prentice handed him an unsealed envelope. 'Caught on a tooth.'

Abbs looked at the tiny thread of dark wool.

'Cole doesn't yet know about this, by the way. He was impatient to tell me my job and be off. I found these later.'

'He should be very grateful to you.'

Prentice made a sound indicative of disgust. 'He'll be dismissive, saying the husband was wearing gloves or mittens, and what of it?'

'He wouldn't be wearing gloves indoors,' said Abbs. 'Granted, it's a harsh April, but surely, not sufficiently cold for a man of Dove's age to wear mittens at home?'

'You don't know him, Abbs. Cole has an answer for everything. He'll say the husband came home and set about quarrelling with his wife, before he took off his hat and gloves.'

'Cole's gone to Kent, searching for him. It's thought Dove will try to flee the country but there's fog in the Channel. He might be trapped in one of the ports.'

'Let us hope the inspector's detained there. I pity his new sergeant. Cole has taken a dislike to him.'

'Sergeant Reeve can look after himself.'

'He's new to the Yard?'

Abbs nodded. 'I know him from the County Police at Exeter. He comes from London, but moved away in boyhood. He was keen to return. Reeve's an able detective.'

'Can we ever go back, though? It's the past men long for in a place, not the present.'

Curious, Abbs gave him a sideways look. 'You may be right.'

'There's one thing more about the body,' said Prentice abruptly. 'She didn't die from hitting her head on the hearth.'

'No? Then how?'

Fetching his long-handled glass, Prentice held it over the wound. 'Observe. There was a second blow, all but masked by the first. See that slight abrasion? That's the edge of a wound beneath this.' He shifted the lens. 'And here. Some hairs still caught up, but torn from the scalp.'

'Ruthless.' Abbs straightened up. 'She wasn't dead, so they made sure.'

'I'm certain of it. When Inspector Cole has someone in the dock, there'll be no passing this off as manslaughter. Jessie Dove was deliberately murdered.'

Abbs passed the razor carefully over his jaw. All the while, thinking about Jessie Dove's corpse, as he rhythmically scraped and flicked lather back in the basin. An early morning express sounded in the distance, pulling away from London. Down in the street, a dustman was ringing his bell, warning householders to close their windows.

Dr. Prentice agreed the finger bruises were too indistinct to discern the sex of the murderer. Jessie Dove had been a small woman, hardly up to his shoulder when she'd opened the door. Not inconceivable that a strong woman had subdued her. You weren't long a constable without seeing women fight like furious cats. Hair-dragging was a frequent means of injury.

The bell forced in her mouth was appalling. Prentice was right, surely the deed of someone who hated her? Her, or what she stood for? He wondered about someone cheated by a fake message from a dead, loved one. Would Silas Dove also be dead if he'd been at home?

Officially, Jessie Dove's death was none of his concern. He had a week to find the murderer of Rowland Ellis. What if there was simply no evidence to be found and he never managed to bring him or her to justice? Louisa Maitland or Hester Ibbotson could have slipped away from the Institute, killed Ellis and returned. Frederick or Ambrose Buckley might have left their home and returned, without the other knowing. They'd found no one who'd seen them.

Thomas Ibbotson was the closest to Lindholm. Although time was tight, he could conceivably have crept out, done the deed and returned to the vicarage. He'd found no trace of a motive for either of the Ibbotsons. The idea that Rowland and Hester were conducting a liaison, went against all accounts of Ellis's grief. Try as he might, he couldn't imagine the vicar's wife lost in illicit passion. He was missing something. None of them seemed a likely murderer. Was there anyone he'd overlooked?

Drying his face, Abbs went over his next tasks. Back to Kennington to see Miss Maitland. He had to solve the puzzle of the woman at the pawn-broker's. At least, his inquiries were once more legitimate. Thanks to Inspector Sheppard, he was to meet the journalist that evening.

He would take his landlady's advice and summon young Caleb for an errand. See if the lad lived up to his name. His mother should be helping downstairs, where a whiff of kippers was rising from the kitchen. It occurred to him, as he knotted his cravat, that Mrs Newsome had mentioned keeping the books for her husband's business. She struck him as a shrewd lady. If she could spare a little time after breakfast, she might be able to tell him a thing or two about the building-trade.

~

Abbs stood by the railings of Kennington Park. Frustrated, for Miss Maitland was again not at home, he studied the building on the opposite corner. The white-painted Horns Hotel looked well over a century old, a Grecian-style portico at the door and three rows of tall, sash windows. A side-arch led to the stables, he suspected some of its out-buildings had been lost to modern premises.

Further down the road, he could see another church, in the style of fifty or sixty years ago. An indication of when the Common was destroyed, the ugly buildings in London brick put up and the need for a new parish arose, beyond Mr. Ibbotson's ancient church. A toll-house stood nearby, boarded-up, as most were now.

He found it difficult, with the omnibus and 'factory wagons, to imagine the rough turn-pike road the coaching-inn's occupants had formerly looked out upon. This was the ancient highway from the south coast to the capital, following the Romans' route of Stane Street.

The orderly park, its pruned shrubs and swept gravel, was the tamed earth of the wild Common. Sheep had grazed perhaps, where he stood on paving, amid the tumult of passers-by and jolting growlers, a gas-works looming in the distance. He recalled the wistful remarks of the man he hoped to see.

The public bar was busy, few tables remaining unoccupied. The men were mostly clerks and traders, Abbs guessed, as he waited to be served. Ordering brandy for them both, he had but a short time to wait before Henry Searle came in, looking about him as he unwound his muffler.

'Thank you for coming, Mr. Searle.' He indicated the tray as the clerk took his chair. 'I hope this will suffice.'

'Indeed, it will serve to keep out the cold, sir, thankee. Such a raw breeze for the time of year. I had your note, as you see.'

'Was the lad who delivered it discreet?'

'He waited, I think, until our errand-boy left. He came in directly I was alone at the counter. A polite boy. He didn't stay an instant and refused a coin, saying he'd been paid.'

'Good. I hope it wasn't difficult for you to get away? We met before about this time, I recollect. I thought you'd prefer your employer not to see us together.'

'No, indeed, Inspector, you did aright. This is generally my time to step out. What may I do for you, sir?'

'I want you to tell me about Mr. Buckley's part in the business. When we spoke previously, you were reticent, Mr. Searle. I understand your loyalty, but time is pressing. I had the impression you might have said more. I want to know what you took care not to relate.'

'Oh, dear me. This is very difficult.' Removing his wire spectacles, he produced a handkerchief and began to polish furiously, looking down at his task. 'I don't know what to say to you, Inspector.'

Abbs waited while he fitted back his ear-pieces and began folding his kerchief on his knee. He passed one of the bumpers he'd filled. 'Drink up, if you will.'

The clerk took a sip. 'Thankee, that's warming.'

'Perhaps I might help you begin,' said Abbs. 'I've been speaking to someone who knows about the building-trade. Crooked builders have various ways of cutting costs, it seems. A frequent ploy is building walls of insufficient width, using half-bricks.'

'Bats,' Mr. Searle nodded. 'That's what they're known as in the trade.'

'They make money on the side. You mentioned the partial collapse of a building in Globe-town. I hear unscrupulous builders sell the gravel beneath their feet. They construct homes on rotting rubbish, covered with a thin layer of earth. At best, an unhealthy miasma rises. Unfortunate tenants suffer damp, fever, afflictions of the lung. At worst, the walls teeter like the sword of Damocles above their heads.'

'I fear you were not misinformed, sir. Those are only two ways of profiting. It baffles me that landlords have no care for their deteriorating property, provided they make rents. They would never live in such wretched dwellings themselves.'

Abbs took up his drink. 'I suppose a crooked architect might nowingly employ such men and take his cut. My sergeant tells me e bumped into an unsavoury fellow on your premises.'

'A most unpleasant person in his manner.' Searle held his glass in oth hands. 'He is a builder, not one Mr. Ellis would have used, but know of no complaints against his work.'

'An architect would be a fool, indeed, to get a name for his walls inking. Mr. Buckley is not a fool. He's a man set on a reputation for restigious buildings. So he won't cut corners these days, but I wager, e's done so in his time?'

Searle nodded unhappily. His shoulders stooped, seeming to unch himself lower in his chair. Abbs was minded of a horse fearing he whip. Not for the first time, he wondered how he could do this o people. Was he any better than Cole or Grainer?

'Mr. Buckley is ambitious. He always chafed under Mr. Ellis's autious reasoning. But he is not a wicked man, sir.'

Abbs forbore to point out that a workman died in the accident at Globe-town. A man, who disregarded the possible consequences of is actions, may well not be wicked. Nevertheless, Buckley might be ulpable.

'I set to wondering how an architect might increase his share of the rofits, without harming his designs. It occurred to me he might lefraud his partner by inflating his fees. Too risky, I thought, with a usy, working partner, meeting clients, conversing with men at his lub. But if that partner was semi-retired, someone who'd lost interest n the business, who only called in once a month. Then it would be imple. Write down a lower fee for the books, charge the client a igher amount and pocket the difference.'

Searle's hands trembled as he set down his glass. 'I know you'll hink I should have warned my employer. I owed much to Mr. Ellis. Please believe me, Inspector Abbs, I have no proof of any irregularity. There was only something I overheard, a client quoting a higher igure than should have been.'

'Then I'm right?'

'How can I say? I keep the books from the figures Mr. Buckley ives me. I'm handed receipts, I write letters and invoices as I'm told. Everything tallies in the ledger, I assure you. At my age, and without character, I could never get another position.'

'Calm yourself, Mr. Searle. Will you have another drink?'

'Thankee, no. We have no savings, Inspector. I couldn't put us on the streets for a suspicion. I may be mistaken. I... I do make mistakes oft times. I can be foolish and clumsy. Mr. Buckley says it is charity to keep me on at all.'

'I understand, Mr. Searle. Please don't distress yourself. I really don't care what Mr. Buckley got up to. I seek only to eliminate him from my inquiries. Will he be there this afternoon?'

'No. Mr. Buckley has an appointment in Sydenham. I don't expect him back.'

'Will he be at his desk on the morrow?'

'He will, sir, but I fear he'll guess you've questioned me.'

'Nonsense,' said Abbs briskly. 'I shall ensure he does not.'

Mr. Searle departed, brushing heavily against the table as he went, dropping a glove at the door, Abbs returned to the bar, where no one else waited. Catching the eye of the landlord, he produced the creased sketch of Mr. Ellis's companion and reminded him of Grainer's visit.

'Sorry, gov, like I told your sergeant, don't recall either of them. I know Mr. Buckley, he comes in the coffee-room fairly often. I knew he had a partner, but couldn't have told you what he looked like. As for a fellow badly pock-marked, not enough to go on. No regular springs to mind.'

Thanking him, Abbs was about to leave when the landlord tapped the sketch.

'That's one of young Ambrose's, isn't it?'

'Yes, it is. You know him?'

'Thought so, his style's unmistakable. Know him? He's a good customer, him and his pals. I've got one of his somewhere. Tried to settle his slate once with a drawing of my missus. I wasn't having that lark. Told me I should hang on to it, all the same, 'cause it'll be worth good money one day.'

'Is he often low in funds?'

The landlord pulled a dismissive face. 'You know what they say, a fool and his money are soon parted. Double that for a young fool. I've seen it often enough.'

His resplendent moustache, and erect bearing, proclaimed him a military man. An ex-sergeant was Abbs's guess. 'A spendthrift or gambling?'

'Both, I'd say. One of his pals is a baronet's son. He's another fancies himself as a painter. I've heard him talk of spending their winnings at Kate's and boasting over their losses, as if they're of no account.' He shook his head. 'Cards lead to ruin and whores to ruination. I've seen a young officer shoot himself over debt afore now. And I've seen what happens when the mercury don't work.'

Abbs didn't doubt the landlord knew what he was talking about. The consequences of syphilis could be horrifying and certainly, not unknown in the army.

He left with a great deal to think about. He was tempted to question Ambrose Buckley at once, but Chelsea was a good way off. Ambrose might not be there. Better to see what Frederick Buckley had to say, on the morrow, then return to his son.

The landlord was sure Kate's wasn't a local night-house. Grainer would probably know of it. A baronet's son might well frequent an establishment in the West-end. Life would get easier when he knew London as his colleagues did.

After Townsend's revelation, he didn't particularly want to talk to Grainer at all. Besides, he was gone all day on other inquiries. It occurred to Abbs, Sheppard might know where this Kate's was to be found. He'd be seeing him that evening.

THIRTY-NINE

'A clear evening for once,' said Abbs.

The two detectives passed through a pavement arch of Temple Bar. Horse-traffic jolted beneath the great central arch, its upper floor straddling the thoroughfare. Abbs looked back at the majestic edifice, the statues of long-dead monarchs weathered in their niches. He knew this was the boundary into the square-mile of the old City of London, the financial heart of the Empire.

'It won't last,' said Inspector Sheppard. 'Don't trust him, that's all I'm saying.'

'I'll bear that in mind.'

'That's where March earns his crust.'

They were in Fleet-street, otherwise known as the river of ink. Abbs looked up at the building, *The Daily Inquirer* incised in the stonework. He made out the dull clatter of printing presses, coming from an alley.

'Not that he's a bad sort, I don't say that. He can be useful. Put a tip or two my way in his time.' Sheppard tapped his craggy nose. 'But you know what they say about supping with the devil. No journalist is a friend to us.'

'Townsend said much the same. He also said don't bring Grainer.'

Sheppard chuckled. 'You had a useful lesson there, old chap. Toby Grainer's an old washer-woman.'

Abbs sighed. He'd given Grainer considerable thought, deciding he couldn't remonstrate with him for discussing a case with another inspector. They had to work together, after all, but he'd remember. He couldn't quite trust his sergeant.

'I'll introduce you and be off.'

'This is very good of you, Sheppard.' Abbs stepped aside as a pair of gaudily-attired women weaved too close to them. Their upper bosoms were goose-pimpled in the cool evening air.

Declining their offer of company in few words, Sheppard pushed past without breaking his stride. 'Ugh, I swear I stink of cheap scent now. My good lady won't miss that when she brushes my coat.'

'I expect she's used to it,' said Abbs drily. He rather regretted it when Sheppard slapped him on the back, giving a great bellow of laughter.

'Shall you brave Kate Sullivan's, then?'

'Not unless I have to.'

'Haven't seen her in a long while. Don't mistake me, Abbs, I've only ever been there in the course of work. There's not a girl down south can hold a candle to a Yorkshire lass, I can tell you. Our five might have stretched my Sal's figure a mite, but plumpness becomes a woman. She'll do me. You must come to supper and meet her.'

Abbs thanked him, liking the affection in Sheppard's voice. 'You said Mrs Sullivan is unusual?'

'She's right skinny, not showy at all. Suppose she doesn't need to be. Her whores are reputed to be some of the prettiest in town. Don't know what her old man saw in her. The rumour is she was never one of his girls.'

'Her house doesn't give us trouble?'

'Wouldn't last if she did. Not with her visitors.' Sheppard shrugged affably. 'The best night-houses are discreet as a bishop's palace. Harry March would like a list of her customers, I'm sure.'

'I don't doubt it.' It sounded expensive for Ambrose Buckley.

'She's choosy who she lets in. Won't stand for her girls being knocked about by any man.'

'I should think not.'

Abbs studied his surroundings as they made their way among fellow pedestrians. Many of the tall buildings housed newspaper offices, among stationers' shops, tobacconists and taverns. Lanterns glowed along the street, marking the narrow throughways. The great dome of St Paul's cathedral rose beyond the roof-tops, pale in the moonlight.

This way.' Sheppard, indicated a covered passage between buildings. 'Shame you weren't down here a few years since. You might have seen Mr. Dickens one night.'

Abbs smiled to himself. His colleague had an endearing habit of saying *down here,* many years after moving south. 'I should have liked that.'

'I saw his funeral cortège pass. Magnificent, it was. Reckon he had more mourners than the Prince Consort. People were weeping in the street.'

'I was sorry he didn't get his wish to be buried in Kent.'

They emerged in a court where the ancient inn's thick-paned

windows cast but a subdued light from within. Abbs could just make out the notice, about a debating club, pinned to the battered door. The Cheshire Cheese had been described to him as a haunt of writers and orators, built anew after the Great Fire of London, in the seventeenth century.

The interior was gloomy, as they made their way through several small rooms of smoke-stained ceilings and oak-panelled walls. Men, who'd drawn up their chairs to the fireplaces, were hogging the warmth.

'In the corner booth. I'll get these and leave you to it.'

Abbs looked across the room to see the Indian from the séance, a tankard and a folded newspaper on the table before him.

Sheppard ordered more ale, carried them over and introduced the two men.

Half-rising, the journalist extended a thin hand. 'We meet again, Mr. Abbs. Mr. Sheppard said you wanted to talk.'

'I'm obliged to you, Mr. March.' Abbs seated himself opposite, as Sheppard returned to the bar. 'Your good health. I'm interested in why you were at Mr. Dove's house?'

March smiled, revealing sound teeth. 'I guessed you were a jack, soon as I saw you.'

'I rather thought our hosts did.'

He shook his head dismissively. 'No, that was me they rumbled. I don't know how, but my guess is they get an instinct, same as you or I would. Want to know what gave you away?'

'Why not? It might be useful in the future.'

'Only two kinds go to those meetings. Fools who want to be entertained, that's men as well as women. Then the ones who are desperate to talk to their dead. You were neither. You were too watchful.'

'I'll bear that in mind,' said Abbs, a second time. 'I take it you were there in the course of your work?'

'Our readers take a keen interest in matters scientific.'

Abbs glanced at the newspaper. 'It isn't the fraudulent element that interests the *Inquirer?*'

'That too, mankind being what it is. The public love reading about crime. As well as those who detect it. You're new to the Metropolis, are you not, Inspector? We'd pay for a profile. Readers like to get to now the detectives in the 'branch.'

'Oh, I'm really not that interesting,' said Abbs lightly. His blood ran cy at the thought of Townsend reading about him over his devilled kidneys.

'Time will tell. I warn you, one of our rivals may take you up. *The Illustrated Police News*, for instance.'

'I'll take the chance. What drew your attention to Silas Dove in particular, might I ask?'

March shrugged. 'He's the latest of several mediums I've investigated. He's attracted a lot of interest in a short time.'

'How many of his meetings have you attended?'

'This last was the fourth. He's very good at what he does. Shame you didn't get to see. Spirit-flowers are tossed on the table by an unseen hand. Bells ring with no one near, ghostly scent perfumes the air. My guess is they rig up something with oil for that. Above the ventilation-grille, hidden in the ceiling rose. The table's placed directly beneath, if you recall.'

'No doubt it can all be explained.' Setting down his ale, Abbs reached in his pocket. 'Did you see this man there? A Mr. Rowland Ellis.'

'The dead architect? So that's your interest.' March studied the face before passing back the stiff card. 'Never saw him.'

Abbs hid a stab of disappointment. He still had no proof Ellis had ever met Silas Dove. Despite all Miss Maitland said, he might have been handed the card by a third party.

'Heard you're in charge of that one. Any progress?'

'The case is developing,' said Abbs.

'Come now, Inspector, it's customary to trade.'

'You haven't given me anything, Mr. March, though I appreciate our meeting.'

'Not at all, it's useful to get to know the jacks. When you do make an arrest, the readers of the *Inquirer* would like to be first in the know.'

'May I ask what you found out about Silas Dove?'

'Nothing to suggest he's a wife-killer. I suppose you won't say a word about that?'

'I'm not involved in that inquiry. I must refer you to Inspector Cole.'

'He'll tell, long as it's all to his credit.'

Abbs studied the journalist without comment. Middling thirties, a year or few younger than himself. Smudges, darker than his skin, pooled beneath his eyes. He sat back, one arm along the settle, with an easy grace. His signet-ring glinted in the candle-light.

'You think the two murders are connected?' March spread his fingers in a disclaiming gesture, as Abbs hesitated. 'You're not looking at Dove for nothing. You went there before Mrs Dove was killed.'

'There may be no connection at all. I'm eliminating everyone Rowland Ellis met. By all reports, he was still grieving for his wife.'

March smiled lazily. 'I don't believe in coincidence.'

Neither did he, and in a curious way, Abbs felt heartened. Somehow, Silas and Jessie Dove had to be mixed up in Ellis's murder.

'What interests me is you didn't go and interview the Doves. You turned up at one of their circles like any mark.'

Chief Inspector Townsend had said much the same, if couched differently. It was unlike him to be impetuous. He'd learnt how costly it could prove. 'And encountered you doing likewise, Mr. March.'

'Fair enough. You were sniffing around like a good jack.' March leant forward. 'Tell you what, I haven't found out that much but I'll give you what I know, for goodwill.'

'I appreciate your public-spiritedness.'

March chuckled. 'The Doves came to Kennington before Christmas. Started advertising as spiritualists, word of mouth soon got around. Their marks are always looking for a new sensation. They linked up with others of their ilk and branched into public performances. That lot like to stick together, back each other up. He's the medium, said to be amazingly convincing. Mrs Dove did the side-stuff, automatic-writing, working the planchette board.'

'And you agree Dove's performance was more accomplished than most?'

'Decidedly, from what I've seen of these sharpers. *The Inquirer* has been unmasking fake mediums for a long while. We see it as our duty to the public. Have you come across Mr. Maskelyne's show in the provinces?'

'I don't recall the name.'

'You will. I saw him at Crystal Palace last summer. He's a remarkable illusionist. He and his partner took a room at The

Egyptian Hall before Christmas. They're still on. Audiences love them. This fellow can see through all the mediums' tricks. He does everything they do on stage and more besides. And he doesn't need near darkness. It's all done in full gas-light.'

'Might they put an end to spiritualists in time, when word gets round?'

March curled his lip. 'I doubt it. People are credulous to a remarkable degree.'

'I fear so. You were about to relate what you found out about the Doves?'

'So I was. They kept to themselves, no mixing with the neighbours. No maid kept, only a woman in the mornings to do the rough. Had a discreet word with her.' March rubbed his fingers.

'What did she say?'

'She was never allowed in their parlour, opposite the room we were in. Mrs Dove saw to that, herself. Must be where they kept their equipment. She said it smelt funny sometimes. Not perfumed, chemical. The char cleaned the séance parlour. Said it gave her the creeps. There was another room she wasn't meant to see, at the top. Mrs Dove told her it was empty but she's a nosy besom. Crept up there once, when she was doing the bedroom. Reckons she saw trunks and hat-boxes.'

'Not singular in an attic,' said Abbs. 'Interesting though, why Mrs Dove should lie.'

'She wasn't talkative, but did let slip they'd come from the south coast.'

'Brighton?'

March lifted his tankard in a mock toast. 'Very good, Inspector. You have been digging.'

Abbs shook his head. 'A guess. There was a picture in the hall.'

'I missed that. Too busy playing the part of a sorrowing betrothed.' A brown eye closed in a slow wink.

'Did your interest extend to going to Brighton?'

'Nah. But now, who knows? Mrs Dove's murder is a turn-up. I hear Inspector Cole is chasing Dove. He was a fool to flee if he's innocent. But I can't say I'd want to be left to Cole's tender mercies.'

'You're well informed, Mr. March.'

'Have to be. Mine's a dog eat dog profession. Or is that just the world we live in?'

'I'd like to think not,' said Abbs.

'Not an idealist, Inspector? You'll never last in the Metropolis, if that's the case.'

As he walked back to his lodgings, Abbs hoped the journalist's words would not prove prophetic.

FORTY

Kennington-road, on a crisp forenoon, was thronging with people, vendors and conveyances. A small group of passers-by were gathered about a patterer on his regular spot. The blood-curdling ballad, he declaimed, was a new tale. Rowland Ellis's murder was old news. When... if he caught the killer, thought Abbs, no doubt the patterer would make up some verse for the hanging.

A scolding voice behind him caught his attention. A female assistant was telling a match-seller to move away from the smart frontage of a milliner's. Turning back, he purchased a box from the girl. As he waited to cross, a covered wagon went slowly by, a manufactory name in large lettering across the canopy. Belmont Candle-works.

He heard Grainer's voice, remarking on the stench of tallow, as they travelled through Lambeth on that first morning. Belmont, the same as the false street-name given by the woman at the pawn-shop. He was almost sure now, who she must be.

Frederick Buckley was outside his premises, thumbs in his patterned waistcoat, sporting a satisfied air. He had a likeness to his son. Buckley was watching a workman remove the name-plate beside the entrance. In answer to Abbs's greeting, the architect pulled out his watch.

'I'm expecting a client. I trust this won't take long.' He addressed the labourer, now reaching for his tool-box on the step. 'Careful with that. I don't want your grubby finger-marks on it. And mind you align the screw-heads.'

'Y'sir, right enough.' The look the fellow gave him was akin to a spit.

Abbs read the new plate. Buckley's name and the letters of his professional body stood out on the gleaming brass.

'Very sad and all that, but life must go on.' The architect led the way inside. 'I'll be making many changes, now it's all mine. Cutting out the dry rot.'

Abbs looked through to the back room, where the cabinet had been pulled away from the wall. Wide, shallow drawers, full of paper, were stacked on a table. Wiping his brow, Mr. Searle looked out at them.

Abbs bade him a perfunctory good day, as he followed. Knowing he deserved the shadow of dislike in the clerk's gaze.

'Take a seat.' Buckley sank back in his chair. 'Well, Inspector, are you any nearer to finding who killed Ellis?'

'We draw closer, sir.'

'Is that so? Glad to hear it. Can I tell you something that will assist you?'

'I hope so, Mr. Buckley. You'll appreciate, we work by eliminating suspects from our inquiries. In consequence, we learn things that people would prefer to remain hidden. These matters must be cleared out of the way.'

Sitting up straight, Buckley frowned. 'I'm not sure I care for your remarks. Out with it, Inspector, if you've something to say.'

'Very well. I'm speaking of your practice, Mr. Buckley. I've been acquainting myself with various deceits used by some builders.'

Buckley opened a box, removing a cigar and reaching for his cutter. It was considerably larger than the ones offered by Chief Inspector Townsend.

'I like your tone even less, Inspector. Who've you been speaking to? That old fool out there wouldn't dare tattle about my private affairs. The lad knows nothing. If it's anyone in my employ, I'll have their hide.'

'My information comes from a reliable source connected with the building-trade. To my certain knowledge, they have never been employed by you.' He hoped that would be sufficient to deflect second thoughts about Mr. Searle.

Applying himself to puffing furiously, Buckley waved out his match, tossing it in the ash-tray. 'Some of these labourers will say anything in their cups. But I dare say you've been tattling with a builder I won't use. What of it?'

'It's claimed that, in the past, you've turned a blind eye to shoddy construction in the buildings designed by this practice. I understand there are financial gains to be made. If this is true and was done without Mr. Ellis's knowledge...' Abbs shrugged. 'If he found out, it does seem to give you a motive.'

'Now you look here, Inspector.' Buckley waved away his pungent smoke. 'If you go spreading scurrilous rumours, they could harm my reputation. Have you any idea how many architects there are in London? Plenty to choose from, let me tell you, when there's a juicy ommission on offer. I demand to know where you got this?'

'No need to raise your voice, sir. Rumours are rife among all professions. The detective-police have no interest in relating them.'

The architect grunted, his bluster deflated. 'I don't deny I've made enemies. All successful men have rivals. You've had Hollins sniffing round, I dare say?'

'Would you care to comment on the veracity of the rumours, Mr. Buckley?'

'What of it? I don't deny it. Most builders scamp at some time or other. It's common enough at the lower end of the trade. Ellis knew that as well as I. It's not something we discussed or needed to. I'd be a damned fool to let it be done now on a private commission. Any building I put my name to, has no expense spared. They shall be my legacy. No, you're way off the mark there, Inspector. You'd best seek elsewhere for a motive.'

Watching Buckley breathe a drift of smoke towards the cornice, Abbs found he believed him. 'Very well, I accept what you say, but it's still possible Mr. Ellis's murder is connected with this business. My sergeant learned of a manufactory you had built in Globe-town, a few years ago. A labourer was killed when a gable collapsed. There is the question of revenge as a motive. Could someone have held Mr. Ellis responsible?'

To his surprise, Frederick Buckley grinned. 'Let me stop you there, before you make a greater fool of yourself. I mind the time well. We were exonerated of all blame, as you must be aware.'

Abbs nodded. 'I am, sir. There is the possibility of a relative of the man who died.'

'There was no family. It was gone into at the time. Doyle, that was the name. An Irishman. I'm blessed with an excellent memory. He might have had a score of relatives back in the bog-country, but none who came over with him. These men have accidents from time to time. Look at navvies, dock-labourers, they always know it's a possibility. All very unfortunate, but their kin don't go murdering share-holders. As for the other fellow, he had no more than a broken leg. Hazards of their trade, Inspector. They accept the risks. Believe me, they're glad of the work.'

'I take your point, Mr. Buckley.'

'That's cleared up, then. Whatever short-cuts I may have taken in the past, my practice is beyond reproach. I trust that's the last I'll hear on the subject.'

Abbs rose to leave. 'There is the matter of the night of the murder. I understand your servants live over the stables. Their habit is to retire to their quarters at nine of an evening.'

'What of it?'

'You neglected to mention your son has his own set of rooms on an upper floor. It's perfectly possible for either of you to have left that night, and returned without the other knowing.'

Buckley paled. 'Now, look, Inspector. I see you're determined to hang someone but you're seeking in the wrong place. You're paid to have suspicions, but you're wasting your own time and mine. Neither of us had the slightest reason to kill Ellis. My life was going along very well, before all this happened, and I'm more than capable of providing for my own son.'

'Does that include paying his gambling debts?'

'Gambling?' He looked taken aback, rallying swiftly. 'Young men will always have debts. They're trifling. My son has a fine future before him.'

'I'll need to see Mr. Ambrose Buckley again.'

Buckley's satisfied air returned. 'That won't be possible for some time. You've missed your chance, Abbs. My son is presently travelling somewhere in France. Until he writes, I don't know where, myself.'

~

A clarence was waiting in Church-walk, the coachman, Tandy, by the door. Increasing his pace, Abbs reached the vicarage gate, together with the Ibbotsons.

'Inspector Abbs, good day to you, sir.' Mr. Ibbotson passed a small leather bag to Tandy, a prayer-book in his other hand. 'You seek me? I regret I'm expected elsewhere, a parishioner's sick-bed. I must not delay over-long, but if it's important?'

'My thanks, sir, but it's Mrs Ibbotson I need. It won't take a moment, ma'am. Some information you can give me.'

The vicar's brow cleared. 'In that case, I shall take leave of you. My wife was taking the carriage on. A trivial matter that might easily be postponed. You may get up, Tandy.'

'I do not call it trivial,' murmured Mrs Ibbotson. She looked pensive.

'Forgive me, ma'am, I'll not keep you.'

'What do you wish to know, Inspector?'

Mrs Ibbotson wore a subdued hat with a veil put up. A spray of fresh violets was pinned to her mantle. The vicar had left off the black arm-band he'd worn at the reading of the will. The customary three weeks' mourning, for the death of acquaintance, were not up.

Bowing slightly at him, Abbs asked his question. The vicar climbed inside, not waiting to hand in his wife.

Mrs Ibbotson gave him his answer. Fortunately, she knew without looking up the direction. He was surprised she didn't demand to know why he wanted it.

'Thank you, ma'am.' He slipped his notebook in his pocket. 'My apologies if I've made you late.'

'No one is expecting me, sir. My appointment is not with the living. I bid you good day.' Gathering her skirt, Mrs Ibbotson climbed into the carriage, taking her seat beside her husband.

Abbs watched them recede down the street, the mare's shoes ringing the cobbles. He considered Mrs Ibbotson's parting comment, reminded he hadn't yet made time to visit Rowland Ellis's grave. Reading the floral tributes might prove interesting. He decided to do so at the first opportunity, but it would not be today. He needed to see Sergeant Hollins urgently.

FORTY-ONE

Their arrival had invaded this female domain, thought Abbs, bringing in their wake, a miasma of fear. That had not been his intention, inevitable though it was. The sudden, heavy boots sounding through the house, the gruff voices of Hollins and Grainer would alarm any servants. Above all, would be the significance of the closed maria on the drive. The uniformed constable waiting at the rear, by the small, barred opening. All this must be worse in the absence of the mistress of the house.

Mrs Wilmot shook her head, her countenance fraught with worry.

'It is imperative you tell me the truth,' said Abbs patiently. 'The last time I was in this room, you contrived to slip something down the side of your armchair. Was it a flask?'

'It's only something to keep the cold out. I'm no sot, sir, Maggie will tell you. I couldn't do my work if I was. I'm as sober as a Lord, every God-given minute.'

She'd chosen a dubious example to liken herself to. 'Is it there now? May I see?'

Crossing the few paces of her sitting-room, she felt beside the cushion and handed him a hip-flask. 'It was my husband's, God rest him. I put a nip in my tea of an evening, that's all.'

Abbs noted the dented metal and lack of hall-mark. Cheap, worn things moved him in a way that affluent objects never did.

'There's no harm in it, sir.'

Unscrewing the cap, he sniffed rum. 'None at all. I dare say it makes you sleepy, Mrs Wilmot, after a long day's work.'

'I don't deny it.' Taking the proffered flask, she placed it in the corner-cupboard, turning to face him. 'But I didn't doze off on the night the master was murdered. Bertha didn't do it. Thief she may be, but she was here with me all evening, as God's my witness. She only stepped across the passage to make us a pot of tea. I could hear her the whole while. I'll swear for her in court, if I have to.'

'That won't be necessary. I believe you. Shall we repair to the kitchen?' Abbs ushered her before him.

'Ready when you are, Inspector,' said Hollins, looking pleased with himself.

Grainer was whistling nothing under his breath. The table was laid with the women's interrupted mid-day meal, the air clotted with boiled cabbage.

Maggie stood by the dresser. She took a step towards him. 'Shall I go for the mistress? She's doing charity-work with Mrs Ibbotson. They might be back at the vicarage by now.'

'I should. Tell Miss Maitland we'll be at Kennington-lane station. Bertha will be charged with theft.' He felt the others look at him.

'Sir?' said Hollins. 'A sight more than that...'

'We're done here.' Abbs spoke over him. 'Let us go.' He waited while the two men walked into the passage. Maggie was removing her apron. Mrs Wilmot picked up a plate, set it down again. Hesitating, he went to say something to them. The words died in his mouth.

'This way.' He heard his voice, unnecessarily harsh, at Grainer's heels.

Rather than troop back through the house, he took them out by the tradesman's gate, to their waiting growler. The custody-carriage was gone, leaving only the tang of warm horse and wheel-ruts in the gravel.

~

'Jennet Fry,' said Sergeant Hollins. 'Protested her innocence at first. Struck dumb ever since, I'm told.'

The woman Abbs saw, through the peep-hole in the cell door, was sitting on the slatted bench, arms crossed over her shawl. They must have given her no time to put on her bonnet. Bare-headed, wearing a shabby gown, she was a faint ghost of her young daughter. As they entered, she went to rise, sinking down again.

Abbs eyed the stained, bunched palliasse, straw poking from a gaping seam. The narrow room stank. He tried not to identify the separate odours.

'You've been told why you're here, Mrs Fry,' he began.

'I've done nothing. You got the wrong woman.'

No emotion in her voice. Her London accent was without energy, without hope. Abbs sighed. He'd had this conversation so many times. Like trying to blow on the embers of a near-dead fire. She had not even the fear of a trapped creature. Life had exhausted her.

Her only brightness came from the red glow on her cheeks. Thin to the point of emaciation, he wondered if she was feverish. 'You went to Glossop the pawn-broker, with a valuable piece of china taken from Mr. Ellis's house. Your daughter's late employer.' She ignored him. 'It's no use, you know. We shall send for Mr. Glossop to pick you out, if need be.'

'Waste everyone's time and it'll go harder for you,' said Hollins. 'We'll tell the beak you were troublous.'

Jennet Fry moistened her cracked lips, looking somewhere between them. 'I didn't filch nothing. Found it, didn't I?'

'A likely story. Let's be having the truth and quick about it.'

For an instant, Abbs wondered. He motioned to silence Sergeant Hollins. 'How did you come to have it?'

'It was hers. Bertha's. How do I know where she got it? Thought it come off a stall, didn't I?'

'Where did you find it, Mrs Fry?'

'In her hidey-hole. Same place she's always kept things she don't want me to see. I ain't saying no more.' She folded her arms.

'Shall I get the girl in, sir? See what she has to say for herself?' Hollins looked eager for the finish.

'Very well. We'll see how Grainer's getting on. There's no room in here. Is there somewhere else where we can continue?'

'Follow me, sir.' Hollins paused at Latham, waiting in the passage. 'Hear that? Fetch the sergeant and the girl. Then bring this one.'

They stood in Hollins's room, the window overlooking the rear yard. 'We've sent out for the woman who serves as matron, sir,' he said. 'She's the widow of a former constable.'

Bertha was brought in. The girl was reluctant to enter, Grainer pushed her forward.

Abbs waited for Mrs Fry to be escorted in by Latham, directing the females be given chairs. 'Thank you, Constable.' Dismissing him, he gave his attention to the girl. 'You know why you're here, Bertha. It will fare better with you if you speak up truthfully. How did you come by the china figurine?'

She stared at the worn floor. 'It was lying on the carpet.'

'Speak up,' he said, not unkindly.

Bertha met his gaze, her expression defiant. 'The morning the master was found, I saw it in the study. Behind the chair. I hid it in my apron. They all thought it'd been thieved by the one who cut him.'

'When was this?'

'After they took him away. I crept in to see the blood-stains.'

Sergeant Hollins snorted. 'Your master was murdered and you saw chance to profit by it. Did you let the killer in?'

Terror flared in her eyes. 'All I did was take the lady, after. Gawd elp me, that's all I did.'

'Mrs Wilmot is prepared to swear, you were never out of her resence long enough to harm your master,' said Abbs. 'Bertha, do ou know anything more about his murder? Tell us now, if you do. 'his is your last chance.'

'I don't know nothing about any of it, sir. I'd peach if I did. Me and Cook didn't hear a thing. Someone came in the dead of night, that's vhat we reckon. I only took the lady 'cause they were saying things vere missing. What was one more?'

Considering her carefully, Abbs believed her. Her voice wavered ne unmistakable ring of veracity. She was speaking for her life.

'Why did you take it?'

Grainer stirred in the corner. 'Thought she'd have more bunce nan she'd ever seen afore. Look where your sticky fingers have unded you now, missy.'

'Let her speak,' said Abbs. He glanced at Jennet Fry, looking down t her hands. She seemed resigned to her fate. Bertha gave a tiny hake of her head, biting her lip to hold it still. Her eyes glistened.

'Cat got your tongue,' said Hollins. 'The magistrates are sitting this fternoon, sir. We can take her straight across.'

Abbs looked at Grainer. 'See if there's any sign of Miss Maitland.'

'Sir.'

Watching him depart, Abbs knew if Louisa Maitland didn't refuse) press charges, there was nothing he could do.

'When we spoke on the pavement, later that morning,' he resumed, lid you have the china hidden in your basket?'

Bertha nodded. No wonder she looked furious when Mrs Ibbotson urned her back to the house.

'You took it home the next day. Miss Maitland allowed you to visit our mother, as you pretended to be distressed by the murder. Is that ight?'

'Yes, sir. I didn't mean any harm. She thought it was gone. I didn't nink it'd matter.'

'Don't give us that,' said Hollins. 'You know right from wrong. You vere brought up Christian, weren't you? You know the penalty for stealing.'

Abbs hid his irritation.

'You stupid little bitch,' said Jennet Fry flatly. She might have been reproving her child for some trivial mishap.

'No one'd know if you'd kept your hands off her.' Bertha's voice rose. 'You had no right to pop her. She was mine. I can't have nothing in that house. I hate you.'

'Shut yer stupid mouth.' Again, her mother spoke without animosity.

Bertha jumped up, tears running down her cheeks. She hurled herself at her parent, striking out with her fists. 'It wasn't to sell, d'you hear me? It wasn't yours. She was mine.'

The chair fell back as Jennet got to her feet. Ignoring the flailing arms, she tugged a handful of Bertha's hair, jerking back her head while kicking hard at her skirt. The girl screeched as Hollins forced Jennet's fingers free, wrenching her arms behind her.

Bertha crumpled, sobbing, as Abbs set her down on the chair. 'I didn't ever mean to sell her. Not ever. I've never had anything that lovely. I just wanted to keep her.'

Abbs watched Louisa Maitland sign the receipt. She'd removed her gloves, they looked new, in finest black kid. The square-cut gem on her finger was the colour of sealing-wax. He wondered if it was the garnet ring, bequeathed to Hester Ibbotson.

'There you are, Inspector.'

Thanking her, he blotted her signature and handed over the parcel. 'Is it damaged?'

'Fortunately, not at all. Bertha said she saw it lying on the carpet behind Mr. Ellis's chair. It seems likely it was knocked from the mantel-shelf when the miniatures were snatched from the wall.'

Miss Maitland frowned. 'Was a thorough search made of the mother's home? It seems to me, the girl might have stolen them also.'

'Sergeant Hollins's men did search, yes. Nothing more was found.'

She was undoing the string as she spoke and slipped the figurine from its wrapping, as if she doubted his word. 'I did not think to see this again. I was always fond of her.'

'It's a family piece?'

'From before my grandparents' time. It used to be kept in the bow cabinet in the morning-room, when I was a child. I was never allowed to touch it, naturally. It's a valuable piece.'

'Bertha grabbed it on a whim,' said Abbs impulsively. 'I believed her when she said she wanted to keep it. She broke down and kept saying it was so pretty.'

'She betrayed our trust. The girl's a common thief. I had no choice but to press charges.'

'That was your right, of course.'

'It was for her own good, Inspector.'

Abbs looked beyond her. 'It's done now. I'll ring for the clerk to show you out.'

'I'm greatly obliged to you for returning my property.' She wrapped the china, testing the knots. 'Tell me, how did you realise Bertha had taken it?'

'The pawn-broker had had an earlier visit from the same woman.' He told her about the skirt and handkerchief.

'That's why you wanted to see me, but didn't return? Mrs Wilmot told you the skirt was mine?'

'She described the handkerchief as being one you'd mislaid. A gift from Mrs Ibbotson.'

'That skirt was one I wore as a governess. It had plenty of wear left, but I disliked the association. Mrs Ibbotson convinced me I wouldn't need my work-attire again. Bertha must have removed it from the garments I'd set out for charity. So you see, Inspector Abbs, she had stolen before.'

'She gave it to her mother. That's why Mrs Fry pawned the skirt, rather than sell it at a slop-shop. She knew Bertha would expect to see her wearing it. Mrs Fry told us she intended to redeem it. She had little money to feed her children.' He wondered what would become of them, while Jennet Fry was locked up.

Miss Maitland's features hardened. 'I've sent food with Bertha. Mrs Ibbotson is aware of their plight. There are many like them. Poverty can never justify theft, or where would society be? Did you decide then, the thief could only be Bertha?'

'Mrs Fry gave the pawn-broker a false direction, Belmont-street. I'd recently heard the name. Belmont's is a manufactory in North Lambeth. I knew the Frys lived there. People who give false information often take inspiration from their surroundings. She probably passed the place every day. It seemed too great a coincidence.'

'I know the candle-works. The hall where the Ibbotsons run a soup-kitchen is nearby. It seems very clever reasoning to me, Inspector.'

'It's simply experience, ma'am. You'd be surprised how many people give the same false names. People often keep their own initials. Useful for their luggage.'

'You must have wondered if I was involved.' She rose, smoothing her gloves on her wrists. Smiled thinly when he remained silent. 'We will, none of us, feel free from suspicion until my brother-in-law's murderer is found.'

Mottram knocked and entered, saving him from further comment.

When she went, Abbs stood at the window, waiting for her to appear in the quadrangle. Feeling obscurely disappointed, he thought over the previous day. In truth, he had expected her to refuse to press charges. Bertha had already left London, beginning her sentence at the Female Convict Prison in Woking. The law had to be upheld. But this time, there was little satisfaction in it.

Miss Maitland came in sight, looking smart in her new mourning-attire. No dull crape or dyed paramatta for her. She lifted her face to the sunshine. Someone raised his hat as their paths crossed.

When she was gone from view, he considered what she'd told him. Her words were ambivalent. Certain remarks by Mrs Wilmot seemed to fall into place, but he couldn't be sure. Who might he ask without alerting Louisa? That ruled out the cook, Maggie and the Ibbotsons.

~

The hour before sunset held a lingering light, reluctant to leave the fading sky. Abbs shivered in the cold wind blowing up from the river. Despite the chill, there was a feeling of the days drawing out, the year turning on. The pigeons were seeking their nooks along the pediment of St Martin's, their green-sheened greys merging with the shadows.

The tavern was situated along a lane off Trafalgar Square. Sufficiently distant from the Yard to avoid their fellows in the detective-branch. He walked in behind stable-hands from the nearby barracks. A whiff of their toil hung about them.

Reeve was conversing amiably with a bar-maid. His profile revealed the familiar port-wine birthmark, staining from his brow into his hair. He still looked younger than his years, an impression enhanced by his habitual, cheerful air. They exchanged greetings, carrying their ale to a table, cornered by a screen.

Abbs studied him covertly. He appeared hale, his movements easy. Hard to tell if there was a new wariness in his gaze.

'Are you quite recovered?'

Reeve looked surprised. 'The police-surgeon, back in Exeter, said I'm good as new, sir. Even the scar's nothing much.'

They were silent a moment. 'I still feel a great measure of responsibility,' said Abbs abruptly.

'No need for that, sir. It was my own fault. Taught me a useful lesson. I'd got soft in the country. Have to watch your back here.' He eyed him up and down. 'D'you carry anything for protection, sir, if I might ask?'

Sighing, Abbs reached in his ulster. 'It was given to me by a village constable. A family friend. He seemed to think I couldn't look after myself in London.'

'That's a useful neddy for its size.' Picking up the short life-preserver, Reeve tapped the hidden lead-weight in his palm. 'Do a pate some serious damage. I heard about the bit-fakers, sir. That was a good collar.'

'Inspector Sheppard's, not mine.' Abbs pocketed the weapon. 'So you achieved your ambition, Reeve?'

He grinned. 'Took me eighteen years to get back here.'

'Are you lodging with relatives?'

'No, I'm in Palace-place till I find somewhere. There's only my brother and his family still here. He and his missus are too full, with their own, to put me up. They wanted to, but it wouldn't be fair.'

Watching Reeve, Abbs decided, whatever else had changed, he was still a poor liar. 'I thought they did us very well in the section-house.'

'The grub's all right. Don't dole out enough, mind. I heard you weren't there long, sir?'

'I was fortunate to find agreeable rooms in St Pancras.'

'Where I first drew breath. My brother's in Charrington-street. If you ever need to question a cabby, sir, you'll find him on the stand at Euston. Ask for Bart Reeve. Or knock at number five.'

Abbs thought quickly. 'It so happens, he might be able to assist me now. There's a man I'm seeking. He took a hansom from a cab-stand in Kennington, some weeks ago. The local cabbies didn't know him. The description is little to go on, but I do have a good likeness to show around.'

'I could ask him, but most of his fares will stay north of the river. That goes for the other cabbies he'll be acquainted with.'

'It's worth trying, I think. My sergeant returned twice to cover all the men. This fellow isn't known in Kennington. He may reside anywhere in the Metropolis.'

'Bart can ask around. If you'll give me the likeness on the morrow, sir, I'll catch him at the stables after work.'

'I'm much obliged. I can let you have it now, in fact.' Abbs produced the folded sketch from his pocket-book.

Reeve suppressed a grin. 'Tell you what, sir, if it's urgent, I'll catch him before he sets out.'

'I wouldn't want you to miss your breakfast,' said Abbs drily, 'before you go on duty.'

'I won't be late, sir. You might be lucky. All the cabbies know one another.'

'Please give your brother my thanks for his trouble.'

'He's a good sort.' Stretching, Reeve looked about him. 'Talking of which, remember the Shaws sir? They came to visit me in the infirmary.'

'Is that so?'

'Very good to me, they were. Brought a basket of grub. Don't know why they felt they should, but I was glad of it. I suppose it's what church-folk do. They'll be in Bloomsbury now. Funny old world, that we should all end up in the Metropolis. None of us dreamt that, back in the autumn.'

'Indeed, we did not.' The course of many lives were changed by murder. The repercussions rippled outwards, like a stone flung in a horse-pond. The Seaborough case had altered their lives too.

'I told them I meant to try for the Yard, when I was passed fit. They pressed their new direction on me. Said to keep in touch, if ever I needed assistance. Miss Shaw spoke well of you, sir.'

Abbs watched some old men playing shove-halfpenny. Inhaled the queasy blend of sawdust, spilt beer, strong spirits and tobacco. 'I knew Mr. Shaw was retiring,' he said unwillingly. 'I hope they'll settle well in their new home.'

'They were very kind. He's a decent old cove and I don't doubt he meant it at the time, but I couldn't take them up on it. I'd only feel awkward. I'm not their class and there's no getting across it.' Reeve shrugged, dismissing the subject.

Abbs looked down at his ale. 'How are you faring with the Dove case?'

'We drew a blank at the ports. You know Dove was traced to Charing Cross, sir? That was the cabbies knowing him by sight. There the trail ends. We've covered Folkestone, Dover and Ramsgate. It's possible he was heading for a pal and he's lying low. In that case, he might nip over the Channel yet.' Reeve took a hearty draught, wiping his mouth. 'That's what Inspector Cole reckons. He's having the locals keep watch on the passengers boarding.'

'What do you think?'

He grinned ruefully. 'First time I've been asked that in a long while. Reminds me of Seaborough.'

As he continued, Abbs thought about the small watering-place where they'd encountered Mr. Shaw and his daughter. Reeve was quite right. He, too, had their direction, but would not presume on their kind acquaintance, made in the darkest of circumstances. He did not expect to meet them again.

'Trouble is, sir, there'll be sightings of Dove high and low. You know what's it's like. A man with a dark beard, he'll be spotted from Edinburgh to Boulogne. The real Dove will have had his razor out, long since.'

'You need to get to know the man, Reeve. Find out about his old haunts... if that isn't a pun. They came here from Brighton. I met a journalist who's been investigating them, exposing fake mediums. He was among those outside the house, on the day Mrs Dove's body was discovered. Inspector Cole has spoken to him by now, I dare say?'

'If he has, I don't know of it, sir. Does the rat-catcher tell his dog where they're going?' Reeve set down his tankard with a thud.

'We all have our different way of working.' He had no intention of encouraging Reeve, however much he sympathised with his predicament. The proprieties of rank must be observed. 'It's none of my affair, but I have good reason for my interest.' He recounted the bare facts of the Ellis case.

Reeve listened avidly. 'Sounds like something to really get your teeth into, sir. I like a puzzle.'

'Chief Inspector Townsend is of the opinion I'm taking too long. The glass is running out.'

He waved a hand airily. 'You'll do it, sir. You did last time.'

'We did, Reeve. I'm not sure our superior shares your sentiments.' Abbs reached for the earthenware jug, smiling faintly as he poured them more ale.

'Sir.' Hesitating, Reeve traced a finger in a damp ring on the table. 'Have you been told about the notes Mrs Dove kept?'

Abbs leant forward. 'I have not. Tell me.'

'The inspector found a book in a bureau, a woman's hand. Seems to be notes on their marks. Names, where they live, details about them. They're scrappy, who was a widow, who wanted to contact their dead child, Christian-names. You can imagine the sort of stuff. Anything useful to a spirit-monger. If your Rowland Ellis is among them, Inspector Cole can tell you.'

'You would think so,' said Abbs grimly. 'You don't recall the name, yourself?'

Reeve shook his head. 'I wasn't allowed to go through it. Only had a quick peek.'

'I appreciate your telling me. I'm afraid it won't go unnoticed. I must see this book.'

'Inspector Cole didn't remove it to the Yard, sir. He's so sure Dove's our man. It's still in the bureau in the parlour. The house is secured, of course. We found a key.' He looked regretful. 'That'll be in his desk. I can't get hold of it.'

'I should think not, indeed.'

'Wouldn't dream of it, sir. Mind you,' he said casually, 'the inspector's not above rooting round places he's no business in.'

Abbs made no answer, gazing at his drink. Looking up, he found Reeve regarding him speculatively. He was minded of a terrier, ears aquiver, straining at the leash.

'Absolutely not, Sergeant. Don't even think of it.'

'I was only wondering if you still carried your bettys, sir?'

'We're here to uphold the law, Reeve,' said Abbs severely. 'Not take up house-breaking.'

FORTY-THREE

A clock chimed the half-hour as they left the cab, a street away. The moon, nearing full, vanished and reappeared, as clouds blew across the dark. A clear night, when a certain amount of fog would be helpful. A stiff breeze lifted a ballad-sheet, sending it skittering along the gutter.

'Shame about the back door,' said Reeve. 'I bolted it myself.'

'No matter. Climbing over the wall might attract more attention. People live in the back in these terraces.'

Reeve had turned up his collar, hiding his pale cravat. His new suit was patterned in regrettably loud checks. Abbs supposed he didn't look like a detective. Indeed, Reeve's get-up would be just the thing on Derby-day, when they'd all be on duty mingling, like the pick-pockets, with the race-goers.

He halted near the corner, beyond the light from the street-lamp. Unfortunately it was situated by the Doves' house. He could do what he needed by feel. No one was abroad in Gannon-street. Laurels were rustling in the garden of the end house. The '*To Let*' sign creaked as the breeze caught it.

He murmured. 'This is as far as you come.'

Hands in pockets, Reeve was taken aback. 'Not with you, sir?'

'That's the idea. You will render me a great service if you watch for the beat-constable. You can loiter here out of sight. I'll be as swift as I can. If you see him in time, tap the glass. Quieter than the knocker. I'd sooner not run in to him as I leave.'

'But, sir, I'd best come in with you. I can lead you straight to the book. You'll need a light held.'

'You've told me where it is. I can manage. I take it there are candles on the mantle-shelf?'

Reeve nodded reluctantly. 'It was me who let you know about the book, sir. I could keep watch from inside.'

'What I'm about to do is on my head, Sergeant. The last time we worked together, I almost got you killed. I'll not be responsible for getting you dismissed. You've only just arrived. Any trouble and you were never here. There's an end to it.' Reeve knew he'd brook no argument.

Giving a sheepish grin, he placed a foot on the low wall, vaulting easily over the gate. 'You can rely on me, sir.' His form vanished among the dark mass of shrubs in the side-garden.

The house, neighbouring the Doves', was unlit at the front, the curtains drawn. Checking the street and the dwellings opposite, Abbs produced a bunch of slender, metal wands, the length of keys. His dark back inconspicuous, he hoped, he hunched within the open porch. Trying the lock, he guided each pick by feel, careful not to scratch the surround. After only a few attempts, he felt the tumblers click and release, closing the door quietly behind him.

In the narrow hallway, Abbs waited for his eyes to adjust, straining to listen. He was certain the house was empty. As a young constable in Norfolk, he'd trailed village poachers. In time, he'd acquired the knack of moving near silently in the dark, along with the ability to sense when he wasn't alone.

Feeling for the door-knob on the left, he entered the parlour. The drawn curtains were sufficient to make the darkness absolute. Even so, he dared not turn up the gas-light, lest the glow showed in the street. He struck a match, the sudden flare enabling him to cross the room without bumping into furniture, before waving it out. A candle-stick stood at each end of the mantle-shelf. Lighting the nearest, he held it aloft, looking at the room.

The book was in the top drawer of the bureau, but first, he intended to have a swift look at the rest of the house. His nature was always to save what he particularly wanted until last. He was curious to see the contents of the attic, forbidden to the char-woman.

The parlour opposite, where Jessie Dove had been murdered, smelt musty. A mixture of ashes, stale air and perhaps, the lingering oil of phosphorus. Had the plan been to kill them both? This room had an unlived in feel, a stage kept in readiness to receive paying visitors. The other parlour was homely, scattered with the appurtenances of daily life.

He glanced in the kitchen and scullery, where a beetle scuttled from the candle-light. A pan of stew stood on the cold range, a faint tang of butchery, a fawn scum of congealed fat.

The room over the séance parlour had the carpet rolled back. An oil lamp stood in an enamel dish on the middle of the boards. Harry March had been right about the ghostly fragrance.

The Doves had shared the other front bedroom and here, in

219

skewed drawers, were the signs of Silas Dove's flight. An empty travelling-case, thrown open on the eiderdown, had evidently been rejected as too large.

A steep stair led into the attic. His heart leapt as he caught sight of a figure in a corner. Quietened as he realised it was a dress-maker's model, similar to the one his sister used. The frame was hung with a plain travelling-dress. An old-styled bonnet, set on a wig-stand, was fringed with grey curls.

Three trunks stood on the floor-boards, beside hat-boxes. Abbs lifted the lid of the nearest, releasing a harsh whiff of moth-balls from folded costumes. Another was packed with gentleman's attire, beneath a fitted case of false beards and whiskers, pots and powders, a white jar of bear-grease.

Inspector Cole's men would have undone the straps, but the contents were undisturbed. Silas Dove had not had recourse to disguise. The last trunk revealed only a roll of old play-bills. The Doves had decided there was more money to be made in the spirit business.

Moonlight cast a pathway from the bare window. Abbs glanced down at the street. No one in sight but he could hear footsteps coming nearer. A draught from the ill-fitting casement touched his cheek, slanted the candle-flame. The steps were not the firm, rhythmic tread of a patrolling constable, but he shouldn't linger.

As he returned downstairs, he thought about the tray, resting on an old, wooden chair. The stock of a street-hawker, feminine trifles, such as may be sold door-to-door, lavender bags, pin-cushions and packets of pins, handkerchiefs, ribbons.

Back in the parlour, he noticed one of the doors of the bureau was ajar. Stooping, he inspected the contents; a length of gauzy material, wire, finer than his bettys, a stoppered jar of viscous liquid, other shapes in the dark depths of the cupboard. Abbs smiled sourly. The upper shelf housed a planchette-board and slates. He was only surprised not to see an angel's trumpet or a tambourine.

The book was in a drawer among nibs, pen-knife, bottles of ink, the customary necessities of a desk. He took it to the table, noting the place-setting laid for one. Silas Dove had been out that last evening. The contents, as Reeve had said, were clearly an aide-memoire for their deceitful trade. Rarely written in full sentences and littered with nder-linings and question marks. The first entry referred to a Mrs Cartwright, whose son Edmund had died young. The word 'lame' as under-scored.

Holding the candle close, he leafed quickly through, tense lest the hot wax dripped on a page, aware of the passing seconds. An early entry made him hesitate. He raced on and there it was. Proof, at last, that Rowland Ellis had visited this house, consulted these charlatans. His wife's name, a line or two about how she spent her days. He could guess who'd supplied those telling details, quite unknowing. The occasion had been related to him, if he had but known it.

Abbs copied the entry in a hurried hand, turned back and copied the lines relating to a Mrs Smith. This night's unorthodox enterprise had been doubly worthwhile. He thought he knew now how Ellis had found the Doves.

~

They left their cab in Westminster, where Reeve, spying the flickering candle-lamps of a stall, expressed a familiar need for sustenance. He purchased a ham sandwich which readily disappeared, between sips of cocoa. Taking their mugs to be refilled, he returned, balancing a slice of currant cake and a hard-boiled egg.

As he nursed his tea, Abbs watched the other customers, their faces wan in the moonlight. Some were obviously regulars, weary shop-assistants on their way home at last, night-porters on their way in, a trio of street-walkers, lively as parrots. The swells, with their cloaks and canes, were passing strangers, like themselves. Nowhere was society more level than in the cluster about a London coffee-stall.

'How come they knew so much about their marks, sir? If it were me, I'd take good care to let nothing slip.'

'I've an idea about that. Some of them would give much away,' said Abbs. 'Nervous people talk too much. We see it, do we not?' Reeve nodded, his mouth now full. 'When I went there, I deliberately didn't give my name, but Mrs Dove took my things elsewhere to hang up. She had time to go through the pockets, with the chance of finding a card-case or a letter.'

'A name in a label.' The response was somewhat muffled.

'Exactly. No doubt, some clients are sanguine about giving their name. Easy enough to look them up in a directory, just as we would.'

'And make inquiries about their circumstances.'

'How would you go about it, Reeve, if you didn't have our authority?'

'Pump local tradesmen, maybe the servants.'

Abbs smiled at the prompt reply, thought of Grainer. 'Did you search the attic?'

'No, sir, one of the constables did it.'

'But you know about the contents? The Doves clearly started out as players. They must have decided spiritualism would be more lucrative than the stage. I was struck by the tray of bazaar-goods, housewifes, ribbons and the like. There was a dress hanging up, along with a bonnet and false hair. Mr. Ellis's cook told me, herself, she'd bought a ribbon from a woman at the back door, a couple of months ago. She's a gossipy sort, likes having her tea-leaves read.'

'That's a good ruse.' Reeve gestured with his remaining cake. 'Nobody really looks at hawkers. Apparently, the Doves were getting quite a reputation. Maybe a rival done her? They went to some trouble, sir. Would it really be worth their while?'

'Like any fraud, there are great profits to be made. There were cases in Devonshire, if you recall, though I never worked on one.'

'Nor me. Beats me how the quality fall for such gammon. I saw one in the 'paper recently. Talk about more money than wits. There was this rich, old cove in Kent, sir. Gave a pair of 'em the use of a house on his estate. Had them dining at his table, just so they could hold séances nightly. Living high at his expense, by all accounts, till his nephew came to stay and caught them out.'

'People whose lives lack nothing except idle sensation.'

Reeve grinned. 'The woman got off with a fine. Her old man's living it up in Maidstone Gaol now.'

'I doubt the Doves were after the grieving poor. They can't ever scrape up their pennies for a burial club. Their dead are tipped in among strangers. How must that feel?'

Looking discomfited, Reeve examined his last morsel.

'The poor are too busy surviving this world,' said Abbs, 'to speculate about the next.'

FORTY-FOUR

Sunlight filtered through the streets, fingering the first few feet of the dim alleys slivered between buildings. A false brightness, thought Abbs, as he strode along Piccadilly, between pedestrians and street-traders. He only hoped that did not apply to the case. The light had that knife-edge feel, whereby the fickle weather of April might darken in an instant. As for the Ellis murder, questions and answers were gathering pace.

At last, he'd seen proof of Ellis's connection with the Doves. Though once again, he was unable to tell Townsend. For the moment, his superior approved of him, gratified by Bertha's arrest. Abbs reasoned that would change in an instant, if he knew about last night's exploit. How did he, a staunch up-holder of the law, get himself in this fix?

Reeve's brother was asking after the man seen with Ellis, his last hope of identifying him. By nightfall, he should prove or disprove his theory about Louisa Maitland. Both the Buckleys had seemed evasive about the night of the murder. Ambrose had hastened his departure for the Continent. There was more to uncover, he was convinced. He might learn something useful from Kate Sullivan, or he could be wasting his time.

Grainer was off checking on another idea. Abbs rubbed his brow. He'd slept badly, his thoughts whirling with faces and possible motives. If anything, he now had too many possible motives but, with luck, some would be ruled out today.

This end of Piccadilly was a mixture of prosperous shops, public-houses, an ancient coaching-inn among them, and tall mansions, often the head-quarters of some learned society. Looking up from reading one such name-plate, he noticed a curious façade ahead. Recalling his meeting with Harry March, he went to examine the building more closely, handing a penny to a cheerful crossing-boy.

The Egyptian Hall had the mock frontage of an ancient temple, or a pharaoh's tomb. He gazed above the great columns flanking the entrance, at the statues of Egyptian gods, a crocodile, the curves of various arcane symbols. A poster exhorted passers-by to *prepare to be amazed at the mysterious wonders of Messrs Maskelyne and Cook, appearing nightly, with their stupendous, startling illusions.*

It might be intriguing to attend such a performance, himself, and ponder how the conjuring was managed. A shame Hetty couldn't be with him. His sister would love such an entertaining spectacle. He'd promised, at Christmas, to correspond more often.

A small girl was dancing on the pavement. Too tender in years to be on the streets unchaperoned, were she of the moneyed class, she pirouetted, holding out her skirts. A few people had stopped to watch. Londoners were ever ready to be entertained. He pushed on, averting his gaze, as a man encouraged the child to lift her petticoats higher and show a dainty ankle. Another joined in the banter. The pity was, there were not enough coins for them all.

Having memorised the directions, he turned off before the dappled trees bordering Green Park. Kate Sullivan's night-house was to be found in one of those unexpectedly quiet streets, which sometimes lead off a great artery of the Metropolis. Situated to the south of Piccadilly, close to a quarter of gentlemen's clubs, the imposing terrace had the elegance of the previous century.

The front door was approached by stone steps and barley-twist rails. Abbs eyed the immaculate forest-green paintwork, as he waited, the delicate cobweb pattern of the fan-light. External blinds screened the upper windows. The boot-scraper was brushed clean. Nothing indicated this was not a respectable home like any other.

He was greeted by a male servant, formally-attired, somewhat young to be a butler. Hearing an officer of the detective-police wished to see his mistress, his expression remained impassive.

'What's it about, shall I say? She'll want to know.'

'In connection with a Mr. Ambrose Buckley,' said Abbs shortly.

'Buckley,' repeated the fellow, ushering him in. 'Wait in here, if you will.' He disappeared along a passage.

Abbs expected a man-servant, in a house of ill-repute, to look more of a bruiser. Even so, appearances could prove deceptive. Broad-shouldered, he'd be easily capable of ejecting a patron, troublesome in his cups.

The impressive hall was arranged as a comfortable salon, with sofas and chairs grouped for conversation. Gilt-framed looking-glasses dominated the crimson walls. The house was silent. A grand staircase climbed to a galleried landing. He glanced up at the doors off, wondering if the girls were sleeping.

Everything looked fresh, but vases of spring flowers could not mask the taint of smoked cigars, lingering like a ghost of last night. Abbs glimpsed a dining-room through open double-doors, the highly-polished table seating enough for a Lord Mayor's banquet. This house would seem a palace to the bedraggled street-walkers at the coffee-stall, but the deal struck here was the same.

He wondered what the proprietress might be hiding, while he was kept waiting. The servant returned, conducting him to the rear of the house. Brushing his knuckles cursorily, he put his head round a door, unlike any servant Abbs had ever seen. Presumably conducting a brief, invisible exchange, he withdrew, pushed the door wide and departed.

The room disconcerted him. His immediate impression was of light and greenery. The walls were papered in a pattern of ivy. Glossy-leaved plants in green china pots, a fern hung in the window, feathering beyond the bars of a decorative bird-cage. A young woman, also in green, was standing in the sunlight. She'd been attending to the plants in a jardinière, a small, brass watering-can nearby. He could smell damp soil, mossy, familiar.

'Inspector Abbs.' She moved forward, frowning a little. 'D'you come from this division? I thought I knew all the detectives at Little-vine-street.'

He wondered about their dealings. 'I'm from Scotland Yard.' He heard his voice, stiff as his back-bone. 'You may be able to assist me with some information, Mrs Sullivan.'

'I will, if I am able. Will you take a seat?' She gestured towards the sofa by the fireplace, where a tray stood on a low table. A full cup, newly-poured, was steaming by a silver tea-pot.

He pulled out the chair before the desk, waiting for her to sit opposite him. She picked up her cup. To his annoyance, her mouth twitched as she arranged her skirt.

'Would you like a cup?'

'Thank you, no.' He revised his impression of her age, almost at once. Across the desk, he saw the faint interrogative lines on her pale brow, eyes that had screwed up against the light. Her hair had a slight reddish tinge, she was perhaps five and thirty.

'To business, then. You're seeking confirmation that Mr. Buckley was under this roof on a particular night?'

'Not exactly. I told your man I wanted to speak to you in connection with Mr. Buckley. He was not necessarily here at all. I wish to know either way.' He gave her the date. If it meant something to her, he could not tell.

'Certainly, Mr. Buckley is a regular guest in this house. He mostly visits the same girl.' She spoke briskly, without embarrassment.

He was the one who wanted to get out. This room was all wrong for the hostess of a West-end night-house, whereas the public rooms were much as he expected. The brightness of the forenoon cast their end of the room in a wavering, greenish light, broken by leaves. The shadow of the window-frame cast bars across the carpet.

He noticed a bundle of books, still tied in string, the wrapper torn open. He'd promised himself the reward of a few minutes' browsing in the Piccadilly book-seller's. Kate Sullivan was wearing bergamot and lemon, fresh and clean.

'Mr. Abbs?'

He realised she'd been speaking. 'I beg your pardon?'

'I said I'll ask her to join us.' She went to the door. The servant, she addressed him as Thomas, was lurking within earshot.

'You look tired.' She resumed her seat, giving him a swift look as she sipped her tea. 'Sure you won't take a cup?'

He shook his head. 'I've been working some of the night.' When the words left his mouth, he thought, so had she. Presiding over the supper-table, flattering waiting customers. His expression hardened. 'Do you have gaming-tables here, Mrs Sullivan?'

'That, I do not.'

Her voice was Irish. Something she'd had in common with her husband, then. According to Sheppard, old Phineas Sullivan had employed her as a book-keeper, not one of his girls. He could believe it. She was as thin as a youth, her movements quick, her countenance lacking colour. The widow Sullivan must be very comfortably set-up, yet she chose to run her late husband's bawdy-house.

'You're new here, Mr. Abbs? Or you'd know.'

He ignored her question. 'Inspector Sheppard has told me about your establishment.'

She caught the faint pause he left before the last word. Her chin rose. 'He's a fair man. Be sure to give him my regards.'

He knew he was being churlish. 'Mr. Buckley has gaming debts. I ondered if he ran them up here.'

'I've heard nothing of gambling. He doesn't strike me as that kind, ut I wouldn't know. He might have said more to Dinah.' Someone nocked and she bade them come in. 'You can ask her yourself.'

The young woman who entered was very striking, with high heekbones and a mass of dark curls. She looked him over covertly, hile giving her attention to the other woman.

'You wanted to see me, Mrs Sullivan?' She yawned, revealing early teeth.

'Yes, Dinah. Nothing to be worried about. This gentleman is from cotland Yard. He wants to ask you about Mr. Buckley.'

As she turned to him, Abbs caught the musky rose scent of Fleurs e Bulgarie.

Dinah raised her shapely eyebrows. 'What's he been up to? I've no omplaints. He's a real gentleman with me.'

'Dinah,' murmured Kate Sullivan.

'Sorry, Mrs Sullivan.' She took up a demure pose, at odds with her orldly eyes.

Despite appearances, they were not so very different, thought Abbs, om Mrs Jakes and Edith. Concentrating, he asked if Mr. Buckley ad been there on the night of the murder.

'Definitely. I saw him arrive, after supper, it was. We had a drink ogether. Thomas will vouch for what time he let him in.' She smiled o herself. 'He was with me till he left, about dawn. I was awake 'cause ne water-cart went by. A right racket they make.'

'How can you be sure it was that night? Does Mr. Buckley always isit here on a Monday?'

She shook her head. 'We see him once a fortnight, might be on a 'uesday. Always towards the start of the week, when no one ntertains. He likes to see me best. Says I'm his black rose. Once in while, he'll go with Kitty.' She shrugged, as if there were no ccounting for taste. 'I'm sure 'cause it was the night before my little ister's birthday.' She turned to her employer, her face softened. 'You emember, Mrs Sullivan? I took her her present next day.'

'So you did, Dinah.'

She was telling the truth, he could tell. He thanked her, getting to is feet.

'You're welcome, I'm sure. Come again, do.' She gave him a

winning smile. 'You don't look like a peeler. What's he supposed to have done? He's a dear old boy.'

Abbs's fingers tightened on the brim of his hat. 'What did you call him?'

Dinah giggled. 'Well, he seems old to me. Freddie must be nearing fifty, if he's a day.'

~

Gulls wheeled over the Thames against massing, dark clouds, piling above the tall chimneys of the Surrey-bank. Masts and roofs stood out, sharply delineated, against the ominous, grey sky. The temperature had fallen. The day felt heavy with a sense of waiting. A ringing, of hammer on stone, split the air from across the wharfs. Bent figures worked their way along the wet strand, revealed by the lowering tide.

Simple enough, thought Abbs, how it happened. Kate Sullivan's man-servant had merely repeated Mr. Buckley, without his Christian-name. Dinah had heard tell of Ambrose. Freddie – he was still boggling at the picture of the architect answering to such – sometimes boasted of his son, but he'd never been there. Frederick Buckley was no longer a suspect. Careful questioning showed he left his home shortly after Mrs Felton retired, taking a cab straight to the night-house.

There remained Ambrose, but he didn't strike him as a murderer. More likely, the restless young artist had brought forward his travelling plans on a whim. There were no grounds on which he could have him pursued. Throwing the last of his crust to a waiting gull, Abbs made his way back to the Yard.

As he walked along the upstairs corridor, he became aware of a raised voice coming from the room before his own. Someone was silently enduring a tongue-lashing. He only hoped the biting ire wasn't directed at Reeve. The door was part-open. As he drew level, he glimpsed Inspector Cole. At once, Cole strode to his door, giving it a resounding slam.

A footstep made Abbs turn. Mottram was following him.

The clerk flicked a glance at the door. A look passed between them. 'One here for you, Mr. Abbs.' He held out a folder from the sheaf he carried.

Thanking him, Abbs asked if Grainer had returned. They were

upposed to notify Mottram of their whereabouts. This did not
lways happen.

'I believe he's in the building,' murmured the clerk carefully. 'I
aven't seen him myself.'

'Send him up, if you do, will you?'

Abbs entered his room, hanging up his things. Mottram was an
nteresting fellow, discreet, little escaped him. Once or twice, he'd
moothed the way for him to catch Townsend at an opportune
moment.

His notes written up, he was reading through the report on another
ase, when someone knocked on the door. Grainer came in,
otebook in hand.

'Got what you wanted, sir.'

'Did you have any difficulty?'

'The editor was amenable but it took me a long while to find the
ight copy. In poor light, too. Not knowing what time of year to search,
 reckoned a collapse was most likely in winter, so I began with
)ecember. Had to look through the whole twelve-month. Turned
ut to be November. I should have known.' Grainer related this with
he gloomy air of one who expects matters to go ill with him. 'It's a
vicked month for my chest. There'd been a markedly wet autumn.
Rain and mud did for the foundations.'

'The name of the other labourer?'

'Michael Corrigan, domiciled in Mile End Old-town. You won't
now it, sir, near the Docks. I knew you'd want me to be thorough,
o off I went and asked around. He's still there. His leg never set the
ame, so he's scraping a living as a cobbler.'

'Ah,' Abbs bit his lip. 'Then I'm quite wrong. Finding him was a
ood piece of work, Sergeant. Your time wasn't wasted. It had to be
hecked.'

Grainer had splashed cold water on his face. As he passed his open
otebook across the desk, his hand had a barely perceptible tremble.

'Sit down, Grainer.' Abbs reached behind him to ring for a
onstable. 'We've both had a busy morning. Let us have some tea,
vhile we bring each other up to date.'

Rain had fallen unceasingly since mid-afternoon. Abbs was glad he'd obtained a growler, even if the interior did tell of old sweat and damp leather. Better than sardined side by side, with their faces exposed to the elements. There was a chance Townsend might allow the cab on expenses. The wet pavements were getting a greasy sheen, treacherous with the droppings of a day. Pastry crumbs, fruit pulp, lumps of eel-jelly, bones, gristle, spittle, whelk-shells, cigar-butts, dung and more, all mashed by countless heels into slippery sludge.

While he watched the door, Abbs thought what an arrogant fool he could be. Too often, his reasoning ended in a wild goose chase, for he seemed to favour the complicated over the simple. He fancied he saw hidden patterns, where, in truth, there were only plain threads.

Mulling over his notes, he'd fastened on something Miss Maitland said about Mrs Wilmot. The cook's husband had been crippled in a fall, his death hastened by his injuries. He'd had the sudden notion, the fall might have been tumbling brickwork. That Wilmot had been the other labourer at Globe-town, his accident due to the negligence of the architects. He'd been swept away with the thought of Mrs Wilmot blaming Ellis for her husband's death and seeking revenge.

Grainer had emptied cold water on his theory. Rightly, as it turned out. He might also relate his fanciful idea to Inspector Cole, who'd, doubtless, find it highly entertaining. The question was, would his present errand turn out the same way? Even if he was right, it did not mean Louisa Maitland was prepared to kill to get Lindholm.

He timed his arrival for just before the end of business-hours. As he looked across the street, a boy emerged, his sleeves too short, bony wrists holding his jacket closed at the neck. Shoulders hunched against the down-pour, rain running off the brim of his cap, he dodged along the street with the vitality of youth. This must be Dick, no sooner seen than gone.

Shortly afterwards, the tall, spare figure of Henry Searle appeared, encumbered by his stick and a shabby, black umbrella. A man hastened by, bidding him good night with the familiarity of acquaintance. After shutting the street-door and testing the knob, Mr. Searle struggled to open his umbrella. Watching him contemplate the heavens before he set off, Abbs could almost hear him sigh. He wondered how long a trudge, or tedious wait at an omnibus-stop, awaited the clerk. Leaning out, he called a word to the cabby and they covered the few yards to catch him up.

Abbs called his name twice before Searle turned. 'I hoped to catch you. I'd be greatly obliged if you'll allow me a few minutes of your time. Will you step in? I'll see you to your door.'

The clerk hesitated, reluctance in every sinew. 'My time you may have, certainly, Inspector, but there's no need to go out of your way. I'm accustomed to walking in inclement weather.'

Abbs held the door. 'Please, Mr. Searle. You're getting soaked even now. I intended to offer you a ride home. It's the least I can do. Will you give the direction?'

'Very well, sir, if you insist.' Lowering his umbrella, Searle looked up at the cabby. 'Paradise-row, if you please.' Shaking off the raindrops, he climbed in, setting the growler creaking.

Abbs waited while his companion settled himself with his back to the window-light, folding both hands on his stick. One of his gloves was darned, a rent in his umbrella skilfully mended. He was married, or lived with a female relative.

'I'm thankful you didn't come in, Inspector. I told you it would go ill with me if Mr. Buckley saw us conversing.'

'I remembered, Mr. Searle. We do try to be discreet. I trust Mr. Buckley said nothing untoward to you after my last visit?'

'I'm still in his employ, as you see. He'd have dismissed me, if he suspected I'd been speaking about him. You gave me no choice.' He studied the passing scene, his manner distant. 'What more do you want of me, sir? I cannot believe that one of my employers murdered the other.'

He'd forfeited Mr. Searle's good opinion. The clerk saw him as a bully. Too pressing with his questions. Leaning too close, as Grainer sometimes did. An uncomfortable view of himself to live with.

'I'm not here about Mr. Buckley. You mentioned, Mr. Searle, you've lived in these parts a long time. I'm hoping you'll be able to confirm something about Miss Maitland. There's no one else I might ask, without her knowing, or I should not trouble you further. I know you also will be discreet.'

He'd surprised the clerk. They rounded a corner, Abbs gripping the door, as Searle slid along the seat. A curse came from upfront.

231

They felt the sudden jerk as the horse was pulled up short, awaiting a gap in the high street.

'I don't know a great deal about the lady, only what I've picked up over the years. She did not often have occasion to call at the premises.'

'My question is a simple one.' Abbs paused as the rain beat a tattoo on the roof. 'Was Mr. Ellis's house, also Miss Maitland's childhood home?'

Searle looked baffled. 'Why, yes, Miss Maitland grew up at Lindholm. I was clerk to her father, before Mr. Ellis joined the business. Did you not know, Inspector?'

'There was no reason why anyone should mention it,' said Abbs slowly.

'Can this have any relevance to your inquiries?'

'I'm interested in the background. Miss Maitland's father was an architect?'

'Why, indeed he was. Jacob Maitland had Lindholm built to his own design. Both his daughters were born there.'

Abbs sat back as they moved off, his thoughts racing. This time he was right. The thought had hit him when Louisa recalled the figurine from her childhood. Saying it was always kept in the bow-fronted cabinet, in the morning-room. He'd first met her in that very room, the furniture unchanged.

It explained why she'd objected passionately to the old tree being cut down, despite fearing to antagonise Ellis. No wonder she'd told Mrs Wilmot, the house was her rightful home. With all its early memories, how much did Lindholm mean to her? Another puzzle occurred to him.

'So Rowland Ellis married his employer's elder daughter and, in due course, inherited both the house and business?'

'Quite so, Inspector. Mr. Maitland's sons both died before reaching their majority. In some part, Mr. Ellis took the place of his heir. They shared a great enthusiasm for their mutual profession.'

'I see that, of course, but was not Miss Louisa Maitland treated unfairly? Do you know, why she was sent out to earn her living?'

Searle shook his head. 'Mr. Maitland was comfortably off but he wasn't a rich man. He had no other assets, I suppose.'

'Even so, I'm surprised Miss Maitland didn't remain at home till she married.'

He hesitated. 'It is not uncommon for one child to be the favourite.'

Sadly, he was right. And the neat marital arrangement would have eased the father.

Giving a gusty sigh, the clerk continued. 'I am guilty of the same failing, I fear. My daughters are good girls. Both doing well in service, credit to me, but I confess, I think most of my son.' His voice trailed off, wistful and reflective.

'Many men feel the same,' said Abbs. Privately, he did not believe love should be handed out like unequal slices from a pie.

'Alas, his mother and I shall never see him again in this life. I see your expression, sir. Oh, he is not dead, but every bit as lost to us. He took passage to Canada, determined to improve his lot. He's taken up farming there and wed a local girl.'

Abbs wondered, as he often did, about what wasn't said. Entire families, young and old, sailed to a new life together. Much like the warm-hearted Peggotty family, immortalised by Mr. Dickens.

'My Alfred is doing very well in Ontario, in what they call a township. He's hoping to lease his own parcel of land. Forgive me, Inspector, I digress. You did not waylay me to hear of my concerns. Is there anything else you wish to ask me?'

Abbs looked away from the clerk's moist-eyed countenance. 'You've been very helpful, Mr. Searle. I'm sorry I've had to trouble you again.'

'Not at all, sir. One fact occurs to me in answer to your question. You may not be aware that Miss Louisa was the daughter of Mr. Maitland's second wife? That union was rumoured to be not entirely satisfactory. Unhappy circumstances may reflect a difference in attitude, I fear.'

'I did not know. It's possible, of course.'

Mr. Searle looked out. 'Then if our conversation is concluded, it would do very well if you drop me here, sir. I am not far from home.'

Their breath was obscuring the glass. Abbs wiped a patch, peering between beads of water. 'You must let me take you to your street, at least, Mr. Searle. It's quite dreadful out there.'

He thought they'd crossed the borders of North Lambeth, but could not be sure. Smoke, from the manufactories abutting the river, smudged the pewter sky. They were passing through streets jerry-built, he surmised, when the railway was driven through.

Brick terraces with nothing in the way of ornamentation, endless chimneys, slate roofs divided by ugly ridges of fire-bricks. Each property was only a door and sash-window wide. They clung to respectability, by way of Nottingham lace curtains and polished knockers. The door-steps, giving straight on to the pavement, had been whitened that morning, now besmirched with muddy prints.

They followed the railway-line, signals dropping, the stinging scent of cinders on the wet air. Abbs was seized with a sudden longing for green fields and clean rain. Everywhere were sodden advertising bills, their black ink weeping down soot-grained walls, gutters gurgling, rain thudding on cobbles, sluicing the empty streets. So much water, dirty even as it fell, made scant difference to the dingy grime of London.

The horse slowed, harness jingling, as the cabby manoeuvred them in to the side. Mr. Searle picked up his umbrella, managing to let it slip from his grasp.

Abbs handed it to him. 'My thanks again, Mr. Searle.'

'Thankee, Inspector. The *South London Journal* was full of your arrest of the scullery-maid. Was this female in league with Mr. Ellis's murderer?'

'A separate matter.'

'Well, I wish your inquiries swiftly concluded, sir. Then my poor former employer may rest in peace. He is in a better world than ours I do not doubt. I'll bid you good night.'

Abbs held the door for him to descend the iron step. 'Good-night to you, Mr. Searle.'

When the clerk set off, he spoke softly to the cabby. 'Wait a little before you turn, if you will. I'll knock when I'm ready.'

He resumed his seat, half-ashamed of his curiosity. He knew, full well, Searle did not want him to see where he lived. A hard thing for a man to be shamed by his home. For all his fair reputation, Rowland Ellis had not paid his clerk well. Mayhap Frederick Buckley had long controlled the purse-strings. The architect did not stint himself. He thought of the night-house, Dinah, and its hostess.

The rainy evening was bringing on an early dusk. The lamp-lighter had been round. Mr. Searle did not glance back, as he halted at a door down the far end of the terrace. Wiping his feet, he used his latch-key, the collapsed umbrella vanishing last.

Abbs read the sign high under the wall-lamp. The street had the ailway at its back and ended in a forbidding brick wall. Beyond, lighting much of the sky, rose the cylindrical, iron frames of the London Gas-works. Paradise-row, its neighbouring Providence-street and Salvation-lane, had been named by a builder with a taste for religion. Or did he have a grim sense of humour? Purgatory might have been a truer name.

FORTY-SIX

'Evenings are drawing out,' said Bart Reeve. He breathed in deeply. 'There's something about spring-tide.'

By day-break, the rain had gone, leaving the streets misty and puddled. A faint softness in the air seemed to be carried in on the carts from market-gardens, farm-yards and dairies.

A rosy flush lingered in the sky, with dusk waiting. The sounds of horse-traffic were dulled at this time of evening and, for a spell, no trains were coming or going. Clanging and steaming from the locomotive sheds had ceased a while since. One of those brief lulls had fallen, which may be found even in St Pancras, among the busy streets of the great Metropolis.

His brother grunted, uninterested. He patted Liddy, who snickered lifting her head as he smoothed her glossy coat.

'Dare say it were prettier where you came from.'

Ned's head jerked up, not so smooth as the mare's. His port-wine stain stood out against his pasty brow. 'Don't you start, I get enough of that at work. Here's where I come from, same as you.'

His voice was stubborn, gritty like his own eldest's when he were thwarted. Bart had a sudden memory of Ned as a small boy, fists clenched. Mostly, he were bright-natured and he'd always had a feeling for the horses.

He cursed inwardly. Clumsy with his speech, as well as his elbows. 'I know that, course I do. I were only thinking about sweet air and greenery. I'll take her in now.'

He led Liddy in her stall, alongside Dolly, remembering, as he checked all were to rights. Ned would have gone on the cabs, in his turn, if he'd stayed. Then, when Ma died, and Pa couldn't cope with them all, he were packed off to their uncle's. Bound for the West Country, to an Exeter inn, where they could always find work for a growing lad. Who'd have thought he'd turn out a police sergeant, let alone a detective?

Ned had taken the broom and was attacking the cobbles, when he came out. Energetically dispersing wisps of straw and the splashes under the pump.

'Has someone been on at you?'

'My new governor. Won't stop goading me, saying I'm up from the country, meaning I'm a dunderhead. I'm as much a Londoner as he is. He's a foul-tempered b......'

'Then why do him a favour?'

Ned grinned. Eight-and-twenty now, he kept something of a boyish look about him.

'I didn't.'

He wouldn't press him. 'That's why I like being with horses. I've no one to answer to. A bad fare's soon done with.'

'Dare say I'll soon shake down. I'd like to stick one on this cove, but I'm too fly. I'll not lose my place at the Yard over Cole. I did well to get accepted. Never once, did I feel right in Devon. Made no difference where Ma's family came from. Devon folk never let you forget you weren't born there.'

'Can't like somewhere for our forebears' sake. Ma always grieved for the West Country, didn't she? She used to tell me about her young days.'

Ned looked sceptical. 'Don't remember. Aunt Susan used to say she wished she'd gone to London with her, but she wasn't brave enough.'

They were the last ones left in the yard. Bart eased his aching muscles as he watched the dirty water sloshed down the slope. 'Coming back for a bite?'

'I won't, thanks all the same. I'll grab something on the way.'

Another memory. It were all so long ago. 'You were always hungry as a nipper.'

'That hasn't changed at any rate. I fancy a hot pie oozing with peas.'

'Fan don't mean to be sharp, you know? It's only her way. She's got too much to see to, what with the young 'uns and taking the laundering. I feel right sorry we couldn't fit you in.'

'Not to worry, I didn't expect it. The section-house will do till I find some diggings.'

It needed to be said. There was no crossing Fanny. Left to him, they would have made room, somehow. He owed it to this brother who was half-familiar and yet, a stranger.

'You've done me a good turn with this.' Ned tapped the pocket of the smart jacket he was putting back on. He tipped his bowler, also new, at a rakish angle. 'I'll be off now.'

'Any time.' He went to say more but couldn't catch the words. 'See you again.'

Ned was quick in his ways. With a careless lift of his hand, he was striding past the cabs and through the open gates, his stocky figure soon gone from sight.

Bart hung up the pail. Someone was carrying a lamp through the owner's house, as they drew the curtains. A train was chuffing in the distance. The stables were fading into shadow.

Sometimes, he was almost reluctant to leave of an evening. He liked a last word with the horses, their snuffles as they settled for the night, the familiar scents. Warm, huffing breath, fresh straw, saddle-soap, even the steaming muck, piled against the wall, were homely somehow.

~

The great stone archway reminded Abbs of the entrance to the precincts of a ruined abbey. He read the old name, South Metropolitan Cemetery and the date in Latin, swiftly translating 1837. He was just too young to recollect the old king dying.

The village of Lower Norwood looked a pleasant place, leafy avenues, substantial properties and a small parade of shops. A station, opposite the cemetery gates, made the neighbourhood convenient for men who'd travel to the City each day and appreciate the peaceful environs on a Sunday.

He was about four miles from Kennington, the greater distance from the Metropolis making the area markedly rural. This was unlikely to last many years. The railway-lines had already sliced the countryside into parcels. The capital seemed akin to a devouring predator, its long shadow falling across the woods and meadows, with a brick-yard dug out here, a short row of speculative villas put up there. Biting, until one by one, they were all swallowed.

The sunlit forenoon had brought several carriages waiting in the lane by the high wall. Even on this week-day, a flower-stall had been wheeled to the pedestrian gate. He determined to find Rowland Ellis's grave without inquiring at the lodge, having that peculiarly male aversion to asking the way.

The vast cemetery spread up a hill, with its chapels situated on the height. Headstones, tombs and grave monuments surrounded him, punctuated at intervals by dark green cypress. They seemed like sentinels, watching over the dead. Lichened angels with spread wings,

238

...nds in prayer, crosses, columns and obelisks, urns, scrolls, anchors, ...eeling cherubs, all recorded the names of the gone.

Abbs wondered if Ellis had purchased a plot many years ago, in ...hich case, his wife would not be buried among the newer graves. As ...turned out, the earthly remains of the murdered architect were ...sily found. Ellis had chosen a black marble column bearing a ...recian funerary urn, draped with folds of life-like cloth. The bold, ...lt lettering, *Sophia, dearly beloved wife of Rowland Ellis,* stood out ...oove a counterpane of browned wreaths. Below her dates, Abbs ...ad the last line, *In eternal sleep.* Was that what Ellis believed when ... chose the inscription?

He was surprised to see the bright splash of daffodils, dewy fresh ...nd surely, newly purchased from the stall outside. Few other visitors ...ere in sight as he looked across the jagged memorials. Some way off, ...man stooped by an iron-edged plot. A veiled figure was standing at ...grave, near a row of mausoleums. The other occupants of the ...rriages must be in the upper part or walking the gravel paths, ...reened by firs and deliberately-chosen trees of a weeping habit.

...The man stood, head bowed. He'd placed an identical bunch of ...ffodils on the grave he tended. When he replaced his hat and ...oved away, Abbs followed him, meaning to ask if he'd been ...quainted with Ellis.

His quarry set off between the graves, climbing the rise at a rapid ...ce. By the time he reached the chapels, via the main avenue, the ...an was lost to sight. Both buildings were empty within. A range of ...oisters led from the Anglican chapel, a sign-post indicating steps ...own to catacombs, hollowed in the hill. Ever mindful of complaints, ... could hardly intrude and question a stranger in such a spot.

From the clear air, and birdsong, of the Norwood hill-top, he gazed ...the distant spread of the Metropolis, its roofs, spires and industrial ...imneys clouded in smoke. He could think better outside. Would ... tempted to linger if this was an ancient churchyard, full of history. ...ut this place was too recent, ugly in its modernity. It held no answers ...r him.

He disliked the fashion for Sunday-strolling in cemeteries, as if they ...ere promenading in a public park. This was a town of the dead, ...sited by mourners, peopled by ghosts. He was wasting time.

Descending the hill, he took the boundary path, lined with

mausoleums. A shaded walk with gloomy, evergreen oak overhanging the stone roofs. The grass was still damp, the air redolen of earth and last autumn's decay. Intent on reading names and scrap of verse, he looked up, startled as a dark figure stepped out befor him. He touched his hat as the woman lifted her veil.

'Good day to you, Inspector Abbs. Are you seeking me?'

He bowed slightly. 'Good day, Mrs Ibbotson. I had no idea yo were here. I came to see Mr. Ellis's grave.'

She nodded, appearing to find that perfectly reasonable. 'The lettering on the headstone must be amended. I dare say Mr. Penfol has it in hand.'

'I expect so.' Hesitating, Abbs said gently, 'Did you leave th flowers, ma'am?'

'I did. I was buying some for my daughter.' She indicated a nearby grave.

He saw a stone angel at its head. The statue was child-sized, th hands folded and the mottled face bowed over the pitifully small plot Abbs looked at the fresh posy and read the name he expected to se above.

'I am sorry, Mrs Ibbotson,' he said simply.

She searched his face. 'Thank you, sir. I see your words are sincere

'I intended to call on you again, ma'am. I must speak to you abou Mr. Ellis.'

'He understood grief, I'm sorry to say. It is an affliction I woul not wish on anyone.'

'No, indeed.'

She rested her bare hand on the angel's head, as though caressing her child. 'I believe you do understand. You have known sorrow. scarcely expected an officer of the detective-police to be sympathetic.

He hardly knew how to answer. 'Might we sit down?' He gestured at an open, rustic shelter along the path. 'The bench will be dry.'

Nodding graciously, she went ahead, smoothing her skirts, before he joined her in the opposite corner.

'Mrs Ibbotson,' he began, choosing his words with care. 'I don doubt you'll have heard there's been a second murder in Kennington A lady named Mrs Dove.'

'The servants speak of little else. Not in my presence, but I hea them. The parishioners are no better,' she finished tartly.

'Let me be frank. I know you consulted Mr. and Mrs Dove.'

She turned towards him. 'Does my husband know? You must tell me.'

'Not from me, ma'am.'

'But Sergeant Hollins? He is a member of the congregation. My husband asks him about your progress. Please, Inspector, be honest with me. It is vital.'

'Sergeant Hollins does not know you visited that house. Mrs Dove kept a record of the people who consulted them. I don't believe they knew your real name.'

'Then I may yet keep my secret.'

She did not ask how he'd found out. That he'd recognised Mrs Smith, who habitually wore a bunch of silk violets. He would not hurt her by repeating the memorandum about her dead child.

'I must warn you, Mrs Dove's murder is not my case. The inspector in charge may try to identify the Doves' visitors.'

She twisted the strings of her reticule, the veins standing out on her hands. Her gloves were stuffed in the top, the uppermost was damp, doubtless from attending to the flowers.

He continued. 'Mr. Ellis had Silas Dove's card. Did you suggest he go to them?'

She sighed. 'I knew they would help him. He was so in need of hope. One day, I called upon Miss Maitland, but she was out. Mr. Ellis offered me tea. Somehow, we ended up having a real conversation. To my horror, he broke down, utterly stricken. No one understood him, you see. No one else, but secretly, I did.'

He willed her not to stop, keeping his voice discreet. 'Because of your own loss?'

She nodded. 'I am sorry to say, my husband could offer Mr. Ellis no real comfort. Mr. Ibbotson is a man of great conviction, as befits his calling. He forgets, not everyone has his strength. Thomas says there is a season for mourning, then sorrow should be cast off with the black garb. We all must submit, with humility, to the Lord's plan for us. First, we must accept life's burdens, then seek to master them. None of us are ever given a yoke too heavy to bear.'

She repeated words oft-quoted to her. Evidently, Mr. Ibbotson had never seen a crippled donkey.

'Did you suggest, there and then, that Mr. Ellis visit the Doves?'

'I wanted to, but I did not quite dare. I had told no one for so long. I contrived to see him alone, a few days later, when I'd thought it over. I had to help him.'

'When was this, Mrs Ibbotson?'

Her hands had released their grasp. 'In February, Inspector. It had been hard for Mr. Ellis to endure the New Year without his wife.'

'May I ask if you've been consulting spirit-mediums for many years?'

She shook her head. 'I used to believe it was wrong. Wicked. I've always contrived to be a good Christian, sir. I tried to put my grief behind me, as Thomas ordered me to. I devote myself to good works Try to be a good wife and mother, but none of them ever had need of me. The longing for my lost child has never eased.'

She gazed straight ahead. Not seeing, he thought, what was before her. The stern, managing matron was gone. To his relief, she remained dry-eyed. Her grief too old and weary to find release in tears.

'A score of years have passed. But it is akin to having a limb torn off. In my charity-work, I have met people with amputations. They tell me they feel pain from the missing limb, as if it were still attached, invisible to others.'

Reaching for the jet beads above her collar, Mrs Ibbotson showed him a black and gold mourning-brooch, strung and hidden inside her costume. Opening a hinged compartment, she revealed a twist of fair hair.

'This is in remembrance of my Violet. She was taken from us when she was seven. The doctor said it was pneumonia. She was the brightest, dearest little soul. She was my little girl, you see. Thomas left her to me. He made our sons, his. I did not sleep for nursing her myself. If ever a mother's love could have saved her... I fought for her, but in the end, was not strong enough.'

He stayed mute, not caring to make some platitudinous remark. They were strangers, but he truly pitied her.

'When she lay in her white coffin, she looked like a china doll. I placed waxen violets in her little hands. It was not so much the custom, then, to have a likeness taken in death, but I snipped off a lock of her hair for a jeweller. Thomas allowed me to wear my brooch for a half-year.' She tucked it back in her bodice, looking infinitely sad. 'Have you children, Inspector, to comfort you in your loss?'

'No, ma'am.' Secrets breed secrets. He had a sudden urge to tell her something no one in London knew. 'My wife died in child-bed.'

She touched his sleeve. 'I will not burden you with polite expressions of condolence, sir. We recognise one another.'

Abbs became aware of footsteps approaching on the gravel. A middle-aged couple, arm in arm, glanced in at them as they walked by. The gentleman touched his tall hat.

Mrs Ibbotson shrank back on the instant. 'My husband's mama said it was my fault,' she murmured. 'Oh, not to my face. She said I did not manage the servants sufficiently to see the sheets were well-aired.' Her voice was bitter. 'As if I'd put my dear one in a damp bed. Then, when I had a second daughter, they said she would heal my sadness. She insisted the babe be called Violet. Her own mama's name, you see. So I had to say her name over and over again, as if *my* Violet had never existed.'

He could see it was a relief to her to speak. There was much he wanted to understand about Ellis, but he needed to ask the right questions. There had arisen between them a spurious intimacy, as if the bench, and its wooden walls, were a confessional. But he was a detective and she a witness, at the very least.

'What made you take the step of visiting a spiritualist, Mrs Ibbotson?'

She looked pensive. 'Three years ago, I was told some acquaintance had attended a circle. They were slightly shame-faced, knowing I would disapprove. Secretly, I listened, avidly, to all they repeated. So many of us are turning to mediums. The fortunate ones receive hope and solace beyond their dreams. Why, twice, I've seen people, I know by sight, leaving Mr. Dove's house. Fortunately, I was able to avoid them and I was heavily-veiled. I never dared attend a séance myself, lest anyone recognised me, let alone a public performance. I sought only private consultations.'

'When did you first meet Mr. Dove and his wife?'

'Last December. They'd lately arrived in Kennington, when I overheard some ladies praising their abilities. Believe me, Inspector, Mr. Dove's powers are remarkable. He is so attuned to the spirit-world and such a modest gentleman. People are saying he murdered his poor wife. It's wicked to spread such slander. I don't believe a word of it. He's a good man.'

Abbs regarded her thoughtfully. Did she know anything of use to Inspector Cole? He didn't see how he could give him Mrs Ibbotson's name, without her husband finding out her secret. Her enthusiasm saddened him.

'When you confided in Mr. Ellis, what was his reaction?'

'He tried to counsel me against going. At first, I was terrified he'd tell Thomas, but he wouldn't betray my confidence. In the end, he said he'd visit Mr. Dove and see for himself. He thought he was protecting me, but I knew, if he only saw Mr. Dove connect with the spirits, he'd be convinced. And after a time, he was, Inspector. He was certain.'

'He saw them more than once?'

Mrs Ibbotson nodded, her face shining with passion. 'On the first occasion, he remained unsure. The first time is often disappointing. The spirits cannot always communicate easily. Conditions have to be just right. The very presence of someone sceptical can make connection impossible. But we can assist our loved ones to return. Our faith builds a bridge of light between us.'

'What happened to change Mr. Ellis's mind?'

'It happened on his second visit. I tell you, Inspector, Rowland was given absolute proof that his wife was there in the room with him. I have never seen a man so shaken.'

Abbs's resolve hardened. 'Did he continue to see them?'

'I fear he was adamant, he would not. In fact, he implored me not to meddle in such things. He said we are not meant to know, until our time comes. He believed he would be reunited with his wife. Until that day, he intended to think more on the life he had.'

'You will not heed his advice?'

'I cannot. He was simply too fearful to seek beyond the veil. It takes strong nerves to attend a sitting. I have never yet been vouchsafed such a strong proof of survival as Rowland was given, but I live in hope.'

He had to make her understand. Mrs Ibbotson would not stop. She was putting herself in the hands of criminals. He only hoped the truth would not destroy her.

he rocking of the railway-carriage was mesmeric. Yawning, Abbs
ought about Hester Ibbotson. *Grief fills the room up of my absent
ild...* The daughter had died twenty years since. Two long decades
id not blown out the mother's sorrow. The custom of reusing a
ead child's name was common enough, but he'd always found it
stasteful.

Death is irreparable, that's the horror of it. He still wanted his own
mily, of course, he did. But as a rational man, he knew it could not
e.

Bricks and back-gardens blurred past, blacks stung his eyes as he
w Ma and Pa, his sister and younger brothers. Mary, Samuel and
eter, all gone, their bones lying in a Norfolk churchyard now. The
ead are always with us. But the years pass and you learn to manage
ell enough, as they did, in their turn, long before you.

Not so, poor Mrs Ibbotson. As caught, in her way, as one addicted
laudanum, or the vapours in an opium den. He'd tried to tell her
hat the Doves really were. She refused to believe him. Looking away
hen he explained how they came by their information. He would
ot hand her to Inspector Cole, unless he had to.

Abbs considered the people he'd questioned latterly, seeing their
ces ghostly in the rattling glass. Hester Ibbotson was desperate to
eep her visits secret from her husband. No vicar could tolerate his
ife associating with spiritualists.

Publicly, such a scandal would see him summoned before his
ishop, removed from the parish. Seen as unable to control his wife,
is reputation would be in tatters. Privately, he did not think Mr.
botson would be understanding, or forgiving. A chilling vision filled
is mind, a closed-carriage conveying a stony-eyed Hester to a private
sylum.

Leaving Victoria station, Abbs plunged on to the pavements, the
amour assailing his senses. Costermongers were calling out their
ares, news-sellers hollering, a barrel-organ jangling, errand-boys
histling, a balladeer singing, a fiddler scraping, an earnest preacher
undering salvation.

An endless parade clattered by, bobbing horses, bumping wheels,
ursing cabbies, flicking whips. He'd journeyed from the quiet

cemetery, back to a frantic world. His head aching, Abbs reached Scotland Yard as Big Ben chimed over them all.

Standing alone, the detectives' building always seemed aloof from the adjacent four-square terraces. Its walls cast deep shadows for much of the day. Mottram looked out of his room as Abbs entered the lobby.

The clerk sat at a counter facing an internal, open window, not unlike the position afforded to a railway booking-clerk. Rows of oak filing-cabinets lined the wall behind him, hand-bills pinned above. According to Frank Sheppard, Mottram was the real brains of the Yard, holding the progress of all their current cases, and their whereabouts, in his formidable memory.

'Message for you, Mr. Abbs.'

Recognising the carelessly-blotted scrawl, Abbs thanked him as he opened the envelope. The sketch was now somewhat dog-eared. No matter, it had served its purpose.

'Is Sergeant Reeve in the building?'

The clerk shook his head. 'He accompanied Inspector Cole. I don't expect them back before late afternoon.'

'How about Grainer?'

'He came in three-quarters of an hour since. Heading for the sergeants'-room.'

No one else was within hearing. Abbs said carelessly. 'Any news on the Dove inquiry?'

'I understand a brother of the victim has come forward. At least she won't be buried on the parish.'

Not everyone would have troubled to think that, thought Abbs as he took the stairs. A pauper's burial was a dreadful end. Devoid of dignity, one of seven corpses in an unmarked grave. A far cry from the elaborate memorials he'd seen earlier. If Silas Dove was innocent how helpless he must feel. In hiding, everything about Jessie's funeral out of his hands. After all, a criminal might love his wife, as much as any man.

Sergeant Grainer was stretching his meal-break to the utmost. A sandwich, in its paper wrapping, lay on a copy of the *Illustrated Police News*. Chief Inspector Townsend would condemn his choice of reading matter. Abbs averted his eyes from the tooth-marked bite out of the bread, with its frill of left-over meat.

'You want me, sir?' Glancing at the clock, Grainer swallowed his tea, as he fastened his frock-coat.

'Take your time, Sergeant. Don't choke yourself.' The sandwich was brought from home, but no woman's hand had cut those sloping slices.

Abbs wandered to the nearest window, acknowledging the only other occupant of the long room, who was writing industriously. A steamer-horn sounded on the Thames, followed by a distant voice calling out the stages.

'Are we off out, sir?' said Grainer, resignation in his tone.

'Indeed, we are, Sergeant. Fear not, we shall take a cab and hang the expense. We're bound for Angier-street, to find a man with a pock-marked face.'

~

'There it is,' said Abbs, looking across the busy street, as their cab nudged back into the flow.

Grainer joined him, folding the receipt in his pocket-book. 'I wouldn't put too much credence, sir, on what a cabby says. One pitted face looks much like another. Take him there, Charing Cross, my eye. Banbury Cross, more like. They'll always take you the long way round. An' say anything that suits 'em, just to be rid of you.'

'But look next door, Sergeant. What d'you see?'

Grainer waited for a glossy, private carriage to pass by, squinting at the sign. 'The Harriman Gallery.' He snorted. 'Artists.'

'Exactly the sort of place Rowland Ellis frequented, is it not? Which explains why he used this firm. He'd probably noticed their premises. You're too hard on cabmen, Grainer. They're very useful fellows. Not an easy life, up there in all weathers, waiting for a fare. Skilful drivers too, in these streets.' They were awaiting an opportunity to cross.

Grainer screwed up his face. 'Skilful? P'raps you haven't seen a collision yet, sir. You will. Where d'you find this one who gave you the nod, might I ask?'

'I didn't meet him myself. A cabby, on the stand at Euston, agreed to ask among his acquaintance for me. I understand they all know one another by degree.'

'They all hobnob, right enough. There's talk of putting up shelters, specially for 'em to scoff in. *The Globe's* running a campaign.

Already got one in Knightsbridge. They spend their lives on their backsides, if you ask me. They reckon it'll keep 'em off the grog. Half of them's drunk in charge.'

'An exaggeration, surely. Come now, you don't begrudge a working man a hot drink out of the rain and fog?'

Grainer ignored this, returning to the identity of his informant. He could be tenacious when it suited.

'He recognised young Buckley's scribble, as a fare he sometimes picks up hereabouts?'

'Outside Lewin's,' repeated Abbs patiently. 'He thought the fellow works for them.'

He was feeling somewhat guilty about keeping Grainer in the dark. It didn't seem prudent to tell him his source was Sergeant Reeve's brother. Hardly tactful and sure to be reported back to Inspector Cole, which wouldn't do Reeve any good. He'd given Grainer a heavily-edited account of his meeting with Mrs Ibbotson, having to keep in mind, he wasn't supposed to know of the notebook's existence.

It wasn't his custom to give his sergeant less than his full confidence. The ways of Scotland Yard were more tangled than he'd anticipated. *Oh, what a tangled web we weave, when first we practise to deceive...*

They were in St James's, a prosperous district near Piccadilly, where many of the capital's gentlemen's club-houses were situated. Along the southern edge, bordering The Mall, some of the country's oldest families kept their splendid town-houses, overlooking the ornamental garden.

The commercial thoroughfares were full of smart shops and businesses catering for the well-to-do, particularly gentlemen. An entire street was given up to outfitters of all kinds, tailors, hatters, glovers, linen-drapers, hosiers, cordwainers displaying riding boots. Accessories were not forgotten, with watch-makers and jewellers, purveyors of silk umbrellas, walking-sticks for town and country, guns, rods, hip-flasks, dressing-cases and luggage in finest Cordova leather.

They'd driven past tobacconists, wine-merchants, stationers selling silver card-cases, barber's saloons, French restaurants, cigar-divans and supper-rooms. Abbs remarked that Kate Sullivan's night-house was a few minutes' walk away. Angier-street had a number of art galleries and antique shops, in addition to tea-rooms with tempting displays of confectionery. They were the sort of eminently respectable premises where   unaccompanied ladies might seek refreshment, in perfect propriety.

Seizing their chance, they made a dash for it, without the services of the crossing-sweeper, who was occupied further down the street.

'Looks like a dead end, sir,' said Grainer. 'Nothing to do with his murder.'

'I'm not so sure.' He thought he was beginning to see.

Abbs studied the windows below the sign-board depicting H.R. Lewin, House-agents, Valuers & Auctioneers. Bills advertised seven-year leases on expensive properties in fashionable districts. A country villa was to be sold by auction. There was to be a sale of antique furniture, another of pictures. An arch-way led to a cobbled yard, where a pantechnicon van stood by the stables.

'What did Ambrose Buckley tell us about his last meeting with Ellis?' He glanced at the premises next door.

Grainer patted his pocket. 'All in my notebook, sir. D'you want me to read it to you?'

Abbs let it pass. 'Mr. Ellis nearly bought a painting, until young Buckley kindly gave him his artistic opinion. A scene of a market-square in a country town. It might have been this very gallery. Ellis asked Buckley if he ever tired of the Metropolis.'

Grainer studied his boots, his expression long-suffering.

'There's only one way to find out. Let us go in.'

Abbs lifted the latch and they entered an office, where they were greeted by a lady-clerk. On hearing their purpose, she asked to see some proof of rank. He complied swiftly, before Grainer, stepping forward, could open his mouth.

'If you'll wait here, Inspector, I shall speak to Mr. Horatio Lewin.' Adjusting her pince-nez, the clerk nodded pleasantly at him, passing over Grainer.

'I don't hold with women doing this sort of work. She'd be better not taking the crust out of a man's mouth.' He turned his attention to the hand-bills pinned to the wall. 'Strewth. You seen the price of these leases, sir?'

'Women must eat,' said Abbs, his attention on the muffled voice behind the inner door. It was soon opened and they were beckoned in.

The man risen behind his desk looked vaguely familiar. In his forties, he sported an off-the-peg suit, his appearance the living embodiment of Buckley's sketch, save in one respect. His face was unblemished. Grainer shook his head to himself. A gloomy relish, Abbs had come to recognise.

'You wish to know, sir, if we dealt with a Mr. Rowland Ellis in any respect? This would be the very same gentleman recently set upon in his home and callously struck down?'

Abbs agreed that it would. The figure in the sketch was wearing a hat. Mr. Lewin's thinning brown hair was combed from a side-parting, fanning across his scalp like a trained vine. Bushy side-boards confirmed his theory that a balding man often compensates on his cheeks and jaw, as if his hair had slipped. The resemblance was too marked for him not to be a relative.

'We read about the case.'

'Was Mr. Rowland Ellis a customer of yours?'

Lewin nodded reluctantly. 'In a very slight sense. That is to say, he made an inquiry about using our services but he did not subsequently do so.'

'He couldn't very well come back,' said Grainer. 'On account of he was murdered.'

'Ah, no. Very possibly that was the reason. We had no further connection with the gentleman.'

'Nevertheless,' said Abbs, 'you remembered the name. It would have been public-spirited if you reported your dealings with Mr. Ellis to your local police.'

Mr. Lewin spread his hands. 'Come, Inspector. We get a procession of gents through here daily. Ladies and all. We've nought to do with what befalls them after.'

'Bought something here, did he?' said Grainer.

The clerk moved quietly to a cabinet-drawer, made a rapid search with a finger and extracted a thin folder. Holding it out to her employer, he snatched it without acknowledgement.

'He wanted a valuation of his property.' Lewin glanced at the few lines on a single sheet. 'As I said, he didn't follow through with it. Time-waster.'

'May I see?' Abbs held out a hand.

'Keep it if you wish.'

'Thank you. I should like to question the man who met Mr. Ellis. he here?'

'You'd better speak to my brother.' Lewin crumpled his fingers at s clerk. 'I've told you all I know.'

'Mr. Humphrey is in the sale-room. This way,' said the lady-clerk iskly. 'Mind your elbows.'

She led them along a narrow passage left through a crowded store-om. They followed between sideboards laden with lidded tureens, ested meat dishes and silver candelabras. An array of table-lustres nted in emerald, rose and Bristol blue, their crystal pendants uivering as Grainer swept by.

The Lewin brothers were surely twins. Abbs wondered at the garies of fate that had afflicted one brother permanently with the cks and hollows of small-pox, leaving the other as God made him. he roughening looked decades-old.

Mr. Humphrey Lewin eyed them across the long room, as the clerk oke to him. Dismissing a workman, in shirt-sleeves and hessian ron, he then sent her off with a pat on the sleeve. Coming over, he scarded his writing-board, greeting them with the affable oiliness of commercial-traveller. They took seats at the end of a row.

'According to your record,' began Abbs, 'you met Mr. Ellis twice. nce when he called in to discuss selling his house. A second time en you went to Kennington. Were those your only dealings with m?'

'You have it, Inspector. Never seen nor heard of him, before or ce. Leastways, not until I read about him being murdered. Horry, said to my brother, I'd have seen over the study where he met his d. Stood on the very hearth-rug. You don't happen to know of the ir's intentions, I suppose? If the house is still to be sold?'

'Not my concern,' said Abbs shortly. 'We have the dates in March n which you met. Be good enough to tell us everything that passed tween you.'

Lewin, who was sitting side-saddle in the front row, grinned. 'I can't call every word, but it was like this. Gent called in the afternoon. I ppened to be in the outer office and dealt with him from the start. id he'd been considering selling his property and finally made up s mind.'

'Did he happen to say why?'

'Not he. Struck me as a sober-sides. Direct and to the point. No your fellow for a lively quip to lighten the hour. Said gent describe his property, we made arrangements for me to view with an eye to valuation. He owned it outright, you know. Best side of Kennington Popular with City-merchants. Knew we could sell it ten times over That's it in a nutshell.'

Abbs turned his shoulder away from Grainer, intent on working nail between two of his teeth. 'Did you ask if you might assist Mr Ellis in purchasing another property?'

'I see you think like one of us, Inspector. Certainly, I did. Now what was it the old gent said?' He craned his neck at the roof-light for inspiration.

Abbs was certain every word had passed back and forth over the morning headlines. Like too many people, the Lewin brothers had savoured the gore, dismissing it with a turn of the page.

'He was bidding farewell to our fair Metropolis, that's it. This is younger man's world.' Lewin's glance slid unabashed over Grainer's grey weepers. 'He said, himself, his property needed a growing family.'

'Did he mention where he intended to live?'

'He wouldn't be drawn.' Lewin laughed. 'He didn't want us to act for him. Muttered something about Sussex. We don't handle that far out, so I lost interest.'

Abbs risked a raised eyebrow at Grainer. Not a dead end at all. It was always deeply satisfying to track down a witness and reconstruct the voice of a dead person. Fascinating to hear what took place from differing viewpoints. To work out the truth, when every participant saw his own version. It occurred to him that detectives were spirit mediums of a kind, resurrecting the words of the dead.

'Can you recall anything more, Mr. Lewin, about your first meeting?'

'Mr. Ellis gave me his direction and suggested I call in a few days He was most particular about the date and time. These elderly fellows can be pernickety. They have the tin, so humour them, I always say Always the chance he'd want some furniture put in auction, if he was selling up.'

'Now to your second meeting, if you please.'

'That was a decidedly odd affair.' Lewin leant over the chair-back

ager to recount the tale. 'He wanted his property sold by auction, by
the way. Definitely not by private sale. Wanted it off his hands in one
ell swoop. Is all this really what you want?'

'Just answer the questions, sir,' said Grainer gruffly.

Lewin addressed himself to Abbs. 'I turned up for our appointment
and there was Mr. Ellis waiting outside his gate. A very decent
property, well kept up. He all but bundled me down the street,
apologising profusely, and taking me the long way round to see the
tables.'

'How did he explain his singular behaviour?'

'I gathered some family were at home, who'd been expected to be
absent.'

Abbs exchanged glances with Grainer. 'Pray continue your
narrative, Mr. Lewin.'

'Like I say, the old gent apologised handsomely, insisting we take
our business to some hotel coffee-room. He showed me round the
coach-house, very fair accommodation, and opened a gate to show
the garden. I viewed the rear aspect but we didn't venture in. Then,
true to his word, he took me to a very decent place, a short step away.
Excellent amenities all round. I persuaded him we'd be better off in
the saloon, sampling the landlord's ale.'

'We should like to hear everything you recall. Did you converse
along the way?'

'He simply reiterated his apologies. Embarrassed, I fancy. It was
frustrating, I was eager to see round the property, but all in a day's
work. You wouldn't credit how many change their minds,
withdrawing lots at the last instant. I made it my business to set him
at his ease. Put him under an obligation and he'd be bound to give
me the handling.'

'What was said at The Horns?'

'That was it, an old posting-inn, more of an hotel-establishment
now. Good class of customer, I thought. Mr. Ellis was true to his word.
I didn't put my hand in my pocket, though we weren't there long. He
produced a scale-plan of the property for me to see, beautifully drawn.
We had some general talk about our fees, the likely valuation and so
on.'

Lewin mentioned a sum, making Grainer purse his lips, exhaling
audibly. Abbs glanced at him irritably.

'You may well whistle, Sergeant. As I see it, the property will be snapped up by one of the estates and rented out on a repeating lease. The Crown holds a good many free-holds south of the river. Oh yes,' Lewin tapped his nose, 'you might be surprised who owns what. There's the widow of Windsor, the Prince of Wales's own estate, the Church.'

'That lot don't leave much for the rest of us,' said Grainer.

'Way of the world, ever been so. We find City-men favour Kennington. They can easily reach their counting-houses, while their wives can play at being a lady. There's good society, every amenity and the air's cleaner. For myself, I'd rent a newer property with every convenience but Lindholm has an air of distinction. Smacks of old money. Plenty of rising men like that.'

'Was anything more discussed, Mr. Lewin?'

'Mr. Ellis said he'd contact me, when he'd thought over my advice. I believe I made some jocular remark about hoping to see the inside next time. To underline the inconvenience, you know, secure the commission. We shook hands and parted on the best of terms. Tell you what, Inspector, a young fellow stopped to greet Mr. Ellis. Seemed surprised to see him there.'

'Go on, sir.'

'Somewhat dishevelled in appearance, attire well-cut, mind. I always notice such things. On his way to a pair of lively young fellows, lounging in a corner. Seemed quite familiar with the old gent.'

'Do you recall their conversation?'

'They only passed a remark or two. Mr. Ellis greeted him amicably. Said something about calling in at an office. Fellow said someone was away that day. Mr. Ellis started to reply but he'd had already moved on.'

'Do you recall Mr. Ellis's words?' Abbs watched Lewin tap his fingers on the chair-back. He had a black blister under his thumb-nail, tobacco on his breath.

'Wasn't much. It was only an impression I had. You know how you stir yourself to speak, but your companion doesn't notice? The moment passes, you don't press it, if it was of no importance.'

'I follow you, sir. You have an excellent memory.'

Lewin grinned. 'Not much gets past me. "It's not," was all Mr. Ellis said, I fancy. It's not convenient, that sort of line. That's all I can tell you, gents. I made for the high-street and the nearest cab-stand. Didn't look back to see which way he went.'

The sky was darkening. As they left, Abbs looked up at the row of glazed roof-lights, and the first spattering of rain. He had almost all the pieces now.

FORTY-EIGHT

Inside Palace-place, the serviceable linoleum was overlaid with muddy boot-prints. Abbs spared a thought for the woman who'd scrub on her knees next morn, until the lobby reeked of lye for a brief spell.

Supper was over, the mess-hall empty, with chairs pushed back. The long table was littered with greasy plates, smears of mopped gravy, crumbs and small bones on the rim. A whiff of warm meat lingered from the kitchen. The sounds of dishes clinking, and a woman singing, came from the scullery. A rounded matron, in pristine white apron, bustled in with a tray, smiling when she saw him.

'Back to see us, Mr. Abbs.'

He greeted her, making inquiry of her health.

'Mustn't grumble. Looking forward to May-time, and better weather, but it's the same for us all.' She began collecting dishes as she spoke. 'No, no, that's all right, sir, I can manage. How are you faring in your lodgings? I hope your landlady's making you comfortable.'

'She is, thank you, Mrs Stibby. Her cooking is almost on a par with your own.'

'Get along with you.' Her face flushed with pleasure, she tucked a grey wisp back under her cap. ''Tis my opinion you never ate enough when you were with us. I'm glad you're suited, Mr. Abbs, though St Pancras is a tidy step from the Yard.'

'Good exercise though,' he smiled at her, 'and quieter.'

He'd found that the women who looked after the section-house were often widows of police-officers, supplementing their meagre income and toiling long hours. Mrs Stibby was a motherly soul, the single men in her care were well-served.

'Were you looking for someone?'

'Sergeant Reeve, if you know him?'

'That I do, I don't know where he puts it. Mind, I like to see a young fellow enjoying his vittles.' Leaning along the table she collected the salt-cellars.

As she knocked one over, Abbs stared at her hands, red, lumpen knuckles distorting her fingers. He wondered how long she could carry on working.

Pinching a few spilt grains from the cloth, she flicked the salt over r left shoulder. 'He was in for his supper. Have you tried the lliard-room?'

'He wasn't there, nor with the men in the parlour.'

Mrs Stibby nodded to herself. 'He sometimes goes out for his ffee. You could try the stall along by Charing Cross piers, the one oposite the underground. Watch how you go home, sir. Fog's on e way.'

~

bs made his way down to the Thames. He wondered what owland Ellis had meant to say to Ambrose. Things he'd seen, scraps ople had told him, were falling into place. He thought he knew.

Reeve was at the coffee-stall. Sitting on the Embankment wall, he is conversing with a young woman. She had the look of a shop-girl, aybe a milliner's assistant, her hat trimmed with new silk flowers. atching sight of him, the sergeant fobbed her off, with a cheery word, d came over.

'Pray, don't let me spoil your evening, Reeve. You're off-duty.'

'You haven't, sir, I don't know her from Adam. I'd rather hear how u fared.'

His back turned, Reeve did not see the young woman gaze wistfully him, as she handed back her plate and walked away.

'We found our man in Angier-street. What he had to tell us was vealing. I'm greatly obliged to your brother. I should like to shake s hand.'

'I'll be glad to introduce you, sir, but if I know him, he'll be abarrassed and say it was nothing. I'll give him your thanks.'

Good. Another?' Abbs collected a refill for Reeve and a mug of ffee for himself.

Dusk was descending on the Metropolis, the lamp-lighter about his ork some yards off. Abbs watched him climb his ladder, his hand-np swaying. A sudden flare of gas and the soft glow took its place the string of flickering lights along the Embankment. A tinny snatch music drifted from a moored barque. Someone was playing a ueeze-box.

A first intimation of fog was gathering across the Thames. The ildings opposite seemed to be dissolving in twilight and mist.

'It's the shot tower,' said Reeve, in answer to his question. 'At the

257

old lead-works. That's the Lion Brewery by the bridge. They're sti
the same.'

'You must see many changes.'

'Not half, sir. This for a start.' Reeve stamped his foot on the pavin
'This was all river-bed.' He waved an arm at the public-gardens, th
outline of the band-stand in deepening shadow. 'Old mansion
yonder, wharfs and stairs. I never thought to see the Thames tigh
laced in stays.' He looked at the utilitarian rail-bridge. 'I mind the ol
bridge with its great chains.'

Abbs admired the partly-illuminated thoroughfare. The plane tree
were in new leaf, their forms starting to mature. Hard to imagine th
history that had been obliterated a few years since. 'This is intende
to resemble a Parisian boulevard, I read. It's certainly very fine.'

'Greatest capital on earth. The heart of Empire. Didn't I always say
sir, there's nowhere like it?'

'Indeed, you did.' Abbs sipped his coffee. Reeve's voice, brimmin
with boastful pride, was strangely at odds with his expressior
glimpsed in the gas-light. The crest-fallen face of someone with
long-held expectation, who did not receive quite what they yearne
for.

'How are your own inquiries progressing, might I ask?'

'Jessie Dove, sir? We've had a development this very day. /
telegraph came through from Brighton. You were right about th
Doves residing there. And about them being play-actors. A brothe
of Mrs Dove called at the station after breakfast, only that wasn't thei
real name. Silas Dove turns out to be one Samuel Finch and she wa
Julia. The brother saw the account in the newspapers, but he's take
his time about coming forward. He might regret that when Inspecto
Cole sees him.'

'Your superior didn't go straight down there?'

Bumping his mug on the wall, Reeve shoved his hands in hi
pockets. 'He's off to Brighton on the morrow, sir. He won't take m
with him.'

'Is Inspector Cole still of the opinion that Dove, or Finch, killed hi
wife?'

'It'd take the Fenians and their dynamite to shift him, once he'
made up his mind.'

'Yes or no would suffice. Let us not forget Mr. Cole's rank.'

258

'No, sir. Small chance of that.'

Abbs gazed at the river. He disliked waste. Reeve was a good detective.

Nightfall was creeping in, that ever-expected visitor. Another long day gone. He'd put the number to the back on his desk-calendar, to be rotated next month. But these hours were done.

The Albert Embankment would be lit by now, not even pin-pricks showed through the fog. He could hear the water below them, lapping the wooden stanchions of the landing-stage. Some said you could hear the murmuring voices of the drowned, at night. Not he.

'The tiny bell found in Mrs Dove's mouth is curious, Reeve, is it not?'

'I'll say. When we returned to the house, we found why she had it. There was a sewing-basket in use. Looked like she'd been attaching the bell to a garter, when she was disturbed.'

"So a bell might seem to ring without anyone near. Clever,' said Abbs, thinking back to the circle he'd attended. 'Dr. Prentice opined that the murderer must have hated Mrs Dove to do that. It's surely not the act of a rational person, that is if murder, itself, can ever be said to be sane.'

'I'd say Dr. Prentice is right, sir. Someone turned up with a bone to pick with her. But did they mean to go so far? Mayhap something he said angered them so badly, they flew into a rage and did for her?'

'Sound reasoning. You don't believe the killer was her husband?'

Reeve's words were lost as a locomotive thundered over the rail-bridge from Charing Cross terminus. On the iron foot-bridge high above the river, pedestrians were bobbing through the steam, merging briefly, before being swallowed in the fog. Their clanging footfalls faded over the water.

'No, sir, I don't.'

Abbs turned his back on the Thames. The far side of the great thoroughfare was still with them, carriages passing with a regular, hollow beat on the cobbles. Here, the vapour was almost playful, floating, hovering and retreating. Its colour indeterminate, not yet the ghastly yellowish it could be. Its taint was like sniffing the first turn of meat. The fog might worsen. Yet it was April, they might be spared.

He spoke his thought aloud. 'Could it have been seeing Mrs Dove's mask that enraged the killer?'

'Someone she'd gulled? She wasn't expecting a caller, else she wouldn't have been working on one of her tricks.'

'Someone who pushed their way in the room, before she could hide her sewing?' Abbs ran his fingers through his hair. 'Did they know her to be alone, I wonder? Or did her killer expect to confront them both?'

'They could have known she'd be alone, sir. Dove was giving a talk that evening at the Institute in Kennington. He was before an audience until seven. The time ties in with him going straight home, finding his wife's body and fleeing. The cabby reckons it was about five and twenty past eight when he dropped Dove over the way.'

Reeve nodded in the direction of the great bowed roof of the terminus. Its framework of iron and glass glowed faintly in the lamp-light far below on the platforms. Its skeletal outline seemed to waver in the drifts of fog.

'*In my end is my beginning,*' murmured Abbs. 'An event at the Institute is how it all began. Twice that provided an opportunity for murder. I'm surprised Dove didn't bring his wife with him to assist?'

'Wasn't one of his fake performances, sir. He was engaged to address some society and answer questions about spiritualism. They call themselves *The Learned Society for the Study of Unproved Science.* You know the sort of thing. Monied old coves, with time on their hands, who make out they're intellectual. Mesmerism one week, fossil-bones the next.'

'This was not open to the public? How many people would have known Mr. Dove was occupied?'

'Anyone, sir. They allowed non-members to pay on the door. Put a notice in the local 'papers and another outside the hall.'

Abbs came to a decision. 'Regarding my own case, Reeve, I believe I'm almost there.'

Reeve grinned. 'I thought you might be, sir.'

'If I take you into my confidence, this must remain between the two of us for the time being. By rights, I should be speaking to Sergeant Grainer. Are you acquainted with him?'

'Not really, sir, we were introduced in the sergeants'-room. Don't know much about him, only his reputation for being glum. An' his sister keeps house for him. Oh, someone said about his wife running off.'

'What?'

Reeve hadn't been at the Yard above a fortnight, but he was one of those men who conversed affably with all comers. To be welcomed in the servants' hall was a useful quality in a detective. Unfortunately, Grainer seemed to hector people, more often than not.

'His wife ran off to the Potteries, sir, years ago, with a salesman from Doulton's.'

It explained a good deal. Abbs said abruptly. 'I think I know who murdered Rowland Ellis and why.'

Reeve studied him, in the pool of light from the street-lamp. 'You think they did for Mrs Dove and all, don't you, sir?'

'I believe her lies came back to haunt her. It is a dangerous thing, to give false hope to someone desperate.'

'The inspector won't be pleased. I'd like to see his face when you tell him.'

'Hold your horses, sergeant. I need more proof. I think I can lay my hands on some evidence. Unfortunately, it won't be enough. I need one more piece of the jigsaw to link them to the Doves.'

'What about the notebook, sir? Are they in it?'

'I'd have to examine it properly, but I think not.'

'Can I help you in any way, sir?'

'You'll assist me greatly by acting as a sounding-board. Hear my narrative and test the weaknesses.' Abbs held up a hand. 'No, truly, Reeve, you're best out of it. Taking an active part would bring trouble on your head. You know that.' He waited until his companion nodded reluctantly. 'Very well, then, this is what I believe happened.'

Fog dogged Abbs's footsteps as he returned to his lodgings. He'd walked a short way back with Reeve, parting at Charing Cross, near the statue of Charles I. The figure on horse-back, high on its plinth, was beginning to seem less solid, blurring behind browning vapour. The omnibuses were still running, one took him much of the way to St Pancras. In Gloucester-road, Mr. Snow's front windows were unlit, the curtains undrawn. He wanted to ask his neighbour if he'd ever come across Silas Dove, or Samuel Finch, and his wife professionally.

Mrs Newsome had lit his parlour fire. She brought him up a tea-tray, Lachie slipping in at her heels, much as wisps of fog insinuated round the front door, despite their best endeavours. Her cat appropriated the hearth-rug, soon turning in the tight round of an ammonite, as Abbs warmed himself, weighing his next course. Grainer must be told and Chief Inspector Townsend. It was imperative he get his superior's backing.

In the circumstances, Inspector Cole must also be consulted. According to Reeve, he would be back from Brighton by late afternoon.

Some considerable time later, Abbs gave up trying to concentrate. Setting down his book, he went to the far window and parted the curtains. The houses opposite were, for the most part, still visible. Patches of roof and chimney, basement and railings were gone, as if the terrace were draped in a moth-holed gauze. If the weather stayed like this, life would carry on. Worsen and day-break would bring no light. The Metropolis would slow to groping pace.

Moving to his desk, he opened one of the small drawers he rarely used, taking out a folded paper, together with a Christmas greetings-card. He had not looked at them for months. Though Bloomsbury was not so very far from St Pancras, he'd avoided walking there in his explorations.

All his resolve made little difference. He hadn't forgotten Miss Adelaide Shaw. He studied her father's elegant hand, remembering last December. Quite by chance, he'd bumped into the Shaws in Exeter. On their way to take tea at the Royal Clarence hotel, overlooking the cathedral, they'd invited him to join them.

He'd found himself telling them he'd applied for a transfer to the

rd. Mr. Shaw, explaining he'd not yet had new cards printed, asked
waiter for paper and ink. He'd invited him, most cordially, should
be successful, to call on them in London.

He'd bidden farewell to Adelaide in the cathedral Close, lingering
the gateway after she'd returned to her papa. In truth, they scarcely
ew one another. Mr. Shaw, a gentleman, would want someone
her better than the son of a gardener for his only daughter.

And yet, he'd liked Sam Shaw very much. Friendship should not
htly be declined. A small sound, as of agreement, made him turn.
chie opened his eyes, stretching his paws and regarding him
ndly.

He could do nothing while he had this murder to solve. But
nking of Mr. Shaw, turned his mind to Thomas Ibbotson, a very
ferent kind of cleric. He heard again the voice of Hester as they
in the shelter, surrounded by the dead. Something she'd said,
sregarded at the time, might just possibly hold the answer. There
s only a faint chance, but he had to try.

~

ernight, the fog had closed in, bringing a faint uneasiness, as if an
welcome stranger drew closer. A veil hung in the streets, visibility,
places, reduced to a few yards. Horse-traffic was still moving
utiously. Throats thick with the sulphurous stink, people coughed
d wretched behind their mufflers.

At Scotland Yard, the gas-lights hissed, wavering in the draughty
oms. Meagre coals smoked, throwing insufficient warmth to dry
mp top-coats. Accounts were coming in of accidental deaths across
capital. A dock-labourer fallen in Shadwell basin, two drowned in
Surrey canal at Deptford, another crushed in a collision of wagon
d coal-dray.

The courtyard was empty of visitors, a mysterious, hollow place
ere the lamps had not been extinguished, glowing feebly from
seen walls. The horses whinnied fretfully in their stables and
known men appeared out of the gloom.

The chimes were sounding mid-morning by the time Abbs arrived
Kennington. Everywhere was damp, the laurels he brushed along
vicarage drive, his hat, beaded with moisture, and the wet sheen
his face. Roof-tops rose out of the fog, seeming taller, for distances,

shapes, everything on such a day was deceptive. The cross on the vicarage porch stood out, as though held aloft by an unseen hand.

The door was opened by Edith, who brightened when she saw him. Before she could reply, a voice called from the hall.

'Who is there, Edith? I did not hear a carriage.'

'It's the detective-officer, sir, asking for the mistress.' She stood aside as Mr. Ibbotson appeared, frowning.

'Good day to you, Inspector. My wife is not here and I'm expecting a parishioner. Might I know your business with Mrs Ibbotson?'

Abbs greeted him politely. 'A matter she may be able to confirm.'

The vicar fingered his chin through his dark beard. 'This is the second time you have returned to single out my wife. I should not like her upset. She's been greatly disturbed by the disgrace of the Lindholm maid, after she exerted herself to place the girl and assist the family. It has given rise to some coolness from Miss Maitland.'

'The first occasion was simply to obtain Mrs Fry's address.' Abbs regarded him steadily. 'When will Mrs Ibbotson return, sir?'

Ibbotson continued, as though he'd not spoken. 'You should, mayhap, be advised, Inspector, that a further difference has arisen between Miss Maitland and ourselves. You'll, no doubt, recollect the terms of Ellis's will, the token of a ring bequeathed to my wife?'

Abbs nodded. 'I remember, sir.'

'Miss Maitland is unaccountably reluctant to fulfil her obligation and relinquish the ring. Mrs Ibbotson has urged me to let the matter lie. This, I will not do. Miss Maitland has no claim on the ring. It is a matter of property. Property which rightly belongs to my wife.'

He really wanted to say *me*, thought Abbs.

'The ring, I'm told, holds some sentimental feeling for Miss Maitland. Its monetary value is trifling. She has offered a replacement but I cannot accept. A principle must be upheld. I consider it my duty to see Mr. Ellis's wishes are carried out. He was so good as to remember my wife, in admiration of her charity-work. As Miss Maitland refuses to see reason, I fear the matter must be placed in the hands of Mr. Penfold.'

The vicar did not look as though he feared anything, drawing himself up on the high ground, as doubtless, he did in his pulpit. His attention shifted as they both became aware of slowing hooves and a carriage turning in to the drive.

Abbs peered at an approaching brougham. Vapour swirled about the mare's bobbing head, like steam flaring from her nostrils.

'I must bid you good day, Inspector,' said Mr. Ibbotson. 'Here comes my visitor.' He turned on his heel, gesturing dismissively at Edith.

The front door was shut on him. As he stepped from the porch, it opened again.

Edith looked out. 'She's in the church, doing the flowers.' Darting back, she closed the door silently.

As the carriage drew up, he acknowledged the coachman. The solitary passenger, a stout lady, measured him openly. He touched his hat as he passed.

A cluster of old yews were like mourners waiting by the lych-gate. The only sounds, in the streets, were the judder of wheels and a faint ringing of a hand-bell. No birdsong pierced the muffled air. The fog seemed to move when he did, a floating presence, parting to let him through. The churchyard was crowded with grassy mounds, their sloping headstones modest, for the most part. A few slab-topped tombs stood in the lee of the church.

Gravel crunched beneath his feet. Abbs took in the simple lines of the ancient building, which seemed to be lost somehow, belonging among hedgerows and grazing cattle. He noted signs of recent renovation, a weather-vane not long from the anvil, a lightning-conductor. As he drew near, the walls were veined by the ghost of ripped ivy, the old door marred by a thick layer of unblemished paint.

Removing his hat, he went in. Not a sepulchral creak to be heard, the latch and hinges were oiled. Two women turned, one on either side of the nave. They were filling flower jugs on the deep sills below lancet windows. They acknowledged him in subdued voices as he skirted the font, with its pointed oak cover, making his way along the aisle.

Mrs Ibbotson was standing in the chancel. Her walking-dress wrapped in a serviceable apron, she was surveying her handiwork with a critical eye. Evidently, the vicar's wife claimed the privilege of decorating nearest the altar. She greeted him calmly, without a trace of the embarrassment he'd expected.

He felt he should obliquely warn her. 'Mr. Ibbotson was anxious lest I disturbed you, ma'am. He mentioned your difficulty with Miss

Maitland.'

Mrs Ibbotson gave a final tweak to a bough of hazel. 'Miss Maitland is changing.' She angled the vase slightly. 'Perhaps we all are. Nothing seems as it was a month ago.'

Abbs read the grave slab by his feet. The first murder had changed everything for this small circle of suspects. They were taking different paths in consequence. One among them was drawing towards the gallows.

'Is there any word, Inspector, of poor Mr. Dove?'

He told her there was not, simpler that way. Taking up her oil-lamp, Mrs Ibbotson bade him follow her to the vestry. Holding up the lamp, she mentioned various points of interest as they went. The other women remained ostensibly busy at their tasks.

'The poor-box is by the door. What think you of my husband's church, sir?'

Abbs assured her truthfully, the building was very pleasing. He eyed the monstrous organ-pipes soaring towards the beams, recalled the merry scraping of the village band, in his childhood. Fresh plaster-work marked where the old gallery had been torn down.

The vestry did not dare smell of mice and musty hymn-books. Even so, wisps of sour fog ventured through the gap beneath outer door and sunken step. Wrinkling her nose, Mrs Ibbotson began tidying a heap of wet stalks, enfolding them in newspaper.

'What may I do for you, Inspector Abbs?'

'I'm here about something you mentioned, Mrs Ibbotson. You were telling me about your visits to Mr. Dove's' house. Do you recall saying that, twice, you saw someone leaving whom you recognised?'

Glancing at the inner door, Mrs Ibbotson nodded. 'I remember our conversation very well. Indeed, I've gone over our exchange many times.' She hesitated. 'You might wonder why my daughter was not laid to rest here, near her parents?'

'I had not thought of it,' said Abbs patiently. 'Was the churchyard perhaps full?'

'It was closed to new burials a few years after we came here, but there was room still at that time. I wanted her laid close by me. There was a vacant plot by the vicarage path, where the sun falls much of the day... Mr. Ibbotson insisted on the cemetery. He thinks them more suitable in every respect.'

What could he say to her? 'It seems to be the modern thinking. For myself, I rather like peaceful old churchyards.'

'You have an understanding of people, sir. It must be useful in your work. Forgive me, I believe I interrupted you. Pray, ask your questions.'

He moved an enamel water-jug out of her way, striving to sound even. 'I have only one. Will you tell me who you saw in Gannon-street?'

Mrs Ibbotson looked surprised. 'Why, yes, if it will help you.'

She mentioned a name that meant nothing to him, a lady on one of her committees. One chance gone. Abbs felt his heart quicken as he waited. Most probably, he was sunk. He needed that link to the Doves.

'The other was someone most unexpected. Though, I don't know why I should think that. Mr. Dove's reputation is spreading fast in Kennington and doubtless, far beyond. Why, he may appear at the Egyptian Hall, in time. He wasn't there on that occasion. I'd gone to consult Mrs Dove. It was her evening for the planchette-board.'

Abbs breathed out, as finally, Mrs Ibbotson repeated the name he wanted to hear.

~

The fog-horn sounded again, mournful and insistent. Out of the corner of his eye, Abbs caught Grainer stifling a yawn. He felt keenly alert, for all he'd slept badly. Hester Ibbotson had handed him the final piece of the pattern. No detective could see it all. Some things only the murderer could tell and they might take their explanation to the grave. But often, they wanted to justify their deeds. Every last one, he'd met, claimed they'd had no choice.

Chief Inspector Townsend stood at his window, more by habit, than surveying the murky afternoon. His hands, behind his back, were loosely linked, nails meticulously kept. Looking round, he gave a satisfied nod, resuming his seat.

'You've done well, Abbs. Two murders off the books. To practicalities, then. You believe the miniatures are still in the house?'

'I can't be certain, but I believe there's a good chance.'

'Sergeant Reeve will conduct the search,' said Townsend decisively, 'taking a constable to assist. You'll brief them on what they're looking for.'

'Very good, sir.'

'Do you anticipate any difficulty in making the arrest?'

'I think not, sir.' Their eyes met. Abbs knew Townsend was thinking of what happened in Devon.

'Best to be certain. Take Sergeant Hollins along and one of his men.'

'As you wish, sir.'

'I trust you don't find this conference too tedious, Sergeant?' Townsend's quiet tone flicked like a silken whip.

He would have made a good headmaster, thought Abbs, as Grainer flinched, sitting up straight.

'Beg pardon, sir, I am listening hard. It's the weather, coming from the streets into the warm.'

He had a point. Higher rank meant a greater allocation of coal. Abbs glanced at the cheerful flames, burbling like a kettle. Fog without, fug within, their superior's room was a bastion of soporific comfort.

'We all must endure the same weather, Sergeant, some of us without recourse to slumber. Be advised, you'd better be fully alert on the morrow, when you make the arrest.'

Grainer's reply was saved by a knock on the door. At Townsend's command, a young constable entered. New to Abbs, he had a deferential manner, behind a luxuriant moustache.

'Excuse me, sir, telegraph for you. Marked urgent.' Taking in the scene at a glance, he departed promptly.

Something flashed in Townsend's eyes as he read the form, too fleeting to interpret. 'From Inspector Cole.' His voice neutral, he studied them both as he continued. 'He's arrested Silas Dove in Eastbourne. They are on their way back, as we speak.'

ιe forenoon seemed suspended, the fog no better, no worse. Still
his ulster, Abbs wiped a squeaky pane, looking out from Scotland
rd. At least, they could make their way through the streets without
shap. So far, so good. He'd feared the fog engulfing the city by
;ht, as it had at the beginning of the month. The day after they'd
en the bit-fakers, the sky had not shown itself. The murk so thick
it boys were employed to trudge before cabs with flaring torches.
such weather, anyone might find an excuse for not being about
ir accustomed business. There was much that could go wrong.

Someone gave a cursory knock, opened the door and darted
ough the least gap. His nerves already wound tight as a cross-bow,
bs sighed.

It's customary to wait,' he observed mildly.

Sorry, sir,' said Reeve. 'Silas Dove's been released.'

I was informed.'

So all the while, he was hiding with an old friend, eh?'

I don't know the details.'

Used to be an actor in the same company. It was simple once
spector Cole knew Dove's real name. He questioned the brother-
law, went to see the manager of the company and got a list of
yone they'd been close to. Eastbourne was the second one he
ecked. Not a bad piece of detective-work. Shame he was wasting
s time on the wrong suspect.'

Something we've all done, Reeve. It's the nature of our work.' He
smissed Cole from his thoughts. 'Ready to set off?'

Yes, sir. I'll heed what you said.'

Good. Then I wish you success. We shall await you at Kennington-
ιe.'

Rooting through someone's home was a distasteful task, best
rried out by an officer more tactful than Grainer. Townsend was
idently of the same mind.

Sir...'

Not tactful enough to recognise dismissal, mind. Abbs moved his
lendar, as Reeve leant on the edge of the desk. 'We've been
rough this, Sergeant. If it were up to me, I'd gladly include you.
ιur assistance has been invaluable, but here, your involvement ends.

No doubt, you have duties awaiting your return.'

'Yes, sir. It's just that after last time... I'd like to be in at the kill.'

'I know, Reeve, I know. There'll be other arrests.' Abbs ushere[d] him to the door. 'You've nothing to prove.'

Reeve grinned ruefully. 'I won't let you down, sir. If anything[']s hidden there, be sure I'll find it.'

~

The two carriages left Kennington police-station with the sombr[e] pace of a funeral procession. In a strange sense, it was, thought Abb[s.] They heralded the way to the gallows. They rode in ominous silenc[e.] Grainer looked weary, a trace of snuff on his sleeve. The package, i[n] its black-smeared oilcloth, lay on the seat between them. Facing the[m,] Sergeant Hollins looked purposeful, Constable Latham pink wit[h] anticipation.

Four men to make an arrest was too much of a spectacle for h[is] liking. He was under no illusion. Townsend had him on probatio[n.] The inclement weather would, at least, deter a crowd of spectator[s] alerted by the following maria. A barred custody-carriage had bee[n] known to attract a gaggle of jeering urchins.

Abbs consulted his pocket-watch again, as they swayed into th[e] familiar street. The officer on the box pulled up well short of th[e] building, as instructed.

Sergeant Hollins buttoned his top-coat, assuming a look [of] importance. He cast an appraising eye over Latham's tunic. 'Read[y] when you are, sir.'

Grainer leant across to look out, sucking in his cheeks. 'We've g[ot] company, sir. See who's here.'

Craning his neck, Abbs saw a growler outside the entrance. [A] woman, attired in mourning, had her back to them. She turne[d,] revealing her profile beneath a fashionable black hat, its dyed feathe[r] curled. Miss Maitland was paying the cabby. He cursed inwardly. Th[e] others were awaiting his lead.

'Give her a moment to get inside.' He watched as, lifting her hem[,] she entered the premises of Ellis and Buckley. 'Remain outsid[e,] Latham. Stop anyone entering. We don't want a letter-carrier walkin[g] in on us.'

'Very good, sir.'

270

'An' if anyone loiters, send them on their way,' said Hollins.

'Yes, Sarge.' His voice sounded hoarse.

Abbs waited a little, aware of Latham's tension, Grainer's even breathing, like a worn bellows. The sergeants were old hands. 'Well, gentlemen,' he looked at each of them. 'Any questions? Then let us go.'

First to descend, he waited on the pavement. This end of the street was empty of pedestrians, not a servant or trader to be seen. The flower-girl was at her pitch, just before the corner, alone among her pails. No one was stopping in this weather. The reek of fog assailed him, a deadly brew of Lambeth manufactories, Thames marshes and umpteen thousand sooty fires. He cleared his throat. This was no time to break off in a fit of coughing.

He led the way, Grainer at his heels. Hollins hung back by the outer door, Latham planted himself beside the step.

Inside, Abbs took in the scene at a glance. Behind the counter, Henry Searle was on his stool, writing in a ledger. He looked up as they entered, an ink-blot seeping on the page. The errand-boy, fortunately, was absent. The room was busy enough.

Mr. Buckley, in a slate-blue frock-coat and patterned waistcoat, was conversing with Miss Maitland. He broke off as he saw them.

'Inspector, you've picked the wrong time, I fear. Miss Maitland and I have matters to discuss, then I'm escorting her to luncheon.' Buckley smiled at his companion, his tone jovial. 'I've heard from my son, by the by. I can tell you where to write, if you really must. He's staying put for some weeks, so he tells me.'

'Mr. Ambrose Buckley is happily ensconced in Bordeaux,' said Miss Maitland. 'He finds both the people and landscape admirable for his purpose. Have you any news, Inspector?'

'Perhaps you would care to wait in Mr. Buckley's room, ma'am,' said Abbs. 'I think you would be more comfortable there.'

She studied the two detectives, her eyebrows folding closer. 'Very well, if you wish.' Withdrawing without fuss, she closed the door behind her.

Searle had let his pen fall, as he watched them. A scatter of black drops disfigured the page.

'Look here, Abbs, this had better not take long.' Buckley tapped his foot. 'I have a table spoken for.'

Abbs regarded him levelly, conscious of Grainer, fidgeting behind him. 'Our business is not with you, sir.' He turned to the clerk, rigid behind the counter. 'Henry Searle... I'

'No...' The clerk's voice shrilled. 'What d'you want with me? I... I know nothing.'

Abbs gave a sign, without need, as Grainer brushed past him. His hands no longer behind his back, he tossed the package carelessly on the ledger. Abbs winced as the dirty cloth parted, revealing a pair of miniature oval frames, one atop the other.

''pon my soul,' muttered Buckley. He stared at the gleam of silver, a delicate face beneath a sweeping hat. 'You mean he...?' His mouth open, he pointed at his clerk.

'Yes, that's shaken you.' Searle raged at his employer, his words stumbling forth. 'All over, then. Yes, I did for old Ellis, but I should have done for you, you contemptible swine... I hate the whole damned pack of you.' He swung to Abbs, spittle flecking his lips. 'Bully-boys, all of you. You're no better. If you've frightened my wife...'

Sergeant Hollins appeared, blocking the way to the street. Buckley took up a stance by the inner door. Feeling for his silk kerchief, he patted his brow, gazing at his clerk and Abbs.

'Mrs Searle was treated with every respect,' said Abbs sternly. 'These were found in your coal-house, as you well know, being the one who hid them there. Does your wife know anything of your crimes?'

Searle shook his head, dumbly wringing his hands.

'Speak up.' Grainer leant over the counter.

Searle shrank away, his ire burst and shrivelled like a spent balloon. 'My wife is innocent, I swear. She knows nothing. Don't take her. Leave me be...' Wrenching at his collar, he groaned, as if fingering where the rope would rub.

'Give him some air.' Abbs indicated Grainer should return to his side.

'You mean I've been harbouring a murderer under my roof?' Buckley spoke wonderingly. 'Why ever did you do it, you ungrateful wretch?'

'Ungrateful...' Searle's voice shook. 'You're the murderer. Yes, you standing there in your finery. Men, like you, murder the spirit of

272

men like me. You've made my life a misery, since Ellis left. You made me drop things, standing over me with your carping. He calls me a clumsy oaf. Even the boy laughs at me, following his lead. My wrists are red-raw some days, my fingers like fire. If I can't work, you'd put us on the streets. But what d'you care? You'll never know what it is to starve.'

'This is outrageous. I refuse to listen to this diatribe. He's admitted his crime. Arrest him and lock him up.'

Abbs held up a hand, looked at Buckley and he fell silent. He wanted to hear and, if he was any judge, Searle was desperate to tell. The clerk sagged against the wall, as if a puppet had its strings cut.

Fixing despairing eyes on him, Searle began gabbling, before he was taken. 'Ellis deserved everything he got. I went to see him that night, I knew his habits. He'd be alone in his study, she gone to the Institute. I'd been hanging on, counting the weeks for him to come back to work. He'd had long enough to mourn. Fool, that I was, I thought him decent.' He threw a venomous look at Buckley. 'He'd have to leave me be, with Mr. Ellis here.'

'Mr. Ellis told you he would never return,' said Abbs. 'He was selling his house and leaving London.'

'At his age, the selfish old fool. He'd had his life. He was too old for a new one. He wouldn't even lend me the money. I told him I was desperate. He said putting a man in debt wasn't the way to assist him. I begged him, for my son's sake, to reconsider. The money was nothing to him, but he wouldn't be moved.'

'So you stabbed him,' said Grainer impatiently.

'His own doing. I snatched up the paper-knife in my distress. Mr. Ellis came on to it. I went to plead with him. I didn't go there to hurt him...'

As they stared, his eyes moistened behind his spectacles. Putting his fingers to his mouth, Searle trembled, struggling to master himself.

'A likely story. Fell on the knife three times, did he?' said Grainer harshly. 'You knew what you were about.' He poked at the miniatures. 'Why keep them?'

'I.. I was too frightened to dispose of them. They were too valuable to destroy. I burnt his diary, lest he'd made some note about me. The last time he was here, I told him about my boy, asked him for a loan. Ellis said he'd think it over. Playing with me... deliberately raising my hopes. He'd no intention of helping me.'

'Why did you kill Jessie Dove?' said Abbs.

Searle's eyes widened, his arms raised before him, to ward off a blow.

'Didn't think we knew, did you?' said Grainer.

'She was a wicked woman. A filthy, stinking liar.'

'You called to see her on your way home,' said Abbs, feeling his way. 'You knew Mr. Dove would be at the Institute. Mrs Dove wasn't expecting you.'

'I... I wanted to know when my son would send for us. I had to get away. You kept hounding me. You followed me home. I knew you'd not leave go.'

'You caught Mrs Dove sewing a tiny bell on a garter,' said Abbs, his voice implacable. 'You realised then, everything you'd been depending on was false. The Doves' spirit-messages were all lies, the strange happenings contrived by them.'

'I didn't kill her, though I wanted to. Do you know what it is to toy with someone's life? Like a cat torturing a mouse, for amusement. She said my son would send for us. I believed her. It was all lies. She deserved to die. All I did was make her eat her wicked words. She twisted away from me, caught her foot in the rug. I was glad... Glad, I tell you.'

Abbs nodded at Grainer, who pulled a pair of hand-cuffs from his pocket.

'Well done, Inspector,' said Buckley. 'You'll hang, you loathsome blackguard and rightly so.'

Searle launched himself at the counter. 'It's you did this to me,' he yelled at Buckley, spittle flying from his mouth. 'Ellis, that lying bitch, all of you...'

The door opened and Miss Maitland stood on the threshold.

Searle grabbed the heavy glass ink-well, hurling it at his employer.

Miss Maitland stepped back, with a small scream, as the glass smashed on the wall. Frederick Buckley jerked aside instinctively, though Searle's aim was poor. The architect dabbed furiously at spots of ink spraying his frock-coat, condemning him all the while.

Assisted by Hollins, Grainer had the darbies on in an instant. Searle put up no resistance, weeping as they led him away.

Abbs remained for a word with the others. As he endured more

aise, he thought of the two who were dead, the hanging to come,
e wife who must be told. This was always the worst of his work.
Even the ink seemed to resemble dark, clotting blood.

FIFTY-ONE

Two nights later.

The tavern, off Trafalgar Square, was busy that evening. A fire crackled at either end of the saloon, a tobacco fug throughout. At casual glance, the three men, settled in a corner, might be Whitehall clerks in idle conversation.

'When did you know it was Searle?' Leaning back in his chair, D Prentice gestured with his church-warden pipe. A thin twist of smoke drifted past his lean face.

'Not for a long while. He was there in the background, a useful source of information,' said Abbs. 'I grew increasingly sure h disliked me, but no one enjoys being questioned by a detective. pressed him too hard and saw he felt harried. I noticed his hands, h clumsiness, but thought nothing of it.'

Prentice nodded. 'Nothing could have been done. Sufferers nee to keep in the warm and rest the afflicted joints. In other words, n profession can offer no advice the working-classes may take.'

His words were harsh, thought Abbs, if you missed the bitter edg 'Reeve, here, was a great help. He led me to a man we were seekin a house-agent.'

Reeve attempted to look modest. 'Not down to me. My brother's cabby. He found him.'

'This fellow witnessed a slight exchange between Rowland Ellis an Ambrose Buckley. Mr. Ellis said he intended calling at the offic Buckley said his father wouldn't be there that afternoon. The hous agent thought Mr. Ellis said something like 'it isn't...' I kep pondering how that sentence might have finished. One possibility wa *it isn't him I want to see.*' Abbs hesitated, trying to identify when h faint awareness grew into conviction. 'Searle denies seeing Ellis th day. He might have changed his mind.

Once I started to look at Searle, I recalled something Frederic Buckley mentioned. The previous errand-boy had recently bee dismissed for pilfering. That set me wondering. Had Searle bee filching the petty cash? He's admitted taking a small sum here an there. His son had been pressing him to send money for some tim He'd sold the silver ink-stand Ellis left him. When I gave him a li ome, he was terrified lest I invited myself in and asked to see it.'

'And he had the miniatures hidden in his coal-hole,' said Reeve.
'Didn't do my new suit much good, I can tell you. Worth it, mind.'

'The son must have known his father had no money to advance
im.' Reaching for the jug, Prentice topped up their glasses.

'He's a farm labourer, who had the chance to lease a parcel of land.
'eems he has ambitions. Many a man's worked his way up from
othing in the Empire, but he needed the stake.'

'You saw the darn on his glove? The same wool as the thread I
nowed you.'

'Black woollen gloves are to be found everywhere, but I wondered.
'he irony was Searle, himself, told me about his son. It was eating
vay at him. I started to work out what might connect Searle and the
loves. Had he consulted them? Not everyone who goes to these
ogues is grieving. Many people seek their own future, much as they'd
ay a fortune-teller at a country fair. They sit at the planchette-board,
oping to hear of love or riches. Mrs Dove ran a lucrative side-line,
elling people what they long to hear.'

'Cheaper to let a gypsy read their palm,' said Reeve.

'Indeed, or a cook their tea-leaves for that matter.' Abbs shook his
ead. 'No doubt, it seemed a fairly harmless way to make a living.'

Taking up his brandy, Reeve said. 'How can folk be such fools as
o believe in all that?'

'They need hope to cling to,' said Prentice.

Reeve scowled at the stained ceiling. 'Life's harsh, unless you're
onied. Always has been, always will be. No sense in dreaming.
'ount the good times, I say.'

'And if there are none?' inquired Prentice lightly. 'What then?'

'Come now, Doctor, there's always some cheer. You have to get off
our arse and fight back at life.'

'Stout words. But not, I would suggest, quite so easy when you've
ent to find, a family to keep. Your words come, if I might venture,
om a man with youth and vigour on your side. I treat patients who're
efeated by living.' He shifted his legs, as the landlord added a shovel
f sea-coal to the fire. 'We all need hope, Reeve. Men fall in a pit of
heir own making. Then they cannot climb out.'

Something about his tone, made Abbs look sharply at the police-
urgeon.

'Don't tell me you pity a murderer?' said Reeve.

Prentice shook his head. 'Not I, not in this case. I save my sympathy for the dead. I keep thinking about the bell he tried to make that poor woman swallow.'

Silence fell in their corner. Abbs looked up, as someone stood by him.

'Mr. Abbs.' Harry March nodded at the others. 'Gentlemen. Pray excuse my disturbing you.' He placed a folded newspaper on the table. 'You might care for a look at this.'

Abbs read the heading in bold print, turning it to show the others.

The Wronged Husband,' read Prentice aloud. 'In which account Mr. Silas Dove recounts his many woes in his own words, as frankly revealed to our foremost reporter.'

'My congratulations, Inspector. Your success will not go unnoticed. Nor will the failure of your colleague. How about that profile we spoke of? Strike while the iron's hot? Readers of *The Inquirer* are anxious to learn more of the detective-branch's newest star. Fame won't do you any harm at Scotland Yard.'

'On the contrary, Mr. March, I rather think it will. I prefer to remain anonymous, like any working man.'

March sketched a graceful lift of his shoulders. 'It had to be asked. I didn't think you'd change your mind. Remember what I said about our rivals. Some journalists will write you up, regardless.'

'I'll endeavour to ignore them.'

'Two murders cleared up and one of them, not even your case. Take heed, Mr. Abbs. You've made an enemy there.' He bowed slightly, glancing speculatively at the others as he went.

Not long after, the three men left the tavern, a clock chiming as they stepped into the dark street. The fog had lifted at last.

'We go different ways, I think,' said Prentice, pulling on his gloves. 'No doubt, our paths will cross again ere long.'

'Bound to, Doctor,' said Reeve. 'We'll meet over a corpse soon enough.'

'It seems to me,' said Abbs slowly, 'these spiritualists have it all wrong.' He looked back at the detective sergeant, fists in pockets, the police-surgeon, grasping his elegant stick.

'Surely, we are the ones who speak for the dead.'

With a farewell lift of his hand, he walked off into the night. His

278

ootsteps sounded along the shadowed streets of the great Metropolis. Through the darkness pierced by flickering gas-lamps, hemmed in by endless roof-tops, the thousands of chimneys, lost against the black sky. There would be more dead, but this case was done. He had proved himself at Scotland Yard. He was going home. On the morrow, he would write to the Shaws.

He had made a beginning in London.

Historical Note

Kennington is a district of South London, not to be confused with the better-known Kensington. These days, Kennington is probably best-known, to visitors, for the Imperial War Museum and The Oval cricket-ground. In Inspector Abbs's time, it was considered a mainly well-to-do, residential area, popular with City stockbrokers and other professional men.

Kennington lies on the ancient highway of Stane Street, the Roman road that led from Chichester, near the south coast, to the capital. A village in the 18th century, the area began to develop as a suburb after Westminster Bridge was completed in 1751. Terraces of prosperous Georgian townhouses, and garden squares, were laid out.

Kennington Common, on the south-western edge, had long been notorious for nefarious goings-on. The haunt of rogues and highwaymen, it was a place for rowdy fairs, radical meetings and execution. The Surrey gallows was erected at the edge of the Common, by the turnpike road. As the south London equivalent of Tyburn, over 130 executions took place there, including, in the 17th century, burning at the stake. The last hanging was in 1799.

The Common has an interesting history as a gathering place for political protest and dissent. Non-conformist preachers, including John Wesley, preached there in the 1730s to crowds of thousands. In 1792, a rally in support of the French Revolution was quelled by troops. Protesters were prevented from planting a Tree of Liberty.

In 1824, St Mark's church was built on the site of the gallows. This was one of four 'Waterloo' churches in South London, commissioned to commemorate the victory against Napoleon. Its first incumbent campaigned for the Common to be brought under greater control.

From the 1820s, Kennington was a rapidly growing, semi-rural suburb. Its remaining market-gardens and pasture were sure to be snapped up by speculative builders. Some of the several-storeyed, older houses gradually slipped down the social scale, turned over to multiple-occupancy. The Common, increasingly used for dumping rubbish, was nibbled by development. Karl Marx wrote in *Das Kapital,* that 'parts of Kennington were very seriously overpopulated in 1859, when diptheria appeared.'

ectoral hustings took place on the Common for the First Reform
t in 1832. Trade Unionists celebrated the return of the Tolpuddle
artyrs, a few years later. The Chartists held many meetings there.
1848, they held their 'monster' rally, where an estimated 25,000
ended to march on parliament with a petition calling for significant
ctoral reforms. They were prevented by soldiers, under the com-
nd of the Duke of Wellington.

the early 1850s, the decision was taken to enclose Kennington
mmon and replace it with 'pleasure grounds for the recreation of
public.' An act of parliament ended the ancient commoners'
hts to graze sheep and cattle. Swallowed by the Victorian appetite
progress, its wild, Georgian landscape was no more.

nnington Park was opened in 1854, the first public park in South
ndon. John Gibson, who designed the landscape of the much-
aised Battersea Park, was put in charge. The lodge-keeper's wife
s allowed to sell 'ginger beer, lemonade, soda water, biscuits, fruit
d sweetmeats' from her rear window. Interestingly, the spirit of re-
llion lingers on. In recent decades, the park has been used as a
lying-point for a good many marches on Westminster. The Chart-
s' endeavours are still commemorated there.

e Victorian fervour for spiritualism had been underway for over
o decades at the time the story is set. The spiritualist movement is
nerally agreed to have taken off in America, with the Fox sisters. In
48, shortly after moving to an old house in New York, members
the Fox family claimed to be experiencing strange knocking noises
their new home. They claimed this activity emanated from a rest-
s spirit, with whom they learnt to communicate, by means of a sim-
e system of raps.

e two younger Fox sisters, in particular, claimed to be mediums,
ying the spirit was that of a pedlar, murdered in their home. When
ces of human remains were later found beneath the floor of their
llar, the Fox sisters rapidly became famous. Many others subse-
ently claimed to be mediums, some producing a variety of 'proofs'
der test conditions.

ances, public demonstrations and private readings quickly became
despread. Early advocates of the spiritualist movement soon
ossed the Atlantic. Though meeting much scepticism from the

press, and condemnation by the Church and men of science, the fa
cination for 'life after death' was here to stay.

Why did the spiritualist movement become so popular? One reaso
was surely because mid-Victorian Britain was the age of curiosity. Di
coveries were being made in exploration, natural history, industi
and science. Throughout the 1860s, Charles Darwin's ground-breal
ing theories on evolution had rocked Victorian certainty. It is a pe
sistent myth that most Victorians went to church. How new scientif
discoveries fitted in with religious belief, became one of the great d
bates of the age.

In 1855, an artist, named Henry Alexander Bowler, exhibited a pain
ing which summed up this dilemma, soon becoming famous. *Th*
Doubt: 'Can These Dry Bones Live?' depicted a young woman lea
ing on a headstone, contemplating a grave. The name inscribed w.
John Faithful.

It seems likely that the popularity of the spiritualist movement w.
also driven by the high incidence of early mortality. The Victoria:
lived with death in a way that modern medicine has, largely, put b
hind us. Even the rich could not take it for granted that all their chi
dren would live to adulthood. Almost one in five children died befo
their fifth birthday. To be widowed at a young age was commonplac
To illustrate, my own Victorian ancestors were fairly typical. A poo
working-class family, living in damp, crowded conditions, they ha
eight children in the 1860s-70s. Their first-born child died, aged fou
from pneumonia. The description of Mrs Ibbotson's daughter, in he
small white coffin, is taken from family stories handed down. A so
aged five, died from diptheria. Another daughter died from append
citis, aged twenty-six. Her husband, left with two small children, ma
ried again (to his wife's best friend) within a year. Many families su
fered far more tragedy.

Even at the end of Victorian Britain, a generation after the story is se
life-expectancy was only forty-eight. Small wonder there was, fc
many, a longing to contact their dead loved ones – and a ready supp
of 'marks' for fraudulent mediums.

The Horns was a real coaching-inn, situated on the turnpike roa
edging Kennington Common. The former law court building, wher
Inspector Abbs attended the inquest, still survives.

ower Norwood Cemetery, originally the South Metropolitan, is now known as West Norwood. Opened in 1837, it is the second oldest of London's 19th century, metropolitan lawn cemeteries, known as 'the magnificent seven.' Some of the capital's earliest Gothic Revival architecture, and funereal landscaping, make the site an evocative survival of the Victorian way of mourning.

Anne Bainbridge can be contacted at
gaslightcrime@yahoo.co.uk

By the same author

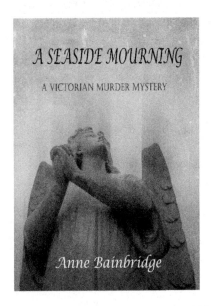

An intriguing Victorian murder mystery. Autumn 1873. Inspector Josiah Abbs and Sergeant Ned Reeve are sent to investigate their first case of murder..

At the small town of Seaborough, on the Devon coast, a wealthy spinster has died suddenly in suspicious circumstances. Some local have ambitious plans to see the seaside resort expand. Was Miss Chorley killed because she stood in their way? Or beneath the elaborate rituals of mourning, does the answer lie closer to home?

Behind the Nottingham lace curtains, residents and visitors have their schemes and secrets. The two detectives must untangle the past to find answers. When a second body is found, time is runnin out to solve a baffling mystery. But uncovering the truth may prove dangerous...

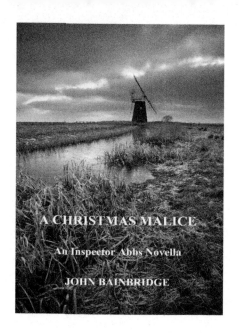

A CHRISTMAS MALICE

An Inspector Abbs Novella

JOHN BAINBRIDGE

December 1873. Inspector Abbs is visiting his sister in a lonely village on the edge of the Norfolk Fens. He is hoping for a quiet week while he thinks over a decision about his future.

However all is not well in Aylmer. Someone has been playing malicious tricks on the inhabitants. With time on his hands and concerned for his sister, Abbs feels compelled to investigate.

Printed in Great Britain
by Amazon

40623588R00162